MATCH ME IF Y

Michele G............ .... One Bestselling author of *The Expat Diaries* series and *Bella Summer Takes a Chance*. She has also written upmarket commercial fiction under the pen name Jamie Scott.

Born and raised in the US, Michele has lived in London for seventeen years. You can find out more about Michele by following her on Twitter, Facebook, Pinterest, Goodreads, or by reading her blog or website. Do chat with her on Twitter or Facebook – she's always looking for an excuse to procrastinate!

Also by Michele Gorman:

MICHELE GORMAN

Match Me If You Can

avon

AVON

A division of HarperCollins*Publishers*
The News Building
1 London Bridge Street
London SE1 9GF

www.harpercollins.co.uk

A Paperback Original 2016
3

A catalogue record for this book is
available from the British Library

ISBN-13: 978-0-00-758566-3

Set in Sabon LT Std by Palimpsest Book Production Limited,
Falkirk, Stirlingshire

Printed and bound in Great Britain by Clays Ltd, St Ives plc

MIX
Paper from
responsible sources

FSC www.fsc.org   **FSC™ C007454**

Acknowledgements

This book probably wouldn't exist if it wasn't for Carolyn, Karl and their little daughter, Robin. Carolyn and my husband are great friends and, once upon a time, they went out together. But it didn't work out and eventually my husband met me and Carolyn met Karl, and on the 8th of April 2014, their daughter, Robin, came into the world.

There I was one afternoon, wandering down my road, mulling over the wonderful phone conversation my husband and I'd just had with Carolyn and Karl after Robin's birth. 'Isn't it funny,' I thought, 'That two people as fantastic as Carolyn and my husband wouldn't be right for each other, yet they're perfect for Karl and me.' Just as I thought that, my gaze fell upon a bank of recycling bins, and *Match Me If You Can,* about upcycling exes, was born.

So thank you, Carolyn, Karl and Robin, for being such lovely friends and the inspiration for this book.

Thanks too to my always amazing agent Caroline Hardman, who was enthusiastic about *Match Me If You Can* from the beginning, and to my editor, Caroline Kirkpatrick, who's been so supportive and willing to deal with me even when I'm being a pain in the arse. Thanks too to my eagle-eyed copy editor, Rhian McKay, whose edits made me laugh rather than cry (the best thing an author can hope for).

And finally, huge kisses to everyone who reads and reviews my books. Without you I'd have to get a real day job, and I've been fired from more of those than I care to remember. So thank you from the bottom of my sofa cushions.

Chapter One

Catherine

'What did you say?' Catherine whispered as Richard calmly sipped the last of his wine. Even as her insides churned, she knew her face gave nothing away. Fifteen years of practice with him gave her the kind of composure that poker players dreamed of.

Only this didn't feel like a winning hand.

'I've asked Magda to marry me,' he repeated, this time at least having the decency to look contrite. He glanced around the busy Soho restaurant. 'Kate, you're not about to freak out, are you?'

'Don't call me Kate. And when have I ever *freaked out*?'

Catherine wasn't a freaker-outer, at least not in public. Richard would have known that when he planned his matrimonial ambush. She glared over his shoulder at an empty spot on the wall. Don't you dare cry, she warned herself. He'll only get the wrong idea and then everything will be really awkward. Besides, it was none of his business any more how she felt. She took a shaky breath. 'I'm . . .' She stopped when the word came out squeaky. 'I'm just surprised, that's all. I didn't know you were so serious after only a few months.'

A few months! She'd been with him for years before she'd even left her toothbrush at his place. And now he was getting *engaged* to a woman he hadn't even known for as long as his Waitrose delivery man.

'It was a year last weekend, actually. We went to the rooftop bar at SushiSamba to celebrate.'

'Oh, she's finally legal then?'

Catherine probably had bras that were older than Magda.

'You know,' said Richard, signalling the waiter for the bill. 'Cattiness isn't flattering on you.'

Maybe not but it was better than letting her real thoughts fly.

'Neither is dating someone who has to ask her dad to borrow the car keys.'

'You know very well that she's twenty-three. She's mature for her age.'

'And firm, I bet.'

A whisper of a smirk played around Richard's mouth, despite the fact that she was savaging his girlfriend.

Catherine didn't wish for her twenties back. Just some of their elasticity. Tall and slim, with thick dark hair that dried straight and swingy, her peaches-and-cream complexion and direct hazel eyes all helped her pull off the classically professional look she'd cultivated for so long. She knew she looked good for thirty-six. As long as she didn't stand beside her ex-husband's new fiancée.

He sighed. 'Let's not fight. I wanted you to be the first to know because you're my best friend. Magda has her heart set on a spring wedding.'

'Which spring?' It was early November already.

His closed-lip smile told her it wouldn't be a long engagement.

'That's only a few months away.'

'Please be happy for me,' he said.

His words shifted Catherine's anger off the boil. She could probably be happy for him in time, but just now she wanted to sulk. It was the contrast that stung. When *they'd* got engaged, he hadn't even officially asked her.

'Just don't expect me to be your best man, or woman, or whatever.'

He smiled. 'Magda might find it a bit too twenty-first century to have you handing out the rings on our wedding day.'

His words caved in her tummy again. 'Well, being from the twenty-first century herself . . .'

Richard shook his head. 'We'll work on your congratulations speech, shall we? I'd like us all to have dinner. Magda is dying to meet you.'

'I can hardly wait.'

Some people sought refuge in the arms of a lover. Others enjoyed the warm embrace of a spicy Pinot Noir.

Red wine just gave Catherine a headache and relationships were usually a pain in the other end. Her job was her sanctuary.

It was a short walk from the restaurant to her office in Covent Garden and her thoughts cleared a little with each step. By the time she reached her doorway on the busy little street and politely moved aside the drunk teen she found there, she knew that her reaction to Richard's news wasn't really about him, or them. It was about her.

She'd just assumed that she'd be first to find love again after their divorce. She was the one looking, not him. So how had someone who never made it out of first gear overtaken her on the road to romance? She'd stalled along the way and her roadside assistance membership was out of date.

The office's security door latch closed with a satisfying thunk, cutting off all the noise from the road. As her eyes swept over her reception area, taking in the colourful oil paintings and the richly patterned overstuffed sofa, the hungry little worm that was wriggling its way into her psyche paused for breath.

Work always did that.

In her office her desktop phone blinked with a message. Should she answer it?

She definitely shouldn't. It was after ten p.m. It could wait till morning.

But the light taunted her. What else are you doing tonight? it whispered. Going home to watch another rerun of *Don't Tell the Bride*? Come on, you know you want to.

She snatched the receiver and punched in the answerphone code.

'You have one new message. Message received at eight fifty-two p.m.'

'Catherine? This is Georgina. Did you mean to set me up with a *dairy drinker*?'

She made it sound like she'd been out with a mass murderer.

'I'm sorry but I can't see him again. The dairy thing is just too weird.'

Well actually, thought Catherine, it would have been weird if he'd shoved a wheel of Brie down his trousers. Pouring milk in his coffee was pretty normal.

But she wouldn't argue with Georgina, even though her client's list of technical requirements made a NASA space launch look simple. If she wanted a lactose-intolerant man who played piano and didn't chew gum, then Catherine would find him.

That was her job, for better or worse.

Matchmakers had it easier before the internet, when clients were just grateful to have a choice beyond their next-door neighbour and the second cousin with the squint.

Now everyone went online, picking out partners like they

did an expensive pair of shoes – they had to fit perfectly and be suitable for the occasion, and be the right height, eye-wateringly beautiful with no sign of wear and tear, coveted by friends and colleagues and impressive to mothers.

Clients like Georgina thought finding love was as easy as ordering from ASOS.

Catherine scrolled through some more options in her database. Georgina hadn't been on their books long but she'd already worked her way through most of their 'A' list. When she'd first signed Georgina as a client she'd seen the stunning, successful, secure thirty-one-year-old as a welcome addition. A woman for whom love was just around the corner. That corner was turning out to be in a maze the size of a football pitch. The dairy disaster was just the latest dead end.

But Catherine hadn't earned her reputation as London's Best Date Doctor (*Evening Standard*, 2014) by giving up. She was a peddler of hope, even when it was hanging by a dairy-free thread.

She could talk to Richard about including the client's world view on ice cream in their Love Match assessment form. But where would that lead? One minute you're measuring gelato love and the next you'd have to sort the toothpaste squeezers from the rollers.

And really, none of that mattered.

If only clients like Georgina would get that through their heads. A partner splurging for dinner or throwing his socks in the laundry didn't make up for jealousy or thoughtlessness or emotional distance. Good grooming was no compensation if your date bored the snot out of you and, at the end of the day, relationships didn't work without that spark anyway.

Despite the fact that she was definitely still mad at him, Catherine found herself thinking of Richard.

Sparks had never been their problem.

He'd made her laugh from the first time they met at uni. By the time classes broke up for the summer holidays he'd been making her laugh for months, as they progressed from shag buddies to something ever-so-slightly more serious. Her spare knickers found their way into his bottom drawer but she didn't stake any claim to his bathroom cabinet or stock her favourite tea in his kitchen. Theirs was a relationship built by stealth over years.

Magda the Marriage-Seeking Missile clearly had a different timetable.

As she chewed over his news in the calm of her office, Catherine knew she didn't mind Richard getting remarried per se. Or even that he'd proposed to someone who probably spoke in texty acronyms (she LOL'd at the very idea). After all, getting divorced was Catherine's fault. Besides, she wasn't in love with him.

It was just that he made it seem so easy with Magda. Where was all the hard work and second-guessing and foot-dragging she knew to be part and parcel of a relationship with Richard?

If it wasn't there, that must mean she'd been wrong. Those things weren't integral to Richard. They were integral to Richard when he'd been with *her*.

That smarted.

It was after midnight by the time she let herself into the quiet house. Eerie blue telly light bathed the front room, where Sarah lay curled on the sofa. She looked like a different person with her expression uncoiled in sleep.

As Catherine turned off the telly, Sarah snorted herself awake.

'I might have nodded off,' she said, wiping her chin with the back of her hand. 'I was watching a proper good documentary just now.'

'You mean a cookery programme, don't you, Sarah Lee?'

6

Sarah grinned at the nickname that Catherine had given her after tasting her lemon sponge.

'No,' said Sarah, shaking her head. 'I mean a real documentary. There was this Greek man who moved to the US in the 1960s and started a pizza restaurant, but his business was stuffed because he wouldn't modernise. It was really sad. He almost lost his family and his livelihood, but he turned it around in the end. It was ace.'

She beamed at this happy ending.

'You're talking about *Ramsay's Kitchen Nightmares*,' said Catherine.

Sarah giggled. 'It was really moving, though Gordon shouldn't shout and swear so much.'

As usual, thought Catherine, she's missing the point. 'It wouldn't get the same ratings if he was nice. Besides, Mary Berry has the market cornered on loveliness in the kitchen.'

Sarah got a faraway look just thinking about her idol. She swung her long legs off the sofa to let Catherine join her.

'You've been running?' Catherine said, noting her housemate's jogging bottoms and baggy wrinkled tee shirt.

'This morning.' She wrapped her arms around herself. 'I don't stink, do I?'

'No. But I'm surprised you don't get a rash from sitting around in sweaty clothes all day.' It drove her nuts that Sarah refused to make any effort whatsoever with her appearance. Granted, she had the kind of wide-eyed, fine-boned pleasant face that didn't need much make-up, but she wouldn't even use moisturiser. That was fine at twenty-eight, but she was asking for wrinkles by the time she was Catherine's age. And it was a crime to keep such pretty, long dark-blonde hair tied back day and night in a messy, occasionally greasy, ponytail. She needed an intervention, really. Maybe they should just drag her kicking and screaming to a salon appointment.

Catherine noticed that Rachel's bedroom light was on. 'Rachel's back from her date?' she asked.

'Not unless she came in quietly while I was asleep.'

They both laughed at the idea of Rachel doing anything quietly.

'It must be going well,' Catherine said, kicking off her suede heels so she could massage her aching feet.

'Maybe we should ring to make sure she's okay?'

Sarah wore her worry like a heavy winter coat, in all seasons. 'She probably won't appreciate the interruption.'

'But it's getting late,' Sarah continued, her green eyes widening even more than usual. 'Something might be wrong. What if her date's got her tied up in his car? Or his basement, or maybe he's taken her to a remote valley in Wales.'

Imaginative didn't even begin to describe Sarah's thought process sometimes. 'Text her if you want to,' said Catherine.

'But what if he's duct-taped her fingers together? He'd only need one piece for each hand, you know.' Sarah wrapped her own slender fingers with imaginary tape. 'Then she couldn't text back.'

'She couldn't answer your call either, could she? Or he might have thrown her phone in the Thames along with all the other evidence.'

Catherine immediately felt bad about teasing Sarah when she saw her expression.

'I'm positive that she's fine,' she conceded. 'If she's not back in an hour, we'll call her, okay?'

But they only needed to wait a few minutes before Rachel careened into the living room. Her deep auburn hair stood up in wild cowlicks and curls and her teal wool coat was mis-buttoned. With pale green tights under her burgundy and yellow wasp-waisted dress, it was no wonder she described her style as 1950s Contrasting Colour Wheel.

She looked like she'd just escaped from Sarah's imagined

Welsh valley, but Catherine knew better. Rachel always looked like she'd been out in a gale.

She flung herself on the sofa, aiming for the space between her housemates but missing due to an abundance of bum cheek. She had all the curves that Catherine and Sarah wished they had. On a shelf together they'd be wooden bookends to her Ming vase.

Sarah drew her arms around her friend as she sat half in her lap. 'It was a good date, then?'

Rachel laughed. 'My bikini wax appointments are more fun. I ditched him after the first drink.'

'But you were out for a long time.'

'I met up with James.'

'You've been seeing a lot of each other lately,' Catherine said.

'Eight hours a day for the past five years. We do work together, remember?'

'And play together, apparently. Still just friends?' Catherine couldn't resist asking.

'Catherine, I wouldn't go back there for all the Prada in Selfridges.'

'It never hurts to ask.'

'It's after midnight,' Rachel said. 'Aren't you supposed to be off duty?'

'As if a matchmaker is ever off duty.'

Chapter Two

Rachel

'You are a really good architect,' Rachel told herself again. 'You are ready for this. You'll nail it.' She studied her reflection. 'But you're a wanker for talking to yourself in the mirror. And your outfit's all wrong.'

She sucked in her tummy and peered at her lilac dress. If she was a little less curvy she could have borrowed something from Catherine's form-fitting monochrome closet. Maybe something in confidence-inspiring beige. Their stuffy corporate clients would probably appreciate that more than her bright swingy frock and loudly contrasting tights.

Not that her clothes were totally to blame for the impression she made. Her hair also had a lot to answer for. Deep red and wavy, it rejected any attempt to look composed. She didn't exactly whisper sophistication so much as shout colour-blind cat lady. And while it was nice to be mistaken for one of the junior architects, today she wished she looked all of her thirty-one years.

She unclasped the chunky red fabric flower necklace and stuffed it into her bag. It clashed with her hair anyway, which was starting to frizz from the damp November day.

Stifling a yawn as she reached her desk, she was tempted

to lay her head down, just for a second. Instead she dialled her mum's office.

By the third ring she knew it would go through to voicemail.

'Hi Mum. I'm just getting ready for my presentation. It's this morning, remember? I just really wanted to . . . Well anyway, I'll let you know how it goes after.' She was about to hang up when she thought she heard a click. 'Hello Mum? Hello? Oh. I thought you picked up. If you get this message before ten thirty, call me, okay? I'll just be going through the presentation one more time.'

Hanging up, she clicked again through her slides. Midway through, the screen began to blur. Just a little rest was what she needed . . .

She opened one mascaraed eye when James set a steaming takeaway cup on her desk. The aroma made her nose twitch.

'I figured you could use this,' he said, handing her a pastry bag to go with her coffee. 'You weren't actually kipping, were you?'

Stretching, she glanced at the wall clock. 'Just a little one. Chocolate croissant?' she guessed. 'Ooh la la.'

'Oui madame, zis eez zee least I can do,' he said in a pathetic French accent. 'Seriously, I'm sorry I kept you out late.' Remorse was written all over his boyish face.

'Don't be,' she mumbled. 'I figured if I stayed up I might be tired enough to sleep. Stupid plan.'

She'd watched her bedside clock pass two a.m., then three, with her mind racing over the pitch this morning.

She sipped the hot sweet coffee. 'God that's good, thanks,' she said. 'You feel okay?'

He slurped the last of his drink. 'No thanks to you.'

'You didn't have to finish the bottle, you know.'

'Oh but I did, Rach. You wouldn't help me.'

Like she'd risk a hangover on the most important

morning of her career. She had the tolerance of a toddler on antibiotics anyway. 'I meant you could have left it unfinished.'

He stared at her like she was insane.

'Sorry. Forgot who I was talking to.' James put the extra pinch in penny-pincher. His guilt must have been over-whelming to splurge on a coffee *and* croissant.

'Better drink up,' he said. 'They'll be here soon. Are you nervous?' His direct blue-eyed gaze didn't leave her face.

She sipped, considering his question. Was she nervous? She used to dream about getting this chance. Now part of her wished she was just a trainee architect again. It wouldn't be so bad doing CAD drawings and photocopying floor plans for the next thirty-five years, right?

Yeah right. Like she'd give up this chance after working her arse off.

'Why should I be nervous? It's only our careers on the line,' she said as the takeaway cup shook slightly in her hand.

He noticed, and put his hand over hers. 'You absolutely definitely shouldn't be nervous. You're going to be great. We both are. We can go through the presentation again if you want?'

They both glanced at her screen. A skyscraper screen saver hid their slides. 'No need. I know it better than the national anthem.'

'You're a star.' James smiled as he strolled back to his office humming "God Save the Queen".

The second he rounded the corner she went back to the presentation. They might be friends but she wasn't about to let a chocolate croissant make her forget that they were also rivals.

* * *

12

She'd just about got her flipping tummy under control by the time he came back with his suit jacket on. 'Ready?' He pulled at his buttoned-up collar and straightened his tie.

She gurned at him. 'How're my teeth?' On account of the big gap between the two front ones, she always checked.

'Clear. Mine?'

'There's something brown in there.' Rachel pointed as he snapped his lips shut.

Panicked, he took a swig from the mineral water on her desk. 'Better now?'

'It looks like . . . no, must be something stuck in there from all the arse-kissing you've been doing.'

'Really, Rachel?' he said. 'You want to joke right now? My arse-kissing got us this meeting, and it's not over yet. Get ready to pucker up.'

She tried to smile as they walked into the conference room but her lips started quivering when she saw her boss making small talk with their most important clients.

Get a grip, Rachel. As far as they're concerned you're perfectly at ease. They don't know that you've aged in dog years or restarted your nail-biting habit over the presentation. They can't see the uncomfortable crotch hammock that your too-yellow tights are making under your dress.

She took a deep breath, resisting the urge to plunge her hand down the back of her tights to make adjustments.

'Ah, Rachel, James, hello.' Their boss stood up when he saw them. 'Gentlemen, allow me to introduce Rachel Lambert and James McCormack, two of our brightest young architects. I think you're going to love what they've come up with.'

His expression warned them not to prove him wrong.

After work, Sarah yanked open the front door before Rachel could get her key out of the lock. Then she nearly wrestled her to the sofa.

13

'Ace, you're home! Let me take that for you!' She grabbed Rachel's giant portfolio case.

'What are you doing?' Rachel protested as Sarah wrenched off one of her brogues. In her tiny hands the shoe looked huge and inelegant.

'You've had a hard day, so you need to relax.'

'And this mugging is supposed to relax me?'

Sarah looked surprised by the shoe in her hand. 'I want you to put your feet up and I'll cook for us.'

Rachel grinned at her sweet, impulsive housemate. 'Thank you. Can I have my shoe back please?'

'Catherine's just changing. Dinner's ready soon.'

Sarah retreated to the kitchen with the shoe still in her hand.

'Do I have to stay here on the sofa?' Rachel called. 'Or am I allowed in the kitchen?'

Slowly she rolled her shoulders, feeling the satisfying tick tick tick of her vertebrae cracking away the tension of the past few weeks.

'Have you been grounded or something?' Catherine said as she came downstairs from her bedroom.

'Sarah stole my shoe.'

Catherine didn't look surprised. 'How'd it go today?'

Rachel couldn't wipe the smile off her face.

'That good, eh?'

'Remember the time I got that flight to Prague for twenty-nine pounds? And the hotel lost my reservation and gave me a suite for the price of a double? Today was better. Seriously, I rocked it! The clients loved our pitch. They made all the right noises about letting us present our ideas. I think they're going to give us a chance.'

She didn't need to tell Catherine that her design would be competing against James's. It was all she'd rabbited on about lately.

'Well done, I knew they'd love it!' Catherine scooped her up in a hug. 'You've told your mum?'

Rachel's face felt like it might split in two. 'She rang me back right after the meeting. She thinks I'm awesome.'

Catherine squeezed her again. 'She's always been the president of your fan club.'

'I know.' She sat back down, resting her head on the back of the sofa and listening to Sarah mangle pop songs at the top of her voice in the kitchen. As much as she loved going out, these rare nights home were bliss. Their rambling, derelict house was the anchor that held them all steady in London.

Or maybe it just seemed like that. She vaguely remembered the same feeling in Catherine's old flat. Which meant it wasn't really the house, but the housemates. They might not spend all their time together like they did in the early days, but she couldn't imagine her life without them.

It was only because of Catherine's extra mortgage that they'd met at all. She'd sunk so much money into the new matchmaking business that she'd needed flatmates to help pay back the loan. Rachel and Sarah had been the first two to answer her advert. Rachel was only a junior architect then, who still went home to her parents' every week for dinner and clean laundry. And Sarah was fresh from uni. That was seven years ago.

And now they had the Clapton house. It had taken blood, sweat and tears to get the money together to buy it at auction. Rachel still cried sometimes, looking at her meagre savings account, but it was an excellent long-term financial decision. Assuming it didn't actually fall down. As the resident architect, she was the one who had to make sure that didn't happen.

'Richard is getting married,' Catherine said, pulling her from her reverie.

15

'No way. Who'd have him?'

'The Hungarian teenager. He wants me to have dinner with them.'

'Why? Is he looking for a grown-up's approval?'

Catherine didn't smile. Rachel always thought that her serious face was her most beautiful. Although that was like choosing which of Thornton's Decadently Dark chocolates she preferred. All of them, obviously.

'What's this mean for you and him?'

'As long as nothing changes then it doesn't mean anything.'

Rachel could see Catherine retreating from her feelings. She rarely went off-kilter. You could detonate a bomb beside her and she'd carry on as normal. Maybe that's what Richard did with his news.

'You're sure about that?' Rachel asked. Just because Catherine called time on their marriage didn't mean it was easy to hear this news.

'Rachel, we just celebrated a happily divorced ten years. Of course I'm sure. As long as he doesn't let this nonsense interfere with the business.'

'Right,' Rachel said. 'That's the business you own with your soon-to-be-remarried ex-husband. Whose fiancée you hate. What could possibly go wrong there?'

'It'll be okay,' said Catherine. With that, she got up and went to check on Sarah.

Rachel couldn't exactly throw stones at Catherine while she had James to deal with at work. She just hoped Catherine wouldn't end up mixing business with displeasure.

Not everyone got to ignore their exes when their tolerance ran out. Sometimes children, social circles, mortgages or, in Rachel's case, office space, made it hard to just delete his contact details and make your friends promise to forget all about that dark period. And sometimes people, like Catherine

16

and Richard, actually wanted to stay in each other's lives. Not only that, they built an entire business model around the idea that other people did too.

It definitely wasn't for everyone, Rachel thought as she followed Catherine down to the kitchen. But after last night's date she had to admit that it might be for her.

She just knew that Catherine was going to be smug about that.

'This looks delicious,' Catherine said as Sarah dished up their dinner – a huge salad of grilled halloumi, rocket, blood oranges and olives – at their battered, beloved kitchen table. It was big and comfortable and never divulged the secrets they shared over it. Like the rest of the house, it had seen better decades.

'So, I've been thinking about RecycLove.com,' Rachel said.

'Oh?' Catherine gave away nothing.

'Because your date was bad? I want details!' cried Sarah as she slid a tray full of shiny white meringues into the oven.

'Please, not while we're eating,' Rachel said.

'How did you meet this guy?' asked Catherine.

'At the pub last Friday. But it was close to last orders so I didn't talk to him that much.'

'That's what you get for going out with someone you don't even know,' said Catherine.

Instead of answering, Rachel dug her phone out, opened Twitter and shared his photo round the table.

'Ah, I see.' Catherine smiled.

'Nice one,' Sarah said. 'He's pretty. I'd overlook a lot to snog him.'

'That's what I figured too. We've been tweeting all week. Just jokey messages, mild flirtation. He suggested a drink near the office. He did seem normal at first. Until he started flirting.' She grimaced.

'But you'd been flirting with him on Twitter.'

'Not like this. At first it was hot.' Her face started to burn. This wasn't the kind of thing you wanted to confess, even to friends. 'We started talking about what we'd do to each other . . . in the bedroom.'

'Rachel!' Sarah exclaimed. 'You don't even know him.'

'Well, obviously, Sarah, at that point I was hoping to change that! It's been a while, you know.'

Both women nodded. The only man who'd been in their house in the last six months had come to fix the boiler.

'So I said something fairly tame like . . .' She lowered her voice. So embarrassing. 'Like I'd wear a body stocking. He said he'd like that. Then he asked if I'd wee on him while *he* wore the body stocking.'

'Wow,' Catherine said, keeping a straight face, Rachel noted. She probably had a tick box on the website for such fetishes.

'That's sick!' Sarah said. 'You should have reported him to the police.'

'For what? Wanting to wee on me? It's not a crime. The crime was that I didn't just get up and leave. But it seemed rude not to finish my drink. That's when it got really weird.'

'*That's* when it got weird?' Catherine said.

'Did he start punching himself?' Sarah asked.

Rachel shook her head.

'No, no punching . . .?'

Sarah's mind worked in mysterious ways.

'It's just that wanting to be dominated probably comes from low self-esteem, maybe self-harm,' Sarah continued.

Then again, Rachel thought, she was a clever woman. She just didn't feel the need to fill the rest of them in on the steps

18

in her thought process. Sometimes talking to her was like being paintballed from all sides.

'So,' Rachel continued. 'I said that weeing on people wasn't really my thing. And then he asked if I've accepted Jesus Christ as my saviour. Because otherwise I was going to hell.'

'Because you didn't wee on him?' Sarah asked. 'That seems harsh.'

'That's when I left.' She turned to Catherine. 'If I join RecycLove.com can you promise I won't have to wee on anyone?'

'I can't make any promises,' Catherine said. 'But it's got to be better than meeting randoms in bars. You're really thinking of joining?'

Rachel nodded. She couldn't believe it had come to this. A decade ago when she was just out of uni she'd never have joined a dating site. It had been too easy to meet guys then, and anyway, online dating reminded her of those WLTM adverts that everyone laughed over in the back of the papers.

But now, unless she developed a fetish or was born-again, she might need RecycLove. 'I'm afraid it's time.'

'That's great, Rachel,' Catherine said. 'Who'll join with you?'

'James, of course. He owes me.'

That was the rule with RecycLove. It was like a normal dating website but she could only join by bringing an ex to upcycle. New joiners gave their ex a romantic evaluation, which could be painful, Rachel thought, even if it was for their eyes only. On the other hand, knowing where she might be going wrong *would* let her make changes if she wanted. Then she'd get access to all those dating prospects . . . all those *improved* dating prospects.

She just had to convince James to join with her. And let himself be criticised for his failure at boyfriendship. How hard could that be?

'But I'll only join if Sarah does too,' she said.

Sarah stared at her housemate as if she'd just asked her to donate a kidney.

Chapter Three

Sarah

Sarah's heart pounded as her running shoes kicked up little dust whorls along the path. The huge plane trees spread their bare branches overhead, shielding her from a bit of the drizzle. Not that bad weather ever stopped her park runs. She'd cemented the habit into her routine when she ran long-distance for her school. Now it kept her jeans from getting too tight when she ate most of her baking. And it let her think.

She never claimed to be the brightest match in the box when it came to reading people but she knew a set-up when she saw one. And last night was one mother of a set-up.

Rachel and Catherine thought she didn't know how they talked about her, that they worried she was turning into some kind of housebound, daytime-telly-watching, tracksuit-wearing weirdo. Like she didn't worry herself. She was about one box set away from hermithood.

But there wasn't really a lot she could do about that at the moment. Besides, her life wasn't too bad, in the scheme of things. So she wasn't dating. At least she didn't have to go through all that effort – the buffing and straightening and shaving and shopping and standing around in uncomfortable shoes, trying to be the most fascinating thing on the planet – only to have a guy want to wee on her.

A few joggers passed her in the opposite direction but none overtook her. Even a decade after she last ran competitively, she was still fast.

She turned through the park gates and started for home. When she got inside she ran straight upstairs to the shower. She didn't want to be told off again by Catherine.

Maybe she'd be happier in her kitchen anyway, she thought as she towelled herself dry. At least there she didn't have to worry about whether she could hold the attention of some guy she'd just met, who might not even be worth her time. Amongst her pots and pans there was no pressure, and things generally ran to plan, unless she dropped a knife on her foot or set something on fire.

The others weren't up yet when she got to the kitchen. Plunging her hands into the tin of flour first, she lifted the sticky bread dough from the bowl where she'd been letting it rise. She could make bread in her sleep. Just thinking about her mum, in the bright yellow kitchen kneading the bread for her and Robin and Sissy, made her salivate.

She began knocking back the dough on the floury tabletop. As usual she couldn't resist the urge to squeeze it through her fingers. Paul Hollywood wouldn't approve but she indulged herself anyway. Few things felt better to Sarah than soft, smooth, living dough between her hands.

Rachel staggered into the kitchen with last night's eye make-up pooling on her cheeks. 'Coffee. Please, I'm begging you.'

'There's a cup left in the pot . . . no, two cups . . . or a cup and a half . . . well it depends on how big your cup is. You look like you've been punched in the face.'

'Call me Dolly,' Rachel said, wiping her thumbs beneath her eyes. 'Parton,' she said in answer to Sarah's confused look. 'She sleeps in her make-up in case she has to face the photographers.'

'If you say so.' The only photographers in Upper Clapton were the ones the police sent out when there'd been a stabbing on the Murder Mile. 'You're more Edward Scissorhands than Dolly.'

'Thanks very much. That for us?' Rachel asked, pointing to the dough between Sarah's hands.

'Mmm,' she said, leaving Rachel in the dark as to the answer. 'I'm going to Sissy's later.'

Sissy loved her sourdough bread. Sarah always felt bad that she couldn't just leave it with her, instead of asking the staff to dole it out slice by slice to her toast-addicted sister.

'Which reminds me,' Rachel said. 'Here.' She pulled some papers from the kitchen drawer.

'My hands are covered. What is it?'

She was just playing dumb. It said right at the top what it was.

'Your application for *The Great British Bake Off*,' Rachel said, popping her coffee cup in the microwave. 'It's about time you applied, Sarah Lee.'

'No way! I'd fall apart at the first signature bake. I'm happy just baking here, for you lot.'

'Bullshit, Sarah. You're not happy. Anyone can see that. This would be so good for you. You need to get your confidence back and this could do it—'

Ding! Her coffee was ready.

Time's up, thought Sarah. That was the end of the morning's round of *Let's Fix Sarah*. Tune in tomorrow. It would probably be a repeat.

'Will you at least think about it?' Rachel asked.

'Yeah.'

Which they both knew meant no.

'It would be so good for you.'

'But Rachel, I'm twenty-eight. Being an adult means that I don't have to do what's good for me.'

'Is that why you won't sign up to RecycLove with me either? You'd rather sit alone in the house and be miserable than do this one little thing to make yourself happy?'

Sarah slammed the tea towel drawer shut. Why did everyone automatically assume that if someone spent time alone she was miserable?

'But I'm not alone. I have you and Catherine.'

She covered the dough with a towel and shoved it back in the boiler cupboard to prove again.

'You know what I mean,' Rachel continued. 'We're no substitute for a normal, honest, red-blooded bloke.'

Sarah got the eggs out. There wasn't enough butter for a Madeira cake, but she could use veggie oil for cupcakes instead. 'Let me know if you find one of those,' she said.

'C'mon, it'll be fun.'

Sarah glanced up. 'That's your idea of fun? Tracking down my ex so that he can tell me everything that's wrong with me?'

'You'll get to do it to him too, though.'

'Oh, well, then it sounds ace.'

She was amazed that Catherine's business model actually worked. Even if there *were* enough people out there who didn't want to stab their exes with a salad fork, how many of those were willing to critique their ex-lover's techniques and relationship suitability and then (shudder) listen to the same thing about themselves?

She could live without that kind of honesty, thank you very much.

'Well I'm doing it,' Rachel said. 'Aren't you even curious to hear straight from the jackass's mouth what he thought of you? You must have wondered what goes through a guy's head.'

About a million times, along with every other woman in the world, Sarah thought.

Rachel continued. 'This might be the one chance we have to find out without caring, if you see what I mean. Nobody wants to hear the truth while they've still got feelings, but now, years later? Bring it on. And then we'll get access to all those men . . . all those *improved* men.'

'I don't even know how to get in touch with any of my exes,' Sarah said, cracking eggs into the glass bowl. 'I don't keep their numbers *after the event*.'

'Except for Sebastian.'

'No way, I deleted him when we broke up.' She laughed. 'Not that he'd be hard to find. He'll be in whichever club has the most Russian models.'

'You could just ask your brother for his number. They *are* friends.'

'He won't do it,' Sarah said, talking about Sebastian, not her brother.

'Why not? You ended on good terms with him. You just weren't right for each other.'

'That wasn't the problem. He thought all women were right for him.'

'He didn't actually cheat though, did he?'

'No, I don't think so. He was just shite at remembering to pay attention to me when pretty women walked by.'

'See?' said Rachel. 'You've already got something for his feedback form. He'll appreciate the advice. Think about it? Please?'

'Will you leave me alone if I do?'

'Of course not. I'll ask you again tomorrow. If James and I join, will you sign up?'

'I'll think about it,' Sarah lied, shoving the *Bake Off* form back in the kitchen drawer.

*   *   *

Sarah tried not to smoosh the cupcakes as she sprinted from the train station to Sissy's place. As she rounded the corner she saw her sister standing outside the facility's front door, looking pointedly at her watch.

'I've got cupcakes,' Sarah called. 'And I'm not late.'

'Close call.'

Sissy was a stickler for time.

When Sarah opened her arms, Sissy threw herself into them with the full force of a small rhinoceros. As they hugged she breathed in the familiar scent of her strawberry VO5 shampoo.

'You brought the bread?' She caught Sarah in her signature laser-beam stare. She had the same colour green eyes as their mum, though they were almond-shaped, whereas Sarah's were more mossy, round and deep-set.

'Of course, I promised didn't I? Shall we have a slice of toast?'

Sissy nodded. 'With jam.'

While Sarah got to work slicing the bread in the communal kitchen, Sissy selected two plates from the cabinet. Carefully she opened the jam jar and unwrapped the butter. When the toast popped up, golden and steaming, she began her process. Nobody did toast as thoroughly as Sissy.

'Want to eat it in the garden?' Sarah asked as she spotted Kelly. Like Sarah, she was in her late twenties, but with a coiled-up energy like those women who taught Zumba classes. She strode rather than walked, with her shiny black hair swinging in a ponytail. She was always easy to pick out, even in the shapeless lilac and black uniform that all the nurses wore. 'I'll just give the rest of the loaf to Kelly, okay? Can you carry mine out too, please?'

'Kelly the bread jailor,' Sissy muttered as Sarah gave her both plates.

'Hi Sarah, all right?' Kelly asked with the same easy manner that all the support workers had.

'All right, thanks. Here's Sissy's bread. We're tucking into some now.'

But Sarah wasn't looking at Kelly as she handed over the loaf. She was watching Sissy as she shuffled at her snail's pace toward the garden door at the end of the corridor.

'As if you'd get out of here without toast,' Kelly said.

'Tell me about it.'

Sissy reached the door but, with her hands full, she couldn't open it. 'Oh, sorry,' Sarah said. 'I should help Sissy.'

Kelly gently touched her arm. 'Let's give her a minute.'

They watched as Sissy stood at the door with the plates in her hands. She looked left and right, for help, Sarah knew. Her heart began to speed. 'I'll just—'

'Leave it just a minute, Sarah.'

Sissy walked into the nearest room and came out a few seconds later with a metal chair in her hands instead of the plates. Carefully she propped the door open with the chair. Then, still not hurrying, she went back into the room for the plates and carried them through to the garden.

Sarah let out the breath she didn't realise she was holding.

'We're trying to let her do as much as possible for herself,' Kelly said. 'She's a clever girl. She figures things out. Why don't you go enjoy your toast?'

As usual, Sarah was in awe of Kelly. She and the others made the care home seem so *normal*. No drama, no fuss and no institutional feel. Despite the emergency call buttons and trained medical staff wandering around, it felt like a family there. Sissy loved it.

Sissy's diagnosis hadn't been a surprise to their mum. When she'd found herself pregnant at forty-two, she'd taken the chromosome disorder test at the insistence of her shell-shocked new boyfriend. Just as a precaution, he'd said.

'It's only precautionary if I'd do something about it,'

she'd told him, her Scouse accent becoming more pronounced with her anger. 'And I won't.' She'd taken the test just to shut him up.

He didn't believe she'd have a Down's syndrome child.

She didn't believe he'd leave her if she did.

They were both wrong.

He probably wasn't a bad person, Sarah conceded when she was feeling generous. He just hadn't planned to father Sissy so soon after meeting their mum.

Their poor mum. Her track record wasn't great when it came to men sticking around once her epidural wore off. Sarah's dad had been the first to run the hundred-yard dash, when Sarah was born and her brother, Robin, was a toddler. She didn't have any interest in knowing her father. Sissy and Robin and their mum had always been enough.

Sissy found a spot under the tree for them to sit. The late autumn sun was weak and their toast turned stone-cold, but Sissy loved the garden.

'I have a boyfriend, you know,' she said.

'Is that right?' Sarah struggled to keep her voice steady. 'Anyone I know?'

Most of the residents in the home were older than Sissy . . . much older.

'Nope.'

'Is he handsome?'

'Yeah, and a bit fat,' she said, nibbling her toast in perfectly even bites along each edge until she got to the last buttery golden mouthful in the middle.

'Oh, well, that's all right, isn't it?'

'I don't mind.'

'How old is your boyfriend?' Sarah asked, holding her breath.

Instead of answering, Sissy brushed the fine blonde hair from her face so it didn't interrupt her snack.

She wasn't sly by nature, but if she got the tiniest inkling that Sarah might get upset she'd avoid her questions.

'Same as me,' she finally said.

At least he wasn't some old perv, Sarah thought. Though he could still be a young one.

'Do you and your boyfriend do fun things together?'

'We paint and watch telly and hold hands.'

Sarah needed to talk to Kelly about this. A shared interest in *EastEnders* was one thing, as long as they weren't shagging during the advert breaks.

It was probably the single biggest worry they had about Sissy. Her trusting nature was to be expected when she was little. Now that she was sixteen it could be dangerous.

As if sexual politics weren't hard enough without Down's syndrome.

'Why don't you have a boyfriend?' Sissy asked, staring at her.

'Do I need one?'

Evasion. It ran in the family.

'It's nice having one,' she said. 'You could bake him cupcakes.'

'But I bake you cupcakes. Would you be happy sharing them with my boyfriend?'

Sissy thought about this for a minute. 'You'd have to bake extra for him.'

Before Sarah left she sought out Kelly again to talk about her sister's budding romance.

'I know it's hard, Sarah, but she's growing up.' The way Kelly said this made Sarah want to crawl into her lap for a cuddle. She had that kind of friendly authority. 'Nature is making changes and it's normal for her to want to explore these. She's done really well so far when it's come to her maturing body, right?'

Sarah nodded. She'd been the one who freaked out about Sissy's first period. Her sister was fine with it.

'We're talking to her about sex and the feelings she's starting to have,' Kelly continued.

'I understand that, but she's got a mental age of nine. How can she understand what those changes mean, or how she's supposed to handle them?'

Kelly squeezed her hand.

Just five minutes in her lap and Sarah was sure she'd feel better.

'We help her understand things the same way we would a nine-year-old,' she answered. 'With a lot of clear explanation in an environment where she's encouraged to ask questions and get honest answers. The boy she's been spending time with is sixteen too. We keep a close eye on them and, as you know, we talk regularly to everyone here about expressing their feelings in an appropriate way.'

'But you can't stop hormones,' Sarah pointed out, remembering her own teenage years. She may not have had sex till well into university but that hadn't stopped her thinking about it a lot.

Kelly smiled. 'I promise we're keeping a close eye on them. And it's good for her to have companionship. Everybody has intimacy needs. It can be unhealthy if they're not expressed. See you on Thursday?'

'Yep, Thursday.'

If her sixteen-year-old sister had a boyfriend, maybe she did need to think a bit more about RecycLove.

Chapter Four

Catherine

Catherine did a double take when she saw her next client. Was the universe just messing with her? After everything these past few weeks, it had to be having a laugh.

Struggling to keep her composure, she said, 'Mr Larson? I'm Catherine. Please come through.'

But the universe didn't answer. And when her client did, it was in a broad Australian accent.

'Aw Catherine, don't be so formal. You can call me Paul. Pleasure to meet ya.'

With just a glance she took in every detail, from his long legs to his shortish, nearly ginger hair and very ginger stubble, from his blue eyes to the quick smile he flashed as he sat in the wingback chair opposite her desk.

The man was the spitting image of Richard. Same aquiline nose, same strong jaw, same full lips and the kind of skin that burst into freckles at the sun's first rays.

But he wasn't Richard. He was definitely Paul. Australian Paul who just happened to look like her ex-husband and wanted her help finding the love of his life. She forced herself to stop staring and do her job.

'So, Paul, I wanted us to meet so that I can get a good

idea about you, your likes and dislikes and what you're looking for in a partner. And I'd like you to feel free to ask me anything at all.'

He glanced around her office. 'How'd you end up in this line of work?'

'Oh, well.' She hadn't meant for him to ask personal questions. 'It wasn't a conscious plan at first. I worked for another introduction service when I first returned from the US. I simply answered her advert.'

'Why were you in the US?'

Catherine felt her control of the interview slipping away. 'I went with my husband when he took a job there. Now, if it's all right, I'd like to talk a bit about you. Maybe you could start by telling me about your dating history?'

'Straight in there, eh?' he said.

Yeah, how's that feel? Catherine thought. She waited for him to answer.

'All of it?'

'You can give me the highlights if you'd prefer.'

He scratched his stubble. 'I wouldn't call them highlights. I've gone out with a few women for a while. Mostly I just date.'

'How long is a while?'

'About twice as long as I should have, according to them.'

Her fingers flew over her keyboard, recording every word he said.

Issues? she typed after his last comment. Her eyes never left his. It was a skill she'd learned from her mentor when she first started in the business. *Don't break eye contact with the client.* The longer you held their gaze the deeper they'd dig to offer up an honest appraisal of themselves, unearthing their habits and quirks in the process. Those golden nuggets of information were what made her so successful in finding love for them.

'Have you ever been in love?' she asked.

Jokey Paul disappeared. Aha, she thought, there's the nugget. 'Tell me about her.'

'We went out in Oz,' he said. 'We were just kids, at school together. Anabelle. Her name was Anabelle.'

'And it ended because . . .?'

He shrugged. 'Nothing dramatic. She moved away, that's all, to Cairns where her mum got a good job. She was a biotech chemist. Her mum, I mean.'

'You didn't keep in touch?'

'For a while, but it was pointless. I couldn't go there and she wasn't coming back. So that was it. Does that mean I peaked romantically at sixteen?'

'I don't think so,' she said, matching his smile. 'There are a lot of women in London.' Though competing with young Anabelle, perfectly preserved in Paul's memory, wouldn't be easy. Catherine ran across that problem quite a lot, actually. The One That Got Away Syndrome. She'd bet anything that Paul dated women younger than him, and got bored when the novelty wore off.

But aside from Anabelle he didn't seem to have any serious hang-ups. She felt like she could work with him.

'So you're in banking,' she said, consulting her initial telephone notes, 'as head of Investment Operations. Is that interesting?'

'S'pose it's all right.' He sounded like a grumpy teen.

'Tell me about it.'

'There's not much to tell, really. It's just a job.'

He wasn't rude about it, or bitter. Just . . . meh. As they talked more about his likes and interests, she had a hard time finding anything to raise him above the thousands of other good-looking, solvent men in London. He'd have to be better than this if he wanted to measure up. Yet she felt he did have something.

'Why are you thinking about using a relationship consultant now?' she asked.

'Is that a polite way of asking if I think I need to?' He smiled. 'Nah, it's not that hard to meet women. Waving your Platinum Amex in the right bars is like chumming the water.'

Catherine felt herself bristle. 'The women are the bait?'

'No, the money's the bait. The women are the sharks. That was fun when I first moved to London but it gets old after a while.'

So she was right about him. 'What are you looking for now?'

He paused. 'Quality, I s'pose. Someone who's got everything I'm looking for and is really together, you know? She's comfortable in her own skin and knows what she wants and doesn't need to play games. But I don't seem to attract that kind of woman.'

'Why not, do you think?' Catherine had to tread carefully here. She wasn't in the business of making people feel bad, but she also didn't want to over-promise.

He laughed. 'I guess I'm too rough around the edges for them. They're used to blokes who know their wines and which fork to use and all that bullshit. I'm just a hick from Queensland who wants to enjoy myself.'

'Are those other things important, do you think?'

When he sighed, Catherine caught another glimpse of the man beneath the Amex card.

'I'm starting to think they are,' he said.

She wanted to disagree with him, but it was true. The women she looked after did expect a certain amount of finesse in their dates. Not that it was the most important thing. It was all just packaging, really.

One of the most important parts of her job was figuring out which of their services would give the client the best chance of finding love. RecycLove was for the people who liked the idea of choosing loads of dates to go out with. It sounded like Paul had had enough of that. The proper matchmaking service, Love Match, was best for would-be romancers who treated dates like they did dental appointments – an inconvenient necessity. She didn't mind these clients who expected her to find a lover to match their requirements. But there was a third, rarer type of client who most interested her.

They were the diamonds in the rough.

The work she did with them didn't have an official name. She didn't advertise it and not even Richard knew much about the details.

People did come to her though, when they heard from former clients about how Catherine was able to mould people into the perfect romantic prospect.

She only had time to take on a few of these clients, so she was very picky. As she listened to Paul, her excitement started to fizz. He seemed to have all the important qualities women looked for. Already she could see that a few tweaks here and there would make a big difference to his chances of finding the woman he wanted. Maybe all he needed was a good polish.

Could she do it? Could she improve him?

She realised she'd gone quiet when she noticed him study-ing her. 'Well, if you don't feel that you've got some of the superficial attributes that your dates look for, I might be able to help you make a few changes.'

She always felt nervous when she pitched like this. She really wanted him to say yes.

'Do I need more kerb appeal?'

She could tell he was teasing her. 'Probably just small things, to help you stand out and meet more of our clients' requirements.'

'So this is a makeover, like one of those DIY programmes where they fill the house with purple velvet and candles?'

'Of course not. Purple velvet clashes with your eyes.' She smiled at her own joke. 'But I could assess you and give you some guidance if you'd like.'

He stretched his legs out in front of him. 'And this is all part of the package deal? Do you really think it'll help?'

'It can't hurt,' Catherine said.

'Thanks for that blinding vote of confidence. I've got nothing to lose then. Where do I sign?'

As Catherine prepared the contracts, she had to wonder whether this was a good idea.

Yes, he did remind her of Richard . . . Richard in the early days before they both got so serious about life.

Of course, they hadn't been serious back then. They'd been only kids, really, when they met. Richard had talked to her first, on the first day of class as they'd crowded into their second year economics lecture at uni. Well, he'd smiled first anyway. Knowing her, she'd done most of the talking. What had started with shared jokes in class soon expanded to shared notes and study dates around exam time. So far so platonic.

Then they ran into each other at a party that some of the third years were throwing. Pressed together by their dancing classmates, heat and alcohol threw their friendship into a sexy new light. At least they did for Catherine. It took Richard a few weeks to catch up, but once he did they spent as much time together out of their clothes as they did in them.

Catherine did start wondering after a while whether there was more to Richard-and-Catherine than shared class notes and drunken fumbling. There was something about him. It wasn't his looks – pale gingers were an acquired taste. But he was comfortable in his own skin, when most of the other boys covered up their self-consciousness with twattishness.

But she wasn't about to spook him with any declarations.

She'd done that to a boy once before, in school. He'd never spoken to her again. This time she planned to make a tentative query about their future that she could totally backtrack on if she needed to.

When he arrived for dinner with a bottle of wine, she kissed him hello like she always did when they were alone (rarely in public though).

'Did you get me over here on false pretences?' he asked, nuzzling her neck.

Had he guessed what she was planning?

'If so, I totally approve,' he said. 'But I'll need to have a snack before we . . .'

She laughed with relief. 'No, dinner is in the oven.' She untangled herself from his arms. 'Wine?'

If he was disappointed that there'd be no naked starter he didn't show it. That was the thing about Richard. He took everything in his stride. Their evening was as relaxed as usual, until they finished their meal.

'I was wondering about something,' she said.

Richard's expression turned serious. She nearly chickened out then and asked if he wanted to watch a film instead of what she really wanted to know.

'Have you lured me into some kind of relationship?' she asked. Yes, a joke. That was good. It didn't sound so threatening.

Her heart hammered as she twirled her wine glass by the stem, trying to look like she didn't care too much about the answer.

'You may have lured me,' he said. 'But I think we are. Aren't we?'

Relief flooded through her. 'I think so too. I just wondered because we didn't start out in the usual way.'

'What's the usual way?'

'You know. Dates and romance and all that.'

He laughed. 'That's never really been my thing.'

'Nor mine. Relaxed and casual is much better.'

It was the first little lie of many.

So, relaxed and casual was how their relationship progressed until graduation. Neither asked the other to join holidays or family visits. They just rubbed along together, with Richard in her life but not part of it. She told him that was fine. Usually she believed it herself.

Besides, she wasn't anxious to have her heart handed to her in pieces again. She did love Richard and she thought he probably loved her. It was enough to be best friends with her boyfriend. It was fun, relaxed and, above all, safe.

But soon their diplomas would be in hand. Decisions had to be made. Coming from England's commuter belt, Catherine grew up dreaming of a career in London. Richard preferred Manchester and started applying for jobs there.

They were about to be geographically unsuitable and she didn't fancy a long-distance relationship. But she didn't want to call quits on it either. So she quietly applied for positions in Manchester too. When she got an offer before Richard, it looked a bit like he was following her. She liked that.

But when he was offered the job in the US a few years later, there was no way for Catherine to move there and make it look like an accident.

Chapter Five

Rachel

Rachel inspected James's office from the doorway. How did he get any work done in such a tip? It looked like an over-full recycling bag had exploded on the floor. Magazines, hardback books and plans were piled everywhere, weighed down with coffee-stained mugs. He didn't even bother putting his files on the shelves the right way around – they were shoved in there on their sides.

Scientists could grow disease cultures on his desk.

She felt her lips pinching with disapproval. It was a signature move inherited from her mum. Ordered space, ordered mind; that was her motto. Rachel had inherited that too.

He was hunched over, sketching furiously. She could see the red pen in his hand. That meant he was working on interior walls. He was as obsessive about his colour-coded pens as they all were.

'James? Want to try the new sushi place with me?'

Light and breezy, that's what she was aiming for. No ulterior motives here.

He glanced up from his tracing paper. 'Thanks, I would but I'm kind of busy right now.'

39

'Come on. I'd rather eat in and you know I hate sitting by myself.'

He didn't look up again. 'Why don't you ask Alison or Beth?'

Creeping across the litter-strewn floor, Rachel hovered over his shoulder. The sketch was good. 'I'll buy.'

He threw himself over the paper like she was trying to copy his exam answers. 'Could you get me takeaway if you're going? You know what I like.'

'Come with me.'

His head snapped up. 'What's up, Rachel?'

Damn.

'Nothing's up. Can't a friend buy another friend lunch?'

He sighed, putting the cap on his Sharpie. 'How long have we known each other?'

'Around five years, I think.'

Five years in January, actually, plus extra credit time for the year they went out.

'And after that long don't you think I can tell when you're up to something?'

'You're no fun to try to manipulate, do you know that?'

She pushed the rolls of tracing paper off his extra chair so she could sit. She'd hoped to do this over maki rolls.

'James.'

'Yes, Rachel.'

She didn't expect him to make it easy for her. 'Do you feel like you're getting everything you want, romantically, from your life? Because I don't.'

She felt too wooden, rehearsed, but she had to push on.

'I keep going out with these guys I meet, and they keep disappointing me. If they don't just want sex then they're too clingy. If they're not too clingy they're emotionally unavailable. If not that then they have a girlfriend already. I'm so sick of it all.'

He nodded. 'Uh huh, I see. Just so I know, Rach, are you just telling me about your dates or is there a question in here somewhere?'

'There's a question.'

'Then can we please . . .' He made a winding-up motion with his finger. 'Make this as painless as possible?'

'You don't want any background at all?'

'Well, you've already told me about the bloke who wanted to wee on you.' He pulled a face.

Rachel sighed. 'Exactly my point. I can't keep meeting random guys in pubs. I need a more structured approach if I'm going to meet anyone worthwhile. I'm joining Catherine's website.'

'Fine, good for you.'

'You know, James, this is exactly why we broke up!'

'Why, Rachel? What do you want me to say? That I'm thrilled you're joining a website to meet guys? Maybe I don't really want to listen to you talk about the shitty men in your life.'

'No! Because you're totally dismissive. Not to mention that you're an absolute pig,' she added, looking again around the office. 'I'm asking for your help.'

'Calling me a pig isn't really making me warm to your request, you know.'

She shrugged. 'I had other words in mind, so I was actually being kind.'

He smiled. 'Tell me what you need, Rach.'

Her tummy churned at the way he said this. It was easier being his friend when he wasn't being tender.

'I can't join unless I bring an ex with me. It's really simple. We sign up and give each other feedback about what we were like in the relationship. You know, an assessment about what we did right and wrong.'

He rubbed his chin. 'Do I really want to know what you think is wrong with me?'

'But you'll get to do it to me too. Just imagine, James. You can outline every single one of my flaws and I'll have to sit there and take it. Besides, nobody else sees the assessment. Only us. Then I write an endorsement telling women why they should go out with you.'

'Hmm, that's interesting.' He leaned back in his chair. 'Tell me more.'

'That's it, really. Once we're on the website we can go out with whomever we want to.'

'No, I mean tell me more about why women should go out with me. You'll throw me this tiny bone, won't you? It might be the only ego stroke I get this year. Come on, Rach, tell me, tell me. Is it my hair? It's my hair, isn't it?' He flicked his head and pursed his lips.

She laughed. James was many things – cheapskate, workaholic, smart-arse – but he wasn't conceited. He never minded making a fool of himself to make her laugh. 'Yeah, I guess you have good hair.' It was a thick dark mop, long and shaggy. He wore it side-combed over his forehead like they did in the boy bands. 'And you're not too short. That would be a plus for women who aren't very tall.'

They were nearly the same height when she wore her high heels and, though he wasn't classically handsome, his regular features were a decent backdrop for the most startling blue eyes she'd ever seen. His mouth was perhaps a bit too small, but it suited his narrow chin which, in turn, suited his slender frame. His personality would attract women as much as his looks.

Of course, he'd rather hear that he was devastatingly god-like handsome.

'Will you do it?' she asked. 'Will you join with me? I have to bring someone with me.'

'Are you saying you need me?'

'Yes, James,' she muttered. 'I need you.'

Thank God that was no longer really true. A few years ago it would have been.

'And all I have to do is fill in a few forms and you'll let me go back to work? I can do that. Wait, this doesn't mean the sushi offer is off, does it?'

'I'll still get your sushi, James.'

'Cool. Extra wasabi please.'

Rachel beamed all the way to the restaurant. That wasn't as hard as it could have been.

The house was empty after work when she unlocked both deadbolts and the door lock to let herself in. They weren't paranoid, fortressing themselves in like this. When they'd first come to look at the house, the door had been patched at the bottom where someone had kicked through it. One of the first things they'd bought was a solid replacement. The little buggers would break bones now if they tried forcing their way in.

Even with the risk of burglary, Rachel loved their house. Back when it was built, Victorian families needed lots of rooms. Clapton wasn't overrun by Poundlands and chicken shops then.

There were little traces of those more affluent days left – ornate cornicing and plaster roses on some of the ceilings, tall sash windows and wide-beam oak floors. But cheap dividing walls scarred the floors where they'd been put up in haste and disintegrated at leisure. Big holes and cracks pockmarked the plaster. Wires and pipes ran in the shortest distance between two points. Basically, they lived in a semi-derelict building site.

But that's what they'd signed up for when they bought the house. None of them could afford their own flat in the area. It might be dirty and dangerous but property prices there were rising faster than Jude Law's hairline. So they bought something together that could eventually be sub-divided. One day, when the time came, they'd each have their own flat. Till then they added a working fridge and settled into the original shabby chic decor. Pictures hung on wires straight from the mouldings. Those covered up the damp-stained walls, and threadbare rugs were strewn over the scratched and splintery floors. They'd scavenged through the charity shops to find velvet sofas and reading chairs to fill the cavernous sitting room.

People paid good money for decorators to give them that kind of distressed look. Their home's distress was authentic.

Still, what a huge tick on her Adult To-Do list. She'd got the degree, she had the job and she'd invested in the house with Catherine and Sarah. Soon she'd be working on the relationship.

Sometimes she had to remind herself that there was nothing wrong with her. Just because she wasn't married or doing the school run each morning didn't mean she had a tail or anything. Millions of women were in the same boat, with high standards and a low tolerance for wankishness.

She made her way down to the kitchen to flick on the kettle, glancing at the 1950s black Bakelite wall clock as she went. It was after seven. She'd kill for a cup of coffee, but the bags under her eyes were now suitcases and she had to sleep. Herbal tea wasn't top of her favourites list but it was better than nothing. And she did feel virtuous drinking grass clippings.

She spotted the *Bake Off* application still in the tea drawer, as unfilled-in as when she'd first printed it off. Not surprising. Sarah was the last person to sing her own praises.

Her eyes darted to the kitchen doorway.

She'd be coming back from Sissy's on the train now, like she did every Tuesday and Thursday. And often at weekends too.

Rachel stared at the application. The teabags were under it anyway . . .

She picked up the sheets.

When the kettle finished its furious boil she poured her tea and rummaged in her bag for the thriller she'd been devouring. There were only around fifty pages left and she was pretty sure she knew who'd done it.

Her glance bounced between the book and the application. She should read her book and drink her tea.

But she *did* know who'd done it.

Her eyes wandered to the *Bake Off* questions.

How long has the applicant been baking?

That was easy. Sarah was already great by the time she moved into the old flat. It was her promise of home-made scones that won her Catherine's vote when they first met.

Her mum had taught her to bake when she was little (the next question). Every year when she got tipsy on her birthday she told them how she'd baked her own Victoria sponge when she turned six. Every year they pretended this was new information.

Glancing again at the doorway, Rachel's hand found a pen. It seemed to have a mind of its own.

I started baking my own cakes at six, she wrote.

Next question: **What did she personally get from baking?**

Sarah never really talked about it but it seemed to make her really happy. She usually sang when she baked, and filled the whole kitchen with a homeliness as she worked through her recipes. Rachel said as much on the form, but skipped the part about the singing in case that might be distracting on set.

Next were a load of questions about skills and knowledge. She had to guess at those. Sarah seemed to know how to bake everything, so Rachel just listed the main categories from one of her cookbooks as examples. The judges probably wanted a broad idea anyway.

When she got to the questions about hobbies and ambitions, it started sounding a lot like a dating profile. *I like long chocolate eclairs on the beach, enjoying sunset cheesecakes, and I live life to the fullest-fat cream.* The questions were handy though, given the conversation she'd have with Sarah when she got in. Two birds, one stone.

She let out a little yelp when the front door opened upstairs.

'Anybody home yet?' Sarah called from the living room.

She shoved the application back in the drawer. Somehow it seemed less sneaky to keep it there in relatively plain sight.

'Been home long?' Sarah said, throwing her bag on the table. 'Whatcha doing?'

'Just finishing my book. I got home a few minutes ago. Have you eaten?'

Sarah shook her head. 'Let's order from the Noodle Shop.'

She moved toward the tea drawer to get the noodle menu.

'Let me do it!' Rachel cried, launching herself at the drawer to shove the application beneath the menus. 'You've just walked in the door. Go change into something more comfy. You want the Thai noodles, right?'

Sarah stared at her jeans and baggy dark blue fisherman's jumper. 'Catherine wants to get me out of my trackies and you want me in them. I wish you'd make up your minds,' she called over her shoulder.

Rachel's heart hammered. So much for feeling less sneaky. Still, Sarah would be grateful if she got the chance to have Paul Hollywood compliment her iced buns.

Twenty minutes later, Aziz was at their front door. His parents owned the Noodle Shop.

'All right?' he said, handing Rachel the steaming plastic bags.

'Good, Aziz, thanks. You?'

Something about him looked different but Rachel couldn't put her finger on it. Was it his hair? Yes, that was it. She could see his hair. 'No helmet? Where's your scooter?'

'Got nicked yesterday,' he mumbled, hunching further into his winter coat.

'Oh no! Your parents aren't making you deliver on foot?'

'Nah, we're not doing deliveries till we get the insurance money to replace it.'

'Well thanks for making an exception for us.'

'No problem, you're our best customers. See you later.'

Poor Noodle Shop family, thought Rachel. As if the people in their neighbourhood didn't have enough trouble making ends meet.

'Aziz's scooter got nicked,' Rachel told Sarah as she unpacked their order.

'That's shite! It's probably halfway to Africa by now.'

'It didn't run away, Sarah. It was stolen.'

'I know. They're selling them in Africa.'

'Are you sure that's not bicycles?'

'Maybe.' Sarah shifted her container of noodles aside to make room for her sketch pad. 'What do you think of this? I'm pitching it at the ideas meeting tomorrow.'

Rachel pulled the pad closer.

She loved Sarah's sketches. No wonder her cards were consistently bestsellers. Her company was very lucky to have her.

She'd done some preliminary colouring in on the pen-and-ink sketch. Two figures stood hand-in-hand beneath an arch of summer flowers.

'What's the theme?' Rachel asked.

The man in the sketch was balding, with a big tummy beneath his suit.

'It's an Asian lady marrying an English man,' she said, scooping up some noodles with her chopsticks.

47

The lithe young woman smiled adoringly at her paunchy groom.

'Seriously?'

'Harry's always looking for ways to expand the wedding cards. I know everybody thinks she's a mail-order bride but sometimes they must really be in love. Don't they deserve a nice card too?'

Sarah was such a romantic at heart. Maybe it was the cause of her success as a wedding card designer. Or a consequence. Either way, it worked for her.

'Well, good luck in the meeting,' said Rachel through a mouthful of steaming noodles. 'It is quite romantic. Speaking of which, I talked to James today. He's joining RecycLove with me.'

Sarah peered at Rachel from beneath her blonde fringe. 'Are you sure you're going to be okay with James dating right under your nose?'

'Womankind is welcome to him! We are *absolutely* just friends. So now you have to join with me,' she continued. 'And don't say you'll think about it. I know that means you won't do it. We'll do it together.'

Sarah sighed, closing her sketchbook. 'Rachel, I don't even know where to start with the profile.'

Rachel thought about the *Bake Off* application. 'But I do. I'll help you. It's probably just some questions about your hobbies and stuff. Please say you will. All you have to do is ask Sebastian. If James said yes, then a horndog like Sebastian definitely will, just to get access to all the women. Please say you will. Please? What's there to lose?'

Sarah ticked off on her fingers. 'My dignity, my self-esteem, hours out of my life, just off the top of my head.'

'At least try, Sarah. If you hate it you can always quit. Nothing ventured, nothing gained . . . Shall I text Catherine and tell her we'll do it together?'

Rachel reached for her phone.

'I'm texting. If you want me to stop, say so. No? Okay. Texting.'

Sarah squirmed, but didn't move to stop her.

'Texting. Texting. Sent. RecycLove, here we come.'

Chapter Six

Sarah

Everyone in the conference room stared between Sarah and her sketch pad.

Her boss was doing that thing with his throat when he got embarrassed.

As if he had anything to be embarrassed about. He wasn't the one being gawped at like he'd drawn willies on the wall.

'Help me see where you're going with this, Sarah,' he said.

But I've literally drawn you a picture, she wanted to shout. Why didn't people ever seem to know what she was talking about?

Instead she said, 'It's simple. Lots of English men and Asian women get married. This card would be for them.'

'You mean mail-order brides?' Harry asked.

Someone sniggered. It was Maria-Therese. That woman spent more time in Harry's back pocket than his own wallet did.

'No, Harry, not mail-order brides! Don't be insulting. It's for Asian women and English men who are in love.'

'I think that might be a little too niche for us, Sarah,' he said.

This time she caught Maria-Therese roll her beady little

eyes. She could never look at her colleague's twitchy needle nose and pinched lips in her thin, washed-out face without thinking of bubonic-infected rodents.

'But we're supposed to be thinking of niche markets. Isn't that what you keep telling us in these meetings?'

'Not quite that niche,' he said. 'Who's next?'

The problem with Harry was that he had no vision. They'd already covered all the usual ethnic combinations, plus gay marriage and their non-standard body type range (which was Sarah's idea).

She didn't mind illustrating traditional boy-meets-girl cards but they were getting killed by companies like MoonPig. At the rate they were going, she'd be sketching tourists for a fiver in Trafalgar Square by this time next year.

Harry's meetings only took an hour but they always felt like they sucked about a week from Sarah's soul. Despite all the evidence – the growth in online cards and all the high-street shops closing down – Harry refused to adapt. He'd only make little tweaks here and there to his family's business. That was like reupholstering the seats on your horse-drawn cart when everyone else was working at Ford.

Sarah didn't know which she hated more – getting bollocked for not bringing an idea to the meeting each week, or getting bollocked when she did.

She hurried toward the lifts, stuffing her sketch pads back into her bag. She didn't have a desk there. None of them did. Harry called it 'flexible working', but he was just too skint to pay for office space. Working from home suited Sarah anyway, with Sissy to think about.

She was waiting as usual just outside the front door when Sarah got there, beneath the big sign that welcomed everyone to Whispering Sands. What a misnomer. Nobody whispered in the care home and the only sand within thirty miles was in the car park, left over from when they gritted it last winter.

'You're—'

'I'm not late,' Sarah said. 'Are you ready to go?'

'I was ready at two thirty,' said Sissy, holding her wrist two inches from Sarah's face.

'Your watch is fast.'

'No, you're slow.'

'Whatever. Let's go. Button your coat.' The November days were closing in. 'We can pick up some flowers for Mum on the way.'

She was only in the next town but travelling back there always gave Sarah pangs, like that sinking-in-the-stomach feeling when you think about an ex that you really liked.

She pushed the feelings aside as they got to the florist near their mum's.

'Do you like any of these bouquets?' she asked Sissy, who was sniffing the flowers in each of the two dozen buckets by the desk.

'These smell nicest,' she said, pointing to the long-stem red roses.

'Yeah, well for three quid a stem, they should. What about one of these?' She pointed to the £10 bunches.

Carefully, Sissy inspected each bouquet. It would take her a while to decide.

Sissy never let Sarah rush her. Her scrupulous attention to detail meant that even the most mundane task took her about a million years. Plus, she liked to touch everything she saw, which made clothes shopping with her an exercise in patience.

'How's everything going with your boyfriend?' Sarah asked as Sissy sniffed a purple and yellow bouquet.

'Good.' Sniff.

'Still holding hands?'

'Sometimes.' She glanced over. 'And kissing.'

'Oh, kissing? Is that nice?'

'Yep.' Sniff sniff. 'This one smells nice.'

'Anything besides kissing?'

She thought for a minute. 'He gave me his jelly.'

'Nothing more? No hugging or . . . sex?'

Sissy rolled her eyes. 'Don't be gross. We're not supposed to do that.'

'I'm just checking.'

'Don't worry.'

Of course she worried.

'I brought a drawing for Mum,' Sissy said as Sarah paid the florist for the bouquet she finally chose.

'Can I see it?'

Carefully, she unfolded the pink sheet.

'Nice one,' Sarah said. 'You're really talented.'

Sissy had covered the whole page with tiny squares, then coloured each one in to create a paper mosaic. It was a zoo scene with elephants, giraffes, lions and monkeys.

'I really like the way you've done the sky. Is there a storm coming?' Sarah pointed to the roiling dark clouds in one corner.

Sissy nodded. 'It's going to rain.'

They walked around the corner from the florist's shop.

'Here we are. Ready to visit Mum?'

Sissy took Sarah's hand and they walked together through the cemetery gates.

As Sarah dropped her sister off she tried not to mind that Sissy never looked even the littlest bit sad to leave her. She might at least wave wistfully every once in a while instead of just returning to her friends without as much as a backwards glance.

Sarah knew she should be happy that Sissy was so independent but the truth was, she wanted Sissy to need her as much as she needed Sissy. Instead she was such a typical teenager.

As Sarah got on the train back to London she called Robin. 'All right?' he said when he answered.

'All right,' said Sarah. 'I just dropped Sissy off. We went to the cemetery. You should see the picture that she did for Mum. It was really ace.'

Kelly at the home was trying to get some funding to start running an art class since several of the residents loved drawing and painting. None of them were as good as Sissy though.

'She's got a boyfriend,' Sarah told him. 'She says they've been kissing.'

'Jesus, that's not good,' he said. 'They should be keeping a closer eye on her.'

'Kelly says it's normal and that we need to be ready for this new phase.'

'Kelly wouldn't say that if Sissy was her sister. She shouldn't be letting guys kiss her. Should I talk to her?'

'Oh I'm begging you, please don't!' Sarah knew how that'd go. When she was in sixth form, Robin had decided to tell her about sex. For some reason he thought it'd go down better if he used all the official words.

Her face still burned thinking about him talking about vaginas.

'We need to let Kelly do the job she's trained for,' she said. 'Please don't talk to Sissy about it. If you spook her she'll never tell us anything.'

'I wish Mum was here,' he said. 'She'd know how to handle it.'

'Me too,' Sarah murmured.

* * *

Their mum could do anything, and Sarah didn't believe that only because she was her child. She had the usual parenting skills – rooting out the monsters from under the bed and kissing away hurts – but Sarah hadn't realised the half of it till she was older.

There hadn't been much spare cash left over from her mum's secretarial job after the rent was paid, but Sarah had never noticed that they were pretty poor. They weren't exactly the sort to splash out in restaurants anyway and why would they want to, with their mum's cooking?

She turned her hobby into a part-time job, to go with her full-time job, when Sarah and Robin were little. She made delicious beef stews, lasagnes and shepherd's pies in bulk for their neighbours, cooking as easily for fourteen as she did for four. And when Sissy was born the few quid she charged per meal were a lifesaver. She had to quit her job then, and their carer's and disability benefits didn't stretch very far.

Their rented terraced house had one of those kitchen extensions off the back that opened on to a long, narrow garden. The appliances and work surfaces spread across the back half of the big room, with overstuffed sofas and the TV beneath skylights at the front. They pretty much lived in those two rooms, till first Robin and then Sarah went away to London.

Maybe if they'd still been at home when their mum got ill, they'd have noticed how run-down she was getting.

At first she wouldn't go to her GP. 'It's nothing,' she'd said. 'Stop worrying and have some more cake.'

But she wasn't eating her own food. That wasn't like her.

Then she got a nosebleed one night when Robin and Sarah were home for dinner. After ten minutes it still wouldn't stop.

'Mum, do you get these often?' Robin asked gently as he passed her another wad of toilet roll and made her keep her head tipped back.

'I've had a few,' she said through the tissue. 'But it's no big deal.'

Robin caught Sarah's eye. *I'm sorry*, his look said, *but watching your mother bleed is a big deal.* 'I'm making you an appointment with the GP tomorrow, Mum.'

This time she didn't fight them, or dismiss the suggestion. Something was obviously wrong. The evidence was right there, dripping down her face.

But Sarah didn't expect cancer. Maybe a sinus infection or haemophilia at a stretch, but not cancer.

She should have been more worried, but she clearly remembered *not* being that worried. She went whole days without thinking about her mum and her nosebleeds. Partly it was because she'd downplayed everything (another of her Parenting 101 skills) and partly it was because Sarah was caught up in her own life. Still pretty new at her job, she was excited about living in London. And she was more concerned with catching the last Tube home than her mother's health.

She should have been bone-freezingly terrified for her.

The GP sent her off for blood tests and when they came back showing that her white blood cells were going haywire, it finally hit Sarah. This was no sinus infection or pollen allergy.

Her mum had lived two days past her six-month prognosis. Acute lymphoblastic leukaemia doesn't like to be kept waiting, and by the time she'd gone to the GP it had already travelled to her spine. Her last weeks were horrible, painful and undignified, yet her only concern had been for them, her children. When Sarah had promised her she'd look after Sissy no matter what else happened, Sarah saw the relief in her expression. They'd already talked about what should happen if the worst came to the worst.

Sarah had wanted to come live in the house with Sissy.

'No you will not,' her mum had said with nearly her usual strength. 'You can give her all the love in the world, but she's only a child and you can't take that responsibility. I've cared for her for thirteen years, every minute of every day and night. Believe me when I tell you it's a twenty-four-hour job and you haven't had the experience or training to do it. She'll need someone qualified to look after her.'

'I could learn!' Sarah said.

'I know you want to, love, but we have to think about what's best for Sissy too. Promise me, Sarah. I mean it. I've got to know that she'll be safe and looked after. There are good facilities that can do that. We'll have to find one.'

Sarah had hated the idea of her little sister moving out of her home but her mum had been adamant.

'It's not just a matter of making sure she's fed and clean and happy,' her mum had said. 'There are medical issues. What if you didn't spot an infection in time? It wouldn't be your fault, you wouldn't know, but have you thought about that? Or have you thought about what you'd do if you came back here? You can't leave Sissy alone in the house all day to work. Would you give up your job and your life to stay with her? Then I'd have to worry about you both while I'm up there knocking on the pearly gates.'

'Don't talk like that, Mum.'

'Why, do you think I'm heading south instead?' She'd pointed to the floor, mustering a laugh. 'Promise me, Sarah.'

She'd had no choice. Every time she had brought it up, her mum panicked at the thought that Sissy wouldn't get the care she needed. So they had a lot of really uncomfortable meetings with social services. Each time, Sarah had felt like she and Robin were plotting behind Sissy's back. She knew her mother was right, but that didn't make it any easier.

Thankfully, Sissy was pretty healthy. They had to watch for the infections but she didn't have the heart defects that many Down's syndrome kids did. And so far there was no sign of leukaemia either. Not that Mum's was hereditary, at least as far as they knew, but Sissy was at a higher risk with her condition. There was so much that doctors didn't know yet about Down's, but what they did know was depressing. Sissy had a one in fifty chance of developing leukaemia by the age of five. Sarah was sure their mum had known this. Not that she'd have worried them with such a potentially deadly fact.

But Sissy was beating the odds (screw you, Fate! thought Sarah).

Each birthday that they celebrated put more distance between her and the disease. She could still get it, but every time she blew out her birthday candles, the odds swung further in her favour.

Chapter Seven

Catherine

'But, Georgina,' Catherine tried again, glancing at the time, 'I'm just suggesting that you might have better luck if you were a little less . . .'

Picky?

Petty?

Unrealistic, spoilt or exasperating?

'. . . less restrictive in your requirements,' she finally said. They'd been on the phone for nearly ten minutes, going round and round. She'd never refunded a client's fee before but she was nearly ready to cut a cheque for this woman.

It was only supposed to be a routine checking-in call. They had them weekly with their Love Match clients, but this had turned into Georgina's bitch session about the quality of the men she'd been set up with.

It was setting Catherine's teeth on edge.

No, hang on, that wasn't really fair, she reminded herself. Yes, Georgina was a pain in the arse, but what was really making her cross was knowing that Richard and Magda were lying in wait to ruin her night straight after the call.

'Are you saying there's something wrong with my

approach?' Georgina demanded. 'Because I've never had any complaints before.'

No, thought Catherine. And you've not had that many dates either.

'But everyone can benefit from an outside perspective,' she said instead of what she was thinking. 'That's my job, after all. In fact . . .'

She knew she'd regret her next words but she also knew that Georgina would never get anywhere in her current state. 'In fact, we do offer another service here that may interest you. It's an advisory relationship.'

'But you already advise me.'

Catherine heard the snarky ditto marks around the word advise. She took a deep breath. Calm professionalism, that's what she needed to get through this call.

'Well, I do guide you towards suitable men, yes. But this is more about working together to overcome any barriers that may be stopping you from finding what you're looking for.'

'What kind of barriers?' Georgina sounded suspicious. 'How much does this cost? I'm not keen to pay more money when, to be honest, I'm not a hundred per cent convinced about the service as it is.'

Catherine bit her tongue. 'It's completely free.'

'I see. And what kind of advice would you give me, for example, if I said yes?'

Catherine glanced again at her mobile as it flashed incoming emails at her.

She was going to be late for dinner. She'd managed to put it off for nearly a month already. Now it would look even more like she didn't want to meet Magda.

But no, this was work. Let Richard wait. Magda would just have to stay up past her bedtime.

'Well, you could streamline your criteria. Home in on the

five or six things that are really critical to you.' She scanned down the long, long list of requirements Georgina had insisted on since she joined. 'For example, are you sure you wouldn't consider someone who golfs? Even the occasional round?'

'But Catherine, it takes four hours to play golf! Four hours, plus getting to the club and back, changing and showering and probably having a drink afterwards. That's my entire weekend day spent alone. If he's a regular golfer, that's *every* weekend day spent alone.'

She had a point. Personally, Catherine wasn't a golfing fan either. 'What about other sports? You said no to any sporting interests. How about football? That only takes an hour and a half and he can do it in the local park.'

Georgina sighed in a way that made Catherine's heart leap. Was she actually going to relax one of her demands? She dared not hope.

'It's a mindset as much as the activity itself,' she said. 'But I suppose, as long as he's not obsessive about it, then it's okay.'

Victory! Catherine wanted to pull the front of her top over her head and run around the office making V-signs.

Of course, she wouldn't do that.

'Rugby?'

'Okay.'

'Billiards?'

'That's not a sport,' Georgina said.

'No, it's more of a pub pastime, I suppose.'

'The pub? Now we're getting into a whole different world of problems.'

Catherine knew when to drop the subject. 'What about beards? Is that a definite no-go? Even if they're handsome and aren't wedded to facial hair? For lots of men it's just a phase, and they can often be persuaded to lose it.'

Georgina made a non-committal noise.

'Is that a yes?'

'S'pose. But I'm not going to go out with anyone who looks like a lumberjack. I don't care if he's got Bradley Cooper's face underneath all that hair.'

'Fair enough,' said Catherine, running her finger down Georgina's list. 'Now, let's talk about language fluency. I know you speak French, so maybe it isn't necessary for him to as well?'

'No, that's non-negotiable. I don't want to be the only one planning our French holidays.'

Catherine thought for a moment. 'What if he's a member of a concierge service like Quintessentially? The consultants there can book the entire thing for you. All you have to do is turn up at the airport with your bag and your passport. In fact, they could plan all your holidays. It really would be a big advantage.'

'Hmm, I like the sound of that,' Georgina said. 'Fine then, please only find me dates who're Quintessentially members.'

Bollocks, that backfired. There were probably even fewer of those than there were fluent French speakers. She let out a sigh. Win some, lose some. She had one more battle to fight, and then she really did have to go.

'Shoes without socks. Georgina, that really is getting too particular. Is it a hygiene issue? Because Boots does decent foot spray and—'

'It's not hygiene,' she said. 'It's Sloaney. I can't stand those South Ken types. You just know he's going to *fnar fnar fnar* at his own jokes and have fond memories of all the times he was bummed at school. No, he *must* wear socks.'

Catherine had to hand it to Georgina. She may be about as flexible as Woody Allen but she did have a reason for every demand she made.

* * *

'So so SO sorry I'm late!' Catherine hurried into the restaurant twenty minutes later full of smiles and excuses.

The blonde young woman bounced up from her chair when Richard stood to kiss Catherine hello. 'I am so happy to finally meet you!' Magda said, nearly pushing Richard out of the way so she could clasp Catherine to her. 'You have no idea how much Richard talks about you.'

'Congratulations on your engagement,' Catherine said, noting the huge round diamond sparkling on her finger.

So this was Magda. Her wide, ice-blue eyes were framed by darkly mascaraed lashes, set in a flawlessly smooth square face that was much more Cameron Diaz than SpongeBob SquarePants.

In the nanosecond that they stood together, Catherine committed Magda's figure to memory. As tall and as slim as she'd been at twenty-three, there was nothing to fault there. Catherine adjusted her beige jumper, wishing she'd worn a dress. But she hadn't wanted to seem as if she was making an effort.

Mission accomplished, she thought crossly.

When she took a seat across from Magda at the small square table, the girl scrunched up her shoulders, gurned and giggled like they were sharing the most exciting secret imaginable.

Maybe that was the attraction for Richard. Magda seemed to be the inverse of Catherine – a bubbly-looking blonde instead of a sensible brunette. Catherine was Hobbs and M&S. Magda was Gucci and, Catherine was betting, Agent Provocateur. And instead of her straight, smooth dark locks, Magda's hair looped in huge curls. If those curls could talk they'd say, *Take me to the bedroom.*

'I got caught up at work,' Catherine said.

'I think what you do is fascinating,' gushed Magda. 'You have to tell me all about it. Richard never tells me anything.'

She pushed out her pillowy bottom lip.

'Oh, well, there's not a lot to tell, really. We've got two businesses – the website and the dating agency. I've been working mostly on the website lately.' She didn't make eye contact with Richard in case he took that as a judgement. 'But I've recently signed an interesting client. I've been meaning to talk to you about it, actually, Richard. But not tonight, obviously.'

'No, no, please do,' Magda said. 'I insist! After all, I am sort of involved now that Richard and I are getting married.'

Catherine saw Richard wince and realised that he was nervous. Though she couldn't work out who he was wincing at.

And really, she should be squirming, not him. She was the one sitting across from her replacement, like the spare laptop that he couldn't quite bring himself to get rid of. But no, it wouldn't even occur to Richard how this might grate on her ego. He was too busy pretending that it was normal for his ex-wife to have dinner with his fiancée.

And, she realised, it *was* more about her ego than her heart. After everything that had happened she couldn't really imagine being with him now. But that wasn't to say she wanted his upgrade to be easy.

Petty? Yes. Understandable? She thought so.

She found herself relaxing as she explained that she'd offered Paul and Georgina the remodelling service. Ah, the sweet influence of work! It was such a clever business model. Clients paid them to be both their customers and their product. The more clients they had buying, the more product they had to sell. So spending a few extra hours to improve their success rate would be worthwhile. She didn't expect Richard to object. After all, she was spending her time, not his.

She was surprised, though, by how many questions Magda asked. That girl wasn't kidding. She did want to know every detail.

'Shall I choose some wine?' Richard said after the waiter went away for the second time with an empty order pad.

He started flipping through the wine menu, running his finger down each page as if he was looking for something special.

Catherine suppressed a smile. He'd choose the fourth or fifth cheapest wine. He always did. He was just too proud to admit he didn't know much about it.

Did Magda know this, or was she impressed by his sommelier impersonation?

'See anything interesting?' Catherine couldn't help asking.

'Hmm, there are a few good vintages,' he said. 'I think we'll like this one.' He pointed out his choice to the waiter.

She wondered what else Magda didn't know.

Did he still claim that he made his own pesto because he'd found the perfect basil at the market? He actually bought it from the Italian deli in Farringdon and froze it. Or that when he said he'd played football with David Beckham, it had been for half an hour when he was sixteen years old, away at football summer camp with a lot of other not-very-athletic boys? The camp's founder knew David's dad from when he fitted his new boiler and got him in as a favour.

Everyone was a little bit false when it came down to it. Catherine only needed to look at herself, smiling at Magda as if they were new best friends.

When she thought about it, that's what she was offering with the client remodelling service: a few tips and tricks to brighten up a sagging façade. They were only cosmetic renovations.

Mentally she filed away Richard's wine gimmick to share with Paul. He wouldn't need to be an expert, only to look competent on a date. Once a woman was in love with him she wouldn't care that he didn't know his Meursault from his Merlot.

'What other changes are you thinking of making?' Magda asked.

'Changes?'

'To the business,' she said, frowning. 'You must have a lot of ideas about how to grow it.'

'It doesn't need growing. It does pretty well as it is,' Catherine said, knowing she sounded defensive.

'But you cannot rest on your laurels.'

'What makes you think that I'm resting on my laurels?'

'Oh, I did not mean to offend you! I just thought that a businesswoman like you would be full of ideas.'

'We can't expand too quickly or we won't be able to give our clients the service they're paying for.'

She did not have to justify her business to this child.

'Catherine is always coming up with new ideas,' Richard said, grasping Magda's hand. 'RecycLove wouldn't exist without her.'

But Magda wouldn't be distracted. 'So this renovation idea,' she continued. 'Giving clients a one-on-one self-improvement, is that not going to stretch the staff?'

'Magda,' Catherine said, knowing she was about to sound exactly like her mother. 'Richard and I talk through all business-related matters and decide together what makes sense for the company.'

She may as well have said, *Your dad and I don't think you need to worry about that kind of grown-up talk. Now go upstairs and do some colouring in.*

'Magda does have a point though, Catherine. *Will* taking on two new clients be too much for you?'

'No! Definitely not. I'll keep track, shall I, and report back to you in a few weeks. Now, are you ordering starters or just mains?'

She'd known dinner would be uncomfortable, but she hadn't expected a work critique.

'Just a main for me,' said Magda. 'With the holidays coming, I need to watch my diet or I will never fit into my dress.'

She rolled her eyes like she was a contestant on *The Biggest Loser*.

Catherine officially hated her.

Chapter Eight

Rachel

James didn't fool her. He might be doodling in his notebook but he'd also hang on every word their boss said. He just thought that pretending disinterest made him look cool.

Rachel, on the other hand, was leaning so far forward that she was practically lying across the table. Missed a trick there. She should have had her nose in her book when Ed came in. But then nobody ever accused her of being cool.

'So what's up?' James asked, as if he and Ed were old pals.

'Thanks for coming,' Ed said, ignoring James's bonhomie. Rachel allowed herself the tiniest smile. Not that his snub meant she'd get promoted to the favourite instead.

'I wanted to touch base about the Zigler pitch,' Ed continued. 'At the risk of repeating myself, you did an excellent job and the client loved your ideas. It's not always easy for young architects to read a meeting correctly, to know just where to pitch your message, but you did it.'

Young architects? Ed was welcome to think of her as a fresh-faced hotshot. She smoothed down her dress – navy polka dots today. Sometimes her style did work in her favour. Though he didn't need to make it sound like he was their grandfather, tutoring them at his wizened old knee and fishing Werther's Originals from his cardigan pockets. She knew for a fact that he'd only just turned forty. His wife had sent an enormous cake to the office a few months ago and embarrassed the hell out of him. There was no arguing with his experience though. He'd been with the company since he graduated, working his way up to partner. The higher he climbed, the more hair he lost. These days his shiny scalp was reflecting a lot more than his success.

When Ed's eyebrows knitted together in concern, Rachel realised she'd been beaming idiotically. Composing herself, she said, 'Thanks, Ed. We worked really hard on it. And thanks for giving us a chance.'

Way to go, she thought. Pitch your message about two notches above kiss-arse.

Ed directed his next comments to James. 'I thought your use of that mood board was excellent. It lifted your idea from a drawing to a concept. Inspired.'

That wasn't James's idea. It was hers. Well, technically she'd nicked it from Sarah. She was always putting mood boards together for her cards. She shredded magazines faster than a hamster when she got a new idea. Even if the house-mates were still reading them.

'And the presentation was slick,' Ed continued as James doodled. 'You used just the right amount of animation to keep their interest. Too much just makes everyone dizzy and lowers the perceived quality of your message.'

Why did he keep looking at James? He'd never been able to work the 3-D program properly. Those animations were hers.

'Actually, Ed, the mood board was my idea,' she said.

Ed's smile creased the laugh lines near his pale blue eyes

and made his face look less narrow than usual. Without the smile he looked like a youngish Richard E Grant.

'Rachel, there's no "I" in team.'

She felt her face go crimson. She shouldn't have said anything. Now she just looked petty, while James confidently doodled. If only she could rewind the conversation and take it back. But she couldn't make Ed unhear her.

Actually, sod that. She didn't want to take it back. She wanted credit where it was due in the first place. Then she wouldn't have to stick up for herself. Because that's all she was doing. She wouldn't get anywhere if her boss thought James did all the work while she sat in the meeting looking pretty.

Ed kept talking to James while she stewed. Then he complimented the pastries they'd ordered for the meeting. This time he looked straight at Rachel.

That figured. James got credit for all the important work. She got pastries. What did that make her – Julia Child to his Mies van der Rohe?

No, she wasn't even Julia. She was Mr Kipling handing out pre-packaged cakes.

'This is ridiculous!' she said. 'There may not be an "I" in team, Ed, but if you change your perspective a bit, you'll see that there is a "me". You seem to have forgotten that.'

Ed stared at her.

James stared at her.

She wanted to crawl under the table and forget the meeting ever happened.

'Rachel, is everything all right? I'm sensing there might be an issue here and, honestly, I need to know that nothing's going to derail you. You and James will be working closely together on this project. Is there a problem?'

She was so incensed at Ed that she hardly heard what he'd just said.

'We've got a shot at the design?' James asked, finally stilling his pen.

'You've got it. Congratulations. Sorry it's taken so long, but I guess they've got a lot on. They just got back to me yesterday. They want to see your preliminary design on the,' he consulted his notebook, 'the twenty-first of next month, so you've got five weeks.'

Well not really, thought Rachel, since the office would shut down for Christmas in a few weeks. Ho Ho Panic Ho.

'It's all yours,' Ed said. 'Well, both of yours. So I need to know if there's going to be any issue with working together. Rachel?'

'What? No, no, of course not. That's awesome, Ed, thanks!' She couldn't wait to call her mum.

'James, what about you? All okay?'

He nodded. 'Absolutely fine, Ed. Oh, and by the way, it really was Rachel who came up with the mood board, not me. And she's a whizz at using the software and all the details that made the clients feel comfortable. If I wasn't so literal – *You want me to design? Okay, I design,*' he added in a simpleton's voice, 'I'd be good at all the touchy-feely stuff like she is.'

The unimportant stuff, he meant. By implication, the actual designs were his. That was bullshit.

'Well as long as you deliver one great design next month, I don't care how you divide up the work.'

Surely, Rachel thought, he meant one design each. 'Ed, we're each submitting our own ideas, aren't we?'

There was that 'me' again. Maybe she did sound like she wasn't a team player.

He shook his head. 'No, you'll submit one concept. You're working together on this. Okay?'

'Sure, fine,' Rachel said. She felt anything but fine.

* * *

71

As soon as Ed left the conference room, James stuck his hand up for a high-five.

So he definitely wasn't expecting Rachel to punch him in the arm.

'Ow, Jesus, what was that for?'

'I'm good at the touchy-feely stuff? James, you made me sound like your assistant.'

He looked stunned. 'I did not, Rach. What are you talking about? It wasn't fair that Ed was giving me credit for work you did. I was just setting the record straight. I was defending you.'

That was exactly the faux-chivalry crap he used to pull when they were seeing each other. He'd always known how to play a room. And the last thing Rachel needed was him wading in with his 'help' when it came to her job.

'I don't need defending, James. I can stand up for myself. I'm here because I'm a good architect, just like you, not some charity case who needs your protection.'

She felt so humiliated. The damage was done in Ed's eyes. No matter what she said, now he'd think she was just trying to grab some credit. She didn't want to have to fight for it. She shouldn't have to.

All the happiness she'd felt at the beginning of the meeting was wiped away. Now she didn't want to ring her mum. 'You made me look like an idiot.'

'I . . . what?' He shook his head. 'I'm really sorry you think that. You don't look like an idiot and I really didn't mean to make you feel bad. I'm not trying to protect you. I know you don't need it. I just wanted to set the record straight with Ed, that's all.'

The fight went out of her. 'Can we please just get on with our jobs?'

He shrugged. 'Are we good, Rach?'

'Yes, we're good.'

'You're sure? This isn't one of those times when you say we're good when you're really still mad?'

She smiled. 'So you do sometimes pay attention. No, I'm not mad. I might have overreacted.' He'd never been malicious. Clueless and exasperating, yes, but not malicious.

'Well, I am sorry. Do you want to go through some ideas now? I've been working on a few things, just some rough thoughts.'

'I've got time. My office?' she asked.

'Or mine. Whatever.'

'Okay, I'll just run to the loo. See you in five minutes in my office then?'

She caught his smirk as she turned toward the loos.

Fine, she was being petty. She still had some power to win back.

She'd composed herself by the time James approached her desk with his pad.

'I see you've been sketching too,' he said, trying to get a look at the drawings already on her desk.

'Just a few ideas,' she said, covering the pages as he sat down.

'I guess if we're working together now we should probably stop seeing each other as competitors.'

'I don't think we're competitors.' She smiled sweetly. 'Do you?'

He shook his head. 'Nuh uh, we're a team. Just like Ed said. So let me see what you've got.'

'Let me see yours first.'

If they were feral dogs they'd be circling each other with menace. Grudgingly, they traded books.

Suspicion hadn't always been the cornerstone of their relationship. There had been a time when she'd trusted him with, well, if not her life then at least her naked sleeping person. For

73

much of that year they were as close as two people could be. How could they not be? They were great friends nearly from day one in the office together. And they'd made good lovers nearly from night one in bed together. Rachel felt like she'd hit the lottery – a boyfriend that she could kiss at work. Bonus.

But the relationship kept mucking up the rest of it, so of course it wasn't that easy. If it had been, they'd be swapping notebooks over breakfast instead of treating it like a hostage situation.

Rachel scanned his drawings to get a feel for the overall look. It was that first glance that set the tone for the client's impression. You only got one chance to make it.

Then she studied them more closely. She knew he was doing the same thing to her designs. She didn't dare look up until she was finished.

'They're pretty different from mine,' she finally said.

'That's an understatement. We couldn't be farther apart if we were drawing from different briefs.'

Rachel studied his sketches again. 'It goes this way up, right?' James's building barely had any solid walls. It looked like a pair of glassed-in Brutalist car parks. 'Well I am surprised by your interpretation,' she said.

He nodded. 'It's all about bringing the outside inside.' He looked very pleased with himself.

'It's not what the brief asked for,' she pointed out.

'Yes, it was. It said that we should work with materials that are consistent with the surroundings.'

'Meaning what? Working with air? The sky? The fluffy white clouds? We're not designing a house in the Caribbean. It's a London office. We have to be practical.'

'The brief didn't say to be practical. It said it has to be functional. This is functional.'

'Oh really. How are they supposed to get from one building to another? Swing over on a rope?'

'You're one to talk about practical. Were you trying to design a giant doorstop? Yours looks like the cheese grater fell over.'

Rachel had drawn an elegant building that tapered from the pavement on one end to twenty-one floors high at the other.

'And what's this supposed to be?' he continued.

'It's an aluminium membrane encasing the external lifts. The brief said to be fun.'

'That means interesting paint, not a water slide down the outside of the building,' he said.

'Clearly we've got different interpretations of the brief.'

'Clearly. Maybe we should let Ed decide.'

'No way, James. He's given us this chance to design for one of the firm's best clients. We've only got a little over a month to do it. How would it look if we can't even agree on the basics? We've got to figure this out for ourselves.'

'Flip a coin?'

'Not funny.'

That was the trouble with working with your ex, thought Rachel. All the things you'd normally not have to deal with any more – the arguments, annoying habits and, in their case, competitiveness – were still there. And without any sex to compensate.

The idea of going out with James might have been fantastic way back when, but the reality gave Rachel the kind of aversion therapy that people paid good money for. She hoped his RecycLove assessment had space for essays.

No, she conceded as he took back his drawings. That wasn't really fair. He hadn't always been a horrendous boyfriend. For every time he'd made her want to throttle him there were probably three when they'd enjoyed themselves. In meteorological terms, he was generally fine with outbreaks of blustery showers. But she'd still got soaked, and that put her off him in a matter of . . . okay, fine, it took months.

Chapter Nine

Sarah

Sarah's brother had a rotten sense of timing. If you wanted someone to spoil your punchline, turn the room awkward with a single question or, in her case, ring the bell when her hands were covered in a papier-mâché of eggy flour, he was your man. With a sigh, she scrubbed her skin. Pasta dough made superglue look like children's paste.

'Just a sec!' she shouted, even though there was no way he could hear her all the way upstairs at the front of the house.

'You're early,' she said by way of greeting.

Robin leaned in to kiss his sister's cheek. 'Nice to see you too. You've got something on your face.'

He pointed, not moving to wipe it off. It probably looked like something had come out of her nose.

'Sorry, I'm in the middle of the pasta.'

'Home-made pasta? Is it a special occasion?'

'Can't I do something nice for my only brother?'

Of course, she wasn't just doing something nice for her only brother. She planned to ambush him while he was in a carb coma.

She didn't usually have to stuff Robin full of spaghetti

alla Genovese to ask for favours. They'd always been close, and especially so since their mum died. But Sarah knew he wasn't going to be keen to do what she wanted without a lot of persuasion.

'Drop your coat and stuff on the sofa.' She kicked her running shoes under the coffee table. 'I've just got to finish kneading the dough and we can eat in about an hour.'

He sidestepped the reading lamp's wire that trailed across the sitting room floor. 'This place is a deathtrap.'

'But it's our deathtrap and we love it.'

'I brought wine,' he said as he followed her down to the kitchen. 'You want some, right?' He began flinging the drawers open like he lived there, which was fine with her. Wall-to-wall dereliction made everyone who entered feel at home. Maybe it reminded them of their student housing. Not for much longer though.

'The opener's in—'

'What's this?'

He held up *The Great British Bake Off* application.

'It's nothing. I was going to say the wine opener's in the drawer to your left.'

'Are you applying?'

'No. It was Rachel's stupid idea. Put it back in the drawer please.'

'It's not a stupid idea at all. You should do it. I love your baking.'

'I doubt Paul Hollywood wants your opinion on it, but thanks. I'm not doing it.' The way Sarah said it made him drop the subject.

Robin was two glasses into the Chianti by the time the water for the pasta started boiling in the huge pot. Both were ready for the next step.

'So, I was thinking about Sissy,' Sarah said, gathering the

soft spaghetti strands from the broom handle where they'd been dangling since she'd pulled them from the pasta machine.

'She was in cracking good spirits when I went up yesterday,' he said, watching Sarah drop the pasta into the water.

'I know. She's been like that for the past few weeks. It's probably because of that boyfriend. Have you met him?'

His expression darkened. 'No, have you?'

Sarah shook her head, watching the timer. 'Kelly says he's very nice.'

'I'm sure he is, for someone who wants to shag my little sister.'

He finished his wine with a gulp.

'Anyway, Robin, she needs a holiday. So I was wondering . . . Maybe you and Lucy could take her somewhere? I'd love to plan something with her but I'll be tied up with the builders for who knows how long. She really needs to get away.'

The builders were meant to arrive the first week in January to start the renovations. Rachel had done all the designs and Sarah was supposed to keep the team of builders under control. It was their way of paying for their share of the house since they hadn't had as much cash as Catherine to contribute towards the purchase.

As she waited for her brother's answer she realised she was holding her breath. She also knew that, if it were up to Robin alone, she'd be breathing fine.

'I'm not sure that'll work, Sarah. There's Lucy to think about. It's not that she doesn't like Sissy. She's just not completely comfortable with her yet. Give her some time to get used to Sissy.'

'Robin, I don't want to tell you how to run your life.'

She was definitely going to tell him how to run his life.

'But she's had over a year and Sissy shouldn't need to be got used to. She's a person. She's your sister. If Lucy wants to be part of your life, she's going to need to let Sissy into hers.'

He leaned back in the kitchen chair. 'I know, and she will. She's never been around someone with Down's before. She just needs some more time. But I don't think a week away together at this point is going to make them bond.'

Nor would keeping them apart. 'So you won't do it?'

'Please, Sarah, try to understand. I know Lucy does your head in but I do love her. What if you and I at least take Sissy away for the weekend? You could get away for just a day or two, couldn't you? Or I can take her myself if you're busy?'

He looked so guilty that Sarah started feeling bad, but no, if she let him get off easily then he'd never force the issue with his girlfriend. If Lucy was going to be in Robin's life then she had to accept them all. That was the deal.

'It's not the same as a proper holiday, Robin, and you know it. It's been over a year since she's been away.'

'Look how well that turned out,' he said.

Sarah grimaced at the memory.

Majorca had seemed like a good idea. Sissy would live on a sun lounger if she could get someone to deliver her toast to her, and though Sarah wasn't much for the sun, she did love the warm weather. Robin had their mum's paper-white skin but wanted to eat his way across the island.

They had walked out to the beach after lunch on their first day, laden with towels and sun cream and snorkelling gear. There hadn't been many other people there but all the sun loungers were taken.

'We'll have to sit on the sand,' Sarah said.

'I don't like the sand,' said Sissy.

'Neither do I but there aren't any free chairs. It won't matter too much. You'll be in the water anyway.'

'C'mon, Sissy, let's swim,' Robin said. 'Race you in!'

Sissy ran into the sea, whooping as she went. As Sarah watched them she thought there was no doubt that they were all related. Robin had the same runner's build and thick dark blond hair as Sarah, with Sissy's round face and vivid green eyes. Their mum was never really far away.

She spread their towels on a patch of sand near some steep rocks. The hotel sat directly on the cove, which was just a few hundred metres across. The hot sun was tempered by a breeze off the water that blew snippets of laughter and conversation from the swimmers. Sarah threw herself onto her tummy with one of the *Artists & Illustrators* back issues she'd brought with her. A week of doing nothing but this! Bliss. She looked forward to these holidays as much as Sissy did.

She read the same paragraph again and again till the David Hockney article blurred. The next thing she knew she was being levered over onto her back.

'Sissy, you're soaking wet! And your hands are freezing.'

Laughing, she dripped seawater on Sarah's face. 'Come swim with me.'

'Your lips are blue. Warm up in the sun first and then I'll go in with you.'

She sat up. The sun had shifted position. 'How long have you been in the water? I was dead tired.'

'It's nearly five now,' said Robin, checking the watch in his bag. 'Have you been asleep all this time? You should cover up. You look burned.'

She pulled the towel around her shoulders. They were already going stingy.

'There are loads of restaurants along the beach,' said Robin. 'We should check one out for tea later.'

That was fine with Sarah. A few glasses of wine would take the sting out of her sunburn.

But they couldn't agree on a restaurant. Sissy was happy with any place that served prawns. Sarah didn't want to spend a fortune on their first night and Robin had his heart set on a restaurant directly on the water. Nothing made them all happy.

'But we're paying for the view,' Sarah complained as Robin loitered in front of one beachfront bistro. 'The food probably isn't even good.'

'There wouldn't be anyone inside if the food wasn't good.'

'Maybe they're all suckers like you, here for the sunset.'

'And the prawns.' He pointed to the menu. 'Look, Sissy, they've got prawns.'

'I want to go here,' Sissy said. Robin smiled.

Sarah shot him a look over their sister's head. Dirty tricks.

She was wrong about the wine. It just made her tipsy and aching. But she was right about the food. It was expensive, with Robin gorging on the ceviche like he was the king of Atlantis.

They went to bed with full tummies and empty wallets.

'Are you awake?' Sissy whispered into Sarah's ear the next morning.

She could see daylight through her eyelids but she knew better than to open them. Her only chance of any kind of lie-in at all was to play dead.

Tap tap tap. 'Sarah, are you awake?' She didn't bother whispering this time.

Sarah kept her eyes screwed shut. 'No. I'm sleeping. What time is it?'

'The sun's up. You're not sleeping. You're talking.'

'Thanks to you.'

'You're welcome.'

They were on the beach before most of the other guests had finished breakfast.

Unfortunately most of the other guests were German.

82

'Here,' said Sissy, choosing three of the sun loungers with umbrellas. 'For your burn.'

'That's very thoughtful, Sissy, but we can't sit there. People have already put their towels down.'

'But they're not here.'

'I know, but they've reserved the seats.'

Sarah knew how stupid that sounded. How was she supposed to explain about this early morning Continental reservation system? Sissy was a linear thinker and didn't usually break the rules. And since there was no actual rule about reserving sun loungers . . .

Sissy moved the resident towel to the sand, laid out her own and settled down with a contented sigh. Sarah knew her sister. It would take an Act of Parliament to move her. So she painfully lowered herself into the next lounger over.

'What are you going to say to the people who come out to sit in their chairs?' Robin asked.

'I'll say that my sister rightly said that beach chairs can't be reserved. They're for people to sit in. Are you joining us?'

'I'll have a swim first.'

In other words, he was leaving Sarah to face the angry tourists. 'Coward.'

He jogged to the water and threw himself in.

'Can I swim too?' Sissy asked.

'Twenty more minutes, I think. Just till your breakfast digests. Robin stopped eating before you did.'

Sissy took Robin's watch from his bag to count down the minutes.

Sarah was shrouded from head to toe from the sun but still enjoying the already warm morning. She watched a couple of eager swimmers who, like Robin, were having a post-breakfast dip.

Suddenly their brother stopped swimming. He must have

got a cramp. It was shallow enough for him to stand up, but he looked scared.

Sarah sat straighter in her chair. What was he afraid of?

He started swinging his arms, rushing for the shore.

Were there sharks?

Jellyfish?

'Robin, what is it?!'

Instead of answering he darted towards the rocks to the left. Then he wheeled around and started running towards them.

But he didn't make it.

As he neared, he slowed.

Then he crouched, still walking, with a look of horror on his face.

'I'm going to . . .'

He squatted.

His face contorted with a mix of mortification and relief.

Right there on the beach in the glare of the sun, in front of the German tourists who were just emerging from breakfast, Sarah's brother shat his swim trunks.

'Don't just sit there!' he shouted. 'Give me a towel.'

And a spade to cover his . . . tracks.

Half an hour later Sarah was paralysed with cramp too, but at least she made it to the room. Just.

That restaurant was emptying more than their wallets.

Luckily Sissy wasn't sick. Her squeamishness about raw fish saved her from the fate of her shitting siblings. But they couldn't leave her to fend for herself on the beach while they dealt with the aftermath of bad seafood. It would have been cruel to make her stay in the room with them on her only proper holiday, so they had no choice but to take turns on the beach, ready to dash to the loo at the next eruption.

Sissy chose a different sun lounger each morning, tipping

the towels onto the sand. Unfortunately she seemed to have a sixth sense about the towel's owner. It was always the same German man. By mid-week, when Robin and Sarah were feeling nearly normal again, he no longer bothered to remonstrate with their stubborn sister, but silently collected his towel and moved along the beach.

They wouldn't be going back to that hotel.

'I know it's not ideal,' said Robin. 'But having a day away, or maybe a weekend, is the best I can do right now. I'll sort out a week in the new year, I promise. I can take Sissy myself if I need to. I know how important it is to her.'

'You are still planning to come over for Christmas, aren't you?'

'Of course, I'll be here.'

It was a new-ish tradition since their mum died. Rachel and Catherine both went home to their families. They always invited her but she wanted to be with Sissy and Robin. So they came to stay for Christmas Eve through Boxing Day and she cooked a feast. They fought over board games and ate their weight in Celebrations. 'All three nights?' She knew she was pushing her luck.

'Definitely,' said Robin. 'Though Lucy will just come on Christmas night and stay for Boxing Day if that's all right.'

It was more than all right. She made a face that she hoped passed for regret. 'Too bad she can't come the whole time, but I understand.'

Robin laughed. 'I bet you're really broken up about it.'

As she stirred the home-made pesto into the hot pasta, she thought, at least he's coming for Christmas. I'm prepared to let Sissy's holiday go. For now.

'Wow, this is good,' she said, when she slurped in the first long strands.

'You're not supposed to compliment your own cooking,

you know. But yeah, you'll make someone a nice little wifey one day. If you ever leave the flat.'

'I'll have you know that I'm joining Catherine's website with Rachel.'

'You're kidding!'

If only, but Rachel wouldn't let her get out of it. 'Thanks for that vote of confidence.'

'You'll be a star, I'm sure. I'm just surprised, that's all. I never pegged you for an internet dater.'

'Rachel's making me. Speaking of which, someone has to join with me. A man.'

'Don't look at me. I'm taken.'

'I mean someone I've dated. I was thinking about Sebastian. Do you think he'd do it? Is he even still single?'

Robin laughed. 'What do you think?'

'Of course he is,' they said together.

He took out his phone. 'Here's his number. Definitely get in touch. I think it's a great idea, you online dating. You've barely been out since Mum died. You should stop punishing yourself.'

'I'm not punishing myself. I've just been busy.'

'Having a relationship with your oven isn't the same as having one with a person, Sarah.'

Like she sat around all day icing cupcakes. He never seemed to realise how busy she actually was. She wanted to see Sissy a lot, but that meant less time for everything else. Add holding down a job and, soon, renovating a house and then see how much time was left for a relationship.

'Shut up and eat your pasta,' she told him instead.

Chapter Ten

Catherine

Catherine hurried to the bar, wishing she'd changed into her ballerina flats for the walk. But after feeling frumpy in her jumper the last time she met Richard, she was back in uniform. The gunmetal grey suede heels perfectly matched her wrap dress. They were worth the bunion-bashing.

Richard hadn't asked her for drinks in months before his wedding announcement. Then dinner with Magda and now this. It could only mean one thing. He had news, and she just bet it wasn't good. She still felt strangely unsettled after meeting him and Magda. Nothing concrete had put her off, just a sixth sense. It was the same sense making her suspicious now.

At least Magda wasn't joining them.

Her anger flickered when she saw that he hadn't yet turned up. What was so important in his life that he got to be late?

At first she'd genuinely believed that his other work commitments were the sole reason for his dwindling commitment to RecycLove. But there'd been too many flimsy excuses. He'd definitely become more selfish since meeting Magda.

She felt like telling him that. They were business partners

first and foremost. She'd have no trouble speaking to one of her staff who wasn't pulling their weight.

Ten minutes passed with no sign of him.

Richard, you're so rude, she texted. *I'm leaving in two minutes if you're not here.*

She heard a phone ping behind her.

'I got our wine,' he said, setting the ice bucket on the table and kissing her cheek. He smelled of an unfamiliar cologne that made her think of car fresheners.

'You're late.'

'Nice to see you too. And I'm not late. I was in the building, at the bar getting our drinks.'

'I didn't see you there.'

'That's because you're too vain to wear your glasses.' He poured the wine.

'You know I hate it when you order for me.'

It was a habit he'd carried over from their marriage.

'You always drink white. What's got you in such a strop tonight?'

'I don't have a lot of time,' she snapped. 'I have to meet Rachel in an hour. And you *are* late.'

'I feel sorry for Rachel then. You're in a mood. Cheers. So how was your day, dear?'

It was no use. Richard never rose to argumentative bait. He was the worst person imaginable to pick a fight with. 'It was busy, as usual,' she said, reaching for her wine. He was right. It was exactly what she wanted.

'Because of the new clients?'

'Partly.'

'And the makeover service, I guess. I've been thinking. We should roll it out to everyone.'

'Everyone?! Richard, do you realise how much more work that would mean?' She could barely get through her day as it was.

88

'You could charge for it, of course. Then you could hire more consultants. And you said yourself that it wasn't taking too much time.'

'Yes, for two clients. It would be too much for the whole business.'

That was so typically Richard. He'd always underestimated the details.

Her mind flicked back to their move to America. Case in point.

Richard had made everything sound so simple when he got the offer to work in Washington DC. It was an adventure and she was welcome to come along.

'Come along?' she'd asked. 'Come along?! What is that supposed to mean? Come along as what, exactly?'

'Well, as my girlfriend, at least for now,' he'd said, looking perplexed. 'We don't really have time to get married before we go. We'll have to do it there. Or fly back to the UK after I start work if you want.'

'You're asking me to marry you?' she'd whispered.

'Well I assumed we would. Didn't you?'

So that was her marriage proposal. *Well I assumed we would.* Not exactly the rooftop declaration of love on bended knee that Magda got.

'We do love each other, right?' she'd asked.

He'd pulled her into his arms. 'Yeah. You're my best friend.'

'You're mine too,' she'd murmured. She was going to marry her best friend.

Richard had loads of ideas about the wedding. She'd bragged about that to her mum during their daily transatlantic phone calls. Not many fiancés would get so involved. Big bands, English sparkling wine, square tables at the reception in her parents' garden, all-white flowers, gingerbread cake, individually tailored party favours and a kebab truck for peckish partygoers near the end of the night. He had new suggestions every day.

But when she realised that all he planned to contribute were suggestions, she had stopped bragging. She was doing all the hard work, while living in a new country five time zones away from the wedding venue. Meanwhile he threw himself into his new job. Aside from the few minutes when his alarm dragged them from sleep, she'd barely seen him in the run-up to the wedding.

By the time the day had arrived she'd just wanted to crawl into bed for a week. She had Platinum frequent flyer status on British Airways and never wanted to stow a tray table or place her seat back in the upright position again. And she'd die happy never to see another fairy light or taste a piece of gingerbread cake.

Richard had turned up on the wedding day as if the whole thing had been put together by magic pixies rather than his bride, who'd had to use extra-strength concealer to hide the dark rings from the photographer's lens.

No wonder she wasn't falling for Richard's enthusiasm now about the makeover expansion. Even aside from the extra strain on the staff, Catherine didn't want to grow too fast. They'd built their business by being sensible. She'd always been the brakes on his racing car.

'We haven't got the bandwidth to expand right now, Richard, especially when it's essentially just me running things.'

She gave him a pointed look. It was the wedding planning all over again. 'I really can't keep doing it all myself, you know.'

'I know you can't, Kate. I've been completely tied up with the other businesses, as you know, and you've been great with RecycLove. I wish I could spend more time there, but . . .' He shrugged. 'I've had a lot on my plate lately. And now with the wedding.'

'I'm sure Magda will have that all in hand.'

He completely misinterpreted her snipe. 'She will. She's amazing like that. And actually, since we're talking about it . . . I think it's time for me to do what's right by the business.'

Finally. 'It really is, Richard. I haven't said anything because I know how much strain you've been under, and I've been managing okay with the team. But it's not really fair to us.'

'I know. I'm sorry. So I'll make it right. You need someone who can be there more. The business deserves it. You deserve it.'

'I'm glad you understand,' she said.

'Magda will need a few weeks to get her feet under the desk but she really is amazing. Well, you've met her, so you know.'

'Magda?'

He fidgeted with his wine glass. 'I've decided to sell my share to her.'

'What?! You can't do that, Richard. You *cannot* do that!'

She put her hand on her chest where her heart was thudding so loudly that he must have heard it. He couldn't sell her business to his girlfriend. Love Match was hers. *Hers*.

His face was starting to match his hair. He'd never liked confrontation. 'It's the best thing, Kate. Listen, I need the capital for another business.'

'Then why can't Magda just invest in that instead? And where's she getting all this money from anyway?'

They weren't worth millions but they were going concerns.

'You probably won't like this, but she's a bit rich.'

'She's *a bit rich*? That's a bit rich.'

'I told you you wouldn't like it. Her family has money, but she's got her own investments as well. Besides, she's

91

interested in Love Match. And since I can't be as involved as I need to be, we've got to have someone we trust to take over for me. And I trust Magda implicitly.'

But I don't, Catherine thought. I don't trust her at all. 'So you've already decided this without even talking to me first?'

'Don't take this the wrong way, but it's not really your decision, is it? I'm the shareholder of my half and I can sell if I feel I need to. You've said yourself. It's unfair for me not to contribute.'

'I know but—'

'Don't you see? This way it's still in the family.'

'So are webbed toes, Richard, but nobody wants those either.'

He ignored her bravado. 'Magda is really excited to work with you,' he continued. 'You'll make a great team. And look at the bright side. This is just a business transaction. It's not like we're getting divorced again.'

He laughed and Catherine's tummy churned, because he was right. Legally he could sell to whomever he wanted. He just so happened to want to sell to his twenty-three-year-old interfering fiancée.

Her head was too swamped by Richard's news to see Rachel at first. What would Magda's investment mean? If it was a matter of swapping one silent partner for another, she could just about live with that. But all those questions about the business Magda had asked when they met – what if she wasn't planning to be silent?

'Catherine?' Rachel said, grabbing her arm as she wandered through the bar. 'You need to wear your glasses. You just walked right past me.'

'I guess I should!' she said, forcing her thoughts aside. She needed more time to think before she talked to anyone about the sale. 'You're early.'

'Well you don't have a lot of free time. I didn't want to waste it.'

Catherine smiled as she ordered a lime and soda from the passing waitress. Why couldn't the men she knew be as considerate?

Stop thinking about men.

And definitely stop thinking about Richard. 'Well it's nice to be out together like this,' she said. 'It's been ages.'

'I know. What's happened to us?'

'Life happened. Sarah couldn't make it?'

Rachel dropped her gaze. 'I didn't invite her.'

'Oh?'

'Not for a bad reason though! I just think we need to talk about her because I'm really getting worried.'

Catherine nodded. 'She's in such a rut, isn't she? I know it must be horrible to lose your mum, and she's got Sissy to worry about, but I hoped she'd be back to her old self by now. It's been two years, hasn't it?'

'Nearly three. She's regressing. It's like she's just given up on a social life. She only leaves the house to run or visit Sissy.'

'Ugh, those jogging bottoms!' Catherine said. 'Seriously, if we can get them off her can we burn them?'

'Definitely. She's got to get her confidence back. I'm going to help her write her RecycLove profile. Otherwise she'll just say she's boring. Then nobody will get in touch.'

They watched the after-work crowd fill in around them. 'Maybe we could join some kind of social club with her,' Catherine finally said.

'Please not a singles club though.'

'No, no, nothing like that. Maybe a theatre club or something we'd do anyway if we weren't so hopeless at organising. I keep seeing those Curvy Girls Club adverts in the *Metro*. They've got interesting events. Too bad we're not curvy or we could join them.'

'Speak for yourself,' said Rachel, glancing at her burgundy dress and green tights. She looked like a dishevelled elf. 'I qualify.'

'Well, you're lucky, but we don't.'

'They don't discriminate.'

'No, but even so. Maybe a cooking class or something like that?'

'Maybe.' Rachel's eyes slid away. 'Oh God, confession time.' She took a deep breath. 'I've sent in Sarah's application for *The Great British Bake Off*.'

'But that's not so bad.'

Rachel closed her eyes. 'It is. She doesn't know I filled it in for her. She's going to kill me.'

'Will you tell her?'

'Not yet. No reason to get her hopes up till she's through, right? The deadline isn't even till March.'

'In other words, you've got time before she kills you,' Catherine said.

'Exactly. Between *Bake Off* and RecycLove, we'll get her back on track. We've got to.'

Yes, they had to do something. They couldn't sit by and watch their friend be ground down any more. Rachel was right: Sarah would kill her when she found out. But once she got used to the idea, hopefully she'd be happy about it.

Now if only she could rewind Richard's decision to sell out to Magda, Catherine could be happy too.

Chapter Eleven

Rachel

Rachel tucked her new chocolate-brown woolly scarf more tightly around her neck and curled up her fingers inside her mittens. As she passed Ladbrokes's window she noticed that they were giving six to one odds on snow for Christmas this year. It felt like a good bet.

Someone grasped her shoulder just as she opened the restaurant door. 'I thought I recognised that hair. Fancy seeing you here!'

She spun around. 'Hi Janet, hi Donald, perfect timing!' She kissed her parents' best friends as they all shed their coats for the cloakroom attendant.

Donald gestured behind them. 'You remember Jonathan, don't you?'

Rachel would know their only son anywhere. His hair was still dark, though thinning, and his small eyes still looked suspicious. How could she forget him? He'd stuffed her favourite teddy down the loo. Her parents said she shouldn't hold a grudge. They'd washed it and declared it good as new. But it was never the same again.

'Of course. Hello Jonathan.'

'Jonathan drove us over. With my knee acting up we didn't

want to take the train, and we wouldn't have missed this restaurant! Darling,' Janet said to her son, 'they're supposed to have the best black cod in London here.'

'Maybe the best in Wimbledon, Mum, but I doubt it's the best in London. You haven't been to Nobu.'

So he was just as arrogant as she remembered.

Janet laughed and shook her head adoringly. 'My worldly son.'

Rachel had a different adjective in mind.

'Jonathan, please join us,' said her mum, Genevieve, as she sprang up from the table.

Rachel felt her excitement slipping away. She'd avoided her mum's questions about the Zigler project all week, just so she could see her parents' faces when she told them in person. She couldn't care less about seeing Jonathan's face.

'You'll love it here,' Rachel's mum continued, grasping his arm. 'The black cod—'

'Is delicious I've heard,' he deadpanned.

'Oh yes, please do stay, Jonathan,' Janet piped up. 'You did say you had no plans tonight.'

No surprise there, thought Rachel.

'And you can drive us home later,' added Donald. Always practical, was Donald.

'Look, there's room for six anyway,' Rachel's dad said. 'Next to Rachel.'

'It must be fate,' murmured her mum.

'You look nice, Dad,' Rachel said. He'd swapped his paint-speckled builder's jeans for a jacket and tie and his sparse greying hair was neatly combed.

'Thank you, love, so do you. All set for the renovations to start?'

Inwardly she cringed. 'All set, Dad. The builders come the first week in January. Thanks again for getting Nate in for us.'

She picked at her napkin.

'I'm just glad he can do it,' Genevieve cut in. 'It's such a big job. Your clients would never have been able to do without you for that long.'

Rachel flashed her mum a grateful smile.

Her dad nodded. 'I do have a lot on. I've got to get that kitchen wall rebuilt before Christmas. And the retiling.'

As much as Rachel hated even thinking it, her dad wasn't the greatest builder in the world. It wasn't that he was unscrupulous. Quite the opposite. He seemed to spend most of his time fixing his mistakes. That was the problem: there were so many to fix. She just hoped his mate Nate would be better.

'Rachel, you and Jonathan have a lot in common,' Janet said. 'You know, Jonathan, Rachel is an architect.'

He didn't look up from his menu. 'Mmm.'

'And Jonathan is an engineer.'

'Oh? What type?' Rachel asked, less out of interest than to force him to say something.

'Architectural.'

'You practically have the same job,' said Janet. 'Isn't that interesting?'

Jonathan mumbled something.

If she wasn't already tetchy about him being there, Rachel might have kept quiet.

'I'm sorry, I didn't catch that,' she said.

'Nothing.'

'No, really. What did you say?'

He finally looked at her, his grey eyes unblinking. 'I said it's hardly the same job, is it?'

'Meaning?'

'Who's ready to order?' her dad asked.

'Meaning that I design buildings and you . . .' he smirked, 'draw with coloured pencils.'

Everyone at the table straightened up at this. Especially Genevieve, who happened to be one of the pre-eminent architects in the country. Jonathan knew this.

What a twat.

'You're right, Jonathan. I draw buildings that I've designed from the ground up to satisfy my clients. You make the calculations about how close the electrics can go to the sewage pipe. It *is* hardly the same job.'

She held his gaze. She'd do it all night if she had to.

Finally he looked down.

'Actually, Mum,' he said. 'I don't see anything here I want so I'm going to take off. I'll pick you up in two hours. Or you can call me and I'll come back.'

Without another word, he got up and left the restaurant.

Everyone stared at Rachel like it was her fault.

'What?' she said, knowing how defensive she must sound. 'Shouldn't I have said anything?'

'Oh, no, darling,' Janet said. 'That was uncalled for. I'm terribly sorry. We just thought that you two might . . .'

'Because of your work,' added Mum.

Rachel stared between them.

So it had come to this. Her parents were trying to find her a date. The sooner she joined RecycLove the better.

The spectre of Jonathan hung over their table after he left, like the smell of boiled Brussels sprouts.

'So, I have some news,' Rachel said, handing her menu to the waiter. 'I've been asked to design the building for Zigler.'

'Oh that's wonderful!' Janet cried, clapping her hands even though she probably had no idea what Zigler was.

But Rachel's mum knew. She pushed her chair back and came round the table to kiss her. 'Darling, you got it. That is terrific, congratulations!'

Rachel felt her face glowing. Jackass Jonathan was forgotten. It *was* terrific. The Zigler buildings were getting to be icons in London, not quite on par with the Gherkin or The Shard or some of the buildings her mum had designed. But well-known enough to make her tummy flip every time she thought about it.

She'd worked for almost ten years for this chance. Studied at school till her head ached and said no to second glasses of wine and stayed at the office when everyone else went home. All the stress and sacrifice would be worth it. Finally, she'd prove that she'd inherited some of her mum's design genes.

She just had to convince James that her idea was better than his.

Chapter Twelve

Sarah

Sorry, Sebastian, I can't make drinks tonight. Thanks, Sarah
  Sighing, Sarah deleted the text. Again.

Rachel would kill her if she cancelled. Plus she'd only make her reschedule, and she had no idea when she'd have free time again now that the builders were there.

Six of them had showed up just after seven yesterday morning. They all looked about twelve years old except for Nate, the foreman, who was in his fifties, grizzled and lined, with arms like Popeye.

After all the horror stories her colleagues had gleefully shared when they'd found out builders were coming, she was surprised to see them at all. And she hadn't expected so many. With everyone running around in hard hats, Sarah had started wondering if it might be a bigger project than they'd thought.

Rachel had redesigned the floor plan so that the house would work as three flats 'when the time came'. Sarah knew what that meant: eventually, when Rachel and Catherine found their soulmates, they'd want their own space and she'd need somewhere to live out her spinsterhood, knitting outfits for the million cats she'd probably have by then.

The builders weren't doing much, structurally, to the

kitchen, sitting room or Rachel's bedroom, but the top three floors were being turned into two self-contained maisonettes. Sarah and Rachel would live in them eventually but, till then, two of the bedrooms would be up there.

It was a case of musical beds for a bit while the living space on the upper floors was being jigged around, but Sarah didn't mind sharing a room, like she had with Sissy.

As if that wasn't enough for Nate and his team to get on with, they were also fixing the electrics, plumbing, floors and whatever else they found wrong.

All while the women lived in the house.

Something told Sarah that she didn't have enough biscuits for the job.

'How long do you think it'll take?' she asked Nate as he directed his team upstairs to start work.

He scratched his greying stubble and looked at the string of exposed electrical cables above their heads. 'About a month, I'd say. All the materials are in stock, so once we get going it shouldn't take too long. You'll hardly know we're here!'

His laugh boomed up the stairs as he followed his boys.

Sarah could live with a month of dust and noise. At least the house was big enough to find a quiet spot to work.

She took her drawing pad into the sitting room and curled up on the sofa with her legs tucked under the pale blue lambswool blanket that Rachel's mum, Genevieve, had given them for Christmas. Despite the old radiators ticking and cracking and popping and rattling, the house was cold now that January officially had London by the bollocks.

She listened to the builders stomping and banging upstairs. They were building her maisonette first, on the second and third floors. She wondered how she'd feel with her bedroom all the way at the top of the house like that. Not that it scared her. The house had loads of creaks and groans but she was used to them. She couldn't wait to have her own bath in a properly insulated room. At the moment they risked frostbite keeping clean in the winter.

She'd miss the old kitchen though, when they eventually broke up the house. It belonged in a country estate, not a Victorian house in East London. It had barely been touched since the 1920s, except for the new fridge and gas cooker. Some of the black and white floor tiles were cracked and a few of the hinges on the cabinets needed adjusting, but it was big and airy and perfect for baking. Sarah wanted joint custody with Catherine 'when the time came'.

She closed her eyes to clear her mind, since thoughts of spinsterhood were the last thing she needed when she was trying to work.

She'd been mulling over an idea for a new card that she thought her boss might like.

Starting with her black pen, she began sketching a couple. The woman was shapely without being too thin. He was tall and broad, with a loose-fitting suit. Then she got to work on her idea. Taking the deep red pencil—

Kaboom! Crash!

She bolted upright, her heart hammering. It sounded like someone had fallen through the floor.

Throwing down her sketch pad, she ran for the stairs. 'Is everyone all right? What's happened?' she shouted as she took them two at a time.

The thunderous crashing continued. Billows of dust roiled out of the top floor door into the stairwell.

'What's happened?' she cried as she rounded the corner.

'Mind your feet!' Nate shouted, moving to block her from entering the room.

Sarah could barely see through the dust cloud.

But she could see clearly through what had once been their wall.

'What have you done?'

'We're taking down the wall. Nearly done now,' Nate chirped.

'Yeah, I can see that. Only, that wall was supposed to stay up.'

'No it wasn't. I've got the plans right here.' He pulled a squashed roll of architecture paper from his back pocket. 'See, right there you've got your wall, which needs to come down to extend this room.' He nodded to his mate, who sent his sledgehammer crashing through another section of wall.

'That's right,' she said over the sound of pulverising plaster. 'The wall needs to come down to make room for the new kitchen . . . on the *second* floor.'

'Right,' he said.

'Right. But this is the *third* floor.'

'What the fuck. It's not, is it? Oh, shit. Sorry about that.' He rubbed his chin in what Sarah suspected might be a signature move. 'Well, it's almost down now. We'll build it back. No charge, obviously.'

Obviously. 'Thanks. Have you got the plans for this floor?'

'Ah, I don't think so. Not with me. I guess we'd better start on the second floor then. That wall wasn't very sturdy anyway. It'll be better new.'

Sarah stared sadly at the remains of the original Victorian wall, its lathes shattered and its plaster crumbling. Nate might be right, but it'd be nice to keep what they could intact. Especially the walls they didn't plan to move.

'If it's all the same, I'll come with you downstairs, just to be sure you've got everything you need.'

It took more than two hours before Sarah was moderately sure that Nate and the team were working to the correct plans and she could get back to her work.

Feet tucked again under the blanket, she picked up her red pencil and began sketching in the groom's scarf.

Red, white, red, white.

She got it just right and any Liverpool fan would instantly recognise it. She'd toyed with the idea of a shirt too but the scarf seemed enough.

Harry should go for it. Even Maria-Therese, who always hated Sarah's ideas, would have to recognise the brilliance of this one. They could do them for all the major clubs. Given that weddings did get planned around major FA Cup matches, there had to be a market.

As she tidied up the sketch, memories washed over her. All of them at Anfield together. Her mum shouting at the top of her lungs for her boys on the pitch. You could take the girl out of Liverpool but you'd never take Liverpool out of the girl.

Sarah's grandparents were appalled that her mum brought them to the stadium.

'They're just children!' her gran would say.

'Nobody's going to hurt a child.'

Her mum was right, and when Robin and Sarah got older and they brought Sissy along, people seemed extra courteous. She was the music that soothed the savage breast.

It didn't stop them cursing though. Sarah had learned her most colourful swear words from the fans of Liverpool FC.

Her mum so wanted to instil her passion in her children that Sarah had pretended an interest in football, but she was really more excited to be together with her family.

She was always buoyed up by the atmosphere though, especially when they started singing. There was something about that song . . . well, none of us wants to walk alone, right?

It had been Robin's idea to play it at their mum's funeral. Sarah knew she'd have loved that, but given how emotional it made Sarah when her mum was alive, she also knew what a blubbering mess she'd be when it reminded her that she wasn't.

She was right.

Oh Mum, she thought, as tears slipped down her cheeks. It was just so unfair. Life was so unfair sometimes. And the worst part was that there was no court of appeals.

Sarah felt strangely calm later when she spotted Sebastian waiting for her outside the Tube station. She wasn't sure what she'd expected. They'd only dated for a few months and it was never serious. It had been nice having someone pay her attention though. She did miss that.

He hadn't changed – same tall, slender frame and dark good looks. Her gran would have wondered suspiciously if he wasn't 'a bit foreign'. But he was as English as they were.

'Hey, Sarah, it's great to see you!' He kissed her firmly on the cheek and she found herself grinning. 'Did you have a nice Christmas?'

An uncomfortable look passed over his face as, she realised, he probably remembered about her mum. She was used to that.

'It was really nice, thanks. Sissy and Robin spent a few days with me at the house. Yours was good?'

A thick wedge of hair fell into his eyes when he nodded. 'I went to St Anton. The snow was okay but the après ski was excellent.'

'I bet it was fun,' she said, mentally replacing *après ski* with *sex*. 'So, thanks for meeting me. Sorry for sounding so mysterious in my texts.'

'I love a mysterious woman.'

Not quite true. He loved all women.

When they'd found a bar that wasn't too full and got their drinks, he said, 'Actually I think I know why you got in touch.'

She doubted that.

'It's about Robin's birthday, isn't it?'

'No, it's not about his birthday. It's more personal than that.'

Concern flitted over Sebastian's expression. 'Sarah, are you all right? Is it . . . something about us?'

'That came out wrong! I'm fine, absolutely fine. And it's not about you and me, don't worry.'

Relief flooded his smile. 'For a second I was afraid you were going to tell me I'm a father.'

'Seb, we went out five years ago.'

'Paranoid, sorry!'

So he was still as commitment-shy as ever. She hadn't even been able to get definite weekend plans out of him when they were seeing each other. He treated short-haul holidays with suspicion and wouldn't get a phone contract in case he found a better offer. That would be top of her list of improvements if he agreed to join RecycLove.

'You remember my housemate, Catherine?' she asked. 'You've never met but I've talked about her, I'm sure.'

Their friends hadn't mixed. Being best mates with Robin, he knew their mum, of course, and Sissy, but they had an unwritten rule that he didn't go to family events once they got together. He was at their mum's funeral though. That was the last time she'd seen him.

'She runs an online dating website and, well, I'm thinking of joining.'

'That's great, Sarah, you definitely should.' He downed his drink. 'You need to get back out there.'

She narrowed her eyes. 'Have you talked to Robin about me?'

'Nah, don't worry! Well, he may have mentioned you over the years. That's normal, right? He is your brother and we are mates.'

'What did he say?'

Sebastian pulled at his collar. 'He just mentioned that you haven't been as social since, since . . .'

'Since Mum died. I know. But I'm trying to change that. There's just one problem with the website. I need an ex to join with me.'

'Ah, you mean RecycLove then. I didn't know your house-mate runs that. Impressive.'

'You've heard of it?'

He laughed. 'Sarah, I know where all the single ladies are.'

She'd need to talk to him about the cheese factor too. 'Then you know the deal. We sign up, give each other a romantic assessment and then we can use the website. Would you think about doing it?'

He seemed to consider the proposition. 'Why not? As long as you don't say anything bad about me, like I have a small penis or something.'

She wasn't about to rise to that ego-stroking bait. 'Nobody else sees the assessment, just us. They'll only see the endorse-ment, and I promise that will be good.'

'Then let's do it,' he said.

'That's ace, thank you!' Sarah's breath hitched in her chest. She was really going to do this.

Chapter Thirteen

Catherine

When Richard had said he was thinking of selling his half of the business to his fiancée, what he meant was that he was definitely selling his half of the business to his fiancée, and he already had the drying ink on the contract to prove it.

Catherine could have resisted signing the papers, but there was really no point. She had no legal basis for her objection, and whining about fairness wouldn't work with her ex-husband. So they agreed a valuation and the deal was done.

Then Magda appeared at the office, as keen as a new intern.

Except that she wasn't an intern, Catherine thought as she led the woman upstairs. She was a fully fledged partner. One who didn't plan to be silent.

Catherine felt sick at the idea.

'I love how you have done the office,' Magda said as she unwrapped herself from her long camel-coloured cashmere coat. Underneath she wore trousers and a fine-knit jumper in the same tone (also cashmere, Catherine was betting). Her chunky, expensive-looking gold jewellery sparkled in the recessed lighting. 'My mother has a similar style in her flat in Budapest. It's quite classical.'

Catherine knew she meant 'old'. 'Mmm hmm. Can I get you a drink?'

'Have you got any herbal tea? I'm not having caffeine.'

That figured. She was probably on some kind of Gwyneth-approved macrobiotic diet. 'Why don't you come this way to the conference room? I'll get your tea.'

'Oh, there is no need for such formality, Kate! I am happy to sit at an empty desk.'

'It's Catherine, actually. I go by Catherine.'

'But Richard calls you Kate.'

'I prefer Catherine, thanks. I'll just get that tea for you.'

She felt like she was on her back foot with Magda. Richard had said only that she wanted to come to the office today. Typical of him to be useless when it came to sharing information.

So what, exactly, do you want here? she wondered when she set her mug on a coaster. Not trusting her voice to ask without bitterness, she just held Magda's gaze.

Sure enough, Magda squirmed. 'I'm really very interested in the business,' she said.

'RecycLove?'

'And Love Match.'

'Well I can run you through how it all works.'

'I am dying to start.' She withdrew a green frog-covered notebook from her bag, but Catherine couldn't help noticing that she seemed a lot more serious than she did around Richard. Was she just putting on the cuddly blonde act for her fiancé?

'It's very simple really,' Catherine said. 'Love Match is for clients who want a bespoke service, where we choose the most appropriate dates from our database.'

'Where do you get the dates' details?'

'They're also clients. We match up clients with each other.'

'But how do you know you will have the appropriate clients to match?'

'Because we vet them before they're accepted. If we don't think we'll have suitable matches, we won't sign them up.'

'But how do you know who will be suitable before they meet?'

'Because I've been a relationship consultant for more than a dozen years, Magda.'

'But why does experience of past clients mean your current clients want the same thing?'

Catherine wanted to scream. It was worse than talking to a child. But she couldn't just send Magda to her room.

After nearly an hour of fielding hostile questions, Catherine found herself flagging. And she needed to prepare for her next meeting. 'Well, I think you've got a good overview of how we operate. As I said, everything relies on strong communication between us and the client and between the consultants. Now, that's probably enough to get your head round for one day. I do have a meeting I'll need to prepare for, so . . .'

'Oh, yes, of course, I have taken up so much of your time!' Magda snapped shut her notebook. 'Should I go talk to the other consultants?'

'No! I mean you don't want to be overwhelmed on your visit, do you?'

'No, you are right. So if you can just show me to Richard's office, I'll get out of your way and let you get ready for your meeting.'

Catherine stared at the girl.

'Richard's office?' Magda prompted. 'Where I will be working?'

110

'I'm sorry, I didn't . . . it's just that Richard didn't really spend time here day-to-day. He didn't have an office.'

Where she'd be working?!

'I'm sure there's a little corner for me somewhere,' Magda said. 'In the meantime, I noticed that there is a table in your office. I can just put myself there until a desk is sorted out. I'm sure it will not take long.'

'Fine. There's a free desk on the other side,' Catherine said. 'Let's walk over and I'll set you up there.'

Magda's smile was triumphant.

This was a woman used to getting her own way, and she hadn't just handed over a cheque to her fiancé to be generous. She was buying half a going concern.

Catherine now saw that she planned to make it *her* concern.

Paul arrived at the stroke of eleven for their meeting, going straight in for air-kisses when they met at the door. Points for promptness, Catherine thought, though she wasn't in the habit of kissing her clients. She should have stuck her hand out to ward him off, but they'd cheek-kissed in their first meeting and now she seemed to be stuck with the greeting.

'I'm ready for my makeover,' he said, leaning back in his chair and stretching his long legs in front of him. Catherine noticed that his socks were stripy red and white. 'Will my office even recognise me when you're done?'

'You don't date your colleagues, do you?'

'Well, I wouldn't say *date* . . .' He shrugged.

Catherine shook her head. 'It isn't clever to fish off the company pier.'

'Maybe not, but we've all done it. You must have too.'

Catherine felt a jolt. 'We're not here to discuss my personal life.'

'That sounds like a yes.'

It was a big, fat yes. And she definitely wasn't going to discuss it with her client. 'I think we should talk about where you want to improve.'

He seemed surprised at the question.

Was it arrogance? Catherine began to feel annoyed. There was only so much she could do for people who didn't want to help themselves. Georgina was a perfect case in point. She may have agreed to allow a bit of stubble into her life but she wasn't budging on much else. That reminded Catherine, she needed to line up a few more dates for her picky client. She'd need to carve out some time in the afternoon to find them.

'You'll probably say I need a complete overhaul,' Paul finally said. 'So how do you plan to assess me? Have you got a test or something?'

She shook her head. That wasn't how it worked on the Love Match side. 'I can get a pretty good sense about you just by talking together, but if you've got any specific areas that you'd like to improve, we can start there. For example, you mentioned wine. We could work together on improving your skills.'

'Sure, Catherine, we could get through a few bottles together.'

'I didn't mean . . . I meant that I could give you some pointers on how to order from the wine list, food pairing and that sort of thing. It's a good place to start.'

'Done. What else?'

'It would be good to know about any shortcomings you feel you have. As a date.'

She left the question hanging between them.

'That's probably something my dates would have more to say about. I've not had any complaints.'

She raised her eyebrow, knowing how well silence worked to loosen a client's tongue.

'Well, nothing beyond the norm anyway,' he continued. 'There've been the usual grumbles from women that I'm not that into, but what do you expect?'

'And how do you let them know you're not into them?'

'Honestly?'

'What do you think?'

'It depends on whether we've slept together. I tell them straight out if we have. If not, then I think silence speaks a thousand words.'

Not really, she thought. Silence generally just speaks two words when it comes from a date. F*** off. So far, so typical.

'What about the women that you do like? Do they have any complaints?'

He shrugged. 'Search me.'

She took a deep breath and tried again. 'Paul, I can only offer generic advice when I don't know what you're like socially. Maybe you could describe exactly what you do on a date.'

But he shook his head. 'Nah, mate, that won't work. I'd only give you my interpretation. You'd need to see for yourself.'

'Well I can hardly follow you around taking notes.' She hoped he wasn't suggesting any secret filming.

'Then come out to dinner with me. For research purposes. That way you can give me an honest assessment about where I'm going wrong.'

'Well first of all, you're a client so I couldn't go on a date with you and—'

'First of all,' he said, raising his finger and clearly mocking her. 'I'm not asking you on a date. If you're serious about helping me, then you said yourself that you need to see where I'm going wrong.'

She felt herself blush. Of course he wasn't asking her on a date. She reached for her Filofax and started flipping through the days.

Paul sat forward. 'I didn't know they still made those. Why don't you just use Outlook?'

'I don't trust online diaries,' she said. Plus she liked seeing her appointments in her own handwriting, and sticking little notes and press cuttings between the pages. 'I could meet for an early dinner two weeks from tomorrow?'

He checked his phone. 'It's a date, then. But not a date, of course.'

She ignored him and rose to signal the end of the meeting. He followed her to the office door. This time she stuck out her hand before he could go for the cheek-kiss.

Magda went straight for Catherine as soon as the door closed behind Paul. 'Who was that?'

'He's one of our Love Match clients, Paul.'

'He doesn't look like he needs any help finding love matches.'

'Well that's the thing about this business; it's not all about appearances,' she snapped. 'People come to us because they need our help. Now, I know you want to be useful.' She tried not to sound like she was speaking to a toddler about making cookies. 'But we're really very busy here. And I'm sure you're very busy too with the wedding plans.'

Magda's smile disappeared.

'Kate,' she said. 'You seem to be under the wrong impression. I have not come in today to pay you a friendly visit or to get your advice about reception venues. I came to check on my new investment. Whether you like it or not I own half the company and, what's more, I will be involved. At least for the next six months.'

'Then what happens? Does your student visa run out?'
She smiled. 'Then I will have Richard's baby. I am pregnant.'

Catherine felt her breath leave her.

Chapter Fourteen

Rachel

At first Rachel wondered if James had turned over a new leaf for the new year when he asked her over for dinner. He wasn't usually the type to entertain at home. He was the type to get pissed in his local and wolf down a kebab after. And that was when they were dating and he wanted to make a good impression.

When he unlocked the door to his flat, the waft of familiarity swept over her. There was also a vague sense of disquiet. She'd often been anxious there. And it smelled a bit of curry.

But he didn't seem to notice any of that as he led them through to the sitting room.

The decor hadn't changed at all. The same poster over the dining table – an oiled-up woman bench-pressing with her legs spread – and the same black leather sofa, unwashed cereal bowls on the table and pile of shoes in the corner. A lad's pad, circa any time after *The Matrix* was made.

'I like what you've done with the place,' Rachel said.

'Yeah, I've had the decorators in. It wasn't easy getting just the right balance of neglect and decay.'

'I'd say you hit it just right.'

She wasn't surprised by James's lack of interior design. After all, she lived in near-squalid conditions. After ten-hour days wrapping her head around design features, who had the energy to do it for fun?

'I'm just going to change,' he said. 'Make yourself comfortable. Well, you know where everything is.'

He emerged from his bedroom two minutes later wearing a grey Franklin & Marshall sweatshirt and matching baggy sweatpants.

She didn't expect him to dress for dinner. But she didn't think he'd dress for bed either. 'Nice to see you make an effort.'

He laughed. 'You should be flattered that I'm so comfortable with you.'

'Hmm. What's for dinner?'

He stared at the kitchen like he was noticing it for the first time. 'There's some pasta in the cabinet if you're hungry. Or we can order something. I thought we were doing the assessments?' He wandered to the fridge. 'Beer?'

That was the James she knew. But to be fair to him, he never pretended to be anything other than Jameslike.

'Well if you won't feed me proper food then let's get started so I can get home.'

He didn't object and they opened their laptops. Once Rachel had logged in to the Wi-Fi network, she said, 'So, Catherine said we just have to sign up and put each other as a reference. Then we'll get an email from RecycLove to confirm that we're joining together and we'll get the assessments to fill in.'

They raced each other to be the first one to sign up.

When Rachel's mailbox pinged first, James licked his finger and ticked the air.

His pinged a moment later.

'So that's it?' he asked. 'We're in?'

117

'It looks like it. Now we can do the relationship assessment.'

Suddenly, doing it in front of James seemed like a terrible idea. 'Maybe you should go in the other room so we don't distract each other.'

'Don't you want to watch me rate you?' he asked.

'Actually I was thinking of your feelings, but whatever.'

They shifted away from each other at the dining table to work through the questions.

James looked over the top of his screen. 'How do you add a rating?'

'See the little pencil icon? Click on whichever number you want. It makes an X.'

'Xs for your ex. Get it? Do I get any last-minute credit for clever comments?'

'If I hear any I'll let you know.'

He punctuated the next ten minutes by constantly asking what question she was on. 'This isn't a race, James.'

'No, but you shouldn't take forever over it either. The first thing that comes to mind is usually the most honest.' He noticed her typing. 'You're writing comments too?'

'Some answers need expanding.'

'Just don't use swear words or you'll hurt my feelings.'

She was on the last question anyway. She tapped the 'Complete Assessment' button. 'I'm finished.'

'I've already sent mine,' he said.

Sure enough, there was a message in her RecycLove inbox telling Rachel that his assessment was waiting for her to complete hers. That got round the retaliation problem in case one person didn't like what they read. Clever Catherine.

'Mine's just come through. Ready? Go.'

They both clicked.

The disbelief built in Rachel's chest as she scanned down the page.

'This is really how you feel?'

Granted, he'd done the questions quickly, but this was ridiculous.

'Like I said, the first thought is the most honest,' he muttered, staring at his screen as she stared at hers.

The RecycLove Relationship Assessment

This assessment is about: **Rachel Lambert**
Assessed by: **James McCormack**

The goal of this questionnaire is to help the person understand their positive traits as well as where they can improve for the best chance of finding a happy and satisfying relationship.

Please rate the person on the following character-istics on a scale of 1 to 4.
1 = Not at all, 2 = Not very, 3 = Somewhat, 4 = Extremely

Feel free to expand in the comments sections.

1. Was this person a good communicator? For example, did he/she get in touch regularly and return calls? Were they clear about things like weekend plans?

    1   2   3   ☒ 4
Comments:

2. Was this person honest about his/her feelings and actions?

    1   2   3   ☒ 4
Comments:

3. Was he/she a loyal person, toward you and others?

1 2 3 ☒ 4

Comments:

4. Did you feel emotionally supported by this person?

1 2 3 ☒ 4

Comments:

5. Was this person secure?

1 2 3 ☒ 4

Comments:

6. Was this person courteous to you and other people?

1 2 3 ☒ 4

Comments:

7. Did you know where you stood in the relationship with this person?

1 2 3 ☒ 4

Comments:

8. Did he/she make you feel like you were important to them, like they wanted to be in the relationship with you?

1 2 3 ☒ 4

Comments:

9. How fun or interesting was this person?

1 2 3 ☒ 4

Comments:

10. Did he/she take a reasonable amount of care over his/her appearance, i.e. not too little or too much?

1   2   3   ☒ 4

Comments:

11. How generous was this person? Generosity could be financial or it may mean a generosity of spirit.

1   2   3   ☒ 4

Comments:

12. Was he/she emotionally mature?

1   2   3   ☒ 4

Comments:

13. How kind was this person, toward you and others?

1   2   3   ☒ 4

Comments:

14. Was he/she attentive to your needs?

1   2   3   ☒ 4

Comments:

15. Was this person ambitious? Did they have goals that they were trying to achieve?

1   2   3   ☒ 4

Comments:

16. How romantic was he/she?

1   2   3   ☒ 4

Comments:

17. Did he/she get along with your friends and/ or family?

    1   2   3   4

Comments: N/A - they never met

18. How committed was he/she to the relationship?

    1   2   3   [X] 4

Comments:

19. Was this person sexually satisfying? Feel free to skip this question if you prefer.

    1   2   3   [X] 4

Comments: No need to go into detail here : -)

He'd given her no criticism whatsoever. As far as James was concerned, Rachel was the perfect girlfriend.

How was that possible?

Her face burned, knowing he was reading her ratings.

The RecycLove Relationship Assessment

This assessment is about: **James McCormack**
Assessed by: **Rachel Lambert**

The goal of this questionnaire is to help the person understand their positive traits as well as where they can improve for the best chance of finding a happy and satisfying relationship.

Please rate the person on the following character-istics on a scale of 1 to 4.
1 = Not at all, 2 = Not very, 3 = Somewhat, 4 = Extremely

Feel free to expand in the comments sections.

1. Was this person a good communicator? For example, did he/she get in touch regularly and return calls? Were they clear about things like weekend plans?

   1   [X] 2   3   4

   Comments: I'm sure you were clear about your weekend plans but I never knew whether to bother shaving my legs or not. You returned my calls/texts about half the time, less at the end.

2. Was this person honest about his/her feelings and actions?

   1   [X] 2   3   4

   Comments: You are honest in your actions – I'm sure you've never lied or stolen anything. Or cheated in a relationship. But you really need to be honest about your feelings.

3. Was he/she a loyal person, toward you and others?

   1   2   [X] 3   4

   Comments: You are a loyal friend.

4. Did you feel emotionally supported by this person?

   [X] 1   2   3   4

   Comments: You always seemed too busy to listen to me, James. Sometimes it's not about anything big. Maybe I just needed to vent about my day, but you're so relentlessly positive that I ended up feeling like I shouldn't be complaining. Even now when I tell you about my crap dates you laugh it all off.

5. **Was this person secure?**

1   2   ☒ 3   4

Comments: Yes, sometimes too secure. It's all right to be vulnerable with people you trust.

6. **Was this person courteous to you and other people?**

1   2   ☒ 3   4

Comments: You are generally courteous but you're not really chivalrous. Do you realise that you always barge in front of me when we go through doors? Try not to bulldoze your dates when you go into the pub. And pull out a chair once in a while.

7. **Did you know where you stood in the relationship with this person?**

☒ 1   2   3   4

Comments: Only at the beginning, when it was really fun and pretty great. And at the end, when you were completely ignoring me.

8. **Did he/she make you feel like you were important to them, like they wanted to be in the relationship with you?**

☒ 1   2   ☒ 3   4

Comments: This one's hard. At first you did but then you changed. Too busy to go out – not making definite plans – cancelling on me – not returning calls. Nobody wants to feel like a waste of time.

9. **How fun or interesting was this person?**

1   2   3   ☒ 4

Comments: I can't fault you here. You're also very funny. Though we could have done more together. Dancing maybe. A good dancer is sexy, you know.

10. Did he/she take a reasonable amount of care over his/her appearance, i.e. not too little or too much?

   1   [X] 2   3   4

Comments: Look down at yourself, James. I rest my case. Though it's nice that you're sporty, it would also be nice to make an effort with your wardrobe once in a while. Your hygiene is pretty good for a man though.

11. How generous was this person? Generosity could be financial or it may mean a generosity of spirit.

[X] 1   2   3   4

Comments: You are totally cheap.

12. Was he/she emotionally mature?

[X] 1   2   3   4

Comments: You might be but I've never seen it. If there is some emotion in there, you should show it in a relationship. It's hard feeling like you're the only one who cares.

13. How kind was this person, toward you and others?

   1   2   [X] 3   4

Comments: Generally, except when you're taking the piss out of me.

14. Was he/she attentive to your needs?

   1   [X] 2   3   4

Comments: Yes, when I asked you to be, but you never told me what you needed. It felt like I was always the needy one. Not a nice feeling.

15. Was this person ambitious? Did they have goals that they were trying to achieve?

    1   2   3   [X] 4

    Comments: It's good that you want to get ahead at work but the relationship couldn't compete with that. It's possible to be ambitious and still realise that other things are important. The relationship doesn't have to be the top priority but it should be a priority, if you like and respect that person. That was really our problem wasn't it?

16. How romantic was he/she?

    [X] 1   2   3   4

    Comments:

17. Did he/she get along with your friends and/or family?

    1   2   3   4

    Comments: N/A, I'm sure you would have if you'd ever met.

18. How committed was he/she to the relationship?

    [X] 1   2   3   4

    Comments: Even a little bit more would have helped a lot.

19. Was this person sexually satisfying? Feel free to skip this question if you prefer.

    1   2   3   4

    Comments: No comment

Finally he said, 'Well, I guess at least you were honest.'

She squirmed in her chair. 'James, it looks worse on paper than it really is. There was only a four-point scale. If I could have put you in the middle on a lot of . . .'

He looked completely dejected. 'I guess I thought I was an okay boyfriend.'

'You were an . . . okay boyfriend!' she said. 'Look, I scored you highly on a lot of the questions. You're loyal, secure, courteous . . .' She scanned down the next page. 'Interesting, kind, ambitious. I'd have rated you higher on appearance if it wasn't for those sweatpants. You do have good hygiene. There's quite a lot in your favour.'

But he wasn't about to be cajoled out of his mood. 'Thanks for saying that I don't reek. Let's talk about the others, like the ones where you wrote essays in the comments box.'

Maybe she'd got a little carried away, she realised as she reread her comments. She wished they hadn't agreed to go through them together.

'I'm cheap?' he asked.

Grimacing, Rachel nodded. 'You really are, James. I can probably count on one hand the number of times you took me out for dinner.'

'Maybe I just wanted to have drinks.'

'Or maybe you suggest drinks so you don't have to pay for dinner.'

He knew he was busted. 'Yeah, all right. But I'm not a total skinflint. I do spend money on some things.'

She followed his eyes to the games console on the sofa. 'Yes but a date won't care that you've got the latest Xbox game. She probably will care if you refuse to feed her. All I'm saying is that a few romantic gestures would go a long way.'

'According to you, I'm as unromantic as it's possible to be. I seem to remember stars and moonlight.'

'Yes, that was romantic. But it was only our first kiss.'

She didn't often dwell on their relationship. What was the

point? But she smiled as she let herself remember how they first got together.

Outlook Messenger had pinged on the afternoon of their first strategy conference. *Meet me out front.*

'Let's get a quick drink,' he'd said when she came downstairs.

'I'm not sure we've got time before the coach leaves.' They'd only been working for the company for a little under a year. Not yet long enough to take liberties.

'Come on, it won't go till at least five thirty. You know you'll just spend that time rearranging your suitcase.'

She blushed. She'd been packed since last week for the two-day piss-up. 'Fine, we can go, but just for a quick one, James.'

They hurried around the corner to their usual after-work pub.

When they came out the coach was gone.

'I knew I shouldn't have listened to you!' she'd fumed as they stood on the pavement with their bags in front of the office. 'That half pint is going to cost me a fortune now in train fares.' And she'd have to spend it too. They couldn't miss the conference. The bosses had hired out an entire country house hotel for it. She'd been so excited to go.

'Please relax, Rachel, I can drive us. Come on, I'm only twenty minutes down the Piccadilly line.'

Much as she wanted to hold a grudge, her anger dissolved with every mile travelled and every song on the radio mangled by two people who really shouldn't have been belting out lyrics at the tops of their voices.

'You realise we'll get crucified when we get there,' she'd said as he navigated the busy traffic along the M4. 'The partners will want to know why we missed the coach.'

He'd smiled as he carefully passed a lorry. 'We've got about eighty miles to think up a good excuse. And you know what? I don't care. This is fun. It's worth the bollocking.'

When they'd safely passed the lorry, James reached over and grabbed Rachel's hand.

That had never happened before. She snuck a glance at him, but his eyes were firmly on the road. What was he doing holding her hand? Friendly gesture? Did friends hold hands? Did he mean anything by it? More importantly: did she want him to?

Interesting question. If she was honest with herself (and what better time for that than when your friend holds your hand for the first time?), her feelings weren't completely platonic. They got along too well, and she fancied him too much, not to wonder about more.

His warm hand felt good in hers.

They stayed like that until he had to downshift off the exit.

Their colleagues didn't know about the motorway hand-holding so their teasing was only because they'd missed the coach. But Rachel knew something had changed. It excited her.

Just before midnight, when they were in the bar together with the whole company, James whispered in her ear.

'Come outside with me.'

They didn't bother with coats, though it was a chilly October night. A nearly full moon illuminated the expansive grounds and formal gardens but, even so, Rachel could see stars blanketing the sky.

'I saw how pretty it looked when I went for a slash,' he'd said. 'I thought you'd like it.'

'Were you weeing in the bushes?'

'I saw it through the windows on my way to the loo.' Then he took her hand. 'Don't worry, I've washed my hands.'

'That's not what I was thinking.'

'What were you thinking?' He spun her around to face him.

'Well, that I was surprised when you held my hand in the car. But I liked it.'

'Good, because I plan to do more of that. And this.'

He'd leaned in and they'd kissed, long, slow, sexy kisses that, to Rachel, didn't feel at all platonic.

All right, it had been a pretty romantic way to start a relationship. He probably deserved a two out of four.

'I gave you all good ratings,' he said, pulling her back to their uncomfortable conversation. 'If it was so bad, why did you stay with me for a year?'

Exasperated, she said, 'It wasn't *so bad*! Just because there are things you can improve doesn't mean you were terrible to go out with.'

'But you were ultimately the one who ended it,' he pointed out.

She snorted. 'Only because you were too lazy to do it. I wasn't stupid. It was obvious that you'd lost interest. Or at least that other things were more important.'

'You mean work,' he said. 'But we were both working long hours. Why was my working a problem if yours wasn't?'

She thought about that. 'Because I didn't do it to the exclusion of everything else. I still saw my friends and my family. And you, when you'd let me.'

She lost count of the number of times he'd backed out of plans she'd made for them. It became a running joke with Catherine and Sarah that they knew she'd be free whenever she had plans with James.

Yeah, that was freakin' hilarious.

'It wasn't hard to read between the lines with us, James. We made better friends than anything else.'

'I guess I have a different opinion,' he murmured. 'But I understand why you think that. I was a cheap, unromantic workaholic.' He pointed to his screen. 'You didn't answer the last question. Is that to save me actually killing myself?'

She could feel the heat creeping up her face. 'The sex wasn't bad, James. That wasn't the problem.'

'Not bad like . . . a two?' He clasped his hands together under his chin. 'Or dare I hope for a three?'

'Okay, if you must know, it was a four.'

She took one look at his face and knew she shouldn't have told him. Now he'd be insufferable.

'As for the rest of it, there are things you should work on. Like . . . well, it all comes from the same place, really. Commitment.'

He made the sign of the cross over his face.

'Exactly. It's not your strong suit.' She shrugged. 'I guess when you meet the right person then the flaws will naturally correct themselves. You'll want to be with them. A woman wants to feel that her boyfriend *wants* to be with her.'

'You didn't think I wanted to be with you?' he asked. 'Just because I didn't send you roses all the time—'

'Or ever.'

'Or take you out for fancy dinners didn't mean . . . I'm sorry you thought that, Rachel. I'm really really sorry.'

'It doesn't matter any more, but thanks. Look, they're just suggestions. Ignore them if you want. And I would like some feedback about myself. There must have been things I could do better.'

He didn't answer right away. Then he said, 'Well, there was one thing. I gave you a four but . . .'

She sat up. 'Yes?'

'Actually more blow jobs would have been nice.'

She punched him harder than she meant to, but exactly as hard as he deserved.

Chapter Fifteen

Sarah

The RecycLove Relationship Assessment

This assessment is about: **Sarah Hamilton**
Assessed by: **Sebastian Mott**

The goal of this questionnaire is to help the person understand their positive traits as well as where they can improve for the best chance of finding a happy and satisfying relationship.

Please rate the person on the following characteristics on a scale of 1 to 4.
1 = Not at all, 2 = Not very, 3 = Somewhat, 4 = Extremely

Feel free to expand in the comments sections.

1. Was this person a good communicator? For example, did he/she get in touch regularly and return calls? Were they clear about things like weekend plans?

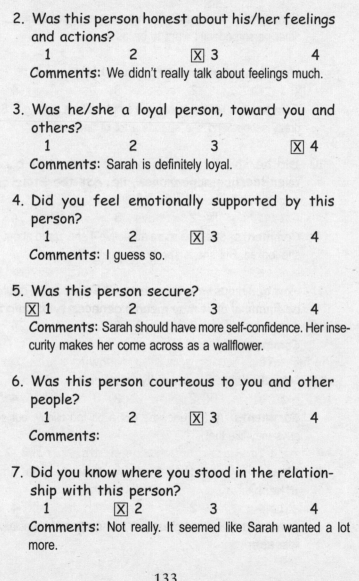

1   ☒ 2   3   4

Comments: Sarah rang me a lot. That's good for someone who wants to talk all the time.

2. Was this person honest about his/her feelings and actions?

1   2   ☒ 3   4

Comments: We didn't really talk about feelings much.

3. Was he/she a loyal person, toward you and others?

1   2   3   ☒ 4

Comments: Sarah is definitely loyal.

4. Did you feel emotionally supported by this person?

1   2   ☒ 3   4

Comments: I guess so.

5. Was this person secure?

☒ 1   2   3   4

Comments: Sarah should have more self-confidence. Her insecurity makes her come across as a wallflower.

6. Was this person courteous to you and other people?

1   2   ☒ 3   4

Comments:

7. Did you know where you stood in the relationship with this person?

1   ☒ 2   3   4

Comments: Not really. It seemed like Sarah wanted a lot more.

8. Did he/she make you feel like you were important to them, like they wanted to be in the relationship with you?

    1   ☒ 2   3   4

    Comments: Yes but that's not always a good thing if the other person doesn't want to be as serious.

9. How fun or interesting was this person?

    ☒ 1   2   3   4

    Comments: I'm sorry, but she's not really a party girl. She's pretty serious and she spends a lot of time baking.

10. Did he/she take a reasonable amount of care over his/her appearance, i.e. not too little or too much?

    1   ☒ 2   3   4

    Comments: She'd be more attractive if she cared about how she looked. But she is sporty and really fit.

11. How generous was this person? Generosity could be financial or it may mean a generosity of spirit.

    1   2   ☒ 3   4

    Comments:

12. Was he/she emotionally mature?

    1   ☒ 2   3   4

    Comments: At the end she got a bit too clingy, but some guys may like that.

13. How kind was this person, toward you and others?

    1   2   3   ☒ 4

    Comments: Sarah is great with her family and especially her little sister.

14. **Was he/she attentive to your needs?**
   [X] 1   2   3   4
   Comments: I really needed someone to have fun with but Sarah wanted a relationship.

15. **Was this person ambitious? Did they have goals that they were trying to achieve?**
   1   [X] 2   3   4
   Comments: Not that I saw. But she is very practical. She built all the Ikea wardrobes in her bedroom herself.

16. **How romantic was he/she?**
   1   2   3   [X] 4
   Comments: She draws wedding cards. It comes with the territory.

17. **Did he/she get along with your friends and/ or family?**
   1   2   3   4
   Comments: Not applic.

18. **How committed was he/she to the relationship?**
   1   2   3   [X] 4
   Comments: A little too committed

19. **Was this person sexually satisfying? Feel free to skip this question if you prefer.**
   1   2   3   4
   Comments:

She'd waited over a week for this? Character assassinations made more glowing reports.

It was so unfair! Clingy, boring and dowdy. And she was supposed to have more self-esteem? Good luck with that now.

Sarah knew she shouldn't get so worked up. After all, nobody else would see the assessment (thankfully). It was just that, deep down, she was afraid Sebastian was right. She was no social butterfly. Now she knew why he'd eventually stopped calling. He'd wanted to spend time with someone he could party with all night long. She only made it past midnight with a double shot of espresso.

And that was before she *really* became a homebody.

Was it any wonder she hadn't been out with anyone but Rachel and Catherine in . . . could it really be years?

'I'm home!' shouted Rachel. 'Glad to see the house is still here.'

It had been her standard greeting since Nate arrived with the sledgehammers and saws and upside-down floor plans. The second floor was starting to come along, but Sarah suspected it might take longer than Nate thought. They were definitely making a lot of work for themselves. Nate had wiped out two of the ceiling lights while carrying materials up the stairs. And when one of his boys had dropped a sledgehammer in the bathtub, it cracked in half. They had to use buckets over the sink to wash now. When she'd asked Nate if he knew when they might be finished, he'd said about a month. She hoped so, although he had said that a month ago.

'I'm in the kitchen,' Sarah called, closing her laptop.

'Shit, what a day I've had.' Rachel unwound her impractically long scarlet scarf from around her neck. 'It's freezing out there.'

'Is it cold? I haven't been out today.'

Oops, wrong thing to say.

Rachel gave her *that face*. 'Honestly, it's great that you get to work from home but you do need fresh air every day. I wouldn't wish a commute on you, but a little walk over to the park would do you good.'

'I meant to, I just got busy.' There was no way she'd admit that she hadn't been outside since her jog on Sunday. 'I'll go out tomorrow, I promise.'

'You're going to get a Vitamin D deficiency.'

'I *said* I'd go out tomorrow, didn't I?!'

'Whoa, what's wrong?'

Sarah shook her head. 'I'm so sorry. I didn't mean to snap at you. I'm just . . . It's . . . it's Sebastian.'

'What's he done?' Rachel demanded. 'Sweetheart, if he's upset you, he'll get a good kicking from me.'

Sarah smirked at the idea of five-foot-nothing Rachel thumping Sebastian with one of her colourful handbags. 'He hasn't done anything to me, exactly. He just gave me the feedback for RecycLove, that's all.'

Sarah watched Rachel's expression shift from anger to guilt. As it should, she thought, knowing that she wouldn't *have* this shite feedback if she hadn't made her join.

'Do you want to talk about it?' Rachel asked.

'Well, I'll have to, won't I, if you're still helping me with my profile. We may as well get on with it.'

'Do you want a glass of wine?' Rachel asked.

'Better chill a bottle,' she said.

'This sounds like a Noodle Shop night. I'll ring Aziz.'

'Actually, it's not as bad as it could be,' said Rachel after she finished reading the assessment. 'You got full marks for being loyal and kind. And he did say you're practical.'

'Ta, Rachel. That makes me sound like a Girl Guide. It's not exactly the ideal candidate for a hot romance, is it?'

'He also gave you credit for being sporty.'

'Ace. We'll sew a fitness badge to my uniform then . . . I know you're just trying to make me feel better but I'm in trouble here.'

She'd forget the whole stupid idea if she wasn't so sure

that she'd never meet anyone on her own. RecycLove might not be the answer, but at least it was amongst the multiple choice options.

Even if she wasn't a total party girl, didn't she deserve to meet someone too? There must be men out there for nice quiet women who didn't mainline fashion magazines or keep up with the Kardashians.

She was getting seriously depressed about the whole thing.

'What if I really am this boring?' she whispered.

It wasn't always fun being inside her head.

Rachel moved so quickly that Sarah flinched. She found herself gathered up in a bear hug.

'You listen to me, you daft cow. You are not boring. If you were we wouldn't be friends. You're funny and clever and, yes, okay, you're a bit of a dingbat sometimes but that doesn't make you boring. The fact that we never know what'll come out of your mouth actually makes you interesting. Now, that's the end of that.'

Sarah sighed, once again grateful for her friend. Only Rachel would think to add an intriguing spin to her muppet housemate.

'Will you let me help you with your profile?'

Sarah shrugged. 'We may as well get this over with. Let's see yours.'

Together they looked at Rachel's online persona. Not only had she put up lots of gorgeous photos, she sounded funny and smart and a little bit sexy. Basically, she was every man's wet dream. 'I'm impressed,' Sarah said.

She didn't stand a chance if everyone on the site came across like Rachel.

'So, the best way to start is by searching for yourself.'

'Hello Rachel,' she sang. 'I'm not on there yet, am I?'

'Hello Sarah,' Rachel sang back. 'Search for someone like

yourself. You need to check out your competition. Then you use the best ideas from those to write the perfect profile. So go ahead, search for a woman, say twenty-six to thirty, non-smoker, university-educated, in London.'

Sarah did as she was told. Six hundred and thirty-one matches came up, page after page of smiling women. 'Now I'm depressed.'

'Don't be! You're way prettier than most of them. Show me the photo you want to use.'

'I don't know. You know I hate having photos taken.'

'Well, I've got some of you on my phone. Maybe one of those will work.'

They scrolled through Rachel's gallery.

'There aren't any good ones,' Sarah muttered. Sebastian was right. She looked serious in every picture.

'We need one of you smiling. I could take one?'

Sarah glanced down at herself, at her jogging fleece and her jeans that were baggy in the knees from daily wear. 'I'm not exactly photo-ready.'

'But you could be. Let me do your hair and make-up, and you must have at least one nice dress. Or you could borrow one of mine. We'll pin it at the back. We can do a photo shoot!' She clapped her hands together in glee.

'Or,' said Sarah, clapping along, 'let's just open one of my veins instead. It'd be less painful.'

'I can't help feeling that you're not embracing this process. Come with me.'

Reluctantly Sarah followed her housemate.

There was no stopping Rachel once she got started. Half an hour and half a ton of slap later, Sarah hardly recognised herself.

'There,' said Rachel, tonging one last bouncy wave into Sarah's dark blonde hair. 'Stop touching your eyes. You'll ruin your mascara.'

'It feels like I've got conjunctivitis.'

'It's just the lashes sticking together a bit. You'll get used to it. I think you look fantastic! What do you think?'

She stared at her reflection. 'I look like somebody else.'

But maybe that's what people wanted.

'No, you look like you, only it's the 2.0 version of you. Still the same program, but with extra enhancements.'

Sarah reached inside her bra and pulled out the gel pads. 'I might not need this much enhancement. What are you doing with these anyway? You don't exactly need more cleavage.'

'I know,' said Rachel, glancing at her bust. 'They came with a bra I bought. You don't really need them either. You've already got a killer figure, with those legs and no tummy. Basically, Sarah, you're hot. You should wear dresses more often. You know you can borrow my boots whenever you like. Or any of my shoes.'

Sarah stared at herself. She vaguely remembered having a sense of style once upon a time, but she hadn't bought new clothes since her mum's funeral. And she'd thrown that outfit into the charity bin the day after. 'If I let you come shopping with me, do you promise not to try to put me in anything you know I'll hate?'

Rachel nodded solemnly. 'And a make-up session too. I mean with a professional. Will you do that? The colours I used on your eyes aren't exactly right, because you've got cool tones and I've got warm ones.'

'Next you'll be dressing my aura,' Sarah said.

'I promise not to touch your aura. Let's work on your profile now and worry about your make-up later. Sarah, do you trust me?'

'Of course I do. I just let you stab a mascara wand at my eyes.'

'Then please listen to me. Sebastian wasn't right to slate

you like he did, but maybe there's some useful advice in that assessment. If we look at it rating by rating, there might be a few things that you *want* to change. I don't mean anything important or fundamental to your personality.'

'Did you and James have a lot of feedback for each other?'

Rachel nodded. 'Sometimes it takes an outsider to show us where we can improve.'

Sarah tried to be offended that she was being asked to change, but she just couldn't. She kept thinking about why she'd agreed to do this. She did want to meet someone. If it took a bit of pretence to do that, it wouldn't be the worst thing in the world.

Chapter Sixteen

Catherine

Catherine's assessment night with Paul came round quickly. Too quickly on the day, as it happened. Magda was in the office again, meddling all over the business.

Catherine wondered at first whether her pregnancy was even real. It was a bit convenient for her to get knocked up so that Richard asked her to marry him. Suspicious. That's all she was saying.

But then Magda threw up over the conference table and Catherine had to concede that it was probably true. Her ex-husband, who she once loved, was going to be a father. And Catherine wouldn't be the mother. She made herself think about this, *really* think about it. She searched every nook and cranny within herself for some feeling of regret, or at least a bit of wistful longing. She even tried forcing out a few tears, just to see if she could get the ball rolling.

Nothing. It didn't bother her. Why didn't it bother her? What was wrong with her?

She was thirty-six. She might never have the chance Magda was getting to be a mother.

Never, she intoned to herself like the voice of doom.

But the only emotion she felt was relief that it wasn't her.

She was, she now knew beyond a shadow of a doubt, childless by choice.

It wasn't like that came as a total surprise. She had considered the question before. She just assumed that when push came to shove, the maternal instinct would kick in. Everyone else seemed to have it. Why not her?

She had tried when she was younger. She played with dolls with her friends, changing their outfits and cooing over imaginary burps. It just wasn't as much fun as playing netball or giggling over boy bands.

And in her twenties, she'd held her friends' babies close and sniffed their heads. She stroked their tiny fingers and kissed their soft cheeks. Then she handed them back till the next time she got to have a cuddle.

It was probably time to face facts. She'd searched for her maternal instinct and failed to find it.

She was okay with that. Magda was welcome to the sleepless nights and expanding waistline. At least it would keep her away from the office most of the time.

Or so she'd assumed.

But she kept turning up, with so many questions that Catherine finally had to give her a project just to keep her busy.

'One thing that we need to do is go through the database,' she said, after Magda's constant chatter had started to give her a headache. 'Client by client, to track how many dates each one has had. Then we have some way to know what the average is.'

They didn't really need to do this, but she wasn't about to trust the woman with anything important.

'I am surprised you have not already done that,' said Magda. 'How do you know if you've been successful without measurements?'

Catherine pointed to the wall of photographs in reception.

143

'That's how, Magda. We've had nearly fifty weddings so far.' And revenues that grew year on year, she didn't add. She didn't need to. Of course Richard had opened their books for his fiancée. 'So you can make a start on that project. It's a big one. It'll probably take you a few weeks.'

Hopefully longer.

Catherine was just checking up on her housemates' profiles when she noticed it was time to go. Sarah had been right about Rachel's profile. It was one of the most popular on the site. And she was thrilled to see that Sarah was getting some interest too. If anyone needed a boost to her self-esteem, it was Sarah.

Thank you, Rachel, she thought, for convincing her to join.

She checked herself one last time in the bathroom mirror – her fitted, cap-sleeved, deep raspberry Hobbs dress and three-inch platform heels said business dinner, just as she intended.

She already had a few things to talk to Paul about. His approach to planning, for one thing.

'Hey Catherine,' he'd said when he'd rung her a few days after they'd agreed the date for his assessment. 'Where do you want to go?'

Catherine had sighed. 'Where would you like to take me?'

'I figured it's easier for you to decide—'

'Stop!'

'What?'

'Paul. It's not about what's easier,' . . . for you, she'd thought but hadn't added. 'Your date shouldn't have to plan her own romantic evening. If you want to give her two or three options then that's fine. But do the legwork to choose them before you call.'

The line had gone dead.

Had he gone into a tunnel or something?

Ten minutes later her phone had rung again.

'Hello Paul,' she'd said smoothly.

'Hi Catherine. About our date. I thought we could try Barshu. It's Chinese. Unless you prefer French, then we can go to Bistrotheque. Or Bocca di Lupo for Italian?'

Catherine had smiled. He *was* trainable! 'How about Bocca di Lupo?'

'Eight p.m.?'

'Perfect.'

'Great, see you there.' He'd rung off.

Though his dismount still needed work.

Paul was already seated at one of the little tables along the back wall of the small restaurant when she arrived. She gave him a few mental points for promptness.

From a purely professional point of view, he was well-presented, looking relaxed and approachable in his pale blue shirt (open at the collar), navy jacket and, yes, she noted as he rose to greet her, nicely fitting jeans.

He kissed her warmly on each cheek. 'You look great!' he said. 'Did you go home to change before coming out? I came straight from the office.'

'No, I wore this to work,' she said, smoothing her dress at the front.

'Hot,' he said, grinning.

Catherine ignored the comment but filed it away for her assessment.

'Have you been here before?' she asked instead.

'Nah, I just googled "best London restaurants" and picked the first three off the *TimeOut* list that came up. From the mid-range price options.'

She hadn't planned to give him feedback until after their dinner but she couldn't stay quiet. 'That's refreshing honesty,

Paul, but it's okay not to share every detail with your date. You could, for instance, simply have said that you got some recommendations.'

Paul's expression soured. 'Just so I know; will you be criticising me as we go along?'

'That's not criticism! We're here to assess you tonight, remember?'

'Well, how am I supposed to be on top of my game if you do a running commentary on me? I should get extra credit for performing under pressure.'

His smile was back and Catherine relaxed. He had a point. Unless they treated this like an actual date the assessment wouldn't be realistic.

'You're right, I'm sorry. I promise no running commentary. We're just two people meeting for a nice dinner together.'

When was the last time that had happened? There had been nothing nice about her dinner with Richard and Magda. And before that . . . God, when had she last gone out with a man?

Rather than dwell on the answer, she shifted her focus back to Paul. 'You're a fan of Italian food?'

'Nope. I'm a fan of all food. Except shellfish,' he said. 'The little buggers make my face swell up.'

'That's a shame with so much good seafood in Australia.'

But Paul shook his head. 'I'm from the interior, not the coast. We eat meat.'

'On the barbie,' Catherine said in a dodgy Australian accent. 'Can you find meat as good in the London restaurants?'

'Nah, that's a waste of money. I cook it myself.'

'Oh, you're a good cook?' That would go over well with her clientele. At-home dinner dates were excellent. They were so much more relaxing than eating in a restaurant. Even when it was a casual pub, she didn't like the way that having other people around changed the dynamic.

'Yeah, as long as you mean throwing meat and a few tatties on the barbie. I'd have to be, wouldn't I, being an Aussie?'

'I suppose so, though I can't cook a roast and I'm as English as they come.'

Paul was good company. Of course, he needed some guidance, but that's why she was there. She just had to think about the ideal man, and then help him get as close to that ideal as possible.

In some ways, Richard did make a good prototype. He might have been hopeless when they were married but he'd been well-trained by all the women he'd dated since then. He liked to share these unwelcome details with her no matter how many times she told him she wasn't interested.

Of course, he was a complete imposter who kept a wine pairing flash card in his wallet, but he got away with it. That was something she could share with Paul without it seeming like criticism.

'Want to know a trick when choosing wine?' she asked.

'Hit me.'

'Once you know whether white or red is best, choose the third least expensive one on the list.'

'I usually pick the cheapest. It all gets you drunk.'

'Yes, well, that's not really the point, is it?'

'Maybe it's not *your* point, Catherine.'

'I mean, you want to choose something that tastes nice and goes with the food.'

'I like a nice meaty red.'

'That's fine, but what if your date is having, I don't know, scallops and cod, or she's a vegetarian? It's easy to remember that white meat goes with white wine and red meat with red.'

'What about pasta?' He gestured to the menu.

'If it's got a red sauce, red wine. White sauce, white wine. See? Easy.'

147

'All right, I'll take a crack at the wine list. What are you having?'

Catherine scanned her menu. 'I think I'll have the pappardelle with hare to start and then . . . the braised ox cheeks.'

'You're just fucking with me, right?'

Catherine looked up sharply. 'No, why?'

'Hare? Hare?! Red or white meat, Catherine? You may as well order rhinoceros.'

'Oh. I see. Well, it's white meat, but since it's game, a red will go nicely.'

'So, red wine with red meat, white wine with white meat, unless it's game, then it's red. Right?'

'Right . . . Except for partridge.' She was starting to regret her instruction. 'White is best with that.'

She cringed when she saw the defeat in his expression. 'There really are just a few basic rules,' she continued. 'I promise, once you get those down, it's easy . . .' She wanted to tell him that when she met Richard he barely knew the difference between wine and beer. And look at him now. So Paul could definitely learn to order a bottle or two on a date.

Should she tell him about Richard? He might feel better knowing someone else was even more hopeless than him.

No, it felt too personal. 'So, that'll be red for me then,' she said instead.

'Right,' said Paul. 'So then we'll have the Refosco dal . . . dal . . . aw, shit, this one.' He pointed to the page.

'Well, yes, or . . . yes, that's fine.'

'Or what? What were you going to say, Catherine?'

She sighed. 'The list isn't in price order, so actually the third cheapest is the Valpolicella. It's here.' She looked into his eyes. 'I'm sorry. This was a bad idea.'

But he smiled. 'Don't blame yourself. Who's to know the damn wine list isn't in order? Wankers,' he said just as

148

the waiter approached. 'Oh, not you, mate. We'll have the Valpolicella, thanks a lot.'

'So, that was easy,' he said, shaking his head. 'We haven't even had starters yet. So far this has been more intense than my job.'

She couldn't be offended by his comment. It wasn't the first time she'd been called intense. Sometimes she envied Rachel's happy-go-lucky personality, or even Sarah's daffy world view. But she'd never been the kind of person to let her hair down. It felt too much like being out of control. She'd only let that happen once, and look where it got her.

Divorced.

Pushing those thoughts aside, she focussed on Paul. At least it was no hardship to have dinner with him. He was just rough around the edges.

'May I compliment your outfit tonight, Paul. You look nice.'

He glanced at his shirt front, seeming to notice it for the first time. 'An ex bought me this, actually. And the jacket. It's a good thing tonight's a one-time-only date. It's the only trendy get-up I have.'

'Then you need to do some shopping,' she said cheerfully.

'Aw, Christ, no way, I can't stand it. My mum sends me work shirts, pants and the like for Crimbo.'

'And I'm sure she's got fine taste, but you need more than one date outfit. What will you do if you take a woman out a second time?'

'I do wash my clothes, ya know.'

'That's good, but you still can't wear the exact same thing twice in a row.'

'It's a shirt and jacket,' he said. 'Nobody will notice.'

'Trust me, she'll notice. I'm sorry, but we may need to go shopping for you.'

He rolled his eyes. 'I've got a better idea. Why don't I give you my card and you can buy whatever you think looks good. I promise I'll wear it.'

'Sorry, Paul, that won't work. Give a man a fish and he eats for a day . . .'

'Teach a man to fish and he'll spend his time at the lake instead of inside some poncy overpriced shop,' he finished. 'Do I have to?'

'I'm afraid so. It won't be so bad, I promise.'

'Can I have a drink first?'

'One drink,' she conceded. 'I mean it. One. And then we shop until I say we're finished. Agreed?'

Reluctantly, he nodded just as the waiter returned with their starters. 'It's a date,' he said. 'But not that kind of date.'

Chapter Seventeen

Rachel

Rachel hadn't been this nervous since . . . she didn't remember when. A long time, anyway. She had an actual date. A proper, grown-up, would-you-like-to-have-drinks-with-me, maybe-we'll-kiss-a-little date. His name was Thomas and he was from Edinburgh. She didn't like to count her Scotch eggs before they were hatched but Thomas had promise. She'd been murmuring that little ditty all week, even at work, until James asked her to please shut up about it.

They were enjoying an uneasy truce in the office, though he'd no more come round to Rachel's design idea than she had to his. What they were able to agree on was that if they didn't find a compromise, they'd both miss the opportunity of their careers. So they had no choice.

'Look,' he'd said. 'The one thing our buildings have in common is that they are buildings. Agreed?'

Rachel had been tempted to disagree, if only to be contrary. 'Uh huh.'

'So if we break each design down into its component parts, both materials-wise and stylistically, we should be able to argue out each component to come to an agreement.'

'You mean mashing up bits of each design into a Frankenstein's monster of a building?'

'Where's your optimism, Rachel? This might turn out to be the most brilliant design that either of us could have imagined.'

'Or it could be a dog's breakfast.'

They didn't have a choice though, with time ticking down. They'd have to show Ed something soon. He wasn't about to let them go unsupervised into a meeting with their most important clients.

Rachel didn't want to think about the negotiations ahead tomorrow. Tonight she planned to have fun.

Her phone dinged with a new message from RecycLove as she applied her lipstick in the office mirror. That website was an eat-all-you-like buffet . . . she knew she was being greedy but couldn't help herself. Just one more taste. She clicked.

And immediately regretted her gluttony.

Hi Rachel! You're hot! And you look fun too! Msg me back and we can go out!
Love Mitchell x

She'd got a bad prawn. Mitchell was at least fifty, paunchy and bald. He did have a nice smile, though probably hadn't bothered to read her profile. Her age cut-off was very clearly thirty-five. If he was thirty-five, then she was Scarlett Johansson.

She stared at her reflection. Maybe a short, plump, ginger Scarlett Johansson.

Tucking her phone away, she hurried from the office to meet Thomas.

All Bar One was already crowded, but she'd looked so often at his photos that she could pick him out of an Interpol line-up.

She squinted when her eye caught a movement at one of the tall tables at the side. It was a man, waving her over. 'Rachel? Hi! I just got here too.' He kissed her cheek. 'Can I get you a drink?'

His Scottish burr sounded lovely to her southern ears. 'I didn't want to give up the table but now that you're here, I'll go get us drinks. What would you like?'

Well for one thing, she'd like to know how old his photos were.

This wasn't Interpol-recognisable Thomas. It was two-stone-later Thomas. 'Hi . . . Thomas?' Just to be doubly sure. 'I'll have a small glass of house white wine please.'

'Right you are!' he said.

She watched him as he made his way to the bar. And she felt like crying. And then she felt stupid that she felt like crying. And *then* she felt stupid that she felt like crying because she'd built Thomas up into some kind of Scottish Ryan Gosling.

No, Rachel, be realistic. It's only fair. She watched him return to the table. He was as tall as he'd said in his profile. And he did have all his hair. It was wavy, dark and a bit messed up, which looked cool.

So he wasn't quite the hottie he'd appeared to be online. Most of his photos showed him doing something sporty – snowboarding, rock climbing, sailing – all things he could still do with a big tummy, she supposed. And he was still on the cute end of the spectrum.

'It's nice to meet you in person,' he said when he got back to the table with their drinks. 'Though it's been fun messaging too.' He sipped his pint. 'I've only been on the site a few weeks so, to be honest, this is my first date. It's kind of a weird concept, isn't it? Joining with your ex?'

'My housemate runs the site,' Rachel said quickly. 'I thought you should know that. Just in case you were about to rubbish it.'

'Oh no, not at all. It's a strange concept but it must work. Like My Single Friend mixed with, I don't know, one of those house makeover shows.'

'*DIY SOS*,' said Rachel.

'Aye.' His smile was nice.

This isn't bad for a first date, she thought. He is easy to talk to.

Though she'd initially thought the same thing about the zealous urinator. 'So was it your idea to join or your ex's?' she asked.

He smirked. 'It wasn't my idea. I don't know many guys who want to fix women. The other way around though . . .'

She took a second to decide whether to be offended by the implication on behalf of womankind. No, he was right.

'Was it your idea to go on?' he asked.

She nodded, proving his point. 'Well, my housemate kept bugging me, so after . . . well, after some bad dates, I finally caved in.'

'Was it hard to convince your ex to join too?' he asked.

She thought about James. 'Not too hard. What about you? Were you against the idea?'

He shook his head. 'Noo. I've been meaning to go online for a while but I'm lazy. I needed a kick up the arse. My ex always did enjoy doing the kicking.'

'Is this where we have the talk about our pasts?' Rachel asked. 'I'm not really up on the protocol.'

He smiled a big dimply grin. 'Me either but aye, we may as well get it over with. Ladies first?'

She sipped her wine, thinking. 'James and I are still friends, well obviously or he wouldn't have joined. We're colleagues actually, and we went out ages ago for about a year.' She shrugged. 'That's it, really. You?'

'Milly, my first real girlfriend, when we were seventeen.

She was my neighbour and our parents are best friends. She's like my sister.'

'Your first girlfriend is like your sister? You do things differently in Edinburgh,' she joked.

Thomas turned serious. 'Milly's a good friend. And she's very popular on the site.'

'Oh, well, yes, I'm sure she is. A friend. And popular.' She could feel her face turning beetroot.

Someone jostled her from behind. She glanced over her shoulder at the three guys getting shouty behind her. They seemed to be friends but their language was pretty colourful.

'Someone started early,' she whispered to Thomas.

The guy knocked her chair again.

'He could say he's sorry,' Thomas said, his brow furrowing with concern.

'Don't worry, it was an accident.' She hoped Thomas wasn't the aggressive type. She was usually a pretty patient person, but she couldn't handle a fighter.

When the guy bumped her chair again she tried to cover it by scooting in.

'He needs to calm down,' Thomas said. His hands were clenched on the table.

Rachel's mind raced for some way to distract him. What was she supposed to do, flash him her boobs?

'Erm, so tell me about snowboarding,' she said instead, saving her boobs as a last resort. 'I saw lots of photos. Where do you like to go? I've been to Cortina, though just once. I'm a crap skier.' She wound her finger into the hair at her temple, a nervous habit. 'But I'm an excellent après skier.'

'I usually go to France,' he said, smiling with obvious pleasure at the memory. 'Or Verbier in Switzerland. I love it. And the snow's been awesome this year. I'll try to get out there again before the season's up.'

'Do you go with a big group?' she asked, wanting to

know more about something that so obviously made Thomas happy.

'Sometimes, but I go alone too.'

Alone? She'd be bored silly after two days on her own. She once took herself off for a long weekend spa break but after the first night by herself in the restaurant she ordered room service for the rest of the stay.

The drunks moved away to refuel at the bar and Rachel could see Thomas relax as he chatted about the beauty of the mountains in winter.

That's what she'd missed from most of her dates lately: passion. Not tearing her clothes off but talking with someone who cared about things. She might not have a huge catalogue of interests, but what she did like, she liked very much. She was tired of asking guys what they liked and hearing variants of 'Dunno. I like the pub.'

'This has been fun,' said Thomas after their second drink. 'I'd love to monopolise your whole night but that wasn't the deal, so maybe we can go out again some time?'

'I'd love to! Hang on, I can check when I'm free. Sorry, I know that's wanky but I have to work late on projects when meetings are coming up.'

As she took her phone out, its face lit up with a text.

How's your date? James had texted. *Don't do that thing with your hair. It makes you look like you're ten. xo*

Rachel unwound her finger from her hair. 'I'm free any night but Thursday and Friday,' she said.

Then she turned her phone off.

'So? You didn't text me back,' James said the next morning as he hovered in her office doorway. 'Does that mean the date was good, or not worth talking about? Or so bad that you've blocked it out?'

She found she didn't want to play this game with him.

156

She liked Thomas. At least she liked what she knew of him so far. She didn't need any of James's snide comments. 'It was good, thanks.'

'And? Don't leave a guy hanging,' he said.

'And what?'

'And aren't you going to talk about it for the next two days like you always do?'

'No, in fact I'm not.'

'Oh,' he murmured. 'Was it really good then?'

'This is me not talking about it, James. Are we working on these designs or not?' She pointed at the drawings under his arm.

'Then I guess you don't want to know about my dates either?' he asked.

'Plural? You've had more than one?'

'Well no, but I might soon,' he said.

'Good. Then I'll be sure to text you a helpful tip in the middle of it, like you did to me. Now, the plans?'

He sighed as he sat in her extra chair. 'The plans. We need one cohesive design for the meeting, so somehow we have to marry your cheese grater—'

'—with your treehouse. Right. So let's take each component and decide whose is best.'

'Let's start with the doors,' he said.

'Okay, that's easy. We can't have yours. Bi-fold doors are fine for a deck off the kitchen, but they're completely impractical for an office building.'

James crossed his arms. 'No more so than they are for a deck off the kitchen. Retail spaces use bi-fold doors all the time. Why shouldn't an office building?'

'Because we're not designing a shopfront. And there's security to think of as well.'

'What's your alternative, revolving doors? Do you really think those would stop a terrorist attack? I'm sure they'll throw down their Kalashnikovs, peel off their balaclavas and go home when they realise they have to enter single file.'

Rachel thought for a moment. 'If I let you have the doors, can I have the external skin over the lifts?'

He sat back. 'Possibly. Let's park the doors for the moment and talk about something smaller.'

'Fine.'

'Did your date have a little package? Is that why you don't want to talk about it?'

'James. Just shut up, will you?'

Chapter Eighteen

Sarah

Sarah's phone chirped just as she walked with Rachel up the last few steps at Bond Street Tube. She reached for it, smiling in anticipation. Her inbox had been steadily filling ever since they'd put up her profile a few weeks ago. Who knew there were so many available guys in London? She might be passing them on the pavement right now and not know it. Someone should make a singles equivalent to those *Baby on Board* badges that pregnant women wore on the Tube. Then she'd be able to pick them out in real-life situations.

Her hand hesitated. No, it would be rude to check her messages with Rachel there. Not when she'd taken time out of her day to meet her.

But she so wanted to look. She'd become one of those obsessive phone people she hated. Must get a grip.

'Thanks again,' she said to Rachel, who was hurrying beside her.

'For what?'

'Signing me up for RecycLove. You were right.'

'Don't mention it, and will you please slow down? Short-arses like me haven't got your stride, you know.'

'Sorry! I guess I'm just excited.'

Rachel grabbed her arm. 'Is this possible? *You're* excited to go shopping?'

But Sarah shook her head. 'No. I hate trying on clothes. I'm excited about the makeover bit.'

In her pocket, her thumb reflexively played with the phone's home button.

Just one little peek. It would take five seconds.

The phone came out with her hand. That thing had a mind of its own.

'What are you doing?' Rachel snapped.

'Nothing.' Guiltily, she slid it back into her pocket and scrunched deeper inside her old coat.

'Were you going to check RecycLove messages?' Rachel's tone was playful rather than accusatory.

'No!'

'Because I will if you will.'

It was a technological Get Out Of Jail Free card. She'd take it.

'Anything?' Rachel asked, scrolling through her messages.

'Just one,' said Sarah, clicking on the icon. 'You?'

'Three. Hellllo, he's not bad.' She flipped her phone around.

A blond man with film star looks smouldered for the camera. 'Oh, never mind,' Rachel said. 'He lives in Leeds. Too far away.'

'Hmm.' Sarah showed Rachel the photo attached to her new message. 'Mine looks like your dad.'

'God, he really does, doesn't he? What's he say?'

Hi Sarah, I never really know what to say in these messages. Not that I write them a lot. Obviously I'm interested in talking with you or I wouldn't be in contact. Maybe that's enough to say? The rest is on my profile and I don't want to waste your time making you

160

read everything twice so I guess that's it. Message me
back if you're interested.
Yours sincerely,
Larry

Rachel pulled a cringy face. 'I'm not sure I could handle having my dad's doppelgänger in his pants sharing breakfast with us.'

Sarah understood completely. The resemblance was uncanny. 'Imagine if I called him Mr Lambert by mistake.'

'If you shouted it from your bedroom I'd need therapy.'

Sarah deleted the message. 'You don't need to worry about that.'

They put their phones away and continued to Fenwick's.

When she walked through the main doors into the jewellery hall, she felt a stab of recognition.

'Mum and I came here,' she told Rachel. 'I was in my tomboy phase so she dragged me. I was a cow to her that day. I didn't remember it till now.'

Rachel put her arm round her friend's shoulder. 'I'm sure you were just being a teenager.'

Sarah shrugged. 'She was gutted. She wanted to buy me all this new clobber, heels and dresses and the like, and I was such an arsehole to her. Make sure you appreciate your parents, Rachel. Because you never know how long you'll have them around.'

'You're wise beyond your years, Sarah Lee.'

Sarah smiled. She knew her mum would be happy to see her there today, so she promised herself not to be too miserable about the shopping.

Rachel led the way towards two women dressed in white at the Clinique counter.

'Aren't you making me shop first?' Sarah asked.

'Nah, we'll do your makeover first.'

Sarah knew it was a pity change of scheduling.

'Besides, it'll be better to have your make-up done already when you try on clothes. That way you can see the whole effect.' She turned to the pretty Asian woman waiting to help. 'My friend needs all new make-up. Could you maybe suggest what colours would suit her?'

'All right, Samira?' Sarah said, reading the woman's name badge. 'I'm Sarah. I don't usually wear make-up so if you could find something that's not too heavy, that'd be great.'

'Ignore her,' Rachel said. 'Make her look beautiful!'

Sarah was about to object, then remembered her mum. It wasn't like she couldn't wipe it all off later if she didn't like it. 'Okay,' she said. 'Make me beautiful!'

Samira got to work. 'Do you have any make-up on now?'

Sarah shook her head, but Samira didn't believe her because she ran a cold wet cotton pad over her face anyway. Like a doctor with a skittish patient, Samira then talked Sarah through every step of the procedure.

After nearly half an hour, during which Rachel gave a running commentary and twice suggested colour alternatives, Samira decided they were finished. She held the mirror up for Sarah.

'Wait, hang on a sec,' Rachel said. 'Take that hair tie out first.'

Obediently, Sarah undid her ponytail and let her hair fall to her shoulders.

She could hardly believe what she saw in the mirror. The woman staring back at her was nearly a stranger. Her greeny-grey eyes looked huge, fringed with thick black lashes, deepened by liner and shadow in a rich plum. The lipstick that Samira had used gave her a killer smile, and she had cheekbones. Actual cheekbones!

Samira had done it. She really did feel beautiful.

'Happy?' Rachel asked as Samira returned Sarah's card. They started for the escalators.

'Happy,' she said, sneaking glimpses in the mirrors they passed on the way up to women's fashion. She never thought a bit of slap could have such an effect. Maybe that Maybelline advert wasn't a complete load of piffle after all.

Upstairs, Rachel stroked a pale blue silk full-skirted print dress. 'Ooh look at this. I love it!'

It looked a bit busy to Sarah. 'Mmm, how about this?' She held up a black and white block print shift dress instead.

'No. That's something Uhura would wear on *Star Trek* for an intergalactic business meeting.'

'I think it's nice.'

'You're too straight up and down, Sarah. You'd look like a wooden plank in that dress.'

'Ta very much.'

'All I mean is that you're athletic so we need to give you some curves.' Rachel ran her hand across a rail of pastel frocks, plucking as she went. 'Let's get a bunch of options. Then we won't have to keep going in and out of the fitting room.'

'These are nice,' Sarah said, moving to another colourful rail in the all-white room. It felt like shopping inside a pillowcase.

'But they won't suit your figure,' Rachel said. 'The nineteen-fifties look is better for you.'

Maybe so, but they weren't really her style. She was tempted to object before she remembered that she didn't have a style. That's why they were there. 'You pick out the dresses for me,' she said. 'I'm happy to try on any clobber you want.'

After searching all the rails, Rachel deposited an armload of frocks on the hooks in the fitting room.

'I'll be right outside,' she said, sitting on the leather pouffe in the corridor. 'Show me when you get them on.'

'How's this?' Sarah said a few minutes later, stepping shyly into the corridor.

'Definitely not with those running shoes! Take them off so I can get a better idea.'

Sarah kicked off her shoes and peeled off the white sports socks. 'Better?'

'Better, but you're still too planky in it. Don't worry about the green one, it'll fit the same. I think the other shape will be better.'

She was right. Four of the dresses gave Sarah curves she didn't realise she had. So she exercised her still-smarting card again and got a new wardrobe to go with her new make-up.

She didn't remember the last time she felt so good.

'Oh my God, I have something to tell you,' Rachel said as she checked her phone on the way back to the Tube. 'Let's go get a drink.' She started looking around for a pub.

'How come we need a drink?' Sarah was suspicious. Nobody makes you drink before giving you good news.

'Just . . . let's get a drink. Trust me.'

Rachel hurried up the road surprisingly fast for someone claiming short-arse legs. 'Where's a damn pub when you need one?'

'Why do we need one?'

'It's a surprise.'

Sarah didn't like the sound of that.

'A nice surprise.'

Still not convinced, she thought.

Rachel steered her into a dark pub. When she got the barman's attention, she said, 'May I have a bottle of house champagne, please?'

Sarah gasped. It must be about Rachel's designs at work! Her boss picked hers. She probably got a promotion. And a raise. And a new office that she'd get to decorate herself and . . .

She threw herself at Rachel, who put her arms out just in time to keep from being knocked over.

'Whoa, what's that for? You don't even know what I'm going to say.'

Sarah mumbled into Rachel's shoulder.

'What? I can't hear you.'

'. . . And your office will be powder blue and then you'll be the most famous architect in the world!'

'What *are* you talking about? Sarah, you are one weird girl. Are you ready for the news?'

'Isn't it that you're going to redecorate your office and be world-famous?'

'Nooo, but maybe you are.' Rachel took a deep breath. 'Now, please don't flip out but . . . I put your application in for *The Great British Bake Off.*'

A chill ran up Sarah's spine. 'You what?'

'And you've been chosen for an audition! Sarah, this is such an opportunity and you were too modest to apply so please don't be mad at me. I just knew you'd be perfect and you're such an amazing baker that you could totally win. But not if you didn't apply. So you did. Or I did. Are you mad?'

'I've been chosen? No way!'

Rachel beamed. 'Look, read this.' She flipped her phone so Sarah could see.

teambakeoff@gbbo.co.uk   6.02pm (12 minutes ago)
To: me

Dear Ms Hamilton,

We are delighted to let you know that your application for *The Great British Bake Off* 2016 has been successful, and we would like to talk with you more about your technical skills and baking aspirations. This is the first step in the *Bake Off* selection process – congratulations! If after this conversation you are chosen to audition, you'll need to bring two bakes, one sweet and one savoury, to the London trials.

We'd like to talk to you at your earliest convenience. The interview will take place by phone so please let us know by return email when would be a good time to ring.

With warm wishes,

Jessica Howzer
Programme Coordinator

'But I can't do that!' Sarah said. Imagine being on national telly. What a horrifying idea. The one time her mum made her join a school play she got so nervous that she threw up all over little baby Jesus in the manger. She wasn't about to vomit into her signature bake. 'I can't go on telly.'

'You don't have to! At least not yet. It's only a phone call at first. They just want to run you through some questions before the audition. I'm sure this Jessica woman is very nice. She must be. She deals with *nans*, Sarah. Baking nans.'

'Oh God, an audition.' She imagined standing on stage in front of the *X Factor* judges, juggling scones and singing 'Pat-A-Cake'.

'Relax, that's probably not for months yet,' Rachel said. 'The deadline for applications isn't even until March so they must be really keen to have you on the show if they're saying yes already. And it's just a phone call for now. You hardly need to swot up, do you? You make loads of delicious cakes.

Any audition would be ages away. Won't you think about it? It's not like there'll be any cameras there, just a few other bakers like yourself.'

'How many others?'

'Well I don't know, do I? Ten or twenty, I guess? And you won't have to bake in front of them. Look, it says here that you'll bring two dishes for the judges to try. You get to bake them ahead of time. Sarah, think about it. You're getting the chance to try out for *The Great British Bake Off*.'

She did think about it as they sipped their champagne. It wasn't like she didn't imagine her signature bakes when she watched the show every year. She did always wonder how she'd do against the others. She fantasised about Mary Berry saying she'd baked the best eclair she'd ever tasted.

But national telly! Could she really do that? Just the thought made her feel ill.

Still, at least there wouldn't be a live audience. It was better than those talent shows.

Listen to her. She still had the phone call *and* the audition to get through.

Did that mean she was going to try?

'I will too have to swot up,' she finally said. 'The interview won't be easy. And then I'll have to bake the best cakes of my life to have any chance.'

Rachel's smile spread across her face. 'You'll do it?'

'I guess I can try.'

At least she'd have something to wear to the audition.

Chapter Nineteen

Catherine

Catherine plastered her smile into place as Magda prattled on. Wedding wedding wedding, nothing but the wedding. And she was probably one of those people who complained that women didn't like her. No prizes for guessing why.

'Catherine? Did you hear me?' Magda held two blue swatches under her nose. 'You are off in fairyland. Which one do you prefer? For the napkins?'

There was virtually no difference between them. 'Erm, that one. Magda, I'm sorry, but I'm a bit busy just now.' With running a business and all. 'Maybe we can talk about this later?'

'Over lunch. Yes, good idea, let's do that.' Magda hurried away to her desk.

'No, I meant . . .' Never.

The woman seemed to have no qualms about bullying her fiancé's first wife into making plans for his second wedding.

Five minutes later an email from Magda popped up. Subject: Agenda. Even her mealtimes were annoying.

But she wasn't proposing to organise their starters, Catherine realised as she read Magda's broken English.

magdasparkles@hotmail.com   11.48am (1 minute ago)
To: me

I want to talk these things please.
makeover
grow
plase settings

thank you

Magda continued her napkin commentary all the way to the restaurant but Catherine hardly heard her. She had her other agenda points to worry about.

It was one of those healthy restaurants where the menu items were all plays on words like Miso Hungry Soup and Absolutely Radishing Salad. Catherine hated it, but Magda was eating only macrobiotic now that she was pregnant.

'So how is the makeover business going?' she asked sweetly when they'd sat down.

Straight into agenda point one.

'It's fine.' Catherine pushed the sprouts off her avocado and looked around for a salt shaker. Of course there weren't any.

Magda waited for more, but Catherine had practically invented that tactic. She could eat her entire lunch in silence if she needed to.

Magda finally broke. 'How many clients are you working with now?'

She couldn't very well ignore a direct question. 'Two.'

'It's not very many, I don't think. When do you plan to increase?'

'It's a bespoke service, Magda. I haven't got time to increase. Besides, not all of our clients need the makeover. They're carefully chosen. And if you don't mind me saying . . .' She didn't give a toss whether or not she minded. 'You seem focussed on growth instead of the business itself. We didn't get where we are today by running off in six different directions. I know how to run my business, thank you very much.'

Magda slowly finished chewing her food. Then she set her fork back on her plate. 'But it isn't your business now, is it, Catherine? It's mine too, and if *you* do not mind, I will say what I think is right for it. I want to expand the makeovers. Maybe I should take on one or two clients as well.'

That wasn't on the agenda! Catherine felt everything she'd worked for slipping from her grasp. All the late nights and weekends spent with her computer instead of her friends. Penny-pinching to afford the website upgrades and forgoing pay cheques to be able to hire another consultant. All for what? So some teenager with her ex-husband's bollocks in a vice could swan in and do what she pleased. That was not going to happen.

But she couldn't confront her directly. What little she knew about Magda told her that she'd fly off in in a fury, like some badly behaved child, if she didn't think she was getting her way.

'That's very kind of you, Magda, and it would be a huge help, thanks. I have one client in mind who could really use your guidance. Would you take her on?'

Magda's eyes shone. 'I will be happy to! I am very busy with the wedding planning, as you know, but I no longer feel as sick, so I can start right away. Should I call her this afternoon?'

'You definitely should,' Catherine said, smiling into her tasteless raw salad.

A few minutes later, Magda patted her tummy. 'Isn't it hard to believe that Richard's baby is in here?'

She wasn't yet ready to let Catherine go.

'Well where else would it be?'

Magda cocked her head. 'Did you not ever want children with him?'

'Haven't you asked Richard about that?' she murmured.

'I did not want to pry into his past.'

Oh but you'll dig straight into mine, she thought.

'It's just that you were together for nearly seven years. Usually people think about children after that time.' Magda laughed. 'Or sooner, in our case.'

'Well, we bounced around between England and the US. And we were ridiculously young. Too young to be responsible for children.'

Magda could hardly miss the barb but she shrugged it off. 'Well, now I know there were no physical problems, at least from Richard's side. More water?'

Catherine wasn't about to give Magda the satisfaction of an explanation. For whatever reason, she hadn't asked Richard about his first marriage, so let her guess what happened. Her imagination was probably worse than the reality anyway, and obviously implicated Richard.

She smiled as Magda studied her.

'What is that for?' she demanded.

'Oh I'm just thinking about when Richard and I were together.'

It was true. Not in the way Magda thought, but so what? Let her think another woman was imagining passionate sex with her fiancé.

The memory was actually much more mundane than that. They had been sitting together on their huge L-shaped sofa. It was an indulgence to buy it when they first moved to Washington and realised everything was bigger in America.

'Catherine,' he'd called from the opposite end of the sofa. 'Do you realise we've colonised this thing?'

'Have we?' She'd glanced up from her book. 'I guess we do each have our end.'

Richard had shifted to his knees and crawled along the seat cushions. He'd wriggled his body between hers and the sofa back. 'I like this better.'

'It's a bit crowded,' she'd joked. Actually she felt a little thrill, as she always did on the rare occasions when he was the one being affectionate.

But he didn't move away.

If they'd stayed crowded on that sofa she might not now be having lunch with Magda.

Catherine had to rush back to the office for her next appointment while Magda faffed around drinking some kind of thistle tea after lunch.

Her new client was already waiting in reception.

'I'm so sorry I'm late, Alistair,' she said, hardly faltering at his appearance.

'Pleasure to meet you.' He extended his hand.

'Please, come through.' She led him to her office and closed the door. 'Would you like something to drink?'

He hesitated. 'I suppose I could have a beer.'

'Oh, I meant a hot drink. Or maybe a soft drink?'

'Sorry!' he said. 'Stupid of me.' His face reddened. At least the bits she could see.

He had the biggest, bushiest black beard she'd ever seen. Their initial phone conversation couldn't have been more misleading. He'd sounded like your run-of-the-mill middle-class Englishman. In real life he looked like a tattoo artist had had a love child with Father Christmas. She mentally crossed him off Georgina's list.

'So, thank you for coming in today. We like to meet with our clients in person, to answer any questions they might have.'

'And make sure they're not total twats, probably,' he said.

'Well, yes, that too.' She smiled. 'As I explained on the

phone, we choose our clients carefully. So we can be sure we'll be able to provide the best service.'

'I guess I don't fit your usual profile.'

She considered his stocky build and the muscular inked arms sticking out from a rather tight Abercrombie-and-Fitch-type tee shirt. And that beard. 'I think you'll find that we look after a wide range of clients. Why don't you tell me a bit about yourself? Did you grow up near London?'

'They're not too far, in Epsom. It's only forty minutes on the train.' He barked a short laugh. 'Everyone from the suburbs says that, don't they? I don't know how Dad did it for so many years. Just so we could have a nice house.' He rubbed the colourful firebird tattoo on his forearm.

Catherine nodded. 'My family was near Hemel Hempstead, so I know exactly what you mean. Even forty minutes adds two hours a day to the commute, by the time you factor in the journey to and from the station. It must have made for long days for your father, and not much time with you.'

'Well I wouldn't have seen him much anyway. I went away to school at twelve, when we moved.'

She resisted the urge to ask how he felt about that. It was important to get into the psyche of her clients, but she didn't want to sound like a therapist.

'Did you like school?' she asked instead.

'I loved it!' He beamed. 'The kids were really nice and not stuck-up at all. That's what I worried about before I went. Well, aside from the buggery, of course.'

'Of course,' she said, smiling. 'And was that an unfounded worry?'

'Oh yeah. I had all the buggery I wanted.'

Catherine knew her face registered surprise.

He grinned. 'Only joking. It was a co-ed school. My sister's a year older and we both went. I think it's good for boys to be around girls. We're savages without them. Though God

173

knows what the poor girls get out of it, having to deal with us spotty hormones on legs. My sister and I had to start a new school anyway when we moved and a lot of our friends in London were starting to go away. You want to do what your friends do.' He shrugged. 'Mum didn't want us to go but she let us convince her. I'm glad she did. I liked the teachers there, and playing sport. I was mad about sport. Rugby and tennis,' he said, anticipating Catherine's question.

She couldn't remember ever giving her full attention to a beard before. Virtually all the men she'd ever known were clean-shaven. When Alistair talked, the bottom half of his face moved a bit like a puppet's, in a smooth up and down motion.

Her fingers flew over the keyboard as he talked about studying economics at uni and moving to London after.

'And now I'm studying to become an accredited feng shui consultant.'

She nearly laughed in his face, until she realised he wasn't taking the piss.

'But I thought you worked in purchasing, Alistair?'

He'd definitely told her that on the phone.

'Call me Alis. I did. I quit. I start the course next month.'

'Alis? Is that what you go by?'

'Yes, my full name is too poncy. Please call me Alis.'

'That sounds like . . .'

'What?'

'It sounds like Alice.'

'It's my name.'

'Well technically it's your nickname. So . . . feng shui. That's an unusual career move for someone who's spent a decade in manufacturing. Is it something you've always wanted to do?'

Nothing in his background suggested this about-face. Had he been dying to wave joss sticks around when he was at

174

his private boarding school, or at the back of his university economics lectures?

If he thought she was being cheeky he didn't show it. 'My reiki teacher introduced me to it.'

'Reiki?'

'It's a way of healing a person's life force energy.'

'I know what it is.' Mostly a load of old tosh, she thought. 'Would you say your life is taking a new direction? I mean, when we talked on the phone you were the head of purchasing for Bravissimo and looking to buy a flat.'

Her clients usually split neatly into two camps: the ones with successful careers that left them no time to manage their own love lives, and the ones who spent most of their time, and a lot of their money, on the latest holistic miracle. Alis seemed to fall between stereotypes.

'I'm still looking to buy a flat,' he said. 'I figure a few more rounds of bone marrow donations and I'll have the deposit nailed. Listen, I'm getting some negative energy here. If you don't want to take me on then that's fine. I just thought I'd try your service because I want to meet someone and you've got a lot of good testimonials on your site.'

Catherine felt bad for knocking his voodoo aspirations. 'I haven't said I don't want to take you on, Alis. I'm just trying to understand a bit about you so that I know whether we'll have suitable dates on our books. I'm sorry if I sounded judgemental. I'm not. Judgemental, I mean. Tell me more about your course.' She fixed her features in a suitably benign expression while he talked about chakras and nerve strokes.

By the end of their meeting Catherine knew Alis was as flaky as a puff pastry but also engaging and solvent enough to suit her list. She had a few women in mind already, mostly yoga devotees who wouldn't mind all that talk about good chi.

Honestly, though, if people spent half as much time just

getting on with their lives as they did trying to reroute their energy or channel their inner child, they'd be a lot better off.

As soon as Catherine ushered Alis out, Magda pounced.

'Who was that?!' Her disdain was palpable.

'His name is Alis, and he may be a new client.'

'Alice? As in Wonderland? You cannot be serious. He is not the kind of client we want.'

'Don't be so elitist, Magda. You can't judge people by looks alone, you know. It's insulting. I happen to think he's a very nice person.'

'He looks like a delivery person. He should be bringing us sandwiches, not dating our clients.'

Catherine bristled, despite having thought the same thing when she first saw him. 'Well, he's also my new client. I'm signing him. So I'll thank you to keep your opinions to yourself.'

He might be the most unsuitable client they'd ever have, but she was not about to let Magda get her way.

Chapter Twenty

Rachel

A text from Thomas pinged Rachel's phone as she walked to the pub where they were meeting.

> *Snagged a table. Should I wait to get a beer? Does that make me sound like an alcoholic? I'm not an alcoholic.*

> *That sounds defensive. Also not defensive.*

> *How do you say that without sounding defensive? Tx*

> *On my way! Get a beer. I won't judge. xo*

They'd talked a lot after their first date, at least by text if not on the phone. With each call or message, he got better looking. Now imaginary Thomas surpassed even his photographs. Maybe he wasn't as plump as she remembered. And there was no denying that his Scottish accent was very sexy when he'd rung.

This time she chose the pub. All Bar One was fine for a first date but she wanted somewhere a bit more romantic, and dimly lit. She suggested The Dove, nearby in Hackney.

Cosy, dripping with atmosphere and candle wax, it was perfect for the blustery January night.

As she walked she scrolled back through Thomas's messages from earlier.

On the bus next to a man who looks like an over-grilled Simon Cowell. Should I ask him if I've got the X Factor? Tx

Take a pic. He'll think he's been papped. Did he bring his rotating chair on the bus?

That's The Voice. Don't you know your celeb TV? Tx

Sorry, I usually read. Anyone on the bus w/X Factor potential?

There's a youth at the back singing with his earphones in. We may get auditions going before we reach my stop. Will let you know if he makes it through. Tx

Can I vote for him?

It'll cost you 35p from your mobile and BT landlines. Calls from other landlines may vary. Voting closes at midnight. Tx

You really do watch too much TV. xo

And yesterday.

I can't believe how expensive okra is. T

That's random.
Did you mean to text me, Thomas? xo

Yeah but I don't want to rush you . . . is it too soon for veg talk?

It's a bit soon TBH.
I usually establish
a solid fruit relationship first. Xo

You guide me. Tx

She loved pinging back answers, knowing his responses would always make her laugh. None of the other guys she was talking to on RecycLove were even half as entertaining.

Her tummy was bubbling with excitement by the time she got to the pub. The windows ran with condensation from so much body heat in the little space. She didn't see Thomas in the front bit so she walked downstairs to the back.

As soon as she spotted him, the bubbles fizzled. She took in his pleasant but portly face and comfy, unstylish fleece.

Why didn't he look like his texts made him sound?

Because then he wouldn't be on a dating website. He'd be married to the luckiest woman on the planet.

'How did the audition go?' She kissed him on the cheek.
'Audition?'

'On the bus. The guy singing with his earphones in.' She giggled, thinking about the texts. Over-grilled Simon Cowell! 'Did he make it through?'

'Oh, he got off the bus before I did. Would you like a drink? I waited.'

'Then you're definitely not an alcoholic.'

He smiled.

She waited for a quip.

179

Nothing.

'Please. May I have a half pint of Fruli?' she asked.

She watched him squeeze between the narrow tables to make his way to the bar.

He was as friendly and smiley as when they first met, but with absolutely no banter at all. Without his phone he wasn't funny. Did that make him a textophiliac?

She had to admit though, as they had their drinks, that she wasn't having a bad time with him. He was perfectly nice. Nice was all right for the moment.

She just preferred Phone Thomas. He had to be in there somewhere.

James where are you? she texted the next morning from her desk. *Mtg starts in 5 and you better be here*

He wasn't usually late for staff meetings. He didn't like to miss his weekly chance to suck up to their boss. Now would be a terrible time to start. They had to show Ed a combined design on Friday and were as far apart on a compromise as when they'd started. Without a united front in the meeting, Ed would start to get nervous. Nobody liked a nervous boss.

She slipped into one of the few remaining empty chairs around the long conference table. 'James'll be here in a minute, Ed,' she said. Normally she'd have no qualms about throwing him under the bus, but with them working together on the project, she needed to save both their faces. 'I think he's having some intestinal issues.'

She may save his face but his arse was still fair game.

'We'll wait a few minutes for him,' Ed said, looking put out. He loved his weekly meetings.

But what if James didn't turn up? Or what if he arrived with an excuse that didn't involve explosive diarrhoea? 'We could start if you want, Ed. I don't know how long he'll be, actually. He might not even be in the building.'

Ed frowned. 'How do you know about his . . . issues?'

'He texted from the loo to tell me.'

Everyone stared at her. She wanted to bury her face in her hands.

'You two have an odd relationship,' Ed finally said. 'All right, let's start then. We're all busy. What's everyone working on?'

Just as her colleague started outlining his work week, James burst through the door. He was out of breath and sweaty. At least her cover story looked plausible.

'I'm not late, am I? I got Krispy Kremes for everyone.' He grinned at Rachel.

That wasn't the act of a man who'd spent the morning on the toilet, but Ed didn't question him.

James chose a jam-filled doughnut and happily munched away as the meeting carried on.

'Where were you really?' Rachel asked him later as they left the conference room.

'I was getting doughnuts,' he said.

'No. I know you. That was a diversionary tactic.'

James always got to the office before her. He purposely left home early to avoid the worst crush of the rush hour. He was very predictable like that.

He shrugged. 'I just ran late today. Hey, I got an idea yesterday after you left. Let me show you.'

He pulled her to his office, where he unrolled a piece of tracing paper. 'What do you think?'

Rachel didn't know what to think as she studied James's redesign of his building. There were still two buildings, which he'd been so adamant about keeping, but they were no longer towers. They were parallel wedges. It was clearly based on her design. 'I thought you hated the cheese grater idea,' she said.

181

'I do, but it's not a cheese grater any more. It's a three-dimensional, tipped-over A.'

He'd drawn a walkway at the midpoint between the buildings, with a completely glassed-in reception area beneath it. 'So when you're in reception it looks like you're still outside. Because of the bi-fold doors.' He smirked.

'Bringing the outside in. I get it.'

'But do you like it?' he asked.

She did like it. She just wasn't comfortable with how it made her feel. There she was, always accusing him of insensitivity, yet he was the one who'd managed to incorporate both their designs into one while she was still arguing over details like door handles. She felt like she'd misjudged him.

'This shows an unusual level of perceptiveness, James. How did you think of it?' She tried very hard not to emphasise *you*.

He shook his head. 'I'm not sure, really. It just came to me as I was thinking about how you'd designed your building. That tapering effect is the most important element of your vision. Am I right?' He pulled a slightly squashed doughnut from his jacket pocket.

At least he'd wrapped it in a serviette.

'So I knew we couldn't lose that or we'd lose the core of your design. This seems like a compromise we can both live with.'

She studied his face as he stuffed half the doughnut into his mouth. The shape of the building was a critical feature. And it was essentially her cheese grater, times two.

Since when did he put his own ambition aside for someone else?

'Do you think we could agree in principle on this new design?' he asked. He had a bit of sugar in the corner of his mouth.

Damn, it was a good compromise. She wished she'd thought of it. 'In principle, yes, I agree. But I don't believe this just came to you. I know you, James. You stayed up all night obsessing over it.' He just loved making everything look so easy when, really, he worked harder than almost everyone else.

'No. I did stay up all night, but I wasn't drawing.'

He waited for her to ask more. When she didn't, he said, 'I happened to have a date last night.'

A date? But he never talked about his love life. Oversharing was her domain.

'So it really did just come to me,' he said. 'Before my date. It was a good night.'

'Who were you out with? Someone from the website?'

'We've been talking online for a few days. She's a nice girl.'

'A first date?'

'Rachel. Don't start judging me just because I slept with her on the first date. She's very nice.'

'You slept with her?' She didn't expect to hear *that*.

'Otherwise I wouldn't have been late this morning.'

'Please.' Rachel put her hand up. 'I don't want any details.'

His expression turned earnest. 'Does it bother you? Me dating other women, I mean?'

'Of course not,' she said. 'As it happens, I had a date too.'

'Oh . . . But you were here on time, so it wasn't as good as mine.'

'Actually, it went very well. Just because I didn't put out like your date doesn't mean I didn't have a great time.' Okay, so that was an exaggeration. But true to form, Thomas's text before bed last night had cracked her up and now she liked him again. 'I assume now that you've slept with this poor woman you'll never contact her again?'

'As it happens, I've already asked her out for this weekend.'

'Really?' She frowned. 'That's not like you.'

'I've matured.'

'No, really. That's not like you. She must be amazing in bed.'

She expected to get a rise out of him, or some disgustingly sexual comment. Instead he said, 'I don't want to be disrespectful to her. This way she knows I'm not a tosser.'

'Did you slip in the shower this morning and hit your head or something?'

'Maybe I just listened to your feedback.'

'Really?'

'Mmm hmm.' He nodded. 'You were harsh, but I had to take some of it on board. Rachel.' He grasped her hands. 'You've *improved* me. I'm a different person. How will womankind ever thank you enough?'

'Shut up.'

He glanced at the doughnut she'd brought out of the meeting. 'Are you going to eat that?'

When she said no, he stuffed it all in his mouth, leaving sugar all over his chin.

She didn't tell him.

Chapter Twenty-One

Sarah

Just get over yourself, ya div, Sarah thought as she got close to Sissy's. It's not like you've had plastic surgery. All the way over on the train she'd fantasised about Sissy's reaction at seeing her looking, well, not too shabby, if she did say so herself.

Each day it got a little easier to put on the make-up she'd bought. Now she hardly stabbed herself in the eye at all. And she'd keep wearing it too, considering what it cost.

Not that it was only about the money. As much as she hated to admit it, people seemed to like her painted face. At first she thought it was just her imagination that smiles were a little brighter and more forthcoming.

But no. There was definitely a difference. The dresses that she'd chosen with Rachel circled her waist and even gave her a bit of a bust. Judging by the number of glances that lingered, she must look good.

And that made her feel amazing.

Her boss, Harry, had asked if she'd been somewhere sunny. Just Costa del Clapton, she'd joked. Even Maria-Therese, who hated everything about her, conceded a grudging compliment.

For the first time in years, she felt wonderful.

'All right, Sissy!' she called as her sister waved from the doorway. 'Ready to bake?'

'Yes.' She stared at Sarah. That wasn't unusual. As long as Sarah kept quiet, Sissy would eventually say what she was thinking. If she asked, her sister would clam up.

'You look like Mum,' she finally said.

Tears sprang to Sarah's eyes. She didn't expect that. After all the time she'd spent in front of the mirror in the past few weeks, she hadn't seen it. 'Do I? Is that okay?'

Sissy considered the question. 'It's okay. I like it.' With that, she threw herself into Sarah's arms. Sarah tried not to cry into her fine blonde hair.

God how she missed her mother. Though it wasn't in that constant grating way that shredded her emotions in the days after she died. And she'd never felt those tides of grief she'd read about either. A tide implied some kind of rhythm, a predictability. That would have been better. At least she could prepare herself, shore herself up against it. But this grief hit her randomly. She might be sitting in a meeting, or on a bus or in the loo, lying in bed or whipping cream or talking on the phone or laughing with her housemates. It didn't matter where or when or whom she was with. The longing that hit her always went through her like a mortar passing through her middle, leaving a hole she could see through. A hole where she wasn't whole.

She didn't have the luxury of going away to lick her wounds though. There was Sissy to think about. She was just as much an orphan and she needed her.

She unpacked her shopping bags and laid out all the baking ingredients on the worktop in the communal kitchen. Sissy stood beside her, rearranging the packets and tins into her own design. When she'd finished, Sarah noticed the symmetry she'd managed to find amongst the jumble of sizes, shapes, labels and colours. That girl had a good eye.

186

Not for the first time, Sarah wondered where their artistic skills came from. Their mum couldn't draw a straight line with a ruler. Had the arty gene skipped a generation on that side? Or had both their fathers been creative? It wasn't like she had anyone to ask. Those details were buried three years ago in the cemetery.

'Right,' she said, pushing aside the dark thoughts. 'I thought we'd make a pound cake today and some biscuits if there's time. I've brought chocolate, vanilla and almond. Which should we use?'

'Chocolate and vanilla.'

'Both?'

'Why not?'

'In one cake? How would we do that?'

'Half and half,' she said. 'You're the baker. Figure it out.'

Sarah laughed. 'You're right, I can do that.' After all, she was auditioning for *The Great British Bake Off*, wasn't she?

She still couldn't believe it. She'd talked to the producer a few days after her makeover at Fenwick's. He had mostly just wanted to have a chat about baking but then he rang back again to ask all kinds of technical questions about working with yeast and hand-raising pies and making choux pastry. She'd got the giggles in the middle of it, thinking how nuts it was to try to describe baking. It was like getting a feel for a porn film using the audio description for the visually impaired.

She had to guess at some of the answers but she must have done okay because he had invited her to audition in March! Half of her wanted to squeal with joy. The other half wanted to ring him up and say it was all a big mistake. She just had to figure out which half would go to the audition.

'Hey Sissy. Do you know the programme, *The Great British Bake Off*?'

She shook her head.

'Oh, well. It's a baking competition on telly where they make beautiful cakes and biscuits and things each week.'

'Sounds boring to watch someone bake.'

'But you watch me bake.'

'I eat the cakes.'

'Well anyway. They've chosen me to audition for the programme. So I might be on national telly in the summer. Would you watch me?'

'When's it on?'

'On Wednesday nights starting in August.'

'Not during *EastEnders*?'

'No. Would you watch?'

'Uh huh. What will you bake?'

'That's what I have to figure out. I need to have two things for the audition. What do you think I should make?'

Sissy didn't answer.

They worked together, creaming the butter, cracking eggs and sifting flour to make the cake batter. Then Sarah divided the mixture in half and Sissy set to work sprinkling cocoa into one bowl and vanilla extract into the other. When they finished, Sissy wiped every inch of the tin's interior with a thin, even layer of butter.

Then she glanced up from the tin. 'I remember Mum,' she said. 'Her dresses.'

Of course. Their mum always wore day dresses, usually with Converse hi-tops in summer and biker boots in winter, always with bare legs. They were a little plainer than the one Sarah wore, but similar enough for Sissy to notice.

'Do you remember baking with her?'

'Yes. Morning muffins.'

They shared a smile. That's what their mum called the carrot cakes she made them for breakfast. Sarah's gran disapproved of cake for breakfast, so their mum devised a 'healthy' muffin instead. It was just carrot cake in another form.

They decided on a marbled effect for their own cake, then popped it in the oven and waited for the delicious baking smell to waft out.

Sarah noticed a young man lurking in the doorway just as Sissy did.

'Ben!' Sissy shouted, stomping across the kitchen to drag the boy by his arm towards Sarah. 'This is my sister, Sarah. This is my boyfriend.'

Sarah smiled. 'All right Ben.' She stuck out her hand. 'It's nice to meet you.'

'Nice to meet you too.'

He had a mop of blond hair and a round face, with a wide, gap-toothed smile and gentle brown eyes. And Sissy was right, he was fat.

'Do you like cake as much as Sissy does?' Sarah asked, noticing him sniffing the air as their marble cake finished baking.

'I don't know how much Sissy likes cake.'

Sarah stifled a laugh. Even after sixteen years with Sissy she sometimes forgot to frame her questions logically. 'Well that's true. Do you like cake?'

'I love it. When's it ready?'

'Ben! Don't be rude,' Sissy said, smiling at him. 'You can't have any until we say. It has to cool first. And then have icing. And then decoration. It'll be hours.'

Ben looked disappointed to hear this.

'I'm afraid she's right, Ben, but we could make some chocolate chip cookies now and it'd be okay to eat a bit of the raw dough before they're baked, if you'd like?'

'But you can't eat any unless you help,' Sissy said.

Ben washed his hands and together they got to work.

A little later, Kelly stuck her head in the kitchen doorway. 'Sarah, could we have a quick word before you go?'

'Is that a hint? Are you trying to get rid of me?'

She laughed. 'Not at all.'

'I'll come now. Sissy, six minutes till the cookies come out, okay? Can you please time it?'

Sissy saluted and peered at her watch.

Ben said, 'Sissy, can we—'

'Sssh, Ben. I'm timing.'

'What's up?' Sarah asked as she followed Kelly down the hallway.

'Let's go outside.'

That sounded serious. Sarah began to worry for Sissy. Was it about her and Ben? Had something happened between them? How was she going to tell Robin? He'd kill the poor boy and start lecturing Sissy about vaginas.

Kelly took a deep breath when they were well away from any of the residents. 'I'm afraid I have some bad news. It's not about Sissy, so don't worry. But it's about Whispering Sands. We've lost our funding and it looks like we may not be able to carry on.'

'You're skint?'

'It looks that way.' Her eyes darted to the doorway. 'Nothing is ever final until the last minute. And then everything just shuts down. That's why I thought you should know now, in case you wanted to start thinking about another arrangement for Sissy.'

'How much time do you think we've got?'

'It's hard to say. It could be three months, or six or more. But if the facility does close, there'll be a lot of people looking for an alternative in the area. There aren't that many options. Do you see what I mean? I want to make sure Sissy gets into another good facility.'

Sarah smiled. 'Thanks, Kelly. You've always been so great about looking out for her. But what'll happen to you?'

'Don't worry about me. I'll find another job. Everyone is short-staffed so it'll be easier for me than it will be for the residents to find other homes. Do you understand what I'm saying?' Her hooded grey eyes bored into Sarah's.

She nodded. 'We should think about jumping instead of waiting to be pushed. Yes, I understand. But there is a chance that the home won't close, right? I'd hate to move Sissy if it's not necessary. She'd be gutted. All of her friends are here. And she loves you all.'

'I know, and it's not an easy decision for you. I'll let you know as soon as I hear any more. We're having a staff meeting on Friday about it. I'm really sorry, Sarah. I wish we didn't always have to worry about where our money was coming from.'

Sarah saw Ben waving from the conservatory doorway.

'Do you need me, Ben?' she called.

'Sissy says it's been six minutes and where are you?'

'Thanks, I'll be right in. We're freezing out here anyway. She's got you running messages for her now, has she?'

'She's kind of bossy.'

'Is that okay?'

'Yes. She's still nice and she shares her toast with me.'

Sarah was glad that Ben seemed to like her sister so much.

Maybe, she thought as she went inside to check the cookies, soon she'd find a Ben for herself online.

She was chatting with a few guys that she wouldn't mind meeting in person, but she was so out of practice! Twice Rachel had had to draft her messages for her. She was like her flirty fairy godmother, waving her wand and working her magic.

'I know what you should make for your show,' Sissy said as she blew on a chocolate chip cookie fresh from the oven. The chocolate was still liquid. 'Mum's morning muffins.'

Sarah smiled. She was hardly likely to win over the judges with such a simple recipe. She'd be up against the country's best bakers – people who could spin sugar in their sleep and hand-raise a pie. Carrot cake muffins weren't very impressive.

On the other hand . . . some kind of wonderful cake that was inspired by the memory of her mother's muffins might be exactly what they were looking for. There were six weeks before the audition. She'd just have to create and perfect the recipe by then.

'Sissy, that's a good idea.'

'I know,' she said, daintily dabbing her lips with a serviette. 'May I please have another one?'

Chapter Twenty-Two

Catherine

Catherine was already regretting taking on Alis as a client. When she'd first said it she'd felt a rush of adrenalin at putting Magda in her place. But that dried up as soon as she rang Alis to offer to sign him up.

'I'll get back to you, if that's okay,' he said. 'Today's not a good day for signing contracts.'

'Oh,' she said. Did he have repetitive strain injury or something? 'Of course. I can send you the forms and you can sign them when you're feeling better.'

'Hmm? I feel fine.'

'It's just that I thought, well, if you can't use a pen today . . .'

He laughed. 'What *are* you talking about?'

'What are you talking about?'

'Mercury is in retrograde.'

'And?'

'And it's Wednesday, which would normally be a good day to do it, but not when Mercury is in retrograde. I'd rather wait till the end of the week.'

He made this sound like the most plausible reason for not signing a contract.

So he was a total flake. 'Suit yourself. I'll put everything in the post today. When I have the paperwork back, maybe we can talk again to go through your requirements?'

That is, she thought, if your astrologer says it's okay.

Magda was waiting to pounce as soon as she got off the phone. 'What is it, Magda?' She'd stopped being cordial weeks ago. It was hard enough being civil.

'Two things,' she said, impervious to subtleties like open animosity. 'First, which of these do you like?'

She held three blue swatches.

'Still deciding on napkins?'

'It is not an easy decision. Which one?'

'The middle one, I guess.'

'Why do you like that one best?'

'I don't know, Magda, because it's the most blue. Happy now?'

'Yes. Also, I want to discuss my client, Georgina, please.'

Magda had developed the annoying habit of rubbing her tummy whenever she talked to Catherine. It was probably her way of gloating over the fact that Richard had knocked her up. Just wait till you get stretch marks and boobs like deflating Zeppelins, Catherine thought. Then who'll gloat?

'Sure,' she said, sounding sweet as treacle. 'Let's talk about your client.'

Georgina had turned out to be about as loyal as an alley cat. She'd been thrilled when she'd heard that Magda was taking over her relationship.

'Georgina should be dating a whole different kind of person,' Magda said. Rub rub.

'Oh really?'

'Yes. You have set her up with the kind of man she thinks she wants, and of course she rejects him because he doesn't meet her expectations. She should meet men that don't fit her list in the first place, because then she won't be disappointed.'

'You're saying we should purposely set her up with unsuitable men because then she won't be disappointed that they're unsuitable?'

'No, that is ridiculous. I mean that the man she will be happy with is not the man who ticks all her boxes. Take me and Richard.' Her belly-stroking picked up speed. 'I've always gone out with worldly rich men who have swept me off my feet.'

She meant stinking rich oligarchs. Richard had bragged about that when they first met. Magda had spent a lot of time amongst England's top football clubs, but she hadn't bothered with the players. She'd gone straight for their owners. Catherine had joked that she'd played more than most of the England squad. Richard hadn't found that funny.

'The weekends on yachts in Monaco, the private jets to Ibiza and gifts from Tiffany,' she continued, sounding exhausted by all that glamour. 'Those men were fun but it gets old. Then I met Richard, who was plain and simple, and here we are, getting married and having a baby.'

It was nice to know that when she'd tired of the exciting, rich jet-setters, simple Richard was on hand to settle for. What a wonderful bridal speech that would make.

'Your point is?'

'My point is that Georgina needs to meet a different kind of man than you have been setting her up with, so she can see what she really likes. I've chosen two for her. I will tell her today. And another thing. I do not think Mahreen is doing well. She has not been giving her clients very many dates.'

Mahreen was one of their most senior consultants. She'd been with Catherine and Richard since they first started. 'How do you know that?'

'The database that you asked me to organise, remember?

I ranked the consultants by how many dates they arranged last month. I think Mahreen is slacking off. I will run another report this week, but I thought you should know.'

What nerve. Mahreen certainly was not slacking off, no matter what Magda's report said. For one thing, she looked after some of their most difficult cases including, Catherine happened to know, two women who were under-going radiation therapy. They weren't exactly in the mood to pop on a wig and meet new people just now. And for another thing, she knew Mahreen. She wouldn't slack off.

But of course Magda wouldn't know about Mahreen's client base or her work ethic because she thought the numbers told her everything.

'It isn't just about data, Magda. It's about people. If you'd talked to Mahreen you'd know that she has good reasons for her clients having fewer dates than the others.'

'I already have.'

'What do you mean?'

'I have already talked to Mahreen. She has a bad attitude, if you ask me, and she is rude. She had better not talk to clients like that.'

'How dare you do that, Magda! You have no right to go behind my back and harass the staff. If I think there's a problem, I will address it. You may not.'

Magda leaned across the desk until her face was very close to Catherine's. 'Why do you think I'm here, Catherine? Do you think this is work experience for me or something? I own half of the company. I will do what I want with it. So do not cross me.'

Catherine was stunned. That's exactly what she'd assumed Magda was – a dimbot who'd tire of playing with the grown-ups before her second trimester was up. Now she saw her for what she really was.

This was no bored soon-to-be-housewife. She was a threat to the most important thing in Catherine's life.

She realised as she locked eyes with this obsessive tummy-caresser that she couldn't bully her. She'd have to be outsmarted.

'I certainly don't want to cross you,' Catherine lied. 'We're partners now, and partners work together. That's all I'm saying. We need to keep each other in the loop when it comes to operational decisions, right? I'll be sure to tell you what's happening and you tell me.'

Magda allowed herself to be mollified by Catherine's words, and left her alone for the time being.

Catherine was still fuming about Magda's meddling when she got to Selfridges early to meet Paul. If she didn't calm down she'd be useless for their meeting.

The champagne bar on the mezzanine overlooked the accessories hall. Clever. Shoppers were tempted from all angles.

'Good afternoon,' said the black-clad young man as he handed her a menu. 'Here's the wine list, and today's food menu.'

'Just a glass of Veuve Clicquot, please.'

'Very good.' He didn't waste any time pouring it and she didn't waste any time drinking it.

Much as she hated to admit it, she was going to need some help with her new business partner. It was ridiculous to have this much trouble with a twenty-three-year-old when the teabags in their kitchen had been around the office longer than she had.

She tapped a text to Richard.

Hi, can we meet please? Need to talk about Magda. Thanks

His response came right back. He was always on his phone.

She's really enjoying working with you. V busy now and out of town next week. Later in Jan? xR

Pick a date. I'll meet you.

. . .

His silence spoke volumes. He knew she wasn't planning a sociable catch-up. And she knew he'd avoid a confrontation if he could. She texted again between sips of wine.

I'm free a week from Tuesday. Or Weds. Or Thurs. Or you could come into the office.

. . .

Don't ignore me.

Not ignoring. Busy.

Not too busy to text back. Set a date at least.

Am away from office. Need to check calendar.

I don't believe you.

Don't be cynical :-) xo

By the time she went to meet Paul under the clock out front, the bubbles had smoothed the edges. But she still knew that Richard was avoiding her.

'Sorry, Catherine, sorry!' Paul boomed, startling the shoppers around him. 'Am I late?'

'No, you're right on time.'

He kissed her on the cheek.

'I had a swift one round the corner,' he said. 'The barman took bloody ages to run my card through.'

'You really needed a drink before meeting me?'

He looked sheepish, just as Catherine recognised a figure rushing towards them. 'Madam, I'm glad I found you here,' said the black-clad waiter. 'You left your card at the bar.'

'Oh . . . Thank you.' She tucked her card into her purse.

'You really needed a drink before meeting me, Catherine?'

'It's not you,' she said. 'Rough day at the office.' Thanks to someone who looks a lot like you, she thought, leading him inside.

'You know your way around in here,' he said as they made their way through the maze of make-up counters and up the escalators to the men's floor.

'It's a perk of the job. Not that I shop much. Or at all, really, unless I need something. I'm not frivolous.'

Like he cared whether his relationship consultant was a spendthrift.

She watched his eyes dart from rail to rail when they got to the vast men's department. 'Do you have any particular style that you like?' she asked.

He looked like he might need to breathe into a paper bag.

'It's okay. Take your time.'

'People can't really like doing this,' he said. 'I'd rather have my teeth drilled.'

'Unfortunately the dentist isn't on our to-do list today.'

'Bummer. There's nothing like a nice root canal to take your mind off shopping.'

'I'm sorry you're doing this without novocaine. What about

something like this?' She held up a Paul Smith shirt. She loved a man in a Paul Smith shirt.

'Or this?' He pointed to a red and white checked combed cotton shirt.

He didn't seem to be joking. 'Mmm. Anything else that catches your eye?'

'What's wrong with the shirt?'

'It's a little too log cabin, if you know what I mean. I was thinking of something more stylish, more fitting for London.'

She trailed him as he walked from concession to concession. 'Stylish like this?' He held up a garish twill checked suit. 'It needs a waistcoat though. Waddya think of this?' He pointed to something ghastly in paisley.

She honestly didn't know if he was taking the piss or just had some kind of clothes-blindness disability. And she didn't want to offend him by asking. Then he'd really hate the shopping trip. 'It certainly does stand out.'

'That's good, right? You wanna stand out when you're dating.'

True, she thought, but not for looking like one of the Marx brothers. Paul would definitely be a fashion project for whomever he ended up with.

'I do like the idea of a suit for you,' she said. 'So that's a good place to start. I'm just not sure this pattern is quite right. Let's have a look around.'

His relief was obvious when she took charge. She already knew what she'd choose for him. A medium blue suit would look nice, maybe with a subtle pinstripe if he really wanted a pattern.

She checked her phone while she waited for him to come out of the fitting room. No texts from Richard. He was definitely avoiding her.

What was taking Paul so long? 'Are you coming out so I can see?'

He emerged in his tee shirt and jeans. 'It looked okay,' he said.

'Let me see.'

'You're taking this consultation seriously. Do you wanna come in with me to make sure I button everything straight?'

Catherine laughed at herself. 'I sound like your mother, don't I?'

'You're worse. My mother doesn't make me try on clothes for her.'

'You're right. I'm sure everything looks nice. If you want to pay for those, I'll just put your next appointment back a bit.'

'You mean we're not done? We've been at this for hours.'

'It's been about forty-five minutes, Paul.'

'That long? I deserve another drink.'

'No more drinks. We have an appointment.'

'Did you schedule the dentist after all?'

'Even better. You're going to love this,' she said, scrolling through her phone to find the number for Ted's Grooming Room.

But instead of loving it, he stood at their reception desk half an hour later with his arms crossed.

'You don't have to have a haircut if you don't want to,' she said. 'But I thought we should freshen up your look.' Paul's hair wasn't bad. It just had a very unfortunate side parting.

'It's not the haircut I'm worried about,' he said, hoicking his thumb at the man getting a wet shave. 'Hair grows back. My lip won't if they slip with that straight razor.'

'Will you at least do the haircut?' She was thinking of something a bit tousled and messy. 'The shave is optional.'

'S'pose so.'

It only took a few minutes for the stylist to transform Paul's head from banker to beach babe. 'What do you think?' Catherine asked as he squinted into the mirror.

Paul smiled. 'It's not bad, actually. What do you think?'

She thought he looked like a different person, and even more like Richard. 'It's a good look. We're getting there, Paul.'

Transforming his manners and giving him a more worldly view would take more work, but they were definitely on the right track. 'Now, are you ready for your manicure?'

'Jesus, really? Is this necessary?'

She grabbed his hand. 'Look at those cuticles. Yes it's necessary.'

There was something extra sexy about a well-groomed man.

'Are you happy with the way things went today?' she asked him later when he kissed her cheek at the Tube. His new aftershave smelled delicious. The earthy cedar scent really suited him.

'I'm just relieved I didn't have my throat cut.'

'You did very well to let them do it.' She might not have been as brave in his place. 'And the suit?'

'It looks all right, but it's not really me.'

'That's why we're doing this, Paul. We're making you better than you.'

Chapter Twenty-Three

Rachel

The doorbell went just as Rachel was lathering her hair over the bathroom sink. 'Shit shit shit . . . You're early!' she shouted through the closed door, even though there was no way the builders could hear her all the way downstairs. She wedged her head under the tap to rinse away as much shampoo as she could. Then, dripping all over the floor, she bolted down the stairs, tying her dressing gown as she went.

'Hi, come in,' she said to Nate.

'Morning,' he said. 'Where's Sarah?'

'She's at her sister's doctor's appointment. I'm working from home today.' She wasn't sure why she felt the need to explain her presence. She did live there. 'I'm Rachel.'

She couldn't shake his hand without flashing him, so she settled for a polite nod. 'I'm just getting cleaned up. There's coffee in the thingy on the hob and tea in the cabinet. Do you know where everything is?'

'Oh yeah, we're right at home, aren't we, lads?' he said to the boys crowded behind him. 'Don't worry about us. You won't even know we're here.'

She stepped aside to let them all in. Instead of going downstairs to the kitchen though, they made their way upstairs.

But she wasn't finished in the bathroom yet. And she didn't like the idea of strangers on the other side of the door.

She rushed to the bathroom as soon as they were safely on the top floor. Poor Sarah! She'd had to be up and ready for Nate every morning for weeks. Yet she'd never complained. That wouldn't be her style.

Quickly she re-rinsed her hair. There'd be no time for conditioner, she thought crossly. And she'd so looked forward to working from home today. Laying out her coloured pens and tracing paper on the big kitchen table. Drinking gallons of coffee. Having a luxurious nap when she felt sleepy after lunch.

There was no way she'd be able to nap with builders in the house.

She jumped when someone knocked on the door. 'Yes?'

'Are you gonna be long?' The boy's voice cracked.

Nate definitely got his workers from the local primary school.

'Erm, well, a few minutes, yes.'

'Okay, I'll wait.'

What did he mean, he'd wait? Outside the door? She crept over to listen. She could hear him shifting around out there.

And if she could hear him moving, then he'd be able to hear her . . .

She wasn't about to poo with a stranger listening. She took a deep breath and tried to ignore her intestines. Summoning all her self-control, she left the bathroom.

'It's all yours,' she told the boy who squeezed through the doorway before she'd even left the room.

Within a few seconds she heard him crapping with abandon. He clearly didn't share her worries about noise travelling.

Just lovely.

She plopped on the sofa with her coffee to answer her emails. The plumbing knocked and rattled as the cistern filled. There was a courtesy flush. Then she heard the door opening.

It immediately closed, and the faecal orchestra began its next movement, with a new conductor.

An email from James popped up.

James.McCormack@DDR.co.uk 8.02am (7 minutes ago)
To: me

Hey, I saw Sarah on the website. She wasn't that hot the last time I saw her. Are you up? Or slacking?

Rachel.Lambert@DDR.co.uk 8.09am (0 minutes ago)
To: James.McCormack@DDR.co.uk

I'm up. Builders are here. They're shitting in my bathroom.

James.McCormack@DDR.co.uk 8.10am (0 minutes ago)
To: me

Where do they usually shit?

Rachel.Lambert@DDR.co.uk 8.11am (0 minutes ago)
To: James.McCormack@DDR.co.uk

It's just rude, no?

James.McCormack@DDR.co.uk 8.12am (0 minutes ago)
To: me

Needs must. So back to Sarah. Is she having luck online?

Rachel.Lambert@DDR.co.uk   8.12am (0 minutes ago)
To: James.McCormack@DDR.co.uk

Why the interest in Sarah?

James.McCormack@DDR.co.uk 8.13am (0 minutes ago)
To: me

Just making friendly conversation.

Rachel.Lambert@DDR.co.uk   8.14am (0 minutes ago)
To: James.McCormack@DDR.co.uk

Go back to work.

James.McCormack@DDR.co.uk 8.15am (0 minutes ago)
To: me

Am working. Typing with one hand, drawing with other.

She closed her laptop as one of the boys came down the stairs. ''Scuse me,' he said. 'Nate wants you.' He picked up two sawhorses that were nearly as big as him and struggled back up the stairs. They bounced along the wall most of the way.

'Can you be a little careful with those?!' They hadn't budgeted to redecorate the ground floor.

He was startled into a spin, where he bashed the horse into the landing wall. A shower of plaster rained from the ceiling. 'Sorry.'

'Just be careful please.'

They were wrecking as much as they fixed.

Now she knew what her dad's clients went through. No wonder sometimes he didn't even break even on his jobs.

The thought made her feel guilty. And sad for him, even though she doubted if he realised how bad he was. He never let on that he did. And they certainly weren't going to tell him that he wasn't in the running for Builder of the Year.

'Ah, Rachel, I forgot to mention,' Nate said when she went upstairs, 'we don't know how to use your coffee maker.'

'Oh, it's simple, really. You just unscrew the top and clean out the filter where the old coffee grounds are. Fill the bottom with water, put the filter in with two dessertspoons of coffee, then screw it back together and put it on the hob.'

He looked at her like she'd just explained nuclear fusion.

'Sarah usually just makes it for us,' he said.

'Oh, right. Okay then.' Because she didn't have anything better to do than be their barista for the day. 'White for everyone? I'll bring up some sugar.'

She stomped downstairs to make coffee for her builders.

They were caffeinated to their back teeth by the time they finished in the afternoon. Between their questions and their banging and their wanton destruction, the day was a complete write-off, work-wise.

And now, thanks to Nate drilling through an electrical cable, they had no lights on the top floor.

She couldn't wait to get to her parents' house. She stuffed a dress into her overnight bag. They'd invited her for dinner but sometimes she just wanted looking after.

She knew she was a mama's girl, though she did stay with them much less than she had in her early twenties. Then she'd slept in her single bed at least once a week, with Kylie Minogue smiling down from the walls in her over-the-knee socks. She'd tried the look, until Micky Flaherty said her thighs looked like chipolatas. The socks went in the bin.

She let herself into the house with her key. Dad's rubble-covered work boots were on the rubber mat by the front door.

Her mum was hunched over her laptop at the kitchen table. 'Is Dad in the bath?' Rachel asked.

'Whirling away,' she said, brushing the strawberry blonde curls from her eyes.

They'd got him the whirlpool bath last year for his birthday after years of trying to convince him to put one in the downstairs bathroom for himself. It was like he was afraid to admit that doing manual labour every day took it out of a man nearing sixty. Which of course it did.

So they'd bought the tub and, controversially, hired a plumber to fit it. Mum had told him it was because he was too busy with his clients. It was sort of true. They only had to look around the house at all the half-finished jobs. The kitchen cabinets had been installed when Labour was in power. They might be in power again before her dad fitted the handles.

The whirlpool was a rare concession from her mum, who usually viewed such things as frivolous luxuries. She could design six-star hotels but would only paint the front door black in case it looked too fancy.

Design unto others what you would not design unto yourself.

'How's the project coming?' Genevieve asked. She didn't need to say which project. There was really only one in Rachel's life at the moment.

Unlike the mothers who liked to wade into the dramas of their offspring, Rachel's wasn't interested in love lives or friendship troubles. Her dad was a better confidante there, as long she told him the Suitable For All Audiences version. But mention a project and her mum was all ears.

'It's good I think . . . James came up with a compromise that might work.'

'Why didn't you come up with the compromise?'

'We've been working together to merge our designs, Mum, so it's not really about who came up with what.'

'Isn't it?'

Rachel smiled. 'Yeah, it totally is. I wish I'd thought of it, but as long as he doesn't take the credit, it's okay.'

'Can I see it?'

'Maybe when it's done.'

Genevieve shook her head. 'I wish you wouldn't be so cagey about showing me your work. I'm sure it's fantastic.'

'I will, Mum, I promise. Just not yet.'

This time she'd have to show her. It shouldn't be a big deal, but what if she didn't like it? Or worse: what if she pretended to like it and Rachel saw that telltale eye-slide that she did when she was trying to be nice? Then it wouldn't matter if everyone else thought it was fantastic. It would make no difference if the client commissioned it or even if she won awards. Her mum's judgement was what she really cared about.

Chapter Twenty-Four

Sarah

'It smells of lavatories,' Robin said, sniffing the air of the care home.

'Disinfectant,' said Sarah.

'What are they disinfecting? The residents?' He glowered at the nurses' station as if that's where they hid the giant human squeegees.

They'd only visited one facility so far and she was depressed already. If this was the standard of the alternatives for Sissy, Sarah would be better off figuring out how to keep Whispering Sands open. 'I suppose at least it's clean.'

'I told you it's a waste of time,' he grumbled. 'We don't even know if Sissy's is closing.'

'We have to be safe, Robin, or we'll be sorry. Kelly said they might not get much warning. Will you take Sissy to live with you until we find her another place? If so, then by all means let's go home and take our chances.'

That shut him up. Of course his girlfriend wouldn't let him take his sister in. He probably wouldn't do it anyway, even if Lucy wasn't in the picture. Family responsibility had always fallen more heavily on Sarah. She didn't usually mind, as long as when she asked him to do something, he did it.

This was one of those times. She knew he'd complain, but he wouldn't let her or Sissy down. Not when they only had each other now.

'We have to get all the information,' she continued. 'Just in case we need it.'

The director was around fifty with jet-black hair and a permanently startled expression. She insisted on being called Ms Bunny, which made Robin cringe.

'We're like a family here!' she gushed when he asked about the residents' age range.

Ms Bunny didn't offer anything else, so Sarah asked, 'Do all the residents have Down's syndrome or other learning difficulties?'

Ms Bunny pursed her mouth into an O, which seemed to be the only expression her Botoxed face still allowed. 'Oh no, Ms Sarah,' she said. 'Most are perfectly fine.'

Sarah bristled. Sissy wasn't *not* fine, you silly cow. She had an extra chromosome. 'Do you have any Down's residents?'

'No, but our staff is fully trained. We know how to deal with them.'

Was Sarah just being overly sensitive? Sissy was a person just like them. She just happened to need more care than they did.

She already knew it wouldn't be this Bunny person providing it. 'Do you have any questions, Robin?' she asked.

He shook his head. She didn't need her sibling telepathy to know their thoughts were in sync. *Let's just get out of here*, his face told her.

'That's two hours we'll never get back,' he said as they walked back to the railway station together.

'Maybe, but that doesn't mean we don't have to do it. Robin, we need to make sure Sissy will be okay if Whispering Sands closes. It's a pain in the arse but you know we've got to.'

If she was honest with herself, the thing that really bothered her wasn't the wasted trips or the possibility that they wouldn't be able to afford the care that was right for their sister. It was no contest between her free time and her sister's safety and happiness. And with Mum gone and Sissy only being sixteen, there were social services funds to help, for the next few years at least.

No, if Sarah was really deep down, middle-of-the-night honest with herself, she'd admit that her conscience was getting hard to live with.

Because Sissy did have another alternative, didn't she? If their mum had still been alive, Sissy would be buttering her toast in the kitchen where she grew up. And despite the promise their mum had extracted, families did look after their Down's syndrome relatives all the time. So shouldn't Sissy be living with her or Robin?

As long as the home stayed open, Sarah could ride along on the status quo, honouring her mother's wishes, letting the people who knew what they were doing keep her healthy, blah blah blah. And Sissy did like living at Whispering Sands.

But what if it closed?

The time was coming to make a new decision.

The last thing Sarah felt like doing after seeing frozen-faced Ms Bunny was to meet her RecycLove date. But Rachel would have a cow if she came home from work and found her slobbing about in the house. She was caught between a date and a bollocking, so she slicked on more make-up and took her hair out of its elastic band so that it bouffed up . . . as much as her long straight hair would bouff. She wriggled into her cornflower blue dress with the gathered bodice and went to meet her date.

One quick drink and she could tell Rachel all about it later while watching *Grand Designs* reruns on the sofa.

She probably wouldn't have agreed to meet Jeremy at all if it hadn't been for his ex-girlfriend's endorsement. 'A kind, shy soul who needs to stop worrying and have more fun'. Birds of a bashful feather, she thought when she read his profile after getting his message.

From: Jeremy
To: Sarah

Hi Sarah, I'm not an expert baker but I do make a mean apple crumble (my granny's recipe). I also know where my local Patisserie Valerie is. Do I qualify for a return message do you think? Hope so! Jeremy

If there was some rule about how long to wait to answer, Sarah didn't follow it.

From: Sarah
To: Jeremy

There's an art to the crumble so if you make it well then, yes, you qualify ☺ I see that you also confessed to liking housebuilding programmes. Any other reality TV addictions? Sarah

From: Jeremy
To: Sarah

I don't know how much to confess to at this point, Sarah. There's a fine line there, as you know. I can probably get away with housebuilding (manly) and cooking, since you're also a fan. I might have to wait till we meet to talk about Don't Tell the Bride. *What do you think? Should we meet?*

213

From: Sarah
To: Jeremy

Only if you're kidding about Don't Tell the Bride! ☺
I'm free on Weds or Thurs.

From: Jeremy
To: Sarah

Wednesday works. It's a date.

He wasn't her usual type, she thought, looking one last time at his photo so she'd recognise him in the bar. She liked tall, dark, handsome men, though after so long on her own, her usual type would be anyone who peed standing up.

It had been almost four years since she'd had a date. Four. Years. Hard to believe, though she tried not to beat herself up too much. Sometimes circumstances got in the way. Romance had been the last thing on her mind while her mum was ill. Even now that she wanted to meet someone, how much free time, not to mention headspace, did she really have to be doing this? And what were the chances of finding anyone anyway? She probably had better odds as the outside bet at the Grand National.

She stifled a yawn. Just one drink, she repeated to herself all the way to the pub. There was always a chance.

He was waiting for her outside.

'Sarah? I thought it might be easier to find each other out here.'

He gave her an easy smile that made his blue eyes crinkle. He was only her height, and slight, with pale blond hair and a smattering of freckles across his nose. He'd buttoned his long navy wool coat tightly against the wintery wind but she could tell that he was as athletic as he looked in his photos. That was good.

It *would* be nice to have someone to play tennis with once the weather got better, or to jog with around the park.

As long as she was ordering her perfect man, she'd take the fully baked, kind guy from the starter menu, and for the main course, a homely boyfriend with a side of funny who was as close to his family as she was to hers . . . with a reputation for being a stallion in bed for pudding.

She bit down the sudden urge to whinny at Jeremy.

Must not be weird, she told herself. 'Please let me get the drinks,' she said when they found a table inside. 'What would you like? I'll be right back.'

Waving away his protest, she went to the crowded bar.

She noticed a text on her phone when she pulled out her purse.

Thanks for making me go today, Robin texted. *Lucy says I was an arse. Sorry about that.*

She doubted that Lucy was really concerned for her boyfriend's little sister. She was just protecting her Down's-free territory.

That's okay, you're my brother, you arse. Sarah x

When she returned with their drinks she found Jeremy scrolling through his phone. 'Sorry, I've just had an email about a club night tonight.' He gave her a winsome smile. 'If we hit it off maybe we'll go later?'

The only club she'd be going to later was the pyjama club. There were no bouncers and it had a very relaxed dress code.

'Do you go to clubs a lot?' she asked, hoping he'd say no. She'd had enough of that during her months as Sebastian's guest list plus-one.

He shook his head. 'Only lately. I'm signed up to a couple of mailing lists. I've been told I need to make more of an effort to get off the sofa.'

His blue eyes caught hers in a pleasing way. There was just a hint of blond stubble on his chin, which she liked.

'I've been told the exact same thing,' she said.

'You? I don't believe it. I had you pegged as a social butterfly.'

She hoped he wasn't disappointed now. 'Being out with people is ace,' she felt the need to explain. 'But I don't get out as much as I probably should. This online dating lark is new for me.'

Now why did she admit that? She was supposed to be cultivating an air of intrigue, not being her normal self. Next she'd be telling him about the time she got piles. Then he'd just finish his drink, make an excuse and delete her details.

'It's fun though!' she said, trying to recover. 'Like online shopping.'

'Because of all the choice?'

'No,' she said, surprised. 'Because you never actually know if the goods will turn up until they arrive.'

His brow furrowed, but then he laughed. 'But you can't do a return on a date. Once you've spent the time, you can't get it back . . . not that I'd want my time back with you! I'm sorry, I need to think before I speak.'

Something else we have in common, she thought.

They ordered from the pub's menu when they got hungry. Through drinks and food and more drinks, one conversation rolled seamlessly into the next. The weirdest thing was, for the first time since she could remember, she didn't feel boring at all.

'Let's go to this club,' he said, much later. 'Do you want to?'

She was surprised to find that she did. 'I'm not exactly in clubbing clobber though. They probably won't let me in.'

'You're joking, right?'

She looked down at her dress. 'No, why?'

'Because you're fit, Sarah. If you don't mind me saying.'

Mind?! If she played deaf, maybe she could get him to say it again.

'Trust me, nobody's going to turn you away at the door. Will you come? Please say yes.'

Could it really be that easy? Just a matter of an enthusiastic yes instead of a bland no? Surely not.

She felt like finding out. 'Yes.'

As she left with Jeremy, he grabbed her hand and suddenly she felt normal. She was just like all the other women who were able to have dates more often than leap years.

Who'd have thought that the secret was nothing more than a little make-up, some new clothes and fighting her instinct to crawl inside her safe, boring little shell?

What a small price to pay. From now on she was saying yes. Yes to dates. Yes to parties. Yes to all-night clubbing. Yes yes yes!

A little queue of people waited for the bouncer to find their names on the guest list. They must have all got the same email as Jeremy. She suppressed a giggle. The only queues she'd stood in lately were at Tesco's when the self-serve tills went on the blink.

'Just a few minutes, folks,' said the brick in the suit at the door. 'It's heaving inside.'

A few of the girls tutted and groaned but Sarah felt herself getting excited. It must be ace if it was heaving!

She stood there watching everyone stream past on the other side of the velvet rope. As she watched them, she knew they were watching her. She didn't feel out of place exactly. She could see that with her new dress, her make-up on, still holding Jeremy's hand, she looked like the other girls there. But she felt like an imposter.

The bouncer checked Jeremy's name off the list and let

them inside, where they were hit by a solid wall of thump thump thumping music.

It took a minute for her eyes to adjust to the lack of light. A few red strobes moved around the big room but the only other light seemed to come from half a dozen crystal-draped chandeliers. It looked like a cross between Versailles and a Victorian sitting room, with deep red flock wallpaper, claw-footed gold tables and gilded mirrors all over the walls. There was nothing Victorian about the crowd though. They could barely move for all the beautiful people.

'This is great!' Jeremy shouted in her ear, looking as excited as she'd started to feel. 'Can I get you a drink?'

They wove their way to the bar, where tanned, muscular men in open waistcoats were shaking cocktails. She couldn't keep her eyes off their smooth, hairless chests. Their arms were bare too. It must cost a fortune to wax all that.

She snuck a look at Jeremy's chest, at the white pinstriped collared shirt hugging his lean torso. He'd unbuttoned another button since the restaurant, and she glimpsed pale hair there. That was a relief. She didn't fancy her date being smoother than she was.

It only took about three sips to finish her peach Martini. It was delicious, and not strong-tasting at all. 'Want to dance?' he asked.

Her head nodded to the music, her shoulders starting to move. The beat made her feel like throwing her arms in the air. People swirled around her, smiling, laughing, talking, dancing. She closed her eyes and let herself feel how good it was to be out, having fun like everyone else got to do. 'Yes, let's dance!'

This time she was the one who took his hand.

Catherine rapped on her bedroom door the next morning. 'Sarah Lee, it's nearly eight. Do you have to go into the office today?'

'Yes,' Sarah said, clutching her head.

'Do you want some coffee? And paracetamol?'

'Yes.'

'Did you have fun last night?'

'Yes! Ow. I think it was after four when I got in. I went clubbing on a date.'

The words felt alien on her tongue.

But she loved the taste.

Chapter Twenty-Five

Catherine

Catherine had to ring Richard half a dozen times before he agreed to meet. After the third or fourth ignored call she thought about phoning from a withheld number, but couldn't bring herself to stoop to such teenage tactics.

She shouldn't have to, she fumed as she made her way to the bar to meet him. How dare he make her feel like this, like she was bothering him, when he was the reason she was having problems with the business in the first place.

It wasn't just the anger she felt as she listened to his phone ring. Every time she thought about it she got annoyed. He was taking up way too much space in her brain lately. It was space she couldn't spare. And space he didn't deserve.

They were supposed to be best friends. Or so he said. Yet she wouldn't treat a casual acquaintance like this, let alone a friend. So just how good a friend did that make him, really?

He was sitting at a small corner table in the crowded bar. Lately he'd started wearing V-neck jumpers with collared work shirts. It made him look a bit granddaddy. She wondered what Magda thought of that.

'Whose turn is it to buy, mine or yours?' he said when she sat.

'Mine.' She wasn't about to give up one iota of control tonight. He was too good at exploiting an advantage.

'I feel like an ale, please,' he said.

She went to the bar and ordered a bottle of Sauvignon Blanc.

If he felt weird about not inviting Magda out with them, he wasn't letting on. But Catherine knew him. To be that relaxed he must have her permission to be there. Richard was no rebel with a cause.

At least she'd get to talk to him alone. Even before he started ignoring her, they hadn't had a private conversation in weeks. Every time he'd rung the office, Magda hovered like she was waiting to hear her test results. She didn't even have the courtesy to pretend she wasn't earwigging.

He raised his eyebrows when she set the wine on the table, but didn't remark.

'I felt like wine,' she said. Something nice and dry and nothing like an ale. 'Would you like a glass?'

'Of course.'

They sipped their wine in stubborn silence, a tactic honed from hammering out divorce details.

'Nice day at work, dear?' Richard finally said.

'Not really, no. We need to talk about Magda.'

He sighed. 'Can't you two sort things out between you?'

'Why?' she asked sharply. 'What has she said about me?'

Richard levelled a look at her. 'Probably the same things you're dying to say about her.'

Touché.

'She's running roughshod over the business, Richard. I know you don't care about that now that you've cashed in, but you need to control your fiancée.'

'What? Catherine, I am shocked. I never pegged you as a chauvinist. Control my fiancée? Is this the nineteen-fifties?'

Catherine reddened at the accusation. 'What I mean is that she'll listen to her elders.'

He smirked.

'Can't you just tell her to slow down a little? She needs to learn some tact.'

When he sat back in his chair she realised they'd both been leaning forward. She sat back too.

'No,' he said. 'She needs to have the freedom to exercise her right to have a say in the business. You, however, need to learn to let go, my dear. Catherine, nothing has changed, really. You owned half the business when I was the other shareholder. You still own half the business. Your problem is that you think you own the whole thing. My fault, probably, because I let you run it.'

'You let me run it?!' she nearly spat. 'Really? Because the way I remember the last year is that you were nowhere to be found. You left me to run the business, Richard. You didn't *let* me run it.'

Instead of acknowledging the truth, he said, 'Magda's just spreading her wings. I thought you'd support a fellow businesswoman.'

'It's not about support, Richard. It's about doing what's right for the business.'

'Well I'm not part of the business any more, so let's talk about something else.'

If she kept harping on he'd just ignore her again. He'd always been like that. Much as she wanted to believe she'd had more influence over him once upon a time, she probably never had. Richard was always a law unto himself.

Besides, this wasn't about Magda's spread wings at all.

Richard had a bad case of whiplash and Catherine was getting the pain in the neck.

Did that mean that Magda had more hold over him than Catherine had had when they were married? The thought bobbed uncomfortably on top of her Sauvignon Blanc.

Looking back, a lot about their marriage made her uncomfortable. Top of the list was her part in ending it.

When she'd first moved with him to the US she hadn't minded not working. With the wedding to plan she hadn't had time anyway. It was only after the confetti had settled that she'd got restless. With him working stupidly long hours she'd had a lot of time to fill on her own and there were only so many ways she could rearrange the medicine cabinet. One morning as she'd stared out the sliding door off the kitchen until her tea was cold, she realised she could sit there staring all day.

When Richard got home she pounced on him. 'I'm going insane. I've got to work.'

'Kate, sweetheart, it's not up to me. It's US Immigration that say you can't. Have you been in touch with those clubs my secretary emailed about?'

'I don't want to just sit around drinking tea with a bunch of other expats. My brain is turning to mush. Do you know what I did yesterday?'

Her glare warned him to wipe the smirk off his face. 'I arranged all the tins in the cupboards. Only I got stuck. Do you organise them by size or colour or type of food? I went round and round and round. Richard, I fell apart sitting on the kitchen floor because I couldn't organise the tins.'

She leaned into his chest when he put his arms around her. 'I'm sorry,' he said. 'I know I've been working crazy hours and you're here on your own. Believe me, I feel guilty about that, but you know you can't work. We can't take the chance you'll get caught, even if you could find something without a work permit. Is there anything I can do?'

'Yes, there is.' She pulled away from him. 'Help me find somewhere to volunteer.'

But that wasn't as easy as it sounded. She figured she'd

need qualifications and experience to find proper work, but to volunteer? Her meagre offering of bar jobs and an eighteen-month marketing stint after graduation didn't get her past the first interview.

She had to give up on the sexy charities – the Greenpeaces and United Ways – and start looking for the ones nobody else wanted to work for.

Finally she found a food bank on the bad side of town that was desperate enough to let her work for free. It wasn't where she'd imagined ending up but at least it saved her from any more breakdowns on the kitchen floor.

She felt like the new girl on her first day of school when she got to the huge warehouse. What if they didn't like her or she screwed up or they said it had all been a mix-up with HR and there was no job for her?

She walked all the way around the building, but couldn't find an obvious office entrance. Nil points for that, she thought.

She crept through one of the giant loading-bay doors instead.

'Excuse me, can I help you?' A stocky young man was piling up boxes. His white button-down shirt hung out of faded jeans and she could see curls of jet-black hair under his vivid yellow hard hat.

'I'm sorry,' she said, realising as she looked around that she was the only one in the cavernous warehouse without headgear. 'I'm here to volunteer. I was told to come for nine but I didn't see where the entrance was. I'm sorry.'

'You can be fired for coming in that door, you know.'

'No, really?'

His caramel skin made his teeth look snow-white when he smiled. 'Nah, I'm just messin' with you. Come on, I'll show you around. I'm Jose.'

They walked through the warehouse together while he

explained the set-up. Tons of food got delivered each month and everything had to be checked for expiration dates, sorted and shelved. That was where she'd play her part with the other volunteers. Then the soup kitchens, food pantries and feeding programmes collected what they needed.

When he showed her the neatly lettered signs above each shelf in the sorting area, she had to laugh.

'Something funny?' Jose said in his sing-song Latino accent that made the word come out as *foney*.

'No, no, not really funny.' She thought of her cabinets. 'It's just that I've had some unofficial experience with this lately.'

From now on she'd be alphabetising tins on a massive scale.

'Well, I've got to get back upstairs,' he said. 'So I'll leave you with Susie here. She's the volunteer coordinator, but really she runs the place.'

Susie, a sixty-something woman in a shiny lime-green tracksuit, joined them when she heard her name. Susie giggled and blushed to her permed grey roots.

'Oh,' said Catherine. 'Are you not with the volunteers?'

Jose laughed. 'Sometimes I wish I was, but no, I'm the director. See you later.'

So he was their boss.

Her back ached by the time she left for home, but she was grateful for the camaraderie with the other volunteers after her solitary confinement. And Jose didn't act like a boss at all. He spent so much time in the warehouse packing boxes that he kept getting told off by the board of directors. But the volunteers loved him and not just because he had more than a touch of Antonio Banderas about him. He was passionate and enthusiastic about more than the charity and they laughed like loons together.

Richard loved that she was working. 'You've got your

mojo back,' he liked to tell her. He was just happy that she was getting out of the house so he didn't have to feel guilty about his manic work schedule. Or the fact that she seemed to be sliding down his priority list at a rate of knots.

It wasn't long before she started looking forward to work for more than the chance to get out of the house.

Who wouldn't want to spend all day with a hot man who talked about modern art and obscure films and Mexican food she'd never heard of? It was a whole new world and it excited her.

If Richard hadn't been so obsessed with work, who knows what would have happened? Maybe she wouldn't have had to listen each night to the same conversation about people she didn't know and processes she didn't understand. Maybe she wouldn't have noticed the contrast between her days at the food bank and her nights with her husband. And maybe she wouldn't have started to prefer one over the other.

She ate lunch every day with Jose and the volunteers in the communal break area. Then one morning, a few months after she'd started, he beckoned her away from the sorting area to the little kitchen.

'Guess what I've got,' he said, pointing to a carrier bag in the fridge. 'My mother's burritos. You have to taste them. Come up to the office at lunch. I've got my own microwave. The others will kill me if they have to smell Mama's hot burritos down here.'

She spent the morning counting the minutes instead of her crates of tins.

'Are you ready?' he asked later, spooning sour cream and guacamole into the warm burrito. Then he sprinkled shredded lettuce and tomato over it and expertly rolled it up.

Her mouth watered. She was more than ready.

She took a bite. 'Mmm. Oh my God. You got to eat these any time you wanted growing up?'

'Any time we wanted. Mom only cooked Mexican food. It killed her when we'd sneak out for McDonald's.'

'I guess we all want what we can't have.'

His deep brown eyes held hers. '*Es una verdad*. That's true.'

From that day on they ate their lunch in Jose's office. If the volunteers thought anything of it they didn't say so.

Technically they were doing nothing wrong.

Chapter Twenty-Six

Rachel

'Do you know what you're going to say?' James asked her as soon as she hung up from the receptionist downstairs. The clients were on their way up.

'Of course I know what I'm going to say,' she snapped. 'Do you know what you're going to say?'

Rachel knew her lines off by heart. They'd only get one chance to pitch their building to Zigler. She just hoped her nerves wouldn't make her barf on the conference room table.

'Teeth check. Okay?' she asked, smiling broadly for James.

'Yep. Mine?'

She nodded. It didn't feel like the time for jokes.

Ed strode towards them. 'Are we ready? The coffee and tea will be here in a minute. They're early.'

'Shows they're keen,' James said, and Ed's face relaxed.

How did he do that? she wondered. He was the Boss Whisperer. Sometimes she did appreciate his false confidence.

If only she had some real confidence of her own. She still couldn't bring herself to show her mum the designs. She would do it, she promised herself, after this meeting, when she knew the clients loved them.

She could hear them coming up the stairs. All four flights.

Snippets of wheezy complaints floated up. She didn't blame them. She hated that climb too.

'Good morning, gentlemen!' Ed welcomed them as they reached the landing. 'Thanks for coming, and for climbing the stairs. You've earned the good client biscuits!'

She was sure he'd said that last time. Maybe he was as nervous as she was.

Eric, George and their boss Philip – or Zig and the Lers, as she'd been thinking of them for months – were all in their fifties and cut from the same pinstriped cloth. Hopefully their taste in buildings wouldn't be as buttoned-up.

She and James had agreed that she'd start the pitch, sprinkled with his well-timed supportive comments. Then he'd take over to talk through the design. As everyone poured their hot drinks and made small talk over the chocolate croissants, she wished he was going first.

But no, that's not how you get ahead, she reminded herself. Despite feeling like she might pass out, she had to ooze confidence. That was half the battle.

The other half depended on her not screwing up.

When everyone began their meeting rituals, opening notebooks, clicking pens, turning phones to mute, she took a deep breath.

'We're really excited to show you our designs today,' she began. She could feel her voice wobble. 'And thank you for giving us the chance. As you know, the firm has a track record of innovation, and we're proud to continue that for you.' Did she sound too rehearsed? She'd only gone over the speech a thousand times or so. 'Just to give you a little background on us,' she ad-libbed. 'James and I have worked together for the past five years and we like—'

'Sunset walks on the beach and piña coladas in the rain,' James quipped.

Everyone laughed.

'Speak for yourself. I was about to say that we like to collaborate on our work even when we're designing for different clients.' That was a lie. The only thing they collaborated on was lunch. 'And for the record, I'm partial to a nice glass of champagne if anybody's offering.'

Their laughter felt like music to her ears. Which meant her speech was all wrong. It *was* too wooden. She'd lose her audience if she kept to the script. She started to panic. Mentally she dismissed her next line, and her next and her next. It was all crap. Amateurish. She had to say something though. Something off the cuff.

'Look, we had a whole speech worked out for this meeting, but you don't need a speech. You just need to know that in our last five years with the firm we've seen some of the most exciting buildings in London designed – the new Standard Union building, 70 Bishops Court and the entire Canary Walk, just to name a few. Influences from some of the best architects in the country have gone into our design. We hope you'll agree. James?'

If he was caught off guard he didn't show it. He talked through their design like he was discussing football scores in the pub.

By the time he finished she was hardly breathing.

Their futures hung on the client's next words.

Finally Philip spoke. 'Thank you, Rachel and James. That was a nice presentation.'

Nice? Nice?! What did that mean?

'I feel like your design does fulfil the brief, so I can't fault it there.'

Where was he going to fault it? Rachel felt sick.

'It's just that . . . something is bothering me.'

Eric spoke up. 'If I may, the building is beautiful, there's no doubt about that. And I can see why you've designed it the way you have. It's eye-catching. It's just not . . .'

'Bold enough,' George finished.

All three men nodded.

'I get the feeling that this is a compromise and maybe that's our fault. We stipulated one design. It might be better to see what you come up with individually when you can design to your own vision. Does that make sense?'

'Absolutely,' Ed said. 'To be honest, Philip, it's what they wanted to do in the first place. They've got some great ideas. Shall we reconvene in, say, two weeks? James, Rachel, is that enough time?'

Numbly, Rachel nodded.

'Sure, Ed, no problem,' said James.

When the clients had clomped safely back down the stairs, Ed said, 'So you've got your wish. You can each present your designs in the meeting and we'll see which one wins.'

Which *one*. Those words rang in Rachel's ears. So much for collaboration or sunset piña coladas.

Sarah couldn't have known that the meeting wouldn't go well, so Rachel couldn't really blame her for planning the celebration after work. It was just the last thing she felt like doing. She didn't even want to leave work. She wanted to lock herself in her office with her coloured pens and not come out until she was sure she'd designed the perfect building for Zigler.

Her face flamed again thinking about the missed opportunity. They hadn't solved a problem with their compromise. They'd only created one.

'We should have just gone with one of our designs,' she'd hissed to James as they left the meeting. 'We've compromised the integrity of the design and now we've got a strike against us going into the next meeting.'

'Well, it was better than fighting it out. Then only one of us would have the chance to present our ideas. This way we both get to.'

'Oh, don't try to make it sound like you planned this all along.'

'I'm just making lemonade out of lemons, Rach.'

She didn't return his smile.

One of their biggest clients didn't think they were bold enough. That implied a lack of vision and there was no more damning criticism for an architect, unless the building you designed actually fell down. She couldn't tell her mum the truth now. She'd have to spin it. They liked it a lot, she'd say. In fact they've asked us each to design another one before they decide. What an opportunity!

She'd do it over the phone. One look into her eyes and her mum would know it was a lie.

'There she is!' Sarah jammed her elbow into Catherine's side. 'Thank Thomas you're here.' She pointed to the champagne bucket. 'Good?'

'Fine with me,' Rachel said. 'Why are we thanking Thomas?' She hoped they hadn't invited him.

'He's your saint,' Sarah explained. 'I went to Swiss Cottage and lit a candle for you.'

'Oh I see. Do I have a saint living in Swiss Cottage?'

Sarah shook her head. 'The patron saint of architects is St Thomas. He's got a church in Swiss Cottage. I could have gone to one in Finsbury Park but that was longer on the train. Do you think it matters that I'm not a Catholic?'

'I think as long as you pay for the candle,' Rachel said, 'then anyone can light one.'

'Pay?' she muttered. 'I'll have to go back tomorrow.'

'So, how did it go?' Catherine asked. Rachel could tell she thought she knew the answer. She didn't have the heart to take a sledgehammer to her bubble.

'Well, the good news is that I'll get to present them with my own design.'

Sarah squealed and made a grab for her.

'But the bad news,' she said into Sarah's shoulder, 'is that they didn't like our combined efforts. So now we'll each show them our own idea and they'll choose between them. That is, hopefully they'll choose one.' She didn't dare think what would happen if the business went to a rival firm.

Sarah pulled back so she could look Rachel in the eye. 'Are you okay?'

'Yes. Well, I will be. I don't really want to talk about it if that's okay. Is that another new dress?'

Sarah grinned. 'You've created a proper monster. These dresses are ace. I see them everywhere now! Like that boy in that film.'

Catherine got it first. '*Sixth Sense*,' she mouthed.

Sarah gave them a twirl without even being asked. That never would have happened a month ago.

'They look good on you,' Rachel said. 'Have you got one in mind for the party?'

Sarah's birthday was in a few weeks. They'd have a party at the house, as long as Nate hadn't destroyed it by then.

'Do you know,' said Catherine, looking from one friend to the other, 'I never noticed before but you look a little bit alike.'

'We do not!' Rachel protested.

'I wish!' said Sarah. 'If I filled out a dress like Rachel did I'd have dates every night of the week.'

'Sarah, you could have dates every night of the week if you wanted to,' Catherine reminded her. 'You're like a different person these days. In a good way!'

She just giggled, which grated on Rachel's nerves.

'Are you seeing that guy again?' she asked. 'The one you were out with all night?'

'His name's Jeremy and it wasn't all night!' said Sarah. 'We're going out on Thursday.'

'Should we expect another four a.m. return?'

'Maybe.' She reddened. 'Let's drink to that!' She grabbed her glass and downed it.

'Whoa, Sarah Lee, slow down,' Catherine said. 'You'll get drunk.'

'Isn't that the point?'

'Rachel, what have you done?' Catherine teased. 'Maybe you *have* created a monster!' Her easy laughter made sure that Sarah wasn't offended.

Rachel just shrugged. 'You're one to talk, for someone who's actually running a business out of remaking people.'

'It's true, but some of them need it. One client is finally making headway but I've got another one who may be a lost cause.'

'You've never said that before,' Sarah said, refilling her glass.

'In this case it might be true. The client's a total flake. He believes in star signs. I'll try to find someone for him who buys into all that, but there are also his looks to consider. He's got a beard that mice could nest in. And he's covered in tattoos.'

'Then why'd you take him on?' Rachel asked. 'You're usually very picky.'

'I let my heart overrule my head,' she said.

Sarah latched on to her words. 'Your heart?'

'No, no, it's nothing like that. It was just to get one over on Magda. She was being such a judgemental cow about him that I wanted to spite her. But the joke's on me. I'm the one who's got to find him dates.'

'Then why don't you make him over too? It sounds like just getting him to trim that beard would make a difference.'

'Hmm, it might . . . yes, maybe you're right.'

Chapter Twenty-Seven

Sarah

Sissy couldn't get enough of the builders. She'd been following Nate and the team around the house all morning. As Sarah finished off the sketch she was working on, she kept an ear out to make sure her sister wasn't getting in the way of their work.

She could hear one of the boys talking to her on the landing. 'What are you doing?' she asked.

'Removing the trunking that hides the cable.'

'Why?'

'So I can chase the cable into the wall.'

'Why?'

'So you can't see it.'

'Why?'

When he didn't answer, she asked again. 'Hello? Why?'

Resistance was futile. She could go on like that for hours. 'Sissy, love, let's go downstairs.'

She popped her head around the corner to look between the stair balusters. 'Why?' She smirked.

'Smart-arse. Leave him alone so he can do his work. I need your help with the baking anyway. Do you want to get your pencils and sketch pads?'

She put a hand on her hip. 'Am I baking or am I drawing, Sarah?'

'You're baking. Sorry. Come on. You can peel the carrots.'

Sissy felt at home in their house and, just now, that was weighing heavily on Sarah. Because wasn't Nate already renovating it for when the time came? Who was to say that now wasn't the time? There'd be just enough room to alter Sarah's new kitchen area and living room. It would mean two tiny single bedrooms and a studio living area, but it could be done. And then Sissy could live with Sarah.

Was it the right thing to do though? That's what Sarah couldn't work out. It would definitely make her feel better to shift the constant guilt from her shoulders. But there was the small matter of the promise she'd made to her mum to make sure Sissy was in a safe facility with professionals to look after her. A promise was a promise, even when the other person wasn't around to enforce it. But what if Whispering Sands closed down and there wasn't another home that was as good?

Round and round she went, feeling guiltier all the time.

'I'm ready,' Sissy said in the kitchen, tying her favourite frilly red and white gingham apron round her tummy. 'Where's the recipe?'

'We'll make it up.'

Sissy didn't look too sure about that.

Of all the things Sarah regretted about her mum's death, not paying more attention when they cooked together was the one that came back most often to bite her. She'd assumed her mum would always be a phone call away to ask how hot the oven should be or how much baking powder to add.

Not that she'd ever used normal measurements – it was all pinches and dashes – so when Sarah did nail a recipe, she made sure she wrote it down.

She didn't get the morning muffin recipe but she did have

a secret weapon: her sister's perfect palate. Sissy would taste when they got the recipe just right.

Sarah was reaching for the flour when she noticed the silence upstairs. The teeth-jangling pounding from the pneumatic drill had died away. There were no startling pops from the nail gun or incessant angry-wasp buzzing from the multi tool.

When Nate had first started the renovations, she'd welcomed these lulls. Now she knew better.

She braced herself just as the swearing started. 'Now what?' she muttered. 'Sissy, I'll be right back.'

She climbed the stairs to the ground floor with a mounting sense of dread. The swearing carried on.

Plasterboard dust billowed from Rachel's bedroom.

And where there's dust there's a hole.

'Sorry, Sarah, we'll fix it,' Nate said as he stepped aside to let her into the room. 'Did you know your party walls are only four inches thick?'

She didn't, but surely a builder should. There was a charred hole in the wall. 'What happened?'

'Dave was chasing in an electrical socket and hit one on the other side. What are the chances of that? Good aim, son!'

One of the boys nervously patted the other on the back.

'You probably want to see if your neighbour's electrics are all right,' Nate continued. 'There was an almighty pop when he hit that socket. We might need to do some work next door.'

Their neighbours, the Rogers-Smiths, weren't thrilled about the renovations as it was. When Sarah first had the quote from Nate about the work, she'd optimistically printed up a detailed works schedule for their neighbours, delivered with a batch of red velvet cupcakes. The schedule went out the window in the first few weeks, along with Nate's promise not to start before nine a.m. 'We'll hit the rush hour if we start too late,' he'd explained. 'We're happy to stay in the vans until it's time to come in.'

They did stay in their vans for the first week or so. Then, as the boys got more comfortable in the house, they started knocking early, asking to use the toilet. She couldn't very well say no to that, and soon they were all in the house by eight thirty promising to be quiet.

They had a different idea of quiet than most people.

'Nate, you're wrecking more than you're building! Is it really that hard to look at the bloody plans before you drill through the walls? You're doing my head in. The instructions are right there in black and white. It really couldn't be simpler.'

Nate's normally jovial face tightened. 'I don't think I like your tone of voice, Sarah. It was a mistake. If you're so unhappy with the work then maybe we should just go.'

She nodded. 'Yes, maybe you should call it a day now.' She was sick of them.

'Fine. We will.' With that he signalled to his boys, who all started packing their tools. Within minutes every screwdriver and hammer, spirit level and machine was packed away.

'Come on, boys,' he said, not looking at Sarah.

They hoisted the heavy bags and toolboxes onto their narrow shoulders and started for the door.

'You can leave your tools here,' Sarah said, suddenly worried that she'd made a big mistake.

'No, thank you, Sarah.'

'You're coming back tomorrow though, right?'

'Sure,' said Nate.

Then the front door closed, leaving the house silent again.

He'll have to come back tomorrow, she thought, once he's cooled down.

But he didn't come back the next day, or the next day. After a week of ignored calls and texts, Sarah had to admit she'd made a huge mistake.

What if he never came back? They'd be left living in a building site with neighbours who hated them.

After SparkGate, Sarah taped a grovelling note to the Rogers-Smiths' door so that the scorch marks on their sitting room wall wouldn't come as a total shock. Unfortunately Nate's team had set fire to the socket that their telly was plugged into. Sarah offered to let Mrs Rogers-Smith watch *EastEnders* at theirs, but she didn't take them up on the offer.

Finally, after nearly two weeks and a dozen unanswered texts, Nate responded.

We can be there tomorrow.

Was all forgiven? Excitedly, Sarah pulled out her baking pans. They'd get such a spread of treats for their coffee breaks that they'd never want to work anywhere else.

'They're coming back!' she told Catherine and Rachel when they got home from work. 'Nate and the team. Tomorrow.'

'I'll be glad to get back into my own bedroom,' Rachel said. 'It's been really disorientating.'

'Plus you can't have sex in the other room,' Sarah pointed out. They had a strict No Sex in Communal Space rule after Rachel had admitted doing it in the shower when the others were out of town.

'You've jumped ahead a bit, Sarah Lee. First I have to have someone to have sex with.'

'Oh. Well I was thinking about your date.'

'You mean Thomas?' She shook her head. 'That's not going to happen. We're meant to go out later this week but I might cancel. He's nice enough but I'm just not feeling the love.'

'You can't just cancel on him,' Catherine said.

'Why, does that break one of the RecycLove rules or something?'

'Well no, but you should probably tell him face to face. You've been out three times?'

239

'Four,' said Rachel.

'And it's been okay?'

'Okay . . . that's the best word for it.'

'I've got ten more minutes till the cake's done,' said Sarah. 'So I'll just tidy up a bit.' She grabbed the broom and dustpan and headed for Rachel's room. She wanted to make it nice for Nate.

The building site was immaculate the next morning when she began watching out the window for Nate's white van. She didn't dare go for her run in case she missed them. Every time a car drove down the road she thought it might be Nate. She waited, listening for the door buzzer.

By ten a.m. they still hadn't arrived. That wasn't like them. They liked to get in early. She fondly recalled how they'd all stand around in the kitchen with their coffees, taking the piss out of each other.

Those were happy days.

Another vehicle approached. Better late than never, she thought, relief flooding through her. She hurried to the kitchen to turn the gas on under the coffee pots.

But when she returned to the sitting room window, there were no white vans outside.

She checked her phone for messages.

It was really unfair. You don't tell someone you're coming and then not turn up. She wouldn't do that to a builder.

. . . Wait a minute. That wasn't right. How would she do that to a builder? She didn't mean builder.

She meant boyfriend. She wouldn't do that to a boyfriend.

Because it was the same kind of feeling, wasn't it? The waiting, the watching and wondering. She was acting like Nate and his team were her fickle boyfriends. What was wrong with her? She was practically replaying their first meeting with the *When Harry Met Sally* soundtrack in her head. Get a grip, she thought. It wasn't like Nate was going to turn up on the doorstep with an armful of spanners for her, proposing to go back to work.

It looked like he wasn't turning up at all. They'd been dumped by their builders.

She went back to the window to wait, just in case he had a change of heart.

She would take him back. All he had to do was ask.

Chapter Twenty-Eight

Catherine

Magda appeared at Catherine's office door clutching her three-ring binder so that it rested on the swell of her tummy. In the last few months that binder had become bloated with wedding minutiae. 'Catherine. I would like to know what you think. I am planning our honeymoon.'

'I'm meeting Alis in ten minutes so I haven't really got time.'

'You know,' she said, cocking her head. 'You haven't been very helpful. You're supposed to be Richard's best friend.'

'In fact, Magda, I have been helpful to Richard. I helped him pick out the groomsmen's outfits, and his own suit.' It was Magda she didn't want to help. 'You do know it's unusual to expect your fiancé's ex-wife to help plan your wedding, don't you? Most people just get on with it.'

'Do you have a problem with our marriage?' she asked.

'Not at all.' She chose her words carefully. 'I couldn't be happier, if he's happy. I just think you should do your own wedding planning. With your friends if you want to, but not with me.'

'But you know Richard well. His best friend should be involved in his wedding.'

She wasn't taking the hint. *I don't want anything to do with you,* she wanted to tell her. 'He's got other friends, Magda. Why aren't you asking them to help?'

'Because I see you every day and you are closest to him. It makes sense. We are deciding between Fiji and Bora Bora.' She opened the binder and let lush brochures flutter to Catherine's desk. 'Fiji is more romantic, I think. But there may be more to do on Bora Bora. Both have good weather in June. Which do you think is better?'

Catherine did not want to encourage any more wedding talk from Magda, but she couldn't help herself when there was such an obvious question. 'I thought the wedding was next month?'

'Yes, March twelfth.'

'You're waiting until after the baby for the honeymoon? Won't that be tricky with a newborn?'

'My mother will take the baby while we are gone.'

'It's a child, Magda, not a houseplant. You may not want to leave it, you know, so soon after it's born.'

'Don't try to talk me out of my own honeymoon, Catherine.'

'Suit yourself. I'm just saying.'

She wondered how Richard felt about the whole thing. Not that he'd ever talk to her about it. He was a stingy sharer of feelings. For years she fooled herself into believing she didn't mind.

And she didn't, till she got to know her boss at the Washington food bank.

She thought back to her life in the States. Without even trying, Jose had reached her on an emotional level, day after day as they worked together. That, along with his nearly black eyes and caramel skin that sometimes made her catch her breath, was why she did what she did.

243

The volunteers had a tradition of celebrating six-month workaversaries so they offered to take her out even though it was a Tuesday. Those grannies jumped at any excuse to party.

Catherine had rung Richard to tell him she'd be late home. She often thought about that call later because it cleanly carved their life together into before and after. But there was nothing to it at the time. He'd been distracted by work and told her to have fun.

There wasn't even anything unusual about the night. Five of them had dinner at an Ethiopian restaurant – a first for Catherine – then drinks at one of the watering holes on The Hill. The other volunteers had peeled off after a round or two, returning to their families or their favourite television programmes. But Catherine and Jose had stayed out.

'I shouldn't really be doing this,' she told him.

'Doing what?' He clinked his glass with hers.

'Having so much fun with you.'

They drank too much and traded stories about their lives. There wasn't anything unusual about that either. They did the same thing every lunchtime, minus the sambuca shots.

It was after midnight when she let herself into the quiet house. She knew Richard was still up – she saw their bedroom light from the road.

He was sitting up in bed, propped against the throw pillows that she always told him to take off so they didn't get ruined. 'They're not for using,' she said.

'Then why do we have them?'

'Decoration.'

'You're weird.'

She felt a familiar swell of annoyance.

'Have fun?' he asked, barely looking up from his laptop.

'It was fun.' She flopped down on the bed.

'It must have been. You're wasted, Kate.'

'I am a bit. Jose made me do shots.' Just saying his name was thrilling.

'He made you, did he?' He laughed. 'You'll all have sore heads tomorrow. Be sure you have a glass of water before bed.'

'The others left before the shots. It was just Jose and me.' Thrill thrill thrill. But something else too.

'Drinking alone with your boss? Should I be jealous?' He was still smiling but she had his full attention now.

'It's nothing really. Just a crush.'

She didn't plan to say that. As soon as she did, she knew it was a mistake. What was she thinking?

That was the problem. She wasn't thinking. She was feeling.

'Whose crush?' he asked levelly. 'Yours or his?'

'Both, I think.' She didn't want to, but she knew she owed him the honesty of eye contact.

'You have a crush on this guy? Is that why you're always so happy to go to work?'

She didn't want to talk about herself. She wanted to talk about him. 'Are you in love with me, Richard?'

'Answer my question.'

'Answer mine,' she shot back.

'Where is that even coming from?'

'It's coming from me. Are you?'

It took a tummy full of Italian liqueur to admit what she'd realised at their wedding. She'd stared into his eyes that day as he made his speech at the wedding breakfast. He respected her. He valued and admired her. They'd been through years of growing up together. She was his best friend, biggest support and confidante.

But he never said he was in love with her. He never said it before and he hadn't said it since. That wasn't the relationship they had.

'I could ask you the same question,' he said.

Deflection again. 'I'm not sure.'

'I see. And is this because of Jose?'

'I'm not sure about that either.'

The eyes that stared at her went as dead as a ventriloquist's dummy. 'Then maybe you should take some time to think about the answer.'

Richard was nothing if not proud.

He gathered his pillow and laptop from the bed. 'I'll sleep in the other room and let you think about your answer.'

But he didn't really let her think about it because the next morning, as the night's shots jackhammered in her head, he packed a bag and left.

She was stunned by what she'd done, but she had to look honestly at their relationship. Maybe for the first time. He'd been a willing participant in it, but would it exist if she hadn't constantly pushed?

Probably not.

Maybe it was the same with Magda, she thought now. She did seem to be doing everything for the wedding.

That didn't make Catherine any more willing to sit through her table placement discussions though.

Alis was on time for his appointment, so maybe his star sign was ascending. Catherine was taken aback again when she saw him. He was just so very hairy, with his mop of unkempt curls and that beard. He had another of his tight tee shirts on that showed off his tattoos.

She directed him to the little table in the corner of her office, swiping away the pile of blue swatches that Magda had been tormenting her with all morning. What was so bloody hard about choosing a napkin?

'I brought you something,' Alis said when he sat.

'Oh, thank you.' Most people just sent their fees straight from their bank account but a few still preferred old-school cheques.

But it wasn't a cheque. It was a small clear plastic box full of . . .

'Tea?'

He nodded. 'It's valerian, lemon balm and camomile. It'll help.'

'It'll help what?'

'With your stress. Though it tastes like an old man's socks until you get used to it.'

'Am I stressed?'

He laughed. 'Are those earrings in your ears, or your shoulders?'

She lifted her head. 'Thank you.' Time for a change of subject. 'So you may be wondering why I've asked you here today.'

'I thought we were going through my profile, but this sounds ominous. Have I got a terminal disease that I don't know about? Where's my box of Kleenex?'

'No, no, not at all. It's just that often we go through the client's requirements on the phone after the first meeting, but I wanted to see you.'

He smirked. 'Did you now?'

She ignored the implication. 'As I said when we met last time, we have some women on our books who I think you'll get on with. But we may be able to increase your chances.'

'If you mean getting them sozzled, I have tried but they usually drink me under the table.'

She smiled. 'I was thinking more about some coaching lessons with me. It's a service that we offer to some of our clients.'

'The hopeless ones, you mean?'

'Well . . .'

'That's okay, Catherine. I've worked out that I don't fit your usual tick boxes. That's okay with me if it is with you, so I'm game to try your coaching. Thank you for offering to help.'

'Oh, well, good then. There's just a form to sign. It doesn't tie you to anything and obviously you don't have to take the advice you're given. It's just to say that we're offering you the service and you agree to be contacted by email or text. You can contact me too, of course, whenever you have questions. My mobile number is right there, and we've got yours already.'

She handed him the form and a pen. 'I don't know if it counts as a contract, if that makes a difference.'

'Mercury is fine today, thanks for asking. So where do we start?' He pointed to his face. 'Here, I'm guessing?'

'How attached are you to your beard?'

'It's not glued on, if that's what you mean.'

'That's not what I mean.'

'I've had it for a long time. It started with Movember and grew from there. Literally. I quite like it.' He stroked his hairy cheek.

'Could you learn to like less of it?'

Just a few inches shorter would make a big difference.

'How much less? I don't want designer stubble like George Michael.'

'So the beard is non-negotiable.'

'I can trim it but, if it helps, some women love it.'

Possibly, but she wasn't sure any of them were her clients. He did have quite nice deep-blue eyes fringed with black lashes. And definitely good biceps.

Looks-wise, she'd have to work with what she had and hope for open-minded clients.

'Let's talk about your approach to dates then,' she said. 'Where would you take a woman out when you first meet?'

'It depends on her star sign.' He appraised Catherine. 'What's yours?'

'Oh, well, it's Aries, but I don't really believe in all that.'

He smiled. 'No, you probably don't. But based on it, I

248

think you'll want options on a date. Somewhere out in public rather than a home-cooked meal. To the races maybe, or a pop-up restaurant, or something VIP. You're competitive so you'd like unique events that you can tell friends about. You've got a lot of energy and you're not the homely type. Am I close?'

Star sign, schmar sign. Personalities were built by nature and nurture, not the fact that one's parents had sex on a certain day. 'That's pretty general,' she said. 'It can be said about a lot of people.'

'But I said it about you. Because you're an Aries.'

'I suppose your star sign suits your personality too.' She tried not to sound too condescending but she completely failed. 'Do you like yoga?' she asked, changing tack.

'Love it.'

'Good. Then I've got a couple of women in mind, so limber up.'

'I'll do my special exercises.' He winked.

She stifled a laugh.

Chapter Twenty-Nine

Rachel

Rachel stepped off the ladder to admire her handiwork. She'd woven strings of fairy lights amongst the exposed cables. A few dozen candles flickered on the tables and window ledges. More fairy lights glowed along the mantelpiece of the old Victorian iron-fronted fireplace. And Sissy's banner hung above it.

'It's uneven,' Sissy said, standing with her back against the opposite wall to get as wide a view as possible. She was already dressed for the party in her pale blue day dress with white swallows on it. A matching blue ribbon held her wispy locks away from her face.

'Is it? Are you sure?'

'Yes.'

Rachel smiled. Of course she was sure. This was Sissy they were talking about. 'Okay, which end should I move?'

'The left. It's too low.'

'How much?'

'An inch.'

Rachel climbed back up the stepladder to untack the drawing pin. 'Is that good?'

'Another inch.'

She moved the pin. 'Good?'

'Another inch.'

'Are you sure?'

'Another inch.'

She repinned the banner. 'Now?'

'It's too high.'

When Rachel turned around to protest, she caught Sissy's expression. 'You're kidding, right?'

'Got you! It's even.'

She climbed down and appraised the sign. It really was beautiful. Sissy had drawn it using her trademark coloured squares. In finely shaded blues and greens against a yellow and orange background, it read *Happy Birthday Sarah!*

'Sissy?' Sarah called up the kitchen stairs.

'Don't come up!' she and Rachel yelled together. Sissy was treating their decorating as a top-secret mission. She'd turned up with her usual assortment of drawing pads and pencil boxes but had yanked Rachel into the kitchen as soon as Sarah went upstairs.

'I made something for Sarah's birthday,' she'd said, rummaging in her bags for the large sketch pad. Folded carefully between its pages had been the birthday banner. Close up it was even more impressive, with fat orange roses and tiny yellow sparrows mosaicked around the edges. 'Don't tell Sarah,' she'd said.

'Never.' Rachel had promised to keep the secret.

Of course, Sarah knew something was up. Sissy was about as subtle as a hand grenade. 'Don't worry, I'm not coming up,' she said. 'I just wondered if you're hungry. I've got the sausage rolls out of the oven.'

'Let's have sausage rolls,' Sissy said to Rachel. 'But don't tell.'

Rachel crossed her heart.

Sarah would have found an excuse to deflect the attention

if they'd admitted that the party was for her birthday. So over the past few weeks it had been branded variously as a celebration of Rachel's work coup, an anti-Valentine's Day party and, when they ran low on excuses, a baby shower for Magda.

The house was already heaving with their friends when Sarah's brother came through the door with an elegant blonde wearing a simple black fitted dress. Behind them stood a hot-looking guy that Rachel didn't recognise.

She smoothed down the front of her blue and green tartan dress and hurried over to play hostess. She still wasn't completely sure about the outfit. She felt like a cross between the Disney princess in *Brave* and a throw cushion. It did set off her auburn hair nicely though.

'Hi Robin, welcome!' She kissed his cheek. 'Sarah's just in the kitchen, I think.'

'No, I'm here,' she said, coming up behind them.

'Happy birthday, old girl,' said Robin, kissing his sister. 'How's it feel to be twenty-nine? Ancient I bet. And look who wanted to come along.'

'Hi Sebastian, hi Lucy,' Sarah said.

Sebastian, Sebastian. How did Rachel know that name? Ah, of course. Sarah's ex, Robin's best friend and destroyer of confidence. He had some nerve turning up.

'Robin!' Sissy bellowed as she lunged.

'Whoa, Sissy, easy there.' He laughed. 'You remember Lucy?'

'Yeah, whatever,' she said, holding her hand up.

Sarah's face went as red as the tea dress she was wearing. 'Sissy! Don't be rude. I'm so sorry, Lucy.'

'Sissy . . .' Robin's tone of voice warned.

'Hello Lucy,' she said glumly, before perking up. 'I made the banner for Sarah.'

'It's gorgeous,' Lucy said, obviously eager to get into Sissy's good books. 'You are really talented.'

'Thanks, I know.'

'Where should we put the bottles, Sarah?' she asked.

'Down in the kitchen please, in the ice buckets if they'll fit. If not, then you can just put them on the side, thanks.'

Lucy grabbed Robin's hand as they made their way through the crowd toward the kitchen.

That left Sarah and Sebastian staring at each other.

Was Sarah uncomfortable with her ex there? They hadn't talked since she convinced him to sign up for RecycLove. com. Maybe for good reason. Rachel felt protective of her friend.

'So, Sebastian, how are you finding the website?' she asked. May as well talk about it.

'It's awesome! That's the other reason I wanted to stop by, Sarah, to thank you.'

'Oh really? That's very kind. You've met some nice women then?'

His smirk told Rachel that he wasn't looking for nice women.

'What about you?' he asked Sarah. 'I bet you're popular.'

He kept staring at her as if he wanted to say more.

Of course she's popular, you buffoon, Rachel wanted to scoff. Not only is she one of the nicest people on the planet, but she's also gorgeous. Just look at her. Her dress gave her curves and the matching red lipstick accentuated the sexy pout of a silver-screen film star. She even had the hang of Rachel's liquid eyeliner flick.

But Sarah was typically modest. 'I've had a few dates with one guy,' she said. 'He seems okay.'

'He's not here, is he?' He waited for her to shake her head. 'Good, then I can flirt with you.'

'Oh, well, yes, I suppose,' she said. 'But I should go say hello to my boss. He's just arrived.'

With that she left Sebastian standing there. Rachel stifled

a laugh. She was sure Sarah hadn't meant to leave her ex high and dry, but he looked like someone just took away his chocolate cake after the first mouthful.

Scattiness had its advantages.

Rachel was just about to tell him off for slating Sarah on the assessment when she saw James come in. She excused herself and went to the door.

'Wow, you don't usually make such an effort,' she said, kissing him on the cheek.

He stared at his suit self-consciously, adjusting his white shirt collar. 'Too much? I didn't wear the tie.'

The grey suit was just woolly enough to look trendy instead of dorky. 'No, no. Suits you.' She rolled her eyes at her own unoriginality. 'Why the fancy dress though?'

'Can't a girl just want to look pretty?' He handed her two decent bottles of red.

'And you've upgraded from Tesco's own brand,' she said. 'Sarah will be impressed.'

That had driven her mad when they'd dated. Just because he drank ales he thought all alcohol should cost less than four quid. He treated his wallet like a time capsule, to be opened every fifty years.

'Speaking of girls looking pretty, you're looking divine tonight, Ms Lambert. New dress?'

'Why thank you, it is. Not too *Braveheart* though?'

'Aye lass, you'd give King Edward a run. I wouldn't cross you. Where's your housemate?'

Rachel caught a flash of red on the other side of the crowded sitting room. 'She's over there. Doesn't she look fantastic?'

He stared at Sarah, smiling. 'Seriously stunning. I know you think I'm just full of shit, but I don't remember her looking that good.'

'That's because she didn't look that good before I made

254

her over.' She wasn't sure why she said that. She didn't own Sarah.

'Crafting her in your own image?' he said.

'Don't be ridiculous.'

'But look at her, Rachel. She's you, only blonde with longer legs.'

Was he right? Rachel watched Sarah for signs of Rachelness.

Oh God, she realised, he might be right. There she was in the cut of her dress and chunky black leather boots and her freshly tonged wavy hair, her own statement lipstick and signature eyeliner flick.

How had she not seen what she was doing?

'Wow, what a narcissist I am,' she said to James. 'This is really bad.'

'It isn't the worst thing in the world to have another Rachel around. You'll come with me to say happy birthday, right?'

She was about to make a crack but he looked rather shy so she bit her tongue.

When Sarah saw James she hugged him like they were long-lost friends. She was definitely a bit squiffy already.

'I take it you remember James then?'

'Of course! We all went to see that film with Sigourney Weaver and the lizards.'

James looked confused. '*Alien*? I don't remem—'

'She means *Avatar*.'

'Ah, that's right. I'd forgotten that. I was thinking about Hyde Park that time during the Christmas market.'

'When you spilled mulled wine down Rachel's back,' Sarah said, looking guilty. 'That was my fault. I shouldn't have asked James for a sip.'

'No,' Rachel said. 'It was James's fault for bringing a drink on a roller coaster. Who does that?' She'd been furious with him for the rest of that night. It was just the kind of thing that she'd hated about going out with him. Everybody else

255

thought he was great fun, but she was the one who had to live with the consequences. She never did get the red wine out of her coat.

'Oh, I almost forgot,' James said shyly. 'This is for you.' He handed Sarah a small envelope.

Rachel recognised the Caffè Nero logo.

'It's nothing, really. I just thought you could treat yourself to coffee.'

Rachel stared at him.

'What?' he demanded. 'Aren't you supposed to give presents at a birthday party?'

'Yes, of course you are,' she said. 'It's just, well, a little out of character for you, if I'm honest. It's nice though. Really nice!'

'Well, maybe I'm a new man.'

He and Sarah grinned at each other like idiots until Sissy turned up and started tapping her sister insistently on the shoulder. 'I want to change clothes, please.'

'Why? You look so pretty.'

'I know. I have another outfit. I have wardrobe changes.'

'Oh well then, let's go. Excuse me, will you? I'm on wardrobe duty.'

She let Sissy lead her away by the hand.

'Excuse me too,' said James. 'Need the loo.'

It was much later when Rachel saw Sarah and James with their heads together again, intent on their conversation. She hesitated for just a second before going over. But that was ridiculous. They were both her friends.

As soon as they noticed her though, they stopped whatever they'd been talking about.

'What's going on?' She tried to keep her question breezy. La la la, I don't really care about the answer.

'Oh nothing,' Sarah said. 'Ace turnout, isn't it?'

James scanned the room, intent on the guests. Whatever they'd been talking about didn't include Rachel.

'I'm getting some more wine,' she finally said, sensing that they wanted to be alone. 'Want some?'

'No thanks,' they both said.

'Suit yourselves.' She went towards the kitchen, feeling left out.

Chapter Thirty

Sarah

Sarah went looking for Kelly when she dropped Sissy off at Whispering Sands the next morning. Even though her head felt like a tombola after their party, she had to find out if there was any more news about the facility's funding.

After she and Robin saw Ms Bunny, they had looked for more options. But most were old age homes, leaving just a handful that specialised in Down's syndrome and other learning disabilities. It was seriously depressing.

They hadn't known how lucky they were to find Whispering Sands.

She caught a flash of sleek black ponytail as she rounded the corner towards the nurses' desk. 'Hi Kelly.'

'Sarah, hello.' She looked both ways. 'Have you got a minute?'

Sarah's tummy churned, wondering if this was going to be another outside conversation.

Kelly grabbed her coat and led her to the courtyard.

Bad news then.

'I'm sorry,' she said. 'There's to be one final meeting, but it looks like the facility is closing down. The staff have all been told to expect it.'

'Oh bollocks!' What about all the nice people who looked after their loved ones? How would they find jobs? They might have to leave the area even though they had family and friends there. Some were in their fifties and sixties. They might never find work again. 'Are you going to be okay?'

She nodded. 'I imagine so. I've been looking around. Listen. We're not supposed to be telling the clients or their families so please don't mention it to anyone. We're still hoping for a miracle donor to fund us but if that doesn't happen . . . they've told us they can't guarantee our pay beyond the end of next month. Have you had any luck with other facilities?'

'We looked at a few but they weren't right for Sissy.'

Kelly nodded. She understood. 'Keep looking.'

Two of the lilac-clad staff came into the courtyard to smoke, glancing curiously in Kelly's direction.

'*EastEnders*, you say?' Sarah said loudly. 'Thanks for telling me. I'll ask Sissy about it.'

As they went back inside, Sarah asked the question that had been nagging her. 'Kelly, do you think she should live with me?'

'That's a big decision that only you can make,' Kelly said. 'What I will say is that since she's finished school her opportunities to socialise are narrower than they were, and this is where the other residents are a real benefit. I know you work from home and she'd love to spend all her time with you, but she's got a social life here, and structured activities. She does enjoy being around a lot of people.'

Sarah smiled, thinking about the party last night. Sissy knew more of the guests by the end than Sarah did. 'I know she loves being here, but what about the next home?'

'Keep looking,' Kelly said again.

She got James's text just as she was getting on the train back to London. Her heart sped as she read it.

It was great to see you last night and I'm going to make you keep your promise! How are you fixed next week? James xo

Great to see you too. Hope you don't feel too rough today. I'm free most days. Sarah x

Tuesday? Xo

It's a date. Sarah x

She could still hardly believe it. He was as fun and nice as she remembered and she could easily have talked to him all night if they weren't at her party. Which, by the way, she'd known all along was for her. She wasn't that dim – Catherine was hardly going to throw a baby shower for Magda, was she?

This was a mad, mad, probably very bad idea, but she'd said yes. Yes, yes, yes. It was her mantra now.

She giggled to herself. Look at her! A text from one guy and going to meet another later. That would never have happened before RecycLove.

It had seemed like a grand idea when Jeremy suggested dinner and dancing the night after the party. And it would have been if Sarah hadn't felt like she was walking through treacle. She popped two more paracetamol and checked her reflection. There were definitely dark circles under her eyes. Hopefully the bright red lipstick balanced things out.

She glanced at the clock on her bedside table. She felt guilty but she didn't really have time for Sissy's nightly call. It would have to be fast to get to the restaurant on time.

She clenched the ringing phone between her cheek and shoulder as she flipped off her heels and dug around in the closet for a different pair.

'Hi Sissy, it's me. How's your day been?' As her sister answered, she made herself sit on the bed to listen. Sissy deserved her full attention and, besides, Jeremy didn't care if she was five minutes late. His whole life seemed to be twenty-four-hour non-stop action.

Sarah thought he was joking when he said their reservation was for ten p.m. She was usually in her pyjamas by then. But must not be boring, she reminded herself. Normal people did go out that late.

She'd forgo her slippers to be a normal person. If she did it long enough it might even be true.

'Sarah!' Jeremy called from behind her just as she pushed through the doors at The Wolseley. 'Sorry, I wanted to get here before you. Damn Tube.' He kissed her cheeks and gave his name to the maître d', who took their coats and showed them to a booth at the side of the room.

'You look nice,' he said as they sat.

'Thanks. So do you.' He wore a collared black shirt with his slim jeans. He was getting Eurotrashier with each date but she didn't really mind as long as he didn't start wearing a white silk scarf round his neck or tucking his sunglasses into the top of his shirt.

'I have a question,' she said as they looked over their menus. 'What's your favourite body part?'

Jeremy looked confused.

'I mean your own favourite body part, not mine!' Talk about fishing for compliments with a trawler's net.

'I'll say this much, Sarah, you always have interesting questions. I'm still deciding which live insects I'd want to eat on a desert island, from when you asked me last time.' He laughed. 'The answer is ants, I think, as long as they're not too big. And I guess my legs are okay.'

Sarah nodded, approving of both his answers. 'And which part do you hate? Bear with me, there is a point here.'

While she was in the shower getting ready, between shampooing and conditioning, just as she was loofah-ing her elbows, she'd come up with the best card idea. The. Best. Idea. She had to tell someone.

'That's easy,' he said. 'I hate my nose. My nostrils are too big.'

She tried not to look up his nostrils which, as he'd mentioned it, were sizeable. 'I do think they suit your nose, though, and your nose suits your face. So what if your wife-to-be gave you a wedding card saying how much she loved your nose? Wouldn't that make you feel good to know that she loves even that? I'm thinking about pitching a body parts wedding card line at work. If someone loves the part of you that you're most sensitive about then they must really, *really* love you, don't you think?'

Sarah fantasised about that man, the one who found all of her quirks endearing. He'd let her know in every possible way that he thought she was perfect, and he'd love to bake as much as she did. Her Prince Charming in a pavlova.

Jeremy didn't look too sure about her idea, but then he wasn't in the wedding card business. He sold computer storage solutions so she forgave his lack of whimsy. Besides, he made a perfectly lovely dinner date.

'So we've got two options for clubs tonight,' he said later as he poured the last of the wine into Sarah's glass. 'There's a DJ I like at Groove Train and a house club night at Ministry. Groove Train's a lot smaller and Ministry is a superclub, so it depends on what you want to do?'

She really just wanted to lie down and have a long sleep.

But then she remembered her new mantra. 'The superclub, I guess?'

It was past midnight by the time they got into Ministry of Sound but between the wine and the thumping house music Sarah found herself spinning with the energy inside. And Jeremy was right, the club *was* super. The enormous room heaved with dancing bodies everywhere. Jeremy bought them drinks and they joined the throng.

She watched the women around her. Most of them undulated like strippers or ground their arses into the men dancing behind them. She copied a few of the less X-rated moves and hoped she didn't look like she needed seizure medication.

Jeremy's hands stroked her hips and sides as they danced. She was getting hot and not just because it was about a hundred degrees. Though these days she got turned on by her washing machine's spin cycle.

He shouted something in her ear as he leaned close. It sounded like 'You're so shit, Sarah', but that would be weird to say to a date, so she assumed he'd said fit.

'So are you!' she shouted back, just in case he had just insulted her.

He stared into her eyes in *that* way. He'd definitely said fit. 'Do you want to sit down?'

No sooner had they found a spot on one of the velvet sofas off to the side when he launched himself on her.

Hold on there, Neil Armstrong, she wanted to say. Before you take us into orbit, I'm not that kind of girl.

Only she found herself quite enjoying his kissing. And his hands. She definitely enjoyed his hands as they roamed up her legs.

So maybe she was that kind of girl. Maybe, for the first time in years, that was exactly the kind of girl she was.

*   *   *

On Tuesday, just as she was locking up her bike behind their office, she caught Maria-Therese and Harry getting out of his car. She wouldn't have thought much about it if he hadn't stared at her in such horror.

She got the feeling he and Maria-Therese weren't just carpooling.

At least that explained Maria-Therese's devotion to their boss. She wasn't getting a leg up on the corporate ladder so much as getting a leg over on Harry.

By the time they all sat round the conference room table for the weekly brainstorm meeting, Harry had recovered some composure. But he turned fuchsia every time he glanced her way. Did he think she was going to grass him up?

Maybe she would have before, but not now. Instead of the revulsion she should feel at the thought of those two naked together, she found herself smiling. If Harry's big arse made Maria-Therese weak in the knees and her ferrety face and caustic tongue gave him the horn, then so be it. Everyone deserved to be happy.

'Even girls with fat knees,' she explained to the table, gesturing to her drawing. Though looking at the woman on the sketch pad, the poor thing looked more like she was suffering from gout. Sarah had been awfully hung-over when she drew it.

'A line of cards pointing out people's flaws?' Maria-Therese said. 'Who'd want those?'

'But it's not mean-spirited,' Sarah said. 'It's to show that nobody's perfect and that the right person will love you anyway.'

Maria-Therese sneered. 'What other . . . shortcomings do you propose to illustrate, Sarah?'

Giggles erupted around the table.

She wasn't about to humour them. 'We could have cards for all the things people usually dislike about themselves.

Maybe they think they're too short or tall or fat or skinny or they don't like their thin lips or big feet or small . . .' Do not say willy. Do Not Say Willy. Or boobs. Definitely not boobs. Though she could sketch a couple of egg cups with something about a gentleman's handful . . . She'd save that one for next time. 'Small teeth,' she finished. 'I don't know. I just think it's a nice sentiment, don't you?'

The others nodded along with Harry. 'It is a nice sentiment,' he said. 'I'm just not sure it's commercial enough.'

'You always say that.' She slammed shut her sketch pad. 'That's it for my ideas this week.'

'Thank you, Sarah,' said Harry. 'Other ideas?'

The meeting moved on and, as usual, Sarah was the butt of the joke. She packed her pens and pads away, trying not to feel so bad.

Chapter Thirty-One

Catherine

Catherine hadn't heard back from either of the clients she'd managed to set up with Alis, so she could barely control her eagerness to hear the gossip when he rang the office.

Ever the professional though, she let him talk at his own pace. It was frustratingly slow.

'Kiera seems nice,' he began. 'But she's very uptight.'

'Oh? How so?' Catherine knew that Kiera sometimes got anxious, but she was devoted to her sweaty yoga sessions and was about a carrot stick away from photosynthesising, so at least she had something in common with Alis.

'She had a real go at me when I ordered a burger after yoga. Up till then we were getting along fine.'

'Oh you didn't.' Keira was a strict vegan. Coming from the countryside, she'd even had a pet cow. And there was Alis, slathering ketchup and pickles all over her beloved pet's cousin. 'I'm sorry, I assumed that because you're a vegetarian, you wouldn't be eating beef for lunch.' She tried keeping the accusation from her voice.

'I aspire to be a vegetarian,' Alis clarified. 'Sometimes I'm not as strong as I'd like to be.'

She started wondering what other things on his profile were aspirational. 'That was the end of the date, I guess?'

'Pretty much, yeah, but that's okay. I'm not sure she was really my type anyway.'

'I'm sorry, but I did match you based on your profile. Usually when people say they're vegetarian it means they don't eat meat.'

He laughed. 'I doubt anybody's values are really that straightforward.'

'Mine are,' she said before she could help herself.

'I doubt that, but you go ahead and believe what you like.'

'I believe it because it's true,' she said.

'I bet I can prove that it's not.'

On the one hand Catherine didn't like having her professional conversation knocked off course like this. But on the other, she did love a challenge. 'Go ahead then.'

He thought for a few moments, then said, 'Okay. Catherine, is it wrong to kill someone?'

'Yes.'

'Always?'

She thought about this. 'Do you mean if they ask you to kill them?'

'No, I mean murder in cold blood. Violently, like shooting someone.'

'Then yes.'

'Always?'

'Yes.'

'What if they're about to kill ten people? Then is it wrong to shoot them first?'

She hesitated. 'Well, that's not a great outcome, but since killing is wrong, then yes.'

'What about a thousand people? You could save a thousand people by killing one. Would you do it?'

'Probably.'

'But you just said killing is wrong.'

'You've got to look at what's worse.'

'Ah, but then you're making a judgement about which lives are worth more than others when you've already said that killing is wrong. That means a life is a life. It's just as wrong to kill one person as it is to kill a thousand.'

'No, there's a question of degree.'

'Sorry, Catherine, but there aren't degrees of death. Either he's dead or he's not, which proves my point. We don't have to be so rigid. Nothing is that simple. Even this conversation. I only rang to report on my dates.'

'Oh well then, by all means don't let me stop your reporting,' she said, glad not to talk any more about death. And glad too not to think about whether he was right. Was she too rigid? 'How was Sajeela?'

She was one of Catherine's favourite clients, a smart, open-minded, vivacious mother of two. She had her life sorted and joined the agency to see if her equal was out there. Who was to say he wouldn't be a horoscope-obsessed walking beard?

'Sajeela was great!' Alis said. 'Thanks for setting me up with her. We had a really nice time getting to know each other. Did you know she used to live in a commune?'

Catherine smiled at his naiveté. 'It's my job to know things like that, and she's a yoga instructor too. That's why I thought you'd hit it off.'

'You were right, we did. But I think I convinced her that I'm not for her.'

'You what?' It was hard enough talking clients into meeting Alis. She didn't need him purposely putting them off.

'Well, we got chatting about where we are in our lives at the moment. She's so level-headed and seems really happy. But with the children and work I wondered why she'd want to invest so much effort in meeting someone just now.'

'And what did she say to that?'

'She agreed with me!' He said this like it was the best outcome he could imagine. 'Her sister convinced her to try, but to be honest her heart isn't in it. She's really quite happy on her own right now. Isn't that wonderful?'

'So you talked yourself out of another date with her?'

He was missing the whole point of her business model.

'Yes, but it's okay. Now she doesn't have to keep looking for Mr Right because she's already Ms Right. She said she'd ring you this week to talk about it.'

Catherine was starting to realise that Alis wasn't only making it hard to find him a date. He might make it hard to keep her clients.

'Alis, it's nice that you two hit it off and you were able to . . . explore Sajeela's motivations together. But the idea was to introduce you to someone to go out with. Not to convince someone to be alone.'

'Oh right. Sorry about that.'

She sighed. 'It's all right. I'll ring you by the end of the week with more options, okay? In the meantime I'll update your profile on the meat-eating issue . . . Just one thing before I go. You seem to spend a lot of time talking about the other person. Would you say that's normal?'

'Who's to say what's normal?'

'No, I mean, do you do it a lot on dates?'

'Well I like to get to know a person by connecting with them.'

'And that's fine, but maybe you could connect without dissecting her? Is it something you'd like to consider?'

'Is this where your coaching comes in?'

'Yes, I think so.'

It was probably the tip of the iceberg.

'When are you free to meet?'

She got the feeling that Paul was going to be a more straight-forward project than Alis. Her rough-and-ready Australian client only needed smoothing around the edges. A little buff here and there and maybe some tucking in or sharpening up.

'I see you're wearing your new outfit,' she said when she saw him on the steps beneath the Doric columns of the National Gallery. With his more relaxed haircut and patterned Paul Smith shirt, he looked like fun. Successful but fun. Armed with a bit of inside knowledge, her clients were going to love him.

'I dress to impress!' He looked curiously at the building. 'I didn't expect a museum today. I figured you'd want me waxed or maybe learning the difference between sushi and sashimi.' He caught her expression. 'I do know the difference. And you thought I was a total cretin.'

'No, a cretin wouldn't wear Paul Smith. Come on. We haven't got much time and we need to go somewhere else after this.'

He trailed behind her as they snaked their way between the tourists inside. 'So if it's not a sushi lesson, are you going to tell me why we're here?'

'Simple. Since quite a few of our clients are mad about art, I'm giving you a crash course on some of the more popular artists.'

'Aw, no, seriously? I'm not much of a student, ya know.'

'Well you'll have to pay attention today. Trust me, it'll be worth it.'

She led them to the back of the ground floor where, for the next thirty minutes, she briefed him on the Impressionists. His interest surprised her, and made her grateful for all those days she spent in Washington's museums trying to validate her new life.

When his eyes didn't glaze over too badly, she risked moving on to Hogarth – one of her favourites. She loved how he combined beautiful art with moral commentary.

Paul whistled, startling the guard sitting in the doorway. 'You're packing in a scary amount of knowledge, Catherine.'

'Too much?'

'Nah, I'm a man. I can take it.'

'This is just an overview really. I don't pretend to be an expert,' she said. 'And I did study up a little for our trip today.' She hesitated for a second, unsure about exposing more. 'But I spent a lot of time in museums when I first moved to Washington.'

'Ah that's right, your time in the US. You never told me anything about that, you know.'

'I know,' she said, moving on to the art in the next room.

Even after a decade she disliked thinking about the end of her US life, but it still sometimes ambushed her from unexpected corners. When Richard had left their home she'd assumed it would be for a night or two, tops. She'd texted to ask where he was. When he hadn't answered, she'd started ringing him. It had just gone through to voicemail.

She'd felt sick knowing she was hurting him. He didn't deserve this.

But she couldn't help how she felt.

And she couldn't lie to herself. Part of her was relieved that it was out in the open. Now that someone else knew her feelings, it must mean they were real. She really was feeling this.

He finally returned her voicemails three days later. 'Have you left me?' he asked.

'Left you? You've left me!'

'No, I've given you space to think. I told you that. Do you know what you want?' For all the emotion in his voice he could have been asking his bank's call centre for an update on his balance.

'Richard, can't we talk about this in person?' Her eyes pricked with tears. Guilt, fear, sadness? Yes, yes, yes.

'That depends on what you're going to do. Have you told your boss how you feel?'

'No.'

'Start there and then let me know what you want.' He hung up.

That wasn't the man she knew. In all their years together she'd never known him to be so cold. So how well had she known him after all?

She tried being as normal as possible at work, not to betray the fact that her husband had walked out on her. But he was right. She had to talk to Jose. Because whatever she was feeling wasn't going away. It was getting stronger.

She felt like throwing up by the time she decided she had to say something. She brought her salad into Jose's office as usual. 'Richard has left,' she said.

'What?' He sprang from his chair to envelop her in his arms. 'I'm so sorry, Catherine.' She was so happy to be there that she nearly didn't say anything else. This was what she wanted – why risk her next words?

'What happened? Do you want to talk about it?'

Typical Jose, she thought, never afraid to get down and dirty in the emotion. 'We've been having some problems.' No, that wasn't true. 'We're having problems.' She took a deep breath. 'I'm not sure I'm as committed to Richard as I should be. I'm not sure how happy I am.'

She searched his face, looking for some clue that he understood what she was saying. Suddenly his face reflected that aha moment as he caught on. He said, 'There's someone else?'

She nodded.

'And it's serious?'

Again, she nodded. 'I think it is.' She took a deep breath and ploughed on. 'I'm not sure he feels the same way though.'

Jose made his that's-the-cutest-thing-I've-ever-heard face. 'Then why don't you ask him?' His tone was playful.

'What if he doesn't feel the same way?'

Jose smiled. 'I guarantee he does. Ask him.' He took her

272

into his arms again as she murmured, 'Jose, do you feel the same way?'

His hug tightened as she went on. 'I've felt so amazingly close to you these past months and I know it's only been a little while but I'm nuts about you.' It was much easier saying these things with her face buried in his neck. 'I feel like my whole world has opened up because of you, and I don't want to go back to the old one. I told Richard the night we went out.'

He pulled away from her, holding her by the shoulders.

She knew she'd made a mistake as soon as she saw his face. He looked surprised, shocked and then, worst of all, horribly embarrassed. She wanted to take it all back.

'I'm so sorry but you've got the wrong idea, Catherine. I don't think of you in that way. If I gave you that impression I'm really sorry. I live with my girlfriend and, actually, I'm going to ask her to marry me.'

She felt like she might faint. Only her pride held her upright.

'Oh yes, right, well . . .' she whispered. 'There you are then. Thanks for clearing that up.' She picked up her uneaten salad and backed from the room. He didn't stop her.

She could hardly believe what she'd done. Was she deluded? Hadn't there been something between them? They got along so well and she loved so much about him. He had to feel the same way . . . though if she'd stepped away from her emotions she'd have seen that he was as friendly with all the volunteers.

Except for the lunch dates, he'd never singled her out.

She did step away from her emotions then. She stepped as far away as she could, until she was out of reach of their impact.

That's when she knew it wouldn't be fair to go back to Richard. Just because Jose didn't feel their connection, she did. It wasn't fair to go back to a relationship that Richard would always know was the consolation prize. Besides, whatever she'd felt about Jose, delusional or not, she and Richard didn't feel for each other.

She left Washington within the month. Richard drove her to the airport.

'Will we ever be friends again?' she asked. She knew she had no right. She couldn't help herself.

'I can't make any promises,' he said.

'That's all right. I don't deserve any.'

'We always were friends, Catherine,' he said. 'Maybe that's been the problem.'

He hugged her briefly at the check-in, and turned away, waving over his shoulder.

So their actual goodbye wasn't the emotional car crash she'd feared. He'd never been overly demonstrative anyway. And her feelings were already safely packed away with the luggage.

The divorce petition from the court came a few months later. That's when she cried. Really cried. Days and days of tears for the relationship she'd fought so hard to win. But she'd never really won it, had she?

She wasn't about to tell any of this to Paul. His agency fee didn't buy him that kind of detail. Besides, it was so long ago that it hardly mattered now.

Paul stood with her in front of Hogarth's *Marriage à-la-mode* series, taking in all the details. 'This guy's pretty good,' he said.

'Yes, he's pretty good.'

He'd probably say that Mozart could carry a tune. 'It's a moral tale, really,' she said. 'About an earl who makes a contract for his son to marry the daughter of a rich merchant, but it's not a happy marriage. Now they've got lots of money from her family and, when the old earl dies, titles from his, but the husband sleeps with a prostitute and catches venereal disease and the wife has it off with their lawyer. Her husband bursts in on them in a rage and the lawyer stabs him. Of course, the lawyer is sent to the gallows for murder and the wife poisons herself in despair. But none of the family money can go to her child because all property is forfeit in the case of suicide. So she's destitute even though she did nothing wrong. A destitute orphan.'

Paul pretended to hang himself with his imaginary tie. 'Thanks, Catherine, that's a real downer.'

She laughed. 'Hogarth was a great moraliser. And a pretty good painter, as you say. Now that you know a bit about him and the Impressionists, with your new look and stylish shirt choice, if I do say so myself, who'll be able to resist you? Come with me. There's an even better series at the Soane's Museum. Then you can go back to your philistine ways.'

'Nah, that's all right,' he said. 'I think I'm coming round to your way of doing things.'

Chapter Thirty-Two

Rachel

Rachel dreamed that she was being chased down the corridor with the Zigler clients throwing cheese graters at her. She was definitely obsessing about work but she couldn't stop now. Not till she was sure she'd designed something really special. So for the third week straight, she dragged herself out of bed before the sun was up, mainlined her coffee and went to the office.

James was already there. 'Morning, sir,' he said, looking up from his drawings when he noticed her in the doorway. 'Is today the day? Today has to be the day.'

He'd asked her if she was finished every day for the past week. Every day she said yes, nearly. Her building was like a mirage in the desert. She never seemed to get any closer. 'Yep, nearly,' she said, and went to her desk.

He followed her to her office. 'C'mon, Rachel, can't I see? I'll show you mine if you show me yours.'

'I don't want to see yours.'

'You've already seen mine, but I'm talking about the drawings. Please? I'll see it eventually, when you show Ed and the clients. I don't know why you're always so secretive.'

'Ha! That's the pot calling the kettle black.' That came out harsher than she wanted.

He looked confused. 'But I always show you my drawings.'

'I'm not talking about your drawings.'

'What then?'

'You know.' She hadn't forgotten about the party. That cosy little conversation with Sarah that she was obviously not welcome to join. 'I mean you and Sarah at the party. Care to elaborate on why you were whispering every time I saw you?'

His eyes flicked to hers and then away again. 'We were just catching up. Why, does it bother you?'

She didn't want to answer that question, even to herself. 'I don't care. It was just rude to monopolise her like that.'

'I wasn't monopolising her. I was talking to the guest of honour. It was her birthday, remember?'

True, but there was definitely something else going on. 'It doesn't matter to me what you and my housemate talk about. You're adults.'

'If it bothers you, Rach—'

'Oh for fuck's sake, *you're* bothering me!'

He kept watching her till she looked away. She heard him leave a few seconds later.

Now her mood was completely ruined. Her drawings were none of his business. Any more than his conversation with Sarah was hers . . .

'Rachel?'

Why couldn't he just stay in his office?

'I thought I should tell you that I'm meeting Sarah tonight for a drink.'

She kept her eyes on her pens. 'Oh? That's nice. Have fun.'

'It's nothing serious, just a drink.'

'Mmm hmm, okay.'

'Are you okay with that?'

Finally she looked up. 'Yes, James, I'm okay with it. You don't need my permission to have a drink with my friend if you want to. Have fun.'

'Are you being facetious?'

'God, you're annoying. You're a big boy. Do what you like.'

'Because if you're not okay—'

'Will you go back to work?!'

'Just thought you should know,' he mumbled as he left.

So that's why they were so secretive at the party. They weren't talking about her. Quite the opposite, actually. She hadn't figured into their thinking at all.

She laid down her pen as an uncomfortable prickling feeling crept up her neck. Did drinks with Sarah mean polite, platonic, definitely friend-zone drinks? Or mild, platonic flirting? Or . . . clothing-optional?

She could imagine how their conversation went. James would do that thing where he tipped his head down to look at you like James McAvoy did in the films. Then he'd be all stammery when he suggested going for a drink some time, staring at her with big hopeful eyes until she said yes out of sheer pity.

Sarah was definitely too kind sometimes. Of course she was just being kind. She wasn't interested in him like that. Especially when she knew exactly why Rachel had dumped him in the first place.

She had liked James's ambition when they first met. It matched hers. The late nights in the office were fun. Junior architects united in solidarity for the cause.

But that was before they had other ways to spend their time. Once they started kissing, Rachel got better at the whole work/life balance.

Not James though.

He did nothing to fit a relationship into his work schedule. The late nights continued. He made and cancelled weekend plans.

She never thought she'd feel jealous of a job. But that was his first love. She felt like a distant second best.

They did talk about it, till they were both sick of hearing her. He'd make an effort for a week or two before slipping back into his routine.

It got so she could tell when she was about to be stood up. Name that excuse in three notes . . .

'Hi Rach, I'm really sorry but—'

'You know what?' she finally said on yet another Saturday that he'd spent in the office. 'Don't bother.'

'Huh?'

'With whatever excuse you were going to say.'

'It's not an excuse. I really do have to—'

'Work. I know. You go ahead and work. Work all you want. I'm done.'

'Can we meet later? I should be finished by ten.'

'I said I'm done.' Her voice hitched. 'You work.'

'No, I'll leave now. I can be with you in half an hour.'

'It's too late.' She was sobbing now. 'A year's enough, don't you think? If you haven't got it through your head by now, you're never going to.'

'You can't just end it like this, Rachel.' He sounded panicked. 'We're friends.'

'Right, James. We're friends. That's exactly what we are.'

She rang in sick for the rest of that week and bawled till she thought her heart would split. Catherine and Sarah, their shoulders sodden with tears, kept her distracted with girl power DVDs.

James rang about ten times a day but she never took his calls. The tiny bit of self-esteem she'd salvaged told her not to.

279

But he didn't give up. When she returned to work, red-eyed but resolved, he wanted to know if she was all right.

'I'm fine,' she lied, knowing that eventually she would be. 'But I don't want to be around you right now.' She could take his aloofness. She could even take his anger (if he'd had any). It was his worry and compassion she couldn't handle.

Now he was probably sitting in his office thinking she was upset about him and Sarah. She wasn't about to let him play the bigger person again.

She strode over. 'James, I might have given you the impression before that I'm not happy about you going out with Sarah. I am. Happy. Thrilled,' she added for good measure, though that might have been overkill.

'If you mean that then thanks. I really enjoyed talking to her. She's funny! Why didn't I know she was so funny?'

'Maybe you should take her to a comedy club then. She'd enjoy that.'

'We're meeting for drinks at Gordon's. She's never been there and I thought she'd like it. What do you think?'

What did she think? She thought it showed a remarkable lack of originality considering she and James had gone there at least half a dozen times. 'Well I always liked it, so yes, I'm sure she will. Maybe I'll take Thomas there. He'd probably like it too. Not tonight though, obviously.'

'Does that mean things are going well with Thomas?'

She couldn't read the look that crossed his face. 'Oh yeah, things are great with him.' Except that she hadn't heard from him recently. 'Joining that website was such a good move, don't you think?'

'Well, I haven't really used it much, to be honest, after that first date.'

'Oh that's riiight. The woman you slept with. Whatever happened to her?' she asked sweetly.

280

Again that inscrutable expression. 'She blew me out. And after I busted some of my best moves on her, too.'

Rachel's hand flew in front of her eyes. 'Please, James, I don't need details. I'll never be able to unhear them.'

'I mean dancing, Rach. I took her out to a club.'

'You did not! James, you've never danced in your life. What has happened to you?'

'I'll have you know that I'm a decent dancer.'

'Then why did you never take me out? I love to dance.'

'I didn't know it was important until you mentioned it on the assessment form. But you were right. Women do find it sexy. I'm irresistible when I'm gettin' down with my bad self.'

He started trying to twerk around the room.

'Oh God, no James!' She put up both hands this time.

'Anyway,' he continued, sounding winded. 'I guess I got lucky at the party.'

Her eyes snapped to his. 'What do you mean by that?'

'I mean seeing Sarah again. Even though she's online now, I got to talk to her in the wild.' When he grinned she wanted to wipe it off his face. 'Hopefully we'll be able to snag a table tonight. We're not meeting till around nine. I have to see my prof first.'

That was an odd thing to say. 'Which prof?'

'My mentor, Doctor Hildegaard. He's looking over the Zigler project with me.'

'You can't do that!' she blurted. 'It's cheating.'

'What are you talking about, Rachel? Cheating on what? This isn't an exam.'

'No, but we're competing against each other. You can't have help with yours.'

'You're using your mother.'

'I am not! She hasn't even seen the sketches. Nor will she.' He stared at her. 'Why the hell wouldn't you? She's one

281

of the best architects in the city. You're nuts if you don't use that. Seriously, Rach, this is your career. Use all the tools available to you. I'm saying that as your friend.'

'I'm not going to cheat. It's not fair.'

'I told you, it's not cheating. It's called getting ahead. I think you've got a screwed-up sense of fair play, but it's your career. I want this project, Rachel. You know that whoever gets it gets promoted, right?'

'Why do you think that?'

'Come on. Ed's been hinting at it since the meeting. Trust me. Whoever wins the Zigler contract gets the promotion. And the other person . . .'

He left the sentence hanging in the air. She didn't need him to finish it. There'd be no prize for coming second.

Chapter Thirty-Three

Sarah

Why couldn't James have picked an earlier time to meet, or another night? Sarah listened for Rachel's key in the front door. He knew she sketched from home. And he also knew that Rachel would probably come back before it was time to leave for their date. What was she supposed to do, hide in the closet for three hours to avoid her housemate?

This had seemed like a good idea at the party when he'd asked her to meet him, but now she wasn't so sure. She just knew she'd bottle it if she had to look Rachel in the face.

She ran her hand over the new dresses in her closet. Black and white polka dots or the watered silk one with cancan girls? The black and white was more elegant but the girls were flirtier. No contest, she thought. It's definitely a dancing girls kind of night. She wriggled into the cinch-waisted frock and popped on her trusty boots. Rachel was right. They did go with everything.

She was right about most things. It didn't take long to get used to the make-up. Now Sarah felt weird without it. The other morning she nearly put on eyeliner before her jog. Step away from the slap, she'd told herself. The squirrels don't give a toss how you look.

Just as she was tonging one side of her fringe, Rachel shouted from downstairs.

'Ow!' Sarah cried as the tongs came down on her forehead with a painful sizzle. 'I'm up here!' she yelled back with her hand over the rising welt.

'Couldn't help but notice that the banister is missing,' Rachel said as she reached Sarah's doorway.

'Oh, that. Nate's replacing it. Apparently it's come loose.' She rolled her eyes. It wouldn't be loose if the workmen didn't swing round the newel post every time they ran up or down the stairs.

Nate had finally shown up again (a week after he said he would) as if they'd never had a falling-out. Sarah still blamed herself for making them quit. But then Rachel asked her dad about it and found out that that's just how builders worked. Nate probably wasn't even mad at her. He'd just taken another job, so it suited him to be away for a few weeks. Now he was back in the house, destroying as much as he fixed, and there was probably another family across town waiting hopefully each morning for a white van.

'So they removed the whole thing?' Rachel asked.

'He didn't want us falling through. He thinks we'll be more careful if there's no banister to rely on.' She'd always doubted Nate's building skills but now she wondered about his intelligence too. She couldn't wait till they were finished. In about a month, Nate promised.

'Getting ready for your date?' Rachel asked.

Sarah inspected the question for any anger, but Rachel kept it neutral. She was just about to say it wasn't a date. But she couldn't do that. 'Yes, nearly ready.'

'What's happened to your forehead?'

'I burned it on the tongs.'

'Ouch. That might blister. Did you put burn cream on it?' She shook her head. 'I don't think we have any.'

'Hang on, I know what to do.'

She ran back downstairs, leaving Sarah a moment to compose herself.

Should she ask Rachel if going out with James was okay? What if she said no? That would stop them in their tracks before they even got started. No, she had to stay strong. She couldn't let herself be talked out of this.

'Here, put this on,' Rachel said, handing her a kitchen towel.

Sarah sniffed it. 'Butter?'

'It helps with burns.'

'Plus it's tasty on toast,' she said, smearing her forehead. 'Do I have to go out like this?'

'No, it soaks in. You may want to wash your forehead though before you go. You might get a bit whiffy otherwise.'

'Thanks,' Sarah said. 'I'm ordering from the Noodle Shop. Want something?'

'Sounds great. Number sixteen for me, please.'

So they were both going to ignore the elephant in the room.

James looked really cute. She'd always thought so, but the past few years had added something extra. He was more man than man-child now. She supposed he was just dressed as he would be for work, since he went to see his prof straight after, and then came to the bar, but he looked stylish. He and Rachel had made an attractive couple.

'You look great,' he said, taking in her dress, the boots, the make-up and half-curled hair. She couldn't face those tongs again after the scalding. 'What happened to your forehead?'

Her hand flew to her head. 'Is it still shiny?'

'No, it just looks like a blister. Why would it be shiny?'

'I burned it. Rachel said butter would help. I'm pretty sure it's a myth, but she seemed really keen to help so I let her.'

'Hmm.'

'What?'

'That's funny. I'm lactose-intolerant.'

Was he also wondering if Rachel disapproved? 'You don't think she . . .?'

'No, no. I mean, come on. I'm hardly going to lick your forehead, am I? What do you want to drink? My round. It's the least I can do.'

They found a little table against one of the walls in the half-empty wine bar. Within a few sips of her wine, Sarah knew she'd been right not to cancel. They settled easily into the same banter they'd had at the party.

It felt nice to be comfortable. Being on the website reminded her how stressful dating could be. Not that she wasn't enjoying her dates with Jeremy. She just felt a bit like a performing monkey sometimes. Tonight she was simply Sarah.

When the conversation turned to RecycLove, James told her about his date.

She wasn't shocked when he confessed to his sleepover, but it was a little insensitive given the circumstances. Still, the more she knew about him the better. 'So will you see her again? I'm asking for a friend.'

'No, but in fairness that's not my fault.'

'Well you would say that, wouldn't you?'

He chuckled. 'It's like you know me already, but as it happens, in this case I mean it. We went out, had a nice time and then, you know. And I did mean to see her again. I even called the next day to arrange something. She said she'd let me know and never called back . . .'

'Maybe you were having an off night,' she said.

'Wow, straight in there, thanks, Sarah, for questioning my manhood.'

She shrugged. Sometimes the truth hurt.

'To be honest, it did bother me,' he said. 'Rachel assassinated me in her evaluation. I guess I've taken it to heart. As usual she was right about most of it.'

'I think you just weren't right for each other.'

He looked stricken.

'I mean you and the woman you went out with. Not Rachel. It feels weird talking about other dates to each other, don't you think?' she asked. 'It's like . . .' She thought for a moment. 'It's like telling your hairdresser that you've had a cut somewhere else.'

'Do you cheat on your hairdresser?'

'Well, I have once or twice,' she admitted. 'I've used the same salon for years and sometimes my usual girl goes on holiday or whatnot when I really need a cut. I have used other stylists . . . always at that salon though! I haven't gone to others.'

James laughed. 'The salon'll be grateful for your loyalty, I'm sure. I go to SuperCuts and couldn't tell you the name of anyone who's cut my hair in the past decade. Maybe I should though. I might look better then. What do you think?'

She thought he looked quite cute as he was. But thanks to Rachel she knew he sometimes fished for compliments.

He did seem like a different person than the one Rachel described though. A skinflint wouldn't have got his round in without a fight, for one thing. And he was listening to her, not waiting till she took a breath so he could interrupt.

'I feel like we should talk about Rachel,' she said. 'Only I feel guilty doing it, like I'm betraying her. I saw her tonight before I left. She didn't say anything, but that was the worst part. It was really uncomfortable.'

'I'm sorry about that, but I did talk to her about it today. I told her. She says she's happy we're out tonight.' A shadow briefly crossed his expression.

By the time it was last orders, Sarah was tipsy and happy.

'Go 'ed, lad, gizza nother,' she said when James offered more wine.

'You've gone all Scouse,' said James. 'You're not from Liverpool though.'

'No, me mam was,' she said, sounding like she'd been born directly into the Mersey. 'I guess I picked up some of her expressions.'

'I like it. There's nothing exotic about my accent, coming from Bucks.'

She laughed. 'I wouldn't call Liverpool exotic! It's not like it's Marrakesh or Timbuktu or the Outer Hebrides.'

He laughed, then said, 'You're intriguing.'

'Am I?' That was very nice to hear. No matter the circumstances, it was nice to hear it from James.

'And you're not nearly as bad as Rachel makes out,' she said.

'Cheers to that. It's nice to know I'm not horrible.'

No, she thought later as they made their way together to the Tube station, he wasn't horrible at all.

It wasn't until the next morning that she realised she hadn't rung Sissy. She got straight on the phone to her.

'Hello? Who's this?' Sissy asked.

'It's Sarah.'

'Who?'

'Your sister? Sarah? The one who bakes you bread?'

'Sorry. I don't remember you.'

'Come off it, Sissy, I'm sorry I didn't ring last night. I was busy.' She felt like an arse as soon as she said it. 'I was stupid not to ring. I'm sorry,' she said again. 'Will you let me off if I bring you a nice loaf tomorrow?'

'You'd bring one anyway. I want muffins.'

The little breadmailer.

* * *

The loaf still held a tiny bit of warmth when she got to Whispering Sands, but Sissy wasn't waiting as usual at the entrance. She really was mad, Sarah thought.

She found her hunched over her coloured pencils at her desk.

'Playing hard to get?' Sarah asked from the doorway.

'I'm busy, that's all,' she said, pushing back her chair. Then she went to Sarah and wrapped her arms around her big sister. 'It's nice to see you.'

Sarah felt herself well up.

They ate their toast in the garden, where the cherry trees were starting to bloom. Sarah didn't let herself think about where she might be next. Every time she glanced at Sissy she wanted to tell her what was going on. But sometimes change was hard for her, and knowing about it before anything was certain only stressed her out. So instead they sat munching their toast in the sunshine.

'Look, Ben's here!' Sissy announced. 'Hi Ben, we're eating Sarah's toast.'

He came across the garden from the conservatory doors. 'Can I have some?' His big brown eyes pleaded with Sissy.

Sissy wavered, then said, 'Okay, a small piece. Sarah will cut it. She won't let me.'

'It's not that I won't let you cut it, Sissy. It's that I can't leave you alone with it or you'll eat the whole thing.'

'Guilty!' she sang.

Where did she pick up these things? Sarah went inside to make more toast for Ben.

She was just leaving when Kelly caught up with her. 'Hey, Sarah, I'm glad I saw you. You're not usually here on a Wednesday?'

'Special circumstances. I brought Sissy some muffins. The front desk put them away for her for breakfast. What's up?' She dared to hope for good news.

They automatically started walking outside.

'They're sending out the letters tomorrow,' she said. 'Thirty days. Have you had any luck?'

Sarah's heart sank. Now it was real. 'Robin's looking into more places but they're further away. Will the facility have any recommendations or anything?'

Kelly shook her head. 'They're being useless. They even dragged their feet on a reference for me. I have found something though.' She looked away for a second. 'I'm going to miss everyone.'

Her heart went out to Kelly. Not only did she have to find another job; she was leaving all her colleagues and patients who probably seemed a bit like family. 'I'm so sorry that you have to leave, Kelly, but it's ace that you've found another job. Will it be as nice, do you think?'

She nodded. 'I think so. It's up near Cambridge though, so it means moving. I'll put my flat on the market, so hopefully it'll sell soon. I can't afford to rent and pay a mortgage for very long.' She blew out her cheeks. 'This sucks.'

'It does suck.' In the back of her mind Sarah had hoped that Kelly would find another home close by, one that was as good as Whispering Sands and had a space for Sissy. But Cambridge was too far. They had a month to find an alternative.

Chapter Thirty-Four

Catherine

Before Catherine could say *I don't want to go*, it was the morning of Richard and Magda's wedding. Richard was being uncharacteristically needy, phoning nearly every day about some minor nuptial detail, as if she'd signed on as his wedding consultant. When she told him to piss off with his questions about which negligee to get Magda as part of his wedding gift to her, he'd whined, 'But you're my best friend.'

Was she though? Was she really, when he'd sold off half of her business and stuck her with his fiancée as an officemate?

It was true that they'd been through a lot together, but when she'd left Washington she wasn't even sure if they'd ever talk again.

They didn't for many months, at least not directly. There had been a flurry of activity through solicitors over the divorce details. Then it was like Catherine-and-Richard had never existed. It had hardly seemed possible.

The guilt had been the hardest to deal with in the months after she'd come back. What kind of person was she, to throw away her marriage for an imaginary relationship? Delusional? Selfish? All of the above.

Not foolish though. No matter how badly she felt, the fact remained: she and Richard weren't in love with each other. She had just been sorry that they weren't friends any more, either.

So she'd been shocked when he'd called her for her birthday. That was nearly two years after the divorce. He'd acted like Washington and Jose had never happened. She'd been so grateful to be let in from the cold that she hadn't mentioned it.

That had set a precedent. She'd rung him up on his birthday. They'd talked at Christmas and eventually they'd stopped using holidays as excuses and just rang whenever they felt like it. By the time he'd moved back to London it had been like they'd never been married at all.

Now she understood that when you've spent years sharing your deepest, darkest, most personal self with someone and then cut them completely out of your life, it calls your judgement into question. The ego liked a gentle transition. Best friend was the cosy B&B just down the road from intimacy. It let them both believe they'd made good decisions when it came to love. Even if they weren't really best friends any more.

Richard's wedding day wasn't the time to say any of that. Let him think what he wanted about her. She felt better for having moved him from one box to the other.

She had more immediate things to worry about anyway. She was about to spend the day with all of Richard's friends and family.

So what, exactly, were you supposed to wear to your ex-husband's wedding?

Not white, obviously, though technically the option should still be open, given that the seven-months-pregnant bride wouldn't be wearing it either.

Blue? No, thanks to that stupid *something old, something*

292

new tradition. Not black either. She didn't want to look like she was in mourning. And nothing too ostentatious or they'd think she was trying to compete. Low-key classical risked looking frumpy next to all the summer frocks the other women would wear.

She toyed with the idea of a man's tuxedo or suit, until Sarah pointed out that that's what lesbians sometimes wore to get married.

She finally found something that didn't look disrespectful, dowdy, loud, lesbian or bereaved. It didn't show her cleavage or too much leg, was neither tight nor billowy, not blingy or brazen.

High-necked and sleeveless with a full skirt to the knee, the pale pink background set off large creamy magnolias. It would have to do. She'd run out of time.

She checked her reflection once more just to be sure her make-up was perfect, then balanced the wide-brimmed cream hat on her head and pinned her favourite frog brooch to her summer coat. She'd pin on the fake smile before she got to the church.

Magda wasn't letting anything as trivial as mortal sin keep her from having her dream wedding. Pregnant or not, she was walking down the aisle of Catholic St Etheldreda's near Holborn. The sun shone off the grey stone and dozens of guests were already outside comparing outfits. Catherine tried to quell the butterflies in her tummy, but they flapped like their lives depended on it.

She stood to the side, careful not to catch anyone's eye. She was looking for only one person. Thankfully he was already there.

'Hiya, Catherine,' Paul said. 'Are ya ready for the show?'

He wore his suit and Paul Smith shirt. She'd have to help him find a few more. 'I'm ready. Thank you for coming. I think it'll be instructional in terms of pointers for your dating.'

He waved her words away. 'Aw, no worries. I wouldn't want to go to my ex's wedding alone either.'

'That's not—'

'Let's get inside before the punters take all the good seats.' He looped his arm through hers and ran up the steps so fast that she had to hold on to her hat.

At least it meant nobody could stop her to chat.

She headed for an unfamiliar usher, murmuring 'bride' when asked which side she was on. If pressed she could always say she wanted to fill out that side since she and Magda did work together and, being from another country, she wouldn't have as many guests.

It was only when they were seated that she dared to look around.

They seemed to have gatecrashed a models' casting call. Uniformly slender and blonde, the twenty-something women all around her chattered away in Hungarian or heavily accented English. A few glanced curiously at her but registered no interest. The men in the pews, however, were more appraising and she knew she looked good. Though Paul hadn't said so. She'd remind him later of the importance of compliments.

Richard looked relaxed at the front of the church. He was smiling and joking with friends and family in the front rows. His brows raised in question when he caught her eye. Not about Paul, since he'd known she was bringing him. But why was she on the bride's side? Catherine shrugged, waved and grinned in what she hoped passed for immense jubilation and heartfelt congratulations.

Those were nearly her genuine feelings. If his chosen bride hadn't been Magda, Catherine knew she'd be happy for him. She just hoped he wasn't making a mistake. Did he really love her as much as he needed to for a lifelong commitment? He'd made that mistake once. She didn't want to see him make it again.

All eyes swivelled to the back as the bridal procession music started and Magda made her entrance.

She looked angelic, despite the large bump swelling beneath her dove grey empire-waist dress. Catherine felt herself welling up despite her misgivings. Maybe it would be all right.

The priest went on, sending Catherine's mind spiralling back to her own ceremony, which had been short and sweet, in her parents' garden. 'The quickest route to the party,' Richard had joked. Now there he was, kneeling through religious readings that he didn't believe in and a speech by the priest that seemed to take hours.

Finally they exchanged their vows and Richard officially became a husband again. Catherine expected to feel some kind of tug, some wobble at watching him marry another woman, but she felt strangely subdued. Only the concern that he was making a mistake stuck with her.

They all followed the couple back up the aisle and into the sunshine. It didn't take long before the first of Richard's side approached Catherine.

'Kate, old girl, Richard said you'd be here today. I have to say I'm surprised, but then you never did know when to quit.'

Richard's cousin hadn't improved with age. As ginger as his relative but with none of the charm, he'd disliked Catherine since Richard took her to Ibiza with them in their last year at uni. 'Alfie, always a pleasure.' She wasn't about to rise to his bait. 'May I introduce my friend Paul? Paul, this is Richard's cousin, Alfie.'

Paul put his hand out to shake Alfie's. 'I figured all the gingers here were related,' Paul said, smiling.

'It's Titian, actually,' Alfie sniffed.

'Sorry?'

'My hair is Titian. It is not ginger.'

'Looks ranga to me, mate, but whatever makes you feel better.'

'Bloody criminal,' Alfie muttered, moving away.

'Fanta pants,' came Paul's reply.

She should be cross with him for the social gaffe, but she could have kissed him as they made their way to the reception.

Magda's parents were throwing the party at the Dorchester Hotel. The ballroom looked like Swarovski had vomited all over the tables. Every surface sparkled. Even the chairs looked made of crystal. The only things that weren't snow-white or crystal were those bloody blue napkins. They looked like the first ones she'd chosen.

Most of Richard's other friends kept their distance. They probably weren't sure what to say. His mother wasn't tongue-tied though.

'Catherine, I always wanted it to work out with you two,' she said after a few too many glasses of champagne. Catherine's heart went out to her. In some ways she'd taken the break-up harder than either of them had.

'But you're going to have a grandchild soon,' she said by way of compensation.

Joy swept over her former mother-in-law's face. 'That will be wonderful,' she said. 'And one day I hope you'll be a mum too.'

Catherine smiled tightly. 'Thank you. We'll see what the future has in store.'

She knew she'd have to talk to the bride eventually, but she didn't expect the conversation when it came. Magda slipped into Paul's chair when he went to the loo.

She was literally glowing. Her face sparkled with the glitter powder that only a twenty-three-year-old can get away with. 'Catherine, thank you for coming,' she said.

They kissed on the cheek. 'You look beautiful, Magda. And the napkins are perfect.'

296

Magda puffed with pride. 'Thank you. And I am glad to see you with Paul,' she said.

'Oh, we're not . . . I'm not *with* him, Magda. I told you, he's here in a professional capacity.'

But Magda smiled. 'You do not fool me, Catherine. I've read his file.'

'I don't understand.'

'I know what you are doing. Teaching him about wine? And art? Hogarth? The Paul Smith shirt? The haircut and having him read *Adrian Mole*?'

'I'm just giving him some pointers to round him out and help with his dating, Magda.' She felt cross that this woman had gone into his file. Paul was her client.

'You are making him into Richard.'

'What?! Magda, your pregnancy hormones are getting the better of you.'

But she only nodded, more certain of her discovery. 'It's obvious, Catherine. You are moulding your perfect man. He happens to also be my perfect man, but since Richard has married me, I don't mind you making another one. Ah, Paul,' she said when she saw him approaching. 'We were just talking about you. Thank you for coming. Be sure to have the cake. It's my mother's recipe from Hungary.'

With that she moved to the next table, leaving Catherine stunned.

Not because Magda was so ridiculous.

Because she might be right.

She had been turning Paul into the type of man she'd like to be with, from the refined tastes in wine and food to a love of the Impressionists to his manicures and well-timed compliments.

And a woman with less life experience than a mayfly had figured it out before her.

'Are you all right?' Paul was staring at her. 'Ya look funny.'

297

Her phone rang. Saved by the bell.

It was Sarah. 'Sorry, I have to take this.' She hurried from the ballroom. There was no way she'd tell Paul what Magda had said.

'Hi Catherine, are you at Richard's wedding?' Sarah asked.

'Yes, we're at the reception now. Is everything okay?'

'I've lost my keys and can't get into the house. Can I come get yours?'

'Where are you? Did you come home last night?' She'd still been out when Catherine went to bed.

'Erm, no. Can I come get your keys? Rachel is at her parents'. You're in London, right?'

'Yes, we're at the Dorchester at the bottom of Park Lane. Ring me again when you get to the hotel and I can come out to the lobby.'

At least waiting for Sarah would distract her from the news that she was Dr Frankenstein.

Chapter Thirty-Five

Rachel

'Have you seen James's drawings?' Rachel's mum asked over the family dinner table.

Rachel nodded, fighting down her emotions. Not about his drawings. They were good, and probably better now that his professor had helped him, but they weren't what was giving her the sleepless nights.

Every time she thought about him she thought about Sarah, and what they might or might not be doing together.

But she didn't have the headspace to let the fact that they might be boffing distract her. She hadn't worked so hard for a decade to derail herself now, especially because of a man. Let them have mad, passionate monkey sex. They could swing from the light fixtures for all she cared. That's exactly what she told herself every time that sick feeling rose up to ambush her.

'They're good,' she told her mum. 'He's working with his prof on them.' She waited for her reaction to this obvious cheating.

'So he should,' Genevieve said. 'I've offered to help you too. I wish you'd let me.'

'But I don't want your help!'

She knew how ungrateful that sounded. 'I mean, I appreciate the offer, I really do, but I want to do this on my own.'

'Sweetheart, even with someone else's advice they're still your drawings, your designs. You're the only one who can translate your vision onto the page.'

Rachel felt herself caught up in her mum's direct gaze.

'You have this idea that buildings are created in a vacuum,' Genevieve continued. 'Do you think that Christopher Wren came up with St Paul's from his imagination alone? He was heavily influenced by French Baroque, you know.'

'Maybe,' Rachel conceded. 'But he didn't have Jules Hardouin-Mansart looking over his shoulder, telling him how to design the dome.'

'That's not what I'd do with your drawings,' her mum murmured. 'There's nothing wrong with having a sounding board. I wish you'd stop trying to do everything yourself. Don't you think I've had advice along the way? All architects do, if they're honest. That's not cheating. It's using the knowledge that the design community has built up over decades. And in a way, the building isn't really even yours. It becomes part of the fabric of the city.'

'I just don't want to feel like I'm not able to do it myself.'

Genevieve reached out and squeezed Rachel's hand. 'All I'm saying is that you don't have to, and there's no shame in that. Will you let me see?'

'I don't have them with me.'

'Next time you come then.'

Rachel knew her mum was right. She was designing a public space, not some private indulgence to prop up her ego.

That didn't calm her nerves when she showed Genevieve the drawings a few days later.

Her mum stayed quiet as she looked at them. It was worse than when Rachel had presented her master's project

300

to her prof. He'd sat at his desk peering into the scale model and studying the drawn plans that she'd sweated over for months. He'd seen drafts, of course, but that didn't make waiting for his pronouncement any easier. Every second that ticked by convinced Rachel she wasn't going to make the cut. He'd break it to her gently because he liked her. Then Rachel would thank him and wait till she got outside to cry.

But he hadn't failed her. He said her design showed a solid grasp of the brief, and a nice flair for aesthetics.

Maybe her mother would give her a pass too.

Genevieve took her time. She gave nothing away with the few questions she asked.

Finally Rachel couldn't take it. 'Mum, are you going to say anything?!'

'You said you don't want advice, so I'm trying not to give any. But I do like it.'

That wasn't as bad as she feared. 'But?'

'There's no but. I like it.'

That wasn't enough. 'What would make you love it?'

Genevieve's eyes widened. 'Do you want advice? I thought you didn't.'

'I'd like to know what would make you love it,' she said carefully.

Over the next two hours Genevieve gently made suggestions. Rachel left full of advice about improving her building. She just didn't know if she'd use it.

By the time the Zigler meeting came round, she'd worn down all her rubbers, tweaking her designs. She felt punch-drunk. She just wanted the day to be over.

Of course, she wouldn't tell James that as he studied her design in the few minutes they had to wait before Zigler arrived.

'I'm glad you didn't show me these earlier,' he finally said. 'They're seriously good, Rach.'

'Thanks.' She was too close to the project now to trust her own judgement. But she did think they were good. 'May the best man or woman win.'

'Yeah, about that,' he said, pulling at his shirt collar where his tie cinched his neck. 'Let's agree that, no matter which design they choose, we go out after work tonight to celebrate, okay?'

She was tempted to make a quip about celebrating with Sarah, but stopped herself when she saw his expression. It reminded her of the old days. 'Agreed,' she said just as they heard footsteps on the stairs.

'Show time,' James whispered. 'Good luck.'

Eric, George and Philip trudged up the stairs. They sounded as out of breath as last time. Ed herded them from behind. 'Here we are,' he said. 'You remember James and Rachel?'

'Of course,' said Philip, head of the Ziglers. 'It's a pleasure to see you again. We're looking forward to seeing what you've got today.'

They moved to the conference room. James and Rachel sat next to each other on one side of the table. United front and all.

They'd each have five minutes to introduce their design and then turn over the drawings for the clients to dissect.

Rachel went first. Her voice shook as she talked through her interpretation of the brief and the influences on her design. 'We're all magpies,' she finished. 'We snatch ideas from everywhere.' She didn't look at James when she said this, in case he took that as a judgement.

Then she slid her designs across the table.

Her mum had been full of ideas. They were the kind of ideas that won design prizes, ideas born out of decades of experience. Some day Rachel wanted to have ideas like that.

But she didn't have them yet.

She knew her mum was right. Nobody was completely free from outside influences. But that was different from consciously using another architect's advice to improve your design.

So she didn't do it.

The clients were examining the cleaned-up designs that Rachel had shown to her mum. She just hoped it was enough.

She waited, hardly breathing.

Would this little stroll along the moral high ground be worth it if she lost the commission? What if she had the wrong idea about morality in the first place? Her mum said she'd take the help if it was offered. James already had taken it from his prof. What would Ed have done? She couldn't ask him. It might cast doubt on her designs if he didn't believe she really was asking for a friend. Or it might make him suspicious of James. And no matter what she thought, she wouldn't be the one to rat him out.

Philip finally spoke. 'This is really very good.'

At his words the other two clients nodded emphatically.

'Ha!' Rachel half shouted, clapping her hands together. Possibly not the most professional response. But what a relief. She glanced at James, who was grinning at her. She wasn't sure she'd have been as gracious if roles were reversed.

She soon got the chance to find out.

She watched the clients' faces as they considered the competing design. How much of it was James's and how much was his prof's? She felt bad even thinking that but she couldn't help it. She knew he was a good architect, but was he that good?

Philip thought so. 'I love this design,' he said after a few minutes. 'It's functional and innovative at the same time.'

There was more emphatic nodding and Rachel's heart

sank. Last time nothing seemed to quite please them. Now they acted like James and Rachel farted rainbows. She just hoped her congratulatory smile to James looked real.

'This is going to be a tough call,' Philip continued. 'Thank you, both, for your efforts. We'll take some time to look at the designs in detail and get input from some of the others, and come back to you, all right?'

More waiting?! She wanted to grab Philip by the lapels and scream in his face, *Just make a freakin' decision!* Her nerves couldn't take much more of this.

Instead she calmly said that she looked forward to talking with them again.

And the Oscar goes to . . .

'Look at the bright side,' said James later as he set her wine in front of her. 'At least they won't go to a competitor for the design.'

Except that James was a competitor, Rachel thought. 'Yeah, I guess. Ed wins either way.'

'Your design is really good, Rach. I wasn't just blowing smoke up your skirt.'

'So is yours. Ditto the skirt.' She wanted to ask him about his prof's help. Instead she said, 'I showed my design to my mum.'

'You said you'd never do that. I'm glad you changed your mind. What did she say?'

'She liked it . . . she had suggestions though.'

'Well she would, wouldn't she? She's a great architect.' He looked into her eyes. 'Was it hard to take her advice?'

'I didn't take it. I listened, but I didn't make the changes. I used the same design I showed her.'

He nodded, gazing around the pub. The project was taking its toll on him too, she noticed. There were dark circles under his eyes. Or maybe the late nights with Sarah were to blame.

'I'm not surprised,' he said. 'You're the most independent woman I know.'

'You mean stubborn.'

He laughed. 'Completely pig-headed, but also self-sufficient and secure. You know your own mind, what you want and what you don't.'

She wasn't so sure about that any more.

'I admire you a lot, Rachel.'

She waited for the punchline but it didn't come. He was serious. 'Thanks.'

'This doesn't feel much like a celebration, does it?' he asked. 'I'm just relieved it's over. When they do finally make up their minds, what do you say we go out to properly celebrate?'

Again she wanted to mention Sarah. It was the perfect in. But she didn't want to sound petty, or worse, jealous.

She'd been biting her tongue for weeks now anyway, every time she saw Sarah. She had no right to tell her not to go out with James. Besides, she was the one who got him to sign up for RecycLove in the first place. How unfair would it be to try to tell him who he could date?

'Yeah, we can go out when this is all over,' she said. 'We'll get a magnum of champagne for one of us to cry into.'

He clinked her glass with his pint. 'Seriously, Rach, we both deserve this.'

Yes, but they both knew that only one of them was going to win.

Chapter Thirty-Six

Sarah

Sarah felt like she could sleep for a week. How did celebs go out until the wee hours every night and not look like death warmed up? Forget the herbal tea. She was drinking so much caffeine that her blood type was probably Dark Roast Positive.

She slathered on another layer of under-eye concealer. Now it looked like Nate had trowelled on the bathroom grout. Sighing, she rubbed it off and downed the last of her cold coffee, and went downstairs.

Rachel was reading on the sofa. 'You're off?'

'Yeah. See you later?'

Rachel stared at her. 'Or in the morning.'

If only Rachel would say something. Then at least everything would be out in the open one way or the other.

On the other hand, whenever she imagined that conversation she felt a bit sick. What a coward she was.

But, she promised herself as she bolted the door behind her, if Rachel said one word about it she'd stop the whole charade. The last thing she wanted to do was hurt her friend over a guy.

She probably shouldn't be going out anyway. Not with the *Bake Off* audition in the morning. But every time she started a text to cancel, the boring old sofa-bound Sarah threatened to re-emerge. She didn't want that to happen.

Which was why she found herself later at another trendy restaurant past her bedtime, stifling yawns as she explained her newest card idea.

'So it's for Trekkies,' she said. 'Live long and prosper together.' She gave him the Vulcan salute.

He laughed. 'And you're constantly having to come up with new ideas like this?'

'Yeah, but they're almost always shot down in flames. It gets depressing. Even more depressing is when they take the idea and ruin it. Like my personalised cards. I wanted names. They just put out a bunch of cards with common initials. That's not very personalised.'

'I guess it's better than nothing. And I'd prefer my initial to my name, actually. It's so middle-England boring.' He pulled a face.

'Really? I quite like it.'

'I think I like J better.'

'Well, then I guess I can call you J, though I'm not a big fan of nicknames. I prefer Sarah.' Just so they were clear, she didn't find anything charming about being called Sair or, worse, S.

'What about your sister?'

'Sissy?'

'Yeah. That sounds like a nickname?'

Sarah nodded, smiling. 'And that was my fault too. Her name is Sophie but she had a lisp when she was small. She sounded so cute when she called herself Thofie that I started calling her Sissy so to get her to say Thithy.'

'Nice sister.'

'I know, it sounds cruel now but I swear I love her more than anything in the world. Sissy stuck. She's had a lot of speech therapy since then, by the way.'

'And what about the rest of her care? I guess it must be hard sometimes to look after her. I don't have anything to compare it with but I can imagine you have to deal with the council a lot.'

'A lot, yeah. It's a pain sometimes. There's so much bureaucracy and hoops to jump through but it's got to be done to get residential care for her. Otherwise she'd have no place to live and she's only sixteen. She's not old enough to be on her own. Maybe she can be in sheltered accommodation one day. I'd like that for her, though she's got lots of friends where she is. I'd hate for her to be isolated. I'm not able to see her every day.'

He was probably wondering if that would be an issue. She couldn't blame him. It was a lot to ask for someone to understand. She shook herself. She wasn't exactly being the life of the party. 'Anyway, enough about Thithy and me. Thanks for tonight. This has been fun.'

'It doesn't have to be over yet. Would you like to check out an eighties night? I've heard it's great. Just to prove that my Oyster card does work outside Zone 1, it's out in East London behind an old gasworks.'

'Oh?' They'd never ventured further east than Soho before and even that was a stretch. He claimed that travelling outside a 'W' postcode gave him a rash.

But being so close to her house wasn't part of the plan. She didn't want him inviting himself over. That *would* be hard to explain. Besides, tonight was definitely not a sleepover night. Her conscience twanged again. 'I've got the *Bake Off* audition tomorrow. I probably shouldn't.'

'We could just swing by though. It's still early. If you go home now you'll probably only stay awake worrying about tomorrow. Besides, it's practically on your street. You're going in that direction anyway. Tell me when I've given you enough reasons.'

'You're very persuasive.'

'I don't want to make you do anything you'd rather not.'

'Oh but I'd rather! And I can always just have one drink. The espresso's kicked in anyway.'

It was a quick Tube ride and a pleasant walk to the huge warehouse. Loads of people stood at the door in leg warmers and Day-Glo. Sarah could feel the now-familiar excitement building with the music. Her tummy was even buzzier than usual because she knew all the songs, thanks to her mum's complete love affair with the eighties. 'I'm going to marry that George Michael,' she used to say. Sarah sometimes fantasised about how she'd casually introduce him to her classmates. 'Oh, this is my stepdad, Mr Michael. We just call him George though.'

As if she'd conjured him with the memory, just as they got through the door she heard it.

What's that? Jitterbug, you say?

'Ooh, "Wake Me Up Before You Go Go", I love this song!' She grabbed his hand. 'Come on, let's dance.'

It was impossible not to flail her arms like she'd done with her mum in their kitchen, snappy fingers and swingy hips and laughing like a crazy person.

'You're a natural!' she shouted into his ear as his neck bobbled in time to his flapping arms.

'It's because I've got rhythm in my bones,' he said. 'I know you're impressed.'

She was even more impressed when he head-bobbed seamlessly into 'Karma Chameleon', singing the words like he was Boy George's backup singer.

'This is the best music ever!' she nearly screamed in his ear as 'Flashdance' came on and her feet started pounding the floor along with everyone else's.

The music flowed over them and it felt so good to let herself go that she didn't want to stop.

Later, her throat hitched when Agnetha and Anni-Frid's voices floated over them. 'Super Trouper' was another of Mum's favourites. So maybe he noted her change in mood. Maybe it was just appropriate for a slower song. Either way, it felt nice to be in his arms for the few moments until the song sped up. Then they broke apart and shouted lyrics at each other. She was pretty sure she had the wrong words but it didn't matter.

It was nearly four a.m. by the time she staggered home and fell into bed with her clothes still on. She still had ABBA buzzing in her ears.

Of course, the house was silent when her alarm went off a few hours later. Catherine and Rachel wouldn't leave their beds at sunrise unless their mattresses were on fire.

With just four hours to bake her morning muffins and the savoury rosemary and sea salt focaccia, then quickly shower and get to the audition, she may as well be on the show already. Ready, steady, bake!

She quickly made the focaccia dough so that it had time to rise before she put it in the oven. She could make focaccia in her sleep, which was handy given how she felt.

Then she pulled out all the muffin ingredients and started preparing them. Carefully she buttered the tins and grated the carrots. She'd found them especially for the recipe, sampling so many from the local markets that she could probably see better in the dark.

She never wanted to think about morning muffins again, but at least she was finally happy with the recipe. And most importantly, so was Sissy.

She needed to double the batch to make sure she'd end up with a dozen perfect little treats. She worked quickly, creaming the butter, adding sugar, then eggs and all the other ingredients.

But there was definitely no time to shower and still get everything properly baked. A fully risen focaccia was more important than clean hair. Besides, the aroma of baked goods should cancel out any lingering *eau de dance floor*.

It was harsh to have auditions so early in the day, she thought as she carried her still-warm offerings to the Tube station. No one wanted to turn up with a day-old cake, so they'd all have to get up early to make a start. And since people were coming from all over the UK, at least they'd be as sleep-deprived as she was.

Although she might have underestimated her competition's hygiene habits. She looked around the room in the community hall where the auditions were being held. No one else seemed to be wearing last night's make-up and everyone's hair looked cleaner than hers. She should have remembered that they were being judged on their ability to bake *for telly*. Self-consciously she ran her fingers through her tangles. At least day-old make-up was better than none at all.

Talk about intimidating. Most of the others had gone for complicated bakes. One grandma-type had a clear box filled with choux pastry swans.

Well, let them have their cream-filled birds. She was confident in her bread and muffins. They were down-to-earth, honest offerings, and exactly how she liked to bake.

But as she found a spot on a row of folding chairs with the other contestants she started to wonder how honest she was really being. She had a bit of mascara in one eye that kept making her wink. Her tummy churned from the vodka and Red Bulls she'd drunk at the club and her feet hurt from dancing in heels.

Vodka and Red Bull? A few months ago the only time she had vodka was if a fancy chef spooned it in a cream sauce over penne pasta. And sore feet used to be a sign that she needed to buy new running shoes.

Lately she hardly recognised herself. It was taking a lot of effort to have fun. Was it all worth it?

A woman with a three-ring binder who'd been calling the contestants forward finally came for her. 'Thanks for waiting, Sarah. This way, please, the judges are ready for you.'

Her nerves swooped down as she made her way to the long table where the judges waited. 'We're being filmed?' she asked, staring at the two cameras aimed at the table.

'It's just so we can see how you'd look on air. Don't pay them any attention.'

Yeah, right.

When the judges introduced themselves – Mark and Margaret – Sarah barely squeaked out her own name. They were in their late fifties or sixties and actually weren't scary at all as they asked her questions about why she liked baking. Then Margaret cut one of her muffins in quarters and started to pinch and poke it.

'Nice bake on the bottom,' she said.

'And a good rise,' Mark added.

Margaret was the first to take a bite. Sarah knew instantly that something was wrong. Instead of blissful excitement, her eyebrows knitted together.

'I think something went wrong with the sugar,' Margaret said. 'How much did you use?'

'A hundred and seventy-five grams. No, three fifty. I doubled the recipe.' She kept her eyes on Margaret but she could feel the cameras trained on her.

'Are you sure?' Mark asked gently. 'It's got a more savoury flavour. Here, have a taste.'

'I'm sure I . . .' But was she sure? She was so tired this morning. She remembered cracking four eggs into the bowl, and shredding three big carrots. But had she doubled the sugar?

Obviously not, judging by their faces.

She took a bite. If they had to eat it, she did too. It reminded her of those non-fat muffins that people sometimes pretended were as good as the real thing. She tried not to grimace.

'Let's move on to the focaccia,' Mark said. 'Rosemary and sea salt?'

'That's right,' Sarah said, feeling ill now. She'd made such an amateur mistake. And of all the times to mess up. Why couldn't it have been something unimportant like her birthday cake? But no, everyone had been dead chuffed with that.

Again they pinched and prodded at the spongy bread. 'Is the sea salt in the bread itself?' Margaret asked.

'No it's on the . . .'

But it clearly wasn't on the top. She'd forgotten to add the sea salt before putting it in the oven. She could visualise the box right there on the table too. Fat lot of good it was doing in her imagination. 'I forgot the sea salt. Should I just go now?'

Margaret smiled at her. 'No, no. Let's taste the bread first. It's another very good bake, Sarah, and I'm sure it's delicious.' She took a bite and practically made yummy-yummy-in-my-tummy hand gestures. She was probably just exaggerating to make Sarah feel better, but it did help take the sting off.

She knew it was all over. She took her mediocre baked goods, apologised to the judges for wasting their time, and slunk from the auditorium.

She leaked angry tears all the way home. The judges' kindness only made her feel worse. No matter how many times they claimed she'd made simple mistakes, she knew she wouldn't have made them if she hadn't been out all night pretending to be the party girl of the century.

It wasn't till she got home that she caught sight of herself.

Her mascara had run under her eyes and last night's hair was that morning's rat's nest. She hardly recognised herself. She scrubbed off the make-up, brushed out her hair and crawled under her duvet.

Chapter Thirty-Seven

Catherine

Paul wanted to talk in person and Catherine had the sinking feeling that she knew what it was about.

He kissed her cheek when they met at the office door. Were those lips lingering?

'I've just made a tea for myself. Would you like something to drink?' she asked as they moved towards the little round table in the corner of her office.

'Maybe later, thanks.'

'So.'

'So,' he said.

'You wanted to talk?'

Paul squirmed like he'd been sent to the schoolmaster for having dirty magazines in his desk. 'I had a nice time at the wedding.'

'Me . . .' She was about to say 'me too' but that would have been a total lie. 'I'm glad you enjoyed yourself. Why don't you let me get you a drink? Coffee, no sugar, right? I'll be right back.'

She fled to the kitchen with the memory of the weekend hanging tightly around her neck.

* * *

She hadn't expected the wedding to be easy, so she wasn't surprised to be right. Just not for the reasons she'd thought. She'd so convinced herself that she didn't want Richard marrying the wrong woman that it never occurred to her how she'd feel if he ended up marrying the right one. As it turned out, not nearly as gracious as she'd assumed.

She'd managed to avoid any more of the groom's side, although it meant spending more time in the loo than someone with a urinary tract infection.

When she came out just in time to hear Richard start his speech she was tempted to return to the cubicle, but her former mother-in-law spotted her, so she couldn't turn back.

She wove her way between the tables to find her seat. At least she knew what Richard was going to say. He wasn't one to reinvent the wheel.

Sure enough, he started by thanking his parents and Magda's. He told her bridesmaids how gorgeous they were, as he was contractually obliged to do. He made a crack about the stag do and his best man pretended it was a new joke. Then he spoke to Magda.

'When I met you,' he'd said, 'I didn't believe you were really interested in me.'

Catherine suppressed a snort. It wasn't the time for heckling.

'I mean, look at you! You're so gorgeous, and as I got to know you I realised that you're also smart and fun and warm . . . and you're rich.'

The room erupted in a mixture of hoots and gasps. Richard held up his hands.

'Calm down, dears. Which means, Magda, that you're not with me for the wrong reasons.' He turned to his bride, who had stood to look him in the eye. 'Magda, I am in love with you. Madly, passionately, deeply in love. And I can't wait to spend the rest of my life showing you that.'

316

Magda threw herself into his arms. His microphone was still on to broadcast her next words. 'I love you more than anything in the world,' she said.

Catherine took it all in as the whole room chorused their ahhs. Of course there was nothing unusual about newlyweds professing their love on the big day.

Only, this was Richard. And he hadn't done it the first time around. That's what felt like a kick in the teeth.

She returned to her office with Paul's coffee. 'So, what did you want to talk about?'

'Well, you and me, actually,' he said.

That's what she was afraid of. 'Let me stop you there, Paul. I feel like I may have given you the wrong impression when I asked you to come to the wedding. I truly did think it would be instructional.'

He laughed. 'Aw, that's bullshit, Catherine. Come on, it was a flimsy excuse and you know it.'

Busted. 'Well, okay. I admit I might have had a tiny ulterior motive.' So she didn't want to go to her ex-husband's wedding alone. Anyone claiming it would be an easy day was either deluded or on some serious medication.

'It's just not very professional,' he continued.

That stung, but he had a point. She had no right to use someone as a Rent-a-Date just because her business had a database full of single men. 'I'm so sorry, Paul. It wasn't appropriate.' Where did she get off using one of her clients like that? She could be struck off the register (if matchmakers had such a thing). They'd take away her little black book.

'Now, I'm happy to stay with the agency,' he continued, 'because I still want to meet someone. And you're great, Catherine, but I just don't feel like that about you.'

'You don't . . .'

'No, I'm sorry.'

317

She couldn't decide if it was worse for him to think she liked him, or to know that she'd been turning him into her ex-husband.

The second one, she decided. At least he hadn't noticed that.

She made a regretful face. 'Well, I understand. Thanks for being so honest with me, Paul.'

'I hope you're not too disappointed.'

She kept a straight face. 'Not at all.'

'Don't get me wrong, Catherine. Casual dating is fine as long as both people want it. But if one is really looking for more, ultimately it's a goner. It might be okay for a while, but only because the person isn't being honest with himself . . . Or herself,' he quickly added.

She stared at Paul. He had no idea how right he was. Not about him and her. About her and Richard.

It took Paul one day to realise what Catherine hadn't really admitted to herself until now.

If she hadn't been so bloody-minded about being with Richard back when they were in school, maybe she'd have seen how little he'd really wanted a relationship with her.

But nooo, she couldn't admit that after working so hard for so long. She had to excuse his protests about wanting to be casual, and put any lack of commitment down to his relaxed personality. That was just him taking things slowly, she told herself. Plus, there was plenty of time to settle down.

And if those things weren't true, then that meant Catherine was just trying to convince a man to love her. That would be foolish. Nobody likes to admit they're a fool.

But she had been a fool. Well-intentioned maybe, and hopeful, but still a fool to think that effort could equate to love. Neither of them should have settled. Richard realised that when he met Magda. It was about time it got to be her turn.

'Thank you, Paul. You're absolutely right, and I appreciate your honesty. I'll get working on some more dates for you. We'll find your Ms Right, not just Ms Right-For-Now.'

'Glad you understand, Catherine. And thanks for being cool about it.'

She smiled. Finally she felt like she did understand. 'No problem.'

Magda was waiting outside the door when she opened it to let Paul out. Since the wedding she'd been at a bit of a loss in the office without any planning to do. 'Did you tell him about Georgina?' she asked when he'd left.

'No, Magda, I told you, you need to talk to her first to see if she wants to meet him.'

'Fine. I will do that now.'

'Fine, you do that.'

Catherine was counting the days until Magda went on maternity leave. Hopefully by the time she popped out the sprog she'd have tired of playing matchmaker.

She was back an hour later. 'She will meet him.'

'Really?'

'Why?' Magda asked sharply. 'Is there something wrong with him that I should know about?'

She asked this like she owned the place.

Oh right.

'No, nothing at all,' said Catherine. 'I'm just surprised that Georgina agreed. She's usually very picky. Australians aren't high on her list.'

Magda shrugged. 'We have a good relationship, and I know how to talk to her.'

Implying that Catherine didn't.

'But first she wants to meet your hairy biker. Alis. So please arrange it.'

Something shifted in Catherine's chest. 'Why would she want to meet Alis?'

319

Magda smiled. 'Because I have a plan. I told her all about Alis. She has even seen his photo.'

'But facial hair is non-negotiable,' Catherine murmured.

'It is negotiable if he changes it. So she will meet Alis and then she will think Paul is perfect.'

'You can't lie to clients, Magda. It's immoral.'

'I have not lied. Your notes say that you have talked to Alis about the beard and he would trim it.'

'Yes, but Georgina doesn't like any facial hair. There's a big difference between giving Gandalf a trim and shaving him clean.'

Then something occurred to her. This might just be a way to hurry Magda into early retirement from the business. 'You know what? Never mind. You go ahead and introduce them.'

Georgina would be absolutely livid with Magda for wasting her time like that. She threw a fit when a date put milk in his coffee. Catherine could only imagine what she'd do when she was really angry. In this case, she thought, it would be worth pissing off a client. And since that client was Magda's responsibility, she'd be the one to get it in the neck.

'I'll tell Paul and Alis the good news,' she said.

She rang Paul first. 'There's someone I'd like you to meet. Can I send you her details?'

'Are you trying to suck up to me?'

She laughed. 'Absolutely. I'll email you now.'

Then she phoned Alis. As it rang, her heart began to race. She didn't want to do Magda's dirty work. Though it was, she told herself, all for a good cause.

'Hello?' Alis whispered.

'Alis?' Catherine found herself whispering back. 'Is this a good time?'

She heard chimes sounding in the background.

'My friend has come to feng shui my kitchen,' he said.

'Oh. Do you want to ring me back?'

320

'No, that's okay. He's doing all the work.'

She imagined Alis's friend sweeping bad chi and bread-crumbs from under his cabinets.

'Actually,' he said, still whispering. 'I don't need my kitchen feng shuied, but he's just learning so he needs the practice.'

'It's nice of you to let him practise in your house.' She wondered if a space could be un-feng shuied, in case he got it wrong.

'He was trying to do it in public car parks. I felt sorry for him.'

'Right. Anyway, I'm ringing to talk about another potential date.'

'Great, count me in.'

'But I haven't told you anything about her.'

'That's okay. I trust you.'

His words pierced her conscience.

'She's called Georgina. I'll email you her details.'

Georgina was going to hate him.

Chapter Thirty-Eight

Rachel

Rachel plastered a smile to her face as she answered the door. 'Nate, hi, come in.' He had just three of his boys with him. She wondered if that was good or bad. Ever since he'd flounced off after setting fire to the neighbours' TV they were all paranoid that he'd pull another Houdini. Then the house would never get finished.

'All right. Rachel, isn't it?'

'That's right,' she said.

'I never forget a face. Especially one who makes such good coffee.' He glanced over her shoulder at the stairs to the kitchen. Very subtle.

She sighed. 'You're finishing the bathroom today, right?'

Nate laughed. 'We're gonna try!'

They should bloody try harder, she grumbled as she stomped to the kitchen. If she'd screwed up deadlines like the builders did, Ed would have fired her by now. In what other profession did clients have to beg workers to do the job they were being paid for?

She got herself more and more worked up about Nate. So by the time she sipped the last of her coffee and went into the bathroom to use the loo, and her socked feet went unexpectedly wet, she felt ready to scream.

'Oh God.' That wasn't bath water. She pulled off her socks. 'Nate!'

He popped his head around the corner. 'What's up?'

'The floor in here is soaked with, well, I think you know what it is.'

'Oh. Sorry about that. I guess we should be a bit more careful. Blame the early morning. We're less steady on our feet.' He shrugged as if he'd spilled a bit of tea on the floor.

'It's totally disgusting, Nate, really completely out of order!'

'I'm sensing some tension, Rachel.'

Two of the boys came downstairs to see what the shouting was about.

'If I'm tense it's because it looks like you've sprayed a flippin' fire hose in here!'

The boys giggled.

Nate couldn't look prouder. 'Well I don't like to brag . . .'

Her mobile rang.

'Hey Sarah,' she said, pushing past Nate to go back downstairs.

'Did the builders arrive?'

'Oh yes. They're here. They've pissed all over the bathroom floor.'

'There's a bucket and disinfectant in the cabinet in the kitchen. And a mop that I use just for that.'

'You're serious? You've been mopping up their wee every day?'

Sarah laughed. 'Well they don't exactly do it themselves, do they?'

'That is disgusting. I had no idea you were doing that. Thank you.'

'Not a problem. Be sure to get the mop into the space behind the sink too.'

'Behind the sink? That's nowhere near the toilet.'

'I know.'

They were quiet as they contemplated the acrobatic manoeuvres the builders might be trying in their loo.

'How's the home?' Rachel asked. She and Robin were visiting another potential place for Sissy.

'It's not horrible but definitely not my first choice either. Mum was so lucky to find Whispering Sands. I realise that now.'

'Did she look at a lot of places?'

'Do you know, I'm not sure. She just told Robin and me about Whispering Sands when she found it. She always made everything seem easy.'

'Mums are good at that,' said Rachel. 'You'll find the right place, Sarah Lee, don't worry.'

'I'm trying not to.'

Nate was still working when it was time for Rachel to go. 'This has been a long day for you,' she said to the boy tiling the bathroom wall.

'Simon here can burn the midnight oil to get the wall done,' said Nate, who seemed to be contributing nothing but moral support to the job.

She never thought she'd hear them offer to work longer than planned. 'But you can't stay late tonight. I have a date and there'll be no one here to lock up when you leave.'

Nate sucked his teeth. 'Well then, I'm not sure when we'll be able to come back to finish.'

Rachel glimpsed their future in their half-tiled bathroom.

'Let me check next door,' she told Nate. 'I'll see if they can lock up for us when you leave.' The Rogers-Smiths were going to *love* that. But she didn't have much choice.

She couldn't cancel Thomas. It hadn't been easy to pin him down to another date in the first place. But she couldn't take no for an answer. Not after implying to James that they were practically engaged.

She wished she hadn't done that. She could have said she was dating loads of guys from the website instead. Then she could tell James about someone new when he asked her. Because he kept asking her.

Thomas did seem nice though. At least, he was too nice to reject her when she went through her calendar day-by-day telling him when she was free. And his Scottish accent was still sexy, so that was something. Add a nice dark bar, enough wine and it wouldn't be bad.

But the bar that Thomas chose was bright enough to perform surgery in. It was one of those places that tried to be a bar, a coffee house, performance space and gallery. The kind that had wooden cutlery and plates made of potato starch. They probably hired their staff by beard length.

At least he'd ditched his fleece in favour of a navy jumper. That was progress. A baby step anyway. If only he'd be as funny as his texts.

'Do you want to get some nibbles? I'm a bit hungry,' she said as he poured her some wine. 'I think they have some bigger snacks too, not just these.' She popped a few of the artisan-vegan-socially-responsible-harvested-by-moonlight kale chips into her mouth.

'What are you doing?' he cried.

It was as animated as she'd ever seen him. 'Having some crisps. They're pretty good. Want some?' When she held the bowl out he recoiled like she'd handed him her bowel movement.

'Have you got any idea how many people have had their hands in those? They're bacteria in a bowl.' His normally jovial face was tensely disapproving.

'Oh no, I'm sure they're fine, Thomas. I eat them all the time. How about something from the menu? I can order at the bar.'

He wouldn't be distracted by her offer. 'I don't mean to sound paranoid but there've been loads of studies about it. Even in posh places they find bacteria in the snacks. And E. coli. That's a killer.'

What a downer. Who didn't snarf free snacks when they were drinking? 'A little bacteria never hurt anyone . . . aside from E. coli, I mean.'

But his smile had vanished. 'Two-thirds of people don't use soap when they wash their hands in the loo. A tenth don't even wash at all.'

'Well, we wash ours right? So we don't have to worry about eating each other's wee.' She laughed.

He didn't.

'Anyway, I'll go to the bar for something to eat. Want to share a few things?'

He glanced at the menu, skipping over the cheese page that Rachel had her eye on. From Thomas's point of view the menu must have been fraught with danger.

Olives? Who knew where they'd been? And he might object to pips too on choking grounds. He'd never go for those delicious salty Spanish almonds either, unless they came in an unopened package. Even then she wasn't sure he believed her about the hand-washing.

'How about the meatballs?' he asked. 'And maybe the maple-glazed tempeh?'

'Tinie Tempah's "Maple Glaze"?' she said. 'I don't know that one.' She threw a few gang hand signs and started rapping, '*Yeah, yeah, we bring the stars out. Let's have a toast with maple glaze and get a glass out.*'

He just looked at her.

'Tinie Tempah? The rapper?' She'd learned the song for a

rap duel with James at last year's conference. Best not to elaborate.

'Do you think that's enough food?' Thomas asked, as if she hadn't just made an excellent pun.

So he wasn't familiar with rap stars. She didn't exactly get down with her bitches in the crib at the weekend. Still, she thought, courtesy demanded at least a smile. 'We can always order more if we want,' she said. 'Be right back.'

When she returned to the table a few minutes later he was tucking a wet wipe into his pocket.

'Were you just cleaning the tabletop?'

He shrugged. 'I've got a germ thing.'

'Yeah, I got that from the bacteria talk earlier. I guess you worry a lot about illness?'

'It's probably the worrying that keeps me well.'

'So you think. I never worry about it and I'm never ill. How do you explain that?'

He knocked on the table. 'That's lucky. So far. My mum got a flesh-eating virus.'

'Jesus! Not from bar snacks?'

He laughed. Finally. 'No, she was in Sierra Leone with a medical team. She's a nurse. She's okay now but there's a huge scar on her arm and chest from it.'

'I can see why you're paranoid.'

'I call it prudent, but you're not the first person to tell me I go over the top. Cheers.'

He raised his glass to Rachel's, not allowing them to touch, she noted.

When the waitress brought the food a few minutes later he pulled a Ziploc bag from his coat pocket.

She watched him extract a knife and fork. 'Do you always carry your own cutlery?'

'Are you surprised?' He scrubbed his side plate with a wet wipe so he could scoop some of the meatballs on.

'What about all the chemicals you're probably eating from those wipes?'

'They're baby wipes. They're not dangerous.'

She spooned some of the little meatballs onto her plate.

'Will you have some tempeh too?' he asked.

Under the sticky glaze were lumpy cubes that looked like cellulite. Her dog used to throw up more appetising chunks. 'You go ahead. I'm fine with the meatballs.'

This date was a mistake, Rachel thought as he started talking about university. Much as she wanted to like Thomas, she just couldn't get excited about a joyless man. She loved laughing too much.

Her mind wandered towards James.

James and Sarah.

What did they talk about when they were out together? He probably had her weeing in her pants. Did they meander from one thing to another like Rachel did with him? Did their conversation spark along like lighting one fag off the end of the last?

Knowing Sarah, James probably had no idea what she was talking about half the time. That was one of the loveliest things about her friend. James wouldn't mind it either. He claimed not to know what Rachel was talking about and she wasn't nearly as off the wall.

She knew one thing. He'd have laughed at her Tinie Tempah joke.

'. . . But the distance was too much, so we broke up at the end of my first year at uni,' Thomas was saying.

How long had he been talking? The last thing she remembered about the conversation was that he'd wanted to go into marketing. 'That's too bad,' she said. 'But I suppose at that age it's all about the sex. If you're too far away that makes things difficult, obviously.'

'It wasn't about the sex with Milly and me, though,' he said.

'No, of course not. I wasn't implying . . .'

'We never had sex,' he volunteered.

'Oh, well. Some people start early, that's all I meant.' She could feel her face redden.

'To be honest with you, I'm not an overly sexual person.' He shrugged. 'It's just not that important to me.'

'No, well, of course relationships aren't all about the sex.'

Were Sarah and James having sex? She absolutely didn't want to think about that. But the question kept bashing its way into her head. Sarah had been having sleepovers. So they must be, right? She wasn't one to sleep around, but James would definitely try it on when he got the chance.

She started to feel sick.

'I guess you could say I'm asexual,' she heard Thomas say.

'What does that mean? Like Morrissey? Don't you ever have sex?'

Now he looked uncomfortable. 'Well, not never, but rarely, and under certain conditions.'

Rachel looked at his friendly face and she felt sorry for Thomas. His issues obviously went beyond baby wipes and personal cutlery.

If they ever did have sex he'd probably want to wrap her in cling film first.

She had to wait a decent amount of time after this disclosure to make her excuses. 'I'm sorry, Thomas, but I'm not feeling very well.' This was true. Her tummy was churning. 'Maybe it was the crisps after all. This has been fun, but I'm not sure we're very well-suited for each other. In the long run, I mean. Besides, actually, there's someone else.'

Because the whole time she'd been sitting there with Thomas, she'd been thinking about James. If she hadn't been so cocksure that she knew him all these years, she'd have seen that she hadn't really known him until now.

He wasn't the same person she broke up with. Yes, he was still driven. He was working as hard as she was to win the Zigler account. But he'd also found the balance to make time to take Sarah out. And to join RecycLove in the first place. Sure, he was bolshie, but he also supported her as a colleague and, she realised, as a friend. Add to that that he was kind, fun, engaging and clever, with a connection to her that hadn't dimmed, and there was no denying it. He was exactly who she thought she'd been looking for on RecycLove.

Unconsciously she must have known that already. Where were all the dates she promised herself when she joined the website? She'd had dozens of messages from perfectly reasonable options, but she'd hardly been out every night on dates, had she?

Unfortunately, James had . . . with Sarah.

Thomas smiled. 'I understand, Rachel. Thanks for coming out with me though, and I hope you'll be happy with this other guy.'

'Me too.' There was just the small matter of her best friend being happy with him already.

Chapter Thirty-Nine

Sarah

Sarah didn't need to read the email to know that Paul and Mary wouldn't be judging her next bake. Still, when the message came – a polite but unequivocal no thanks from the producer – she felt the searing shame of the audition all over again.

'You did your best,' said Robin, glancing up from his phone when she told him she wouldn't be Mary's new best friend. Lucy had already rung him twice and now he was texting her. She should just microchip him and be done with it. What did she think he was getting up to with his sisters on a Saturday morning?

They were on the train to Brighton with the rest of London. Never mind that it was the end of March – hardly bikini weather – the sun was shining and everyone was excited about shivering on the windy beach and picking sand out of their sandwiches. Sarah found it a bit tacky there but Sissy loved being by the sea. Add those spinny rides on the pier that'd make her chuck up her candy floss and she was in heaven. She'd nabbed a train seat for herself and was telling the shaven-headed young man sitting beside her all about her plans for the day.

Meanwhile Robin and Sarah stood wedged in the aisle between a girl who kept jabbing her giant handbag into Robin's back and a man who'd actually fallen asleep standing up. He looked like he might be a Brightonian returning home from a night out in London. Every time the train lurched he swayed dangerously, but kept his footing and his grip on the seat.

How did people do a daily train commute? Sarah would be murderous if she had to stand for hours every day in a carriage that smelled of farts and despair.

'Thanks, but I didn't really do my best,' she told Robin as he waited for Lucy's text response. 'I was hung-over when I baked and I screwed up the recipes.'

'*You* were hung-over? What'd you do, have a glass of sherry during *EastEnders*?'

'I was dancing at a club, if you must know, on a date.'

'That's a brilliant idea the night before the audition.'

'Nice one, Robin. Make me feel even shittier.'

'So who's this guy?'

'Just someone I've been seeing for a while.'

'From that website?'

'Uh huh.'

She didn't want to talk about it, and they stood in silence to Brighton.

'Breakfast!' Sissy said as they pushed through the turnstiles at the station and followed the crowd to the waterfront.

'You've had breakfast already,' Robin said. 'You can't be hungry already.'

'What did *you* have for breakfast?' she asked him.

'Just tea. I'm not hungry in the mornings.'

She consulted her watch. 'It's ten thirty-three. Past morning. You should eat.'

He grinned. 'Oh should I? Any idea where?'

'At a caff.'

'Mmm hmm. Will this caff serve toast?'

She shrugged.

The problem with having a toast-obsessed sister was that she saw every outing as an opportunity.

'All right, but we'll split an order. I mean it, Sissy, we're splitting it. One piece each.'

'Fine by me,' she said, like the whole thing was his idea.

'This isn't too bad,' Sarah said later as they sat huddled together on towels spread over the shingle. It might be ten degrees and blowing a gale but at least it was sunny.

'Rock paper scissors?' Robin asked.

'For what?' But Sarah knew. 'Sissy, you don't seriously want to put your feet in? It's cold.'

'Yes I do. Are you coming?'

'We both will,' Sarah said. 'It's not fair for one of us to get to stay warm and dry. Come on, Robin, don't keep your sister waiting.'

She rolled up her jeans and stood up.

'Shit, I've got gooseflesh and I haven't even touched the water yet!' Robin said.

'Think how warm the air will feel when we get out.' She rolled her eyes. That was what their mum always said when she forced them into the freezing sea in Southport . . . though in fairness, not in March.

'You're such a bullshitter,' he said. 'All right, Sissy, you asked for it. Let's go!'

The siblings held hands, with Sissy in the middle, and stepped gingerly over the shingle towards the water. Sissy started to lag behind as they got closer. Sarah and Robin looked at each other over her blonde head, tightened their grip and began to pull her towards the sea.

Anyone listening to her screams would think they were torturing the poor girl . . . if she wasn't laughing so much.

'Oh, oh, that's cold!' Sarah shouted as they ploughed together up to their knees into the English Channel.

'My bollocks are gone,' Robin wheezed. 'And they're not even close to the waterline.'

'You haven't had bollocks for years.'

'Don't say bollocks,' said Sissy.

When Sissy's lips turned a sickly shade of blue they started trying to coax her out of the water. They finally tempted her to shore with the promise of some Brighton rock.

They rubbed themselves warm again, put all their clothes back on and headed for the pier.

Sissy loved the water but the pier was what she'd been waiting for.

Not Sarah. She hated fairground rides. If Sissy wanted to make herself sick, she was on her own. The helter-skelter was about as wild as she could go.

But Sissy wasn't having fun unless she was about to be sick. So they waited together for one of the up-and-down swirly ones to make sure that Sissy got on all right.

She started screaming as soon as the safety bar came down. This alarmed the man sitting next to her.

'Hey, Sissy. Sissy!' Robin shouted, making calming motions with his hands. 'Tone it down a little, will you?'

'You're not the one riding it,' she said.

'She's got you there,' said Sarah.

The ride started and Sissy's screams turned to helpless giggles as she swooped and dove round and round. She loved it.

They put her on every wild ride on the pier. Each time, she screamed while sitting still and giggled when the ride started moving.

It was late afternoon by the time she showed any sign of tiring. But she wasn't giving up.

'One more ride please,' she said.

'One more, Sissy. Just one. You choose.'

This time there was another teenager sitting beside her.

When Sissy started screaming so did the other girl. They locked eyes and screamed, collapsing against each other in hysterics when the ride began to swoop.

Sarah felt ill just watching her.

So what came next shouldn't have surprised anyone. Sissy staggered off the ride, waved to Sarah and Robin, and vomited down the back of the woman in front of her.

'Oh no,' Robin said.

'Do you think it was the Brighton rock?'

'Or the funnel cakes or the fish and chips.'

Sissy was understandably upset. 'It's okay,' Sarah said, finding a serviette in her bag to offer to the woman. 'I'm so sorry. We'll pay to have that cleaned.'

But the woman shook her head. 'That's not necessary. I have children. This top's had worse than vomit on it.' She opened her own bag and pulled out another one. 'Always come prepared to Brighton.'

Sarah wished she had. 'Come on, Sissy, we need to get you cleaned up. Wait here,' she said to Robin. 'We'll be back.'

They found the ladies' loos a little way back up the pier. 'I've got mints,' she told Sissy. 'You can rinse your mouth, then chew one and rinse again. You've got a bit of yuck on yourself. Here.' She wetted a paper towel and scrubbed Sissy's jumper. 'We'll just wash it out, okay? You can wear it with the wet spot or you can just wear your swimsuit with your jacket over it. Your choice.'

'Swimsuit.'

'Okay. I'll take your jumper.' She stuffed it in her bag.

Her phone was ringing. James.

'I have to wee,' said Sissy.

'All right, you go. I'm just going to take this outside, okay? I'll see you in a minute.'

'Sarah, hi,' he said over the din. 'What are you doing? Are you outside?'

'Yeah, I'm in Brighton with my sister and brother. What's up?'

'Not much, just meeting some mates for the football in a little while. Listen, I think we should talk to Rachel soon.'

Just as she feared. It wasn't a casual social call. 'Why now? Has she said something to you?'

'No. That's the problem. She hasn't said anything. I think that means it's bothering her.'

Sarah stared at the growing crowd on the pier. 'I think so too. She hasn't said a word to me. If she felt normal about us she'd have been more nosey than this. We usually talk about everything.'

'That's what I thought. So we should say something to her, right?'

'Do you want to do it?' she asked.

'You should be there too.'

'Do I have to?'

'Well, kind of. She's your friend.'

Sarah snorted at that. Friends didn't do things to make other friends jealous.

'We should do it soon,' he continued.

'I guess so,' she conceded. 'Given the circumstances. I hate to cut you off but can I ring you later? I've got to check on my sister.'

'Oh sure, sorry to hold you up. Have fun. Talk to you later.'

The knot in her tummy grew as she thought about what was coming. What if Rachel threw a wobbly and accused her of being a bad friend?

Who'd blame her? Sarah already thought it about herself. But like James said, they'd gone too far to stop now.

The ladies' cubicles were all full and Sissy wasn't out yet so Sarah waited for her by the sinks. Mothers, children and groups of friends all jostled for space in the long, narrow room. Their voices bounced off the tiled walls. By the time Sarah said, 'No, you go ahead, I'm just waiting for someone' for about the twentieth time, she started losing patience.

'Sissy?' she called. Her sister could spend ages in the loo. 'Sissy? Hurry up please. People are waiting.'

'Sissy?'

She waited for a few more seconds, not wanting to interrupt people in mid-wee.

'Sissy? Answer me, please!'

Sometimes she could be really awkward. 'Sissy, this isn't hide-and-seek.'

She could imagine her holding in her giggles on the other side of one of the doors.

Sighing, she knocked on each one, murmuring 'Sorry' at the exclamations from the other side.

None of the voices were her sister's.

Fear prickled her neck as she hurried outside. What was Sissy wearing? That's right, her swimsuit top. That was black. Did she have her jacket on or not? Her jacket was white. She scanned the heaving crowd, who all seemed to be dressed in black or white.

'Sissy!' She dug out her phone.

'Robin, is Sissy with you?'

'She was with you.'

'I can't find her. She was in the loo and now she's gone.'

'Well she can't have gone far. I'll come toward you. Are you near the loo?'

'Yes, but I need to look for her.'

'Stay there. I'll look for her on the way to you, then you can look and I'll stay by the loo in case she goes back there.'

She could be anywhere, Sarah realised as she hung up and checked the time. She'd thought it had only been a few minutes, but she'd left Sissy in the loo nearly twenty minutes ago. She could be up on the promenade by now, or on the beach. She could be in the water.

What had she been thinking?! It wasn't like she didn't know her sister liked to wander off. The staff at Whispering Sands always kept a very close eye on her. How did they do it with a home full of charges? She'd lost one person in a matter of hours.

Robin was hurrying through the crowd. Now he looked scared too.

'I'm checking towards the front,' Sarah said. If Sissy was back where the rides were then they'd spot her if she passed. If she wandered off the pier via the entrance though . . .

Sarah dodged between all the people, rushing back toward the promenade. At least she was wearing jeans and trainers, not some stupid dress and heels that she'd never be able to run in.

'Sissy!' she yelled at the top of her voice. It wasn't the time for restraint.

People caught her eye sympathetically, and parents reached for their children to check they hadn't wandered off in some sort of mass migration. Like irresponsibility was catching.

She must be out of her mind. What made her think she could look after Sissy full-time when she couldn't even take her to the loo? If anything happened to her because Sarah had done something as stupid, as trivial, as take a phone call . . .

Her mum had been right. As well-meaning as she was, Sarah didn't know how to take care of Sissy, not when she'd never done it before, and her sister was now gaining more independence. She wasn't a little girl any more.

Then up ahead, between the shoulders of strangers who all seemed so much bigger than her, she glimpsed a head of flyaway blonde hair. 'Sissy!'

Sissy stopped and looked around, everywhere but in Sarah's direction.

'Behind you!' Sarah shouted.

Slowly Sissy turned, an enormous grin spreading across her face. 'There you are. You wandered off,' she said.

'I did not! *You* wandered off.'

Sissy shook her head. 'I was looking for you.'

Sarah hugged her. 'I was looking for you.'

'But I was looking first.'

She didn't want to let go of her sister. 'Let's go find Robin. He's worried. Hold my hand.'

Sissy took her hand and said, 'In case you get lost again.'

No chance of that, she thought, gripping hard.

Chapter Forty

Catherine

What she was doing was absolutely unprofessional. Not to mention that she'd feel like a complete tit if she got caught. She just hoped she'd have enough cover from the after-work crowd to get a quick peek through the windows.

Alis was meeting Georgina at a pub in Soho, which was nearly on Catherine's way home anyway. As long as she happened to walk completely out of her way. Why shouldn't she see how they were getting on?

She waited till she knew their date had started, did a last-minute make-up check and left the office. Magda was long gone of course. She was using the office as an excuse to go out to lunch these days.

A pub wouldn't have been Catherine's choice of venue but Alis had sounded really excited about it when he'd told her that he'd arranged the date with Georgina. She'd felt a guilty little stab at his enthusiasm. Hopefully Magda was wrong about her client's reaction.

She saw the giant flaw in her perfect plan as soon as she approached the painted red façade of The Coach and Horses. Yes, it was crowded with drinkers, just as she'd hoped.

Unfortunately they were all sitting outside at the tables along the windows . . .

Along with Alis.

'Catherine?'

'Oh hi!' she said, feeling her face flush. What an amateur stalker she was. 'Was tonight . . .? Tonight was your date, wasn't it?' She looked around like she just realised where she was. 'Here?'

He nodded, smiling. He'd made an effort for Georgina, she noticed. He wore a button-down shirt with little grey and pink flowers on it. The long sleeves were rolled up past his elbows though, so Georgina wouldn't miss his tattoos.

'Nice shirt. Is it vintage?'

'Just old,' he said. 'I like flowered shirts. I'm glad you approve.'

Catherine noticed that there was only one glass on his table. 'Is Georgina not here yet?'

He rubbed his beard thoughtfully. 'I believe she's what's called a no-show in the business. I was just finishing this before I headed home.'

Catherine glanced at his nearly empty pint. That cow. It was bad enough that she was so judgemental about every-thing, but to stand him up? 'Did she at least ring to cancel? Or text?'

He shook his head. 'Nah, but that's all right. It's warm under the heater here and I've been enjoying watching the people.' He leaned closer, lowering his voice. 'There's a couple behind you who broke up last month but they're trying it again. Between you and me, I don't think it's going to work out.'

'Really?' Catherine slipped into the seat opposite Alis. 'Why not?'

'From what I've heard so far, the dark-haired guy called

it off because he thought the blond one was getting too involved. But the blond keeps pushing the other guy to make plans in advance and it's driving him mental.' He smiled. 'Those are his words, not mine.'

'Do you eavesdrop a lot?'

'Every chance I get. Don't you?'

She laughed. 'Of course I do. But I don't usually admit it. I'm sorry you had to waste your time, when Georgina didn't even have the courtesy to ring you. Can I at least buy you another pint?'

'I won't look a gift horse in the mouth, thank you. It's not a waste of time though. I'm happy sitting here.'

Catherine would be spitting feathers if she were him. She'd fumed when Richard was five minutes late, and she wasn't even romantically involved with him.

'But you had to get ready and travel here and wait for her and she didn't even show.'

Clearly he didn't see her point. 'I'm here, Catherine, out in Soho. It's a nice night, I have a pint and an outdoor seat under a heater. What's not to be happy about?'

Seriously? Who was that pleased about being stood up? 'I can make you even happier. Which beer would you like?'

'London Pride, please.'

She made her way to the bar, drafting a strongly worded email in her head to Georgina. Love Match had strict rules about courtesy. Not all clients would be as easy-going about this. If Georgina were in Alis's shoes she'd have rung Catherine already to complain.

She got herself a glass of wine and returned outside with Alis's ale. She could tell by the tilt of his head that he was being nosey again.

'So, what's the update?'

'Well,' he whispered dramatically. 'It sounds like blondie hasn't exactly been sitting home alone pining for his ex while

342

they were broken up. So now he has some nerve being jealous and making demands of the other guy.'

'Are those his words again?' Catherine asked, sipping her wine.

'No, those are mine.'

She laughed.

'You can't make someone love you,' he said. 'You can convince them to be with you, but you can't make them love you. It's too exhausting to try.'

He sounded like he was speaking from experience. Catherine thought back to Richard. Yes, she had done it too, and then he went and made being in love with Magda look like the easiest thing in the world. For love to really be satisfying it had to come of its own free will. She wished she'd learned that earlier.

The more worrying revelation from the wedding was what she'd been doing to Paul. What kind of control freak was she, anyway? Building her own boyfriend? Who did that?

Sick people, that's who. And the fact that Magda was the one to spot it just made it all the more embarrassing.

'I don't think you and Georgina would have been overly compatible anyway,' she told Alis.

'I kind of got that impression when I contacted her about meeting and she sent me a list of dietary requirements.'

'Ha, you should talk!' she said. 'You're a vegetarian.'

'Yes, but I don't lead with that. And as you know, I'm sometimes a lapsed vegetarian. I did wonder why you set us up.'

She gulped her wine. She had to be careful. 'Well, actually she's my business associate's client. It was her idea.'

'Have you met Georgina before?' he asked.

She nodded. 'She's much like you'd imagine from her profile.'

'In other words,' he said, 'she's about as flexible as a steel rod.'

Catherine thought about that. 'No, a steel rod will bend if you heat it up. I am really sorry, Alis. I think it was a mistake to try to introduce you, but Magda is keen to show Georgina that she shouldn't be so rigid in her requirements. And, to be fair, you're a lovely man who she should be mad about.'

He smiled. 'You think I'm a lovely man?'

'Well yes, of course.' Catherine blushed. 'I admit that when I first met you I may not have given you a fair chance.'

'Because you thought I was a scruffy, beardy twat, you mean.'

'No, no, I never thought you were a twat, really. It's obvious that you're a very sensitive and open person.' She glossed over her surprise that he consulted astrologers and aligned the energy in his kitchen drawers.

Those weren't really defining features anyway. They might be part of him but they didn't define him. Any more than her love of Filofaxes defined her. When she thought of him she thought of his kind, laid-back nature and his enthusiasm for the world.

Georgina would be lucky to have a guy like Alis. What right did she have to reject him before she'd even met him? She'd be ringing that woman as soon as she got to the office tomorrow.

She was starting to think that Georgina shouldn't meet Paul either. Yes, with the improvements he was probably her ideal on paper, Aussiness aside, but Catherine wasn't so sure she deserved him.

She thought again about Paul and her Erector Set approach to dating. She'd been like some demented Nigella following her favourite recipe. Even worse, she was the one who always said that love didn't follow a checklist. At the end of the day the only thing that mattered was whether that spark was there. Lactose intolerance, laundry habits, tattoos, beards, none of that mattered . . .

Tattoos? Beards?

Where had that come from?

'If you're hungry at all,' Alis said, 'we can eat upstairs. That's why I picked this pub for drinks. It's got good vegetarian and vegan food. Unless that's too weird for you? We could go somewhere else if you'd rather. I can find something to eat on any menu.'

'No, no, I'd like to try this. It'll make a nice change. I'm not overly familiar with vegetarian food.'

'Yes you are! Everybody is. Every time you have pasta with pesto or roasted potatoes or saag paneer or quattro stagioni pizza you're eating what I eat. It's not a special cuisine or anything. There's no such thing as a dish that's only for vegetarians. They're just dishes without meat. Come on, I'll show you.'

The waitress led them upstairs to a pretty room with huge black-trimmed sash windows, bare floorboards and a large fireplace. The linen-topped tables had mismatched wooden chairs, and mirrors and frames were hung higgledy-piggledy on the pale walls.

'This is nice,' said Catherine. 'It looks like a Victorian tearoom.'

'That's exactly what it is,' he said. 'Soho's secret tearoom. They serve tea till nine, I think. But they also have full meals.'

Catherine eyed the tiered cake stands on a few of the tables. Alis certainly won points for originality and atmosphere. Georgina definitely didn't deserve him.

She picked up the menu. 'Tofush and chips?' she said. 'You are joking.'

He grinned. 'I've had it. It's tasty.'

'Is there no real fish option?'

'Not unless fish grow on trees. No meat, remember?'

'They shouldn't really call this a burger then, if it's not got meat in it. And shepherd's pie without any lamb? If it's only veggies then it's a farmer's pie, surely, or allotment pie.'

'But the word burger has been co-opted in many ways.'

'Pah! A burger is a burger.'

'Actually, not true,' he said. 'It started out as steak tartare in Hamburg, hence the name hamburger. And steak tartare was brought to Russia by Genghis Khan, who fed horse mince to the Muscovites.'

'So we should really call it the Genghis Khan. Do you know a lot of useless trivia like this?'

'All trivia is useful eventually. It just needs the right questions asked.'

'Then I want you on my team in Trivial Pursuit.'

Catherine couldn't remember the last time she felt so relaxed. Certainly it wasn't when she was out with Richard. An undercurrent of business tension always kept her on guard with him. As the diners around them paid their bills and left, Catherine found herself losing track of the time.

When they'd finished eating, Catherine said, 'Well I have to admit that I enjoyed that. It was tasty, with lots of seasoning. Georgina would have been lucky to meet you tonight. I am sorry again about that. I'm definitely ringing her tomorrow to tell her off.'

'No need,' he said. 'This was a better date anyway.'

'But it wasn't a date.'

'Wasn't it? What do you consider a date then?'

She thought about it. 'Well, you have to know it's a date before it can be a date. Otherwise it's just two people getting along and having fun.'

'Two people who are attracted to each other?'

She couldn't deny that.

Uh-oh.

They stood to go back downstairs to the bar. She felt warm as she started to make her way down the spiral steps.

'Do you want to get another drink?' he asked.

'Erm, no, I'd better not. I have to be in early tomorrow.'

Her heart was racing. 'Thank you for such a nice night, Alis. This was unexpected but very fun.'

'Catherine. It's all right to go off script sometimes. You do know that?'

She nodded. 'I know that.'

'So if I was to, say, lean in like this . . .'

His lips were inches from hers. It would be easy to close the gap.

But she couldn't.

She pulled back. 'Thanks again, Alis. We'll talk soon, okay?'

She pecked him on the cheek above the beardy bit and hurried from the bar before she could change her mind.

Chapter Forty-One

Rachel

Ed called the meeting for ten a.m. 'He's telling us which design they've chosen,' James said. Even he couldn't pretend nonchalance now.

'Did he tell you that?'

'No, but it makes sense, doesn't it? We're the only ones on the meeting request.'

'I guess so.' Something bothered her. 'But why put us through the waiting? Why not just tell us in an email instead of building it up?'

'Maybe he's a sadistic son of a bitch.'

'That's what I thought too.'

They waited in silence for Ed to arrive. Rachel wished she had a cup of coffee. But it seemed silly to go to the trouble for what could only be a two-minute meeting. It didn't take long to say *And the winner is* . . . Still, now she wished she had a cup in front of her. Just to have something other than the conference room door to focus on.

Ed strode in with his mug full of tea. Had they misread the situation? 'Everybody all right?' he asked as he lifted the conference phone receiver. He glanced between Rachel and James. 'Don't you want a drink?'

'Are you phoning a friend?' James asked.

'I wouldn't call the Ziglers friends,' he said. 'But they will be after this call. They're running ten minutes late. Go get yourselves drinks if you want.'

'We're having a conference call?' Rachel asked. 'Aren't you going to tell us who won the pitch?'

'I will do as soon as I know.'

'We figured you already knew,' said James.

'And I didn't just tell you when I found out? I'm not that cruel!'

'No, no.'

'Course not.'

They went to the kitchen to make their hot drinks.

'So this is it, Rach. No matter what happens, we go out tonight, right? May the best person win.'

They shook hands, both hoping to be the best person.

Ed was ready to dial when they came back.

'Anything we should know, Ed?' James asked, wearing his bravado rather well, Rachel thought.

Ed shook his head. 'They emailed last night asking for a call with you both at ten this morning. That's all I know. Maybe they have questions, or maybe they just want to tell you the news in person, as it were.'

Rachel was glad it was a phone call rather than a meeting. If she was going to cry, best do it in front of as few people as possible.

Ed dialled. 'Hello, Philip, it's Ed here, and I've got Rachel and James with me.'

'Hi Philip,' they chorused like tuneless backup singers.

'Thanks, everyone, for having the call,' said Philip. 'George and Eric are with me.'

There was silence.

'Philip?'

'I'm here, just getting my notes together.'

Notes? Was that good or bad?

'So,' he went on, 'as you know from our last meeting, we were very impressed with both designs. Rachel, yours was bold and fresh and we can see ourselves going to work in an office like that.'

James made a ridiculous open-mouthed, hands on cheeks, *Home Alone* face at her.

'What's more, it's a bold statement and we feel like you really understand what we're trying to convey.'

She wanted to jump up and down and thank the Academy, but she was waiting for the 'but'.

'But . . .'

There it was.

'James's design is playful and fun and possibly just a little bit more exciting. We showed both designs to our board of directors and key managers. We did focus groups of four or five people at a time to really hone down the feedback. I think we had, what was it, George, eleven focus groups?'

'Ten,' said George. 'We were going to have another but only one person could make it from that group, so we got her feedback separately.'

Rachel wanted to shout at him to get to the punchline. She couldn't care less about their opinion-collecting process.

'So once we collected all the feedback, the result was clear. Although again I want to say that both designs are very very good, and our choosing one isn't an indictment of the other. If we had the budget we'd commission both!'

Ed laughed heartily at this but Rachel could tell he was thinking about Zigler's expansion opportunities.

Philip continued. 'We've decided that the bold, playful option is the one for us. Congratulations!'

They all looked at one another. Which design was that? Rachel pointed at herself, then James, shrugging.

'Erm, thanks for that, Philip,' said Ed. 'Just to clarify, which design have you decided on?'

There was silence on the line again.

'Rachel's.'

She clamped her hand over her mouth. She could hardly breathe. She and James stared at each other across the table. He bowed his head once. Then he smiled.

'Thank you,' she mouthed. 'Wow, thanks Philip and . . .' Her mind went blank. All she could think of was Zig and The Lers. 'And thanks everyone!'

'Thank you, Rachel. We're really excited about this. Ed, I guess there'll be some more letters and contracts to sign, so send those over when you can and we'll get started on all the details. Congratulations again, Rachel, great design.'

'Absolutely congratulations!' Ed said when they'd hung up. 'And they were right, James, they're both great designs. You should be proud too.'

But James shook his head. 'The better design won. Well done, Rach. You deserve this.'

'Thanks.' She searched his face but he seemed genuinely happy for her.

Later, they stood in front of the Jazz Cafe in Camden. When James gave their names at the door they followed a waiter upstairs, where little tables for two lined the narrow mezzanine.

Rachel couldn't hide her surprise. James planning ahead? 'What's all this in aid of?' And with tablecloths even.

'We're celebrating. Plus I felt bad when you called me out about never taking you dancing.'

Wonders never ceased. 'Who's playing?'

'I don't remember, exactly. Poncho Frittata and the Maracas or something like that.'

'It's Latin music, I take it? You don't know how to dance salsa.'

'No idea.' He shrugged. 'I think it's mostly just wriggling about. I bet you can't wait to dance with me now.'

'As long as you don't twerk again.'

The waiter brought their menus.

'Order three courses,' he said. 'I had to prepay for them.'

'You're buying dinner too? My God, man, who *are* you?' She caught her breath. She did know who he was now, didn't she?

His face got suddenly serious. 'About that, Rach. I owe you a thank you. Plus an apology for the way I acted when I read your feedback on me. The truth hurts, and the truth is, I was a pretty shite boyfriend. So I'm trying to make it up to you now.'

Now? He wanted to make it up to her now, when he was probably sleeping with her best friend and she had no hope of going out with him again? Fat lot of good that did her.

And she'd have told him it was too late, if she wasn't so busy hoping that it wasn't.

'Plus,' he continued, 'I'm sure the Zigler account will mean a promotion for you, so it's a double celebration, really.'

The promotion! She hardly dared believe it was possible, but he might be right. They had enough experience now at the firm. Something spectacular could give them a leg-up to associate. But it'd still be a long road. 'Eventually,' she said. 'One win won't do it.'

Their food came about two minutes after they ordered it.

'I guess they don't want us lingering over dinner,' he said. 'But we've got the table for the night.'

'That's okay. I want to get to the part where you dance.'

'Just don't expect any moves off *Strictly*.'

He wasn't kidding. When the band started its hip-swaying rhythm, they held back till the floor filled with competent dancers.

She felt self-conscious. Not at the thought of dancing. She

loved Latin music. She imagined she looked a bit like Shakira when she moved. Probably more like Shrek.

No, she was nervous about dancing with James.

He took her in his arms and they began to move together. He didn't try any flash moves. He just held her and sort of hopped from one foot to the other. Had it been anyone else she'd have made an excuse to stop. She was sure they looked ridiculous.

But she didn't care. It felt too good to be in his arms. Each time he pulled her close she tried not to pant in his face.

By the time the band took its break she wished she hadn't worn a wool dress. She wiped her forehead with the back of her hand.

'Drink?' he asked.

'I'm parched.'

Taking her hand, he led her back to their table.

This wasn't right. Not when he was seeing Sarah. It was one thing to go out, as colleagues, to celebrate a win. Colleagues weren't supposed to cuddle. How would she feel if Sarah had held James's hand while they were going out?

She smiled at the irony of that thought.

Then she dropped his hand.

He turned back to look at her, but said nothing.

The waiter wasn't as keen to get their drinks as he'd been to sling their food at them, but their mojitos finally arrived.

'Cheers.' She raised her glass. 'Thanks for tonight, James, especially for being such a great loser.'

'I like to think that I came a close second, but thanks for—'

When his phone rang he glanced at the screen.

So did Rachel. 'You should get that. It's Sarah.'

'No, that's okay, I'll talk to her later.'

'Don't be daft.' It was one thing to be out dancing with the man her friend was seeing. It was another to ignore her calls. She reached for his phone. 'Hi Sarah, it's Rachel. James is right here, I'll put him on.'

Her feelings were running crazily in her head. She wanted him to ignore the call. Yet Sarah was her friend and she wasn't about to let anyone treat her badly.

'No way!' he said into the phone after they'd said their hellos. 'Hang on, you can tell her yourself. Rach.'

She took his phone. It was a bit wet where his cheek had been. 'Hey, Sarah, what's up?'

'You'll never guess!'

Given that it was Sarah, no, she probably wouldn't. 'Go on, tell me.'

'Guess! No, I'll tell you . . . no, guess. Do you want to guess? Or should I tell you?'

'Just tell me!'

'We've got an ace place for Sissy to live!'

'Yah!' Rachel screamed. As it was still during the band's break, this made everyone around her stare.

'It's in Cambridge where Kelly's working,' Sarah continued, 'and it's a really good facility, especially for people with learning disabilities. Kelly rang just now to say there's a free place and I can email the application first thing tomorrow, but I already know Sissy's going to love it.'

There was so much relief in Sarah's voice. 'That is such fantastic news, Sarah! But isn't Cambridge too far?'

'Yeah, it's going to be a pain to get there, but it's so perfect for Sissy that it's worth the extra commute for me to get her in where Kelly is. They're usually chocka, but a few spaces opened up so it's all moving fast. That's why Kelly rang me just now. They can take Sissy and a few of the others by the end of the week. Though I wonder what happened to the residents who were there . . . maybe I'd rather not know. I'm going up there tomorrow to sign some papers and Kelly says there's even an arts programme at one of the community centres close by. We'll just have to look into transport . . . Oh! Am I interrupting anything?'

'No, no! We're just having a drink to celebrate the pitch.' She'd told Sarah all about it when she'd rung after the meeting. Sarah had wanted to know what the winning building looked like. Knowing her, she'd bake a scale model made of sponge.

'I won't keep you then,' Sarah said. 'I need to ring Catherine now anyway to tell her. I'll see you later?'

'Yep, I won't be long. See you soon.'

She handed the phone back to James.

'What do you mean you won't be long?' James asked. 'There's still a set to go and I haven't shown you my cha cha moves yet.' He wriggled his hips around in his chair.

She mustered a weak smile. Talking to Sarah just reminded her how hopeless she was being. 'This has been nice but I should probably head home. Sarah's really excited about her news and it doesn't sound like Catherine is home.'

She regretted her words as soon as she said them. She wanted to stay with James. And she definitely didn't want him coming home with her to congratulate Sarah in person. Then she'd have to see them together in the house.

She wished Sarah had kept the news to herself instead of calling her.

Actually, she hadn't called her, had she? It was James she'd rung first. Rachel was an afterthought after . . . go on, she thought, say it. Rachel was just an afterthought after her boyfriend.

She was thrilled that they'd found a new home for Sissy, really she was. She just wished she didn't feel like crying into her mojito.

Chapter Forty-Two

Sarah

Sarah glanced around the conference table at the other illustrators. What was all this for, really? They talked every week about new ideas. Harry pretended to consider them and then everyone went away to draw the same cards as the week before. She wondered if he'd even notice if she started pitching the old cards that she'd already designed. He seemed so preoccupied lately that he'd probably approve them. Maybe the sex with Maria-Therese was addling his brain. Just being in the same room with the woman addled hers.

Yes, granted, a few of her ideas might be wide of the mark. But they weren't all crackpot, and she knew she had a corker this time.

Maria-Therese looked even more smug than usual. 'All right?' Sarah asked out of courtesy.

Maria-Therese just stared at her, pretending not to hear. She noticed the other illustrators glancing her way too.

'Have you been ill?' Maria-Therese finally said.

'No, why?'

'Because you look ill, or I wouldn't have asked.'

'Well I feel fine. Thanks for caring.'

God, one meeting without make-up and they thought she was terminal.

Harry strode in, making his usual grandiose entrance. He probably imagined he was Churchill heading up the war effort, not a greeting card salesman whose biggest competition had a pig for a logo.

'Let's hear some new ideas, everyone,' he said.

Sarah shot her hand up. She needed to leave the meeting in a few minutes or she'd be late meeting Robin and Sissy in Cambridge.

Harry scanned the room like he was spoiled for choice. Sarah knew he'd stick to his script even though she was the only one volunteering. Finally, when no one else would meet his eye, he nodded at her.

'I know the Trekkie idea didn't work because of copyright issues but I think you're going to like this one.' She pulled the drawings from her portfolio case. 'Hipster wedding cards. What do you think?'

Her illustrations showed couples with piercings, couples with tattoos, and her personal favourite: the groom sporting a nice, bushy beard. She'd got the idea from listening to Catherine talk about one of her clients. She'd imagined this misfit finding the love of his life and getting a beardy tattooed wedding card on his big day.

'We could do them in loads of combinations of hair and skin colour and beards and tattoos. I really think we can tap into a big market here.'

She sat back to wait for the rejection. What would it be this time? They could take their pick of the excuses they'd used before. The Goth idea was too niche, wheelchair weddings might look exploitative and the London bus theme wouldn't sell outside the M25. Maybe she should start trying combinations of the ones Harry had dismissed. Over the weekend she'd work on a football-loving–lesbian-mail-order-bride card.

Harry mumbled something.

'Well, maybe it's not to everyone's taste but . . . What did you say?'

'I said I like it. I just read an article in the *Telegraph* about beards. They're on trend, I think the kids say.'

She'd never heard any kid say *on trend* ever.

'Draw me some variations, please, and we'll see which ones we could take forward. No one else? Okay, thanks, nice work everyone.'

She smiled all the way to the train station. That made a nice change from the way she'd felt lately, after ballsing up at the *Bake Off* audition. Harry's approval might not hold a candle to Mary Berry's, but at least it was something.

At King's Cross she stood with hundreds of other passengers staring at the departures board, willing her platform to flash up. She felt like a real commuter! The men and women in the crowd didn't know she was an imposter, not a student returning to her halls or a don on a reverse commute or a businesswoman preparing to meet clients. She was travelling to Cambridge to visit her sister.

It didn't take long to arrange Sissy's move once they all went to see the new home together. Sarah felt sick with nerves worrying that it would all be too traumatic for Sissy. So when she started introducing herself to the residents and asking about the dinner options, Sarah could have cried with relief.

It would be a big adjustment but Sissy seemed eager to make it.

Robin and Sarah could have driven up together in their Mum's beat-up Nissan if it hadn't been for Sarah's meeting. The car was a link to happy days and they'd wanted to keep it for Sissy when their mum died. It was bad enough they had to give up the house, which was only rented, and move her away. Hopefully all that upheaval was behind them now.

'Have fun on the train?' Robin teased when she got to Sissy's new room.

'It was a delightful journey, thanks for asking, Robin. The champagne was a touch warm but they had caviar and the orchestra was top-notch.'

'In other words, watery tea and stale sandwiches.'

'Don't forget the guy playing his music at full volume with only one earbud in.'

'Too bad. Sissy and I've been having a good time, haven't we?'

Sissy didn't look away from the wall where she was pinning her artwork.

'Sissy?' Sarah said. Sometimes her sister had to be prised out of her own world. 'Do you like it here so far?'

She didn't answer.

Sarah shot Robin a look. They didn't have a choice at this point if Sissy hated it. Soon there'd be no Whispering Sands to go back to. Some developer was probably planning to turn it into luxury flats or something.

She pulled her sister away from the wall to hug her. 'Sissy? Isn't it nice being here with Kelly? And Ben is here too.'

Suddenly her face lit up. 'Yes. And they're having jelly after lunch.'

Sarah smiled. 'You like it here then?'

'It's good,' she said, crushing Sarah in another hug before returning to her drawing pins.

'I'm just going to find Kelly,' she said to Robin, looking away so he didn't see the tears of relief pooling in her eyes.

'I'll come with you,' he said.

Sissy's new home was built in a series of wings off the main building. The outside was nothing remarkable – just red brick from the fifties or sixties – but inside was spacious and light, thanks to the big picture windows. There was a library and a brightly painted learning centre and a huge dining room that doubled as the residents' disco once a month. She could hear the tock tock tock of a ping-pong ball coming from the games room. The noise floated out on hysterical laughter.

That's what had depressed her so much about the idea of an elderly care home for Sissy. Yes, they could offer Sissy accommodation but there wasn't enough activity for a sixteen-year-old. The residents just sat – in their rooms or in the TV room or on chairs lining the corridors. Sitting sitting sitting, but waiting for what?

'So you're back to normal then?' Robin asked as they walked along the corridor.

'What do you mean?' But she knew.

He pointed from her purple trainers and faded jeans to the once-black, now-grey zip-up hoodie over her tee shirt. 'This. You. Where's the warpaint and the Stepford Wives dress? Just a phase?'

'Something like that.'

'I didn't mind you all fancied up, but this is more you. Face it, Sarah, you're a slob.'

'I like to think of it as low-maintenance,' she said.

They found Kelly talking to one of the other staff. 'Don't let us interrupt,' she said. 'We just wanted to say hi.'

'This is Sarah and Robin, Sissy's family.' Kelly gestured to the middle-aged black woman she was talking to. 'This is Grace. She and Sissy have already met.'

Grace wore her hair in greying dreadlocks swirled up in a giant bun. Sarah tried not to stare at such a large volume of hair on such a tiny woman. She shook their hands warmly. 'Your sister is a welcome addition here. And we're thrilled to have Kelly and the others from Whispering Sands too.'

Grace smiled at her new colleague. She had the same easy, calm and capable manner as Kelly. In other words, the perfect person to trust with their sister.

'I just wanted to thank you again for getting Sissy in here,' Robin said to Kelly. 'It looks like it's worked out for everybody.'

'Yes, thanks to you, Kelly,' Sarah added. 'How are you settling in? It must be weird having to get used to a new place.'

Kelly smiled. 'Probably not as weird as it is for Sissy and the others. As you know, routines are important, so they'll be eased into things here. Your sister was a little put out that we don't have a resident kitchen to toast your bread, so maybe the cooks will do it for her in the mornings. We'll find a way around it, and I've had a quick chat with the director about that art programme too, so hopefully we can work something out once she's settled in. The important thing is that she's here and she's being looked after.'

Tears came again to Sarah's eyes. 'Thank you,' she whispered. *It's all right, Mum*, she thought, *Sissy is safe.*

Chapter Forty-Three

Catherine

magdasparkles@hotmail.com   2.44pm (8 minutes ago)
To: me

I want to talk to you with Richard in person. we will meet after your work.

thank you

Catherine dreaded to think what they wanted from her now. It wasn't like Magda was around to ask. She hadn't been in the office for weeks.

When she rang Richard she half expected it to go through to voicemail.

'Yeess?' he answered smugly.

'What's this meeting about, Richard?'

'We'll talk after work. That's the whole point of having a meeting.'

'I want to know what it's about.'

'Don't I always show you a good time?' he said.

'Hmm, let's think about that,' she snapped back. 'You told me you were getting married over drinks. And that you were selling out half my company. I can't wait to hear what's in store this time.'

He just laughed. 'Trust me, Kate.'

'Don't call me Kate.'

Magda levered herself up from the table. 'You are looking well,' she said, air-kissing Catherine's cheeks.

'So are you,' Catherine said honestly. She'd hoped that Magda had grown huge, but her white baby-doll top gathered in the right place to show off her boobs. In her skinny jeans and stiletto platform shoes she could be on her way to a club. Except for the bump.

'How do you walk in those things?'

Magda laughed. 'Practice.'

'We're having champagne,' Richard said. 'Will you have a glass?'

Catherine looked at Magda, who said, 'I am having a sip.'

Richard poured a glass for Catherine. 'How've you been?' he asked.

So they were doing small talk first. 'All right. The builders are nearly finished at the house. I don't even want to think about when we subdivide it into separate flats.'

'But I thought you loved living with the other two,' Richard said. 'Will you use it as a rental property?'

'No, no, we'll still live there. But there might be other people to consider one day, so Rachel's drawn up two sets of plans. The builders are just finishing the first phase, basically to make sure the old electrics don't burn the place down. They also put in all the walls, electrics and plumbing connections to turn it into separate flats eventually. That way it's ready to be converted. When the time comes.'

She really had been single for too long if it didn't even occur to him that she might one day have a partner to think about. She pushed her aggravation aside. 'What about you? Will you stay in your flat once you have the baby?'

Richard nodded just as Magda said, 'No. We will need something bigger.'

He took her hand. 'Darling, I've told you, three bedrooms are enough for now. When we have another baby then we'll worry about having more space.'

'But where will my sister sleep when she comes to see the baby? Mother will already be in the extra bedroom.'

'Is your mother coming to live with you once the baby comes?' Catherine asked. That would be a barrel of laughs for Richard. She'd met Magda's mother at the wedding. She'd acted like Stalin in stilettos.

'Of course Mother will live with us,' said Magda.

Catherine might have her issues with Richard but she'd never wish a live-in mother-in-law on him. 'Well I suppose that's handy. She'll be able to help with the baby.'

'Oh no, we'll have a full-time nanny.'

'What, from birth?'

Magda nodded. 'She'll come home from the hospital with us.'

'Then you might need a bigger house, Richard,' she murmured.

But he was staring at Magda like she was the most reasonable woman in the world and again it struck Catherine that he really was in love. As long as she didn't have to live with Magda she could be happy for him.

There was no accounting for love. Or lust, or whatever it was.

She'd started thinking that a lot lately.

After seeing Alis, he would not get out of her head. Whenever she saw someone with a tattoo, she saw him. There he was in the vegetable dishes on menus and the never-used yoga mat she kept behind her bedroom door. He was in the *Sunday Times Style* magazine when she made fun of the horoscope. Even the adverts for new kitchen cabinets reminded her of him, thanks to his kindness to his feng shui friend. She had to face the facts. She was falling for a man who looked like he had a groundhog napping on his face.

A sudden move by Magda yanked her out of her reverie. 'Richard?' Magda said pointedly, staring at him.

He snapped to attention. 'Yes, so, we wanted to talk to you about something, Kate . . . Catherine.'

'I guessed that from your invitation.'

'In fact I'm glad you mentioned your house, because that's part of what we wanted to talk to you about.'

She suddenly had the feeling that Magda wanted to get her manicured hands on it. 'We're not selling it.'

'No, no, it's not that,' he said. 'But you must have quite a bit of equity in it now, after the improvements . . .' He finished his champagne and poured another glass. 'The thing is, with Magda's due date only six weeks away, we thought it was best for her to step away from the business. There's still a lot to do before the baby comes.'

'And Magda's mother,' Catherine said.

'Yes, well, and we were wondering how you felt about taking a hundred per cent of the business.'

Did she hear him right? 'Buy you out?'

'We would accept reasonable offers,' Magda said. 'Considering the improvements to the business over the past six months.'

'Improvements?' Catherine sputtered into her sparkling wine. 'Which improvements were those, exactly?'

Magda stiffened. 'The reporting system that I created, for example.'

'I hate to break this to you, Magda, but that was a project I made up just to get you out of my office. We don't need data to tell me how well our clients are catered for, because we actually talk to them.'

'I have turned Georgina around,' she said. 'She would have fired you if it wasn't for me.'

Richard was looking very uncomfortable at the shift in conversation. 'Maybe we can—'

'Stay out of this, Richard,' Catherine said. 'Yes, you turned Georgina around, Magda, but it was wrong to try to use Alis to do it. Georgina is lucky I didn't remove her from our books for standing him up.' It was only because she was so contrite that Catherine relented. She'd let her meet Paul and, to everyone's surprise, the Type A perfectionist had hit it off with the laid-back Aussie.

'Anyway, we can work out the details if you're interested in principle,' Richard said. 'I thought you could use the house to help you raise the capital . . . If you're interested?'

She looked between their tense faces. They weren't doing this out of the kindness of their hearts. 'Do you need the money, Richard? Is that it?'

Magda cut in. 'We do not *need* the money, Catherine. I will be busy with a much more important project than your business, that is all.'

But she didn't believe that. Richard had only sold out to his fiancée in the first place because of cash flow problems. He'd admitted as much way back when he first talked to her. And as far as she knew, there'd been no great boom in the economy to top up his bank account since then.

They needed her to buy them out.

Well well well.

'I am interested, in principle, as long as the price is right.'

'Make us an offer,' said Richard.

She should think carefully about her answer, take time to calculate the best offer she could get. A calm, measured approach was what was needed. It's how she got where she had so far. Not by being impulsive or letting her heart decide things.

366

But she didn't want to be calm or measured. She didn't want to ignore her heart any more.

For the first time in a decade, she wanted to listen to her gut. 'I want a twenty per cent discount on what Magda paid for the shares.'

'No way. The business is worth more now, not less.'

'If that's true it's because of the staff who've worked there for years, Richard, not Magda's contribution.' Her glare dared Magda to disagree again.

'We can't sell at that price.'

'Then you make me an offer,' she said.

'We're doing this here, now?'

She shrugged. 'It's as good a time as any. Look at it this way. You can write off the champagne as a business expense. So?'

'Give us what I paid,' Magda said.

Catherine didn't break eye contact with Richard. 'You know I'm not going to do that. So?'

'Five per cent discount,' he said.

She shook her head.

'No counter-offer?'

'No. Go higher.'

'Seven per cent.'

'Fifteen.'

'No way. Eight.'

'Fifteen.'

'Catherine, that's not how you negotiate.'

'It's exactly how I'm going to negotiate. Richard, I know you need the money, and I will do a deal with you. If it's at the right price. So ask yourself what it cost me to have Magda thrust into *my* business, to have to accommodate her whims for the last six months, to fix the errors in judgement that she's made.' She felt a little guilty about that last part, since it was really just one error and spending the evening with

Alis hadn't exactly been a hardship. 'Where were we? Oh yes, I want a fifteen per cent discount please.'

'Ten, and that's my final offer.'

'Twelve, and that's mine.'

They stared at each other. Magda knew better than to say anything. She's probably not a bad person, Catherine thought, if Richard was in love with her. But she didn't plan to be her friend.

Richard extended his hand. 'Twelve. Agreed.'

She shook it. She knew her share of the equity tied up in the house was enough to cover the purchase. 'I'll get the bank round and we can start looking at contracts.'

She was getting her business back. She could hardly believe it.

She took one more sip of her champagne and stood to leave. It had never been a social call.

'There's one more thing, Catherine,' he said. 'We didn't just want to talk about the business tonight . . . we also wanted to ask about something personal.'

'The business is personal for me, Richard, in case you hadn't noticed.'

He nodded. 'I noticed.' He fidgeted in his chair. 'This is about us. I hope you know how important you are to me.' He sat back. 'Ha, that sounds like the beginning of a brush-off conversation. It's not. I'd like to ask whether you'll be the baby's godmother. Will you? You're my best friend and it would mean a lot to me. Would you do it?'

She sat back down to take in that little titbit. If it was a ploy to make her feel guilty about negotiating so hard, it was working.

They really were in different places if he still thought they were best friends. Maybe he really felt it. Maybe it suited him to think it. But she didn't want to be tied to Richard in that way, especially not when she'd just managed to untangle him and Magda from the business.

Sometimes friendships just ran their course, or at least diminished with time or circumstances. She was okay with that.

'No, Richard, I can't, but thank you very much all the same. I will love your child because it's yours, and we'll always be friends, but you have your life to live now with Magda. And I have mine.'

She'd leave it at that.

She stood and kissed them both goodbye. She could see the relief on Magda's face, and the disappointment on Richard's, but she had to be honest with herself. Richard wasn't her best friend, though he had been once upon a time. Her best friends were Rachel and Sarah.

They were the ones who needed her right now.

Sarah was watching telly in the front room when Catherine got back from the bar. All the way back on the Tube she tried to work out what she was going to say to her. She hated to think that a man, even one as nice as James, was coming between her friends. She had to say something.

'What did Richard want to talk about?' Sarah asked when Catherine came in.

'They're selling the business,' she said.

'Oh no!' Sarah jumped up to squeeze Catherine in a python-like grip.

'It's okay!' she wheezed. 'It's okay. They're selling it to me.'

Sarah tightened her grip.

'Sarah, I can't really breathe.'

'I'm so happy for you!' she said, letting go. 'Haven't we all had proper good news lately? With Sissy's new place and Rachel winning the deal and now you getting your business back.'

'And your hipster cards, don't forget about that.'

She blushed. 'And that.'

'Yes, and that. You should be pleased for yourself too, instead of putting everyone else's happiness before yours.' But as Catherine said it she thought, that's not completely true in Rachel's case, is it?

'There's something else, Sarah.' She wasn't really sure what to say next but she seized the moment. 'Your love life is good.'

Now it was Sarah's turn to blush. 'Uh hmm.'

'Sarah, do you want to talk about this? Because of Rachel?' There didn't seem to be any tension between them, but even so. It had to be bothering Rachel. Didn't it?

'Has she said anything to you?'

Catherine shook her head.

With that, Sarah threw herself over the back of the sofa, landing with a fluffy thump on the seat cushions. If another adult did that Catherine would think she'd fainted. 'Then I'd really rather not talk about James and me, if that's okay.'

'Sarah, what's going on with you two?'

'I can't tell you.' Her face was twisted in anguish. 'Please, Catherine, let's not talk about it.'

'Do you know what you're doing?' Catherine asked.

'God, I hope so,' she said.

Chapter Forty-Four

Rachel

It was a clean win. So why should Rachel feel bad about beating James on the Zigler project? She fumed. She bet her conscience would be clear if she had a penis. The Norman Fosters of this world didn't worry about being on top of their game. They embraced their successes. They were called ambitious. She felt selfish for beating James.

That's probably why, when Philip invited her to Club Gascon to celebrate with a boozy Michelin-star lunch, she magnanimously offered to make it up to James after work. Purely as a friendly gesture.

That's what she tried telling herself.

'Yeah, sounds great,' he said, grinning. 'Where are you taking me?'

She hadn't thought that far ahead. Their usual pub seemed like a let-down, but then again it was where they'd had a lot of fun together.

No, a better idea popped into her head. 'Gordon's?'

'Perfect.'

The old wine vault wasn't too crowded when they got there. Most of the people were at the tables in the back garden area, taking advantage of the unusually warm spring night. 'Are you okay sitting inside?' she asked. 'It looks a bit crowded out there.' Plus, she didn't say, inside was more romantic, with all the candles lit and nearly standing up in their own waterfalls of old wax.

He got them a table in one of the barrel vaults while Rachel went to the bar. As she ordered a bottle of red, she could feel herself starting to sweat. Being underground meant the bar was cool. So that could only mean one thing. Nerves.

Better face facts. They were there under totally false pretences. He thought he was getting commiseration drinks, but it felt like one of those now-or-never situations. The longer things went on between him and Sarah the more Rachel's hopes would fade, and the regret build up. She had to tell him how she felt.

As long as he didn't laugh in her face or say she was just suffering dumper's remorse now that it was too late, or (worst of all) that she was being a completely unfair bitch to move in on Sarah, she'd survive it. No matter the outcome, she had to say something.

James was tucking away his phone as she got back to the table. She tried not to think about who he'd been texting.

As she poured their wine he told her about a building complex his prof had been involved in lately. He seemed happy to do the talking. It was a brief reprieve from the conversation she knew she had to have. She found her mind drifting back to their break-up.

She didn't really see how she could fault her decision at the time. Mother Theresa would have lost patience with him. Nobody wants to feel like a chore in a relationship, and by the end of theirs she ranked a few notches below the washing up.

The trouble with being in a relationship that was going

wrong, she now realised, was constantly waiting to be let down. Every time her phone had rung when they were due to meet she'd assumed it would be an excuse not to turn up. When he had arrived she'd still been stuck with all that angst. Was it any wonder she'd started shying away from him?

'You're becoming quite the wine drinker,' she said when he commented on the spiciness of the Pinot Noir they were drinking. 'The only spice you used to talk about was in a vindaloo.'

'What can I say, I'm a new man.'

It was exactly why she had to say something. 'I don't regret breaking up with you, you know,' she said.

'That's out of the blue, and thanks a lot.'

'I mean it was right at the time. We wanted different things and you drove me insane.'

'I know, Rach. I can see that now, but in my defence I didn't consciously set out to hurt you. I'm really really sorry about that. I was immature.'

'You were a pathetic child most of the time.'

'All right, go easy there.'

'Well you were. Not that we didn't have a lot of fun, but you were just so frustrating. I could have murdered you.'

'But now?'

As she took a deep breath she could feel her face flush. 'But now—'

Then, over James's shoulder, she saw Sarah making her way to the table. 'Sarah's here.'

He turned around and waved. 'I know,' he said. 'I asked her to come.'

Of course he did. Why wouldn't he want his new girl-friend to join them? It was perfectly normal. So she shouldn't really feel as sick as she did.

373

Sarah kissed Rachel on the cheek, then James. Rachel was glad about that. She might lose it to see them kissing properly. 'Hi, sorry, am I late?'

No, Rachel thought, you're just in time to keep me from making an arse of myself. Look at her. James would be nuts not to want to go out with her. Though she was back to her usual jeans and slightly manly jumpers, she was still so pretty with her long legs and peaches-and-cream complexion. She hadn't really needed all the make-up and clothes in the first place.

'No, you're right on time,' Rachel said truthfully. 'Have a seat.' She folded away her emotions as best she could and sipped her wine. It didn't always work out like in the movies. Sometimes people didn't get what they wanted.

That was just life.

Sarah pulled out the chair beside James. 'So, we're celebrating?'

'I hope so,' James said. They both laughed, sharing some inside joke together.

Well, why not? They'd had months to develop all those little intimacies that made a relationship special.

As Rachel sat there watching them, she felt her eyes start to sting. 'Be back in a sec. I'll just get you a glass.' She bolted to the bar to compose herself. She needed to get a grip. Stop being such a selfish cow and be happy for your friend, she thought. For both of your friends. If they'd found what they were looking for then one day she might too. She just had to stop looking in James's direction.

'So, a toast,' she said when she came back with Sarah's glass. Her hand shook a little as she poured the wine but nobody noticed. 'To you two. I hope you'll be very happy together.'

Sarah and James looked at each other. 'Uh, about that,' said James. 'We need to talk about that.'

Just hearing him say those words . . . *we need to talk* . . . snuffed out the last tiny glimmer of hope she had about being with him again. Nobody ever started good news with that line.

Her heart leapt into her throat as she realised now why Sarah was there. They were in love. They were about to tell her in person.

'Rachel, we want to talk to you about . . . us,' Sarah began.

'I'd rather not, if you don't mind.' Her voice was shaking. 'It's not that I'm not happy for you, because I am, or I will be. But I think you'll agree that it's a weird situation. So, no, thank you, I'd rather not.'

Sarah's eyes started to swim with tears. 'I knew this was going to happen!' she said. 'You're upset now. James, I told you this was a bad idea!'

'You did not, Sarah. You were all for it at first.'

'I don't want to hear who was all for what!' Rachel said, louder than she meant to. She wanted to clamp her hands over her ears and sing *La La La La*. 'Maybe you can act like this is no big deal but it's not that easy for me. I just figured out what I want. I can't undo that overnight.'

She grabbed her handbag, ready to make a speedy exit.

'But you don't understand,' Sarah said, grabbing the handbag too. 'It's not what you think.'

'Let go.'

'I won't.' She jerked the handbag, nearly pulling Rachel over the top of the table.

'Can't we all calm down and discuss this?' James slid his arm over Sarah's shoulder.

Seeing that felt like a punch in the chest. 'Please, just don't,' she said.

'Sarah and I aren't seeing each other,' James said, studying her face for a reaction.

'You broke up?'

Now Sarah smiled. 'We were never seeing each other.' She let go of the handbag but grasped Rachel's hand before she could pull it away. 'Please forgive me for not being honest. It seemed like a good cause.'

'But I don't understand. That's not true. You've been seeing each other for the past two months.'

'No we haven't,' James said. 'I'm sorry, Rach. It sounded like a good idea when Sarah and I first talked the night of her party. A way to make you realise that . . . well, I'm sorry but I was desperate.'

'What are you talking about?! Sarah, if you weren't out with James then where were you all those nights?'

'With Jeremy. I've been seeing Jeremy.'

'So you and James never went out?' Her mind was refusing to take in what her ears were telling her.

'Only that first night,' he said.

'Then you did lie to me, James.'

'Nuh uh, for the record, I never lied, and neither did Sarah. We did go out that first night, when I told you I was meeting her for drinks. We came here, in fact.'

'Yes, I remember.' She also remembered how that made her feel.

'You wouldn't ask for any details,' said Sarah, sounding miserable. 'I'd come home from seeing Jeremy and I was dying to tell you the truth because it was doing my head in. I didn't want anything bad to come between us. Even though I agreed with James that you must see that you're perfect together, and this seemed like the only way to show you. Every time I brought it up you changed the subject. I promised James I wouldn't blurt anything out and ruin the plan, but we agreed that we wouldn't lie either. If you'd asked, I'd have told you. I really wish you'd asked, Rachel.' She sounded exhausted.

But Rachel hadn't asked. She hadn't wanted to hear any details about them. She hadn't wanted to know if James was doing the same things with her friend as he had with her.

'Let me get this straight,' Rachel said. 'You pretended to go out with each other just to make me jealous?'

James grimaced. 'It wasn't just to make you jealous. It was to make you see . . . I don't know, I was desperate. Rachel, I was so unbelievably stupid to screw up with you the way I did. But I was also too stupid to see it till it was too late. And then when you asked me to join RecycLove I knew there'd be loads of guys who were smarter than me. Of course they'd see how incredible you are. I was afraid you'd fall for one of them, and that would be it. The best thing I've ever had in my life, gone. I didn't know what else to do. You didn't seem to care if I went out with other women, even when I told you I'd slept with someone. And how was I supposed to show you that I have changed in a relationship if you're not in the relationship with me? I thought maybe you could see it through someone you knew.'

'So you didn't really sleep with that woman on your first date?' she asked.

He looked sheepish. 'I did.'

'To make me jealous?'

'Nah, Rach, I am a guy. She seemed like a nice woman, until she jettisoned me, that is, and she was good fun. Besides, you didn't seem to care.'

He was right, wasn't he? It hadn't really stirred any strong emotions when he'd told her.

Why not?

Because then, as far as she knew, he was still the old James. One bitten, twice . . . well not so much shy as nuts to take that chance again.

But he wasn't the old James any more. While she'd been busy congratulating herself on how well she knew him, he'd been busy growing up. He was right. She'd never noticed.

Though pretending to date one's best friend wasn't the act of a mature person. 'So you tried to trick me into liking you?'

'No, not trick!' Sarah said. 'Just help you realise what you wanted, that's all. I promise, we weren't trying to trick you . . . are you really mad at me?'

With anyone else she might have suspected ulterior motives, but Sarah didn't have a mean bone in her body, let alone a tricksy one. She put her arms around her friend and hugged. 'I'm not angry,' she said. And then more quietly, 'Thank you.'

Sarah smiled when she pulled away. 'Then my work here is done. I'll leave you two alone. You've got a lot of talking to do. Bye James!'

'Thanks again, Sarah!' he said, sounding like she'd just given him a lift home. 'So,' he said when she'd left.

'So. I think you'd better explain from the beginning,' she said.

'Should we get more wine?'

'Let's wait until I hear what you have to say.'

'Okay,' he said. 'Here goes, full disclosure. You were right to dump me. I took you for granted. There you were, such an amazing friend and the perfect girlfriend, and I just thought I could carry on doing whatever I pleased, that you'd put up with being fitted in around my schedule. I was such an arrogant twat. I realised that after we broke up, but what could I do? Even if I could completely change, you weren't about to give me another chance, and I couldn't blame you. All you wanted to do was get over me. The trouble was, I didn't get over you.'

378

'But you never said anything, James. It's been almost four years. That's a lot of water under the bridge.'

'I did say I was sorry for the way I treated you. I said that a lot, and I meant it.'

'I know.' It was because he'd said it, and meant it, that she'd been able to stay friends with him.

'What else could I say that would have made a difference? *Sorry I was such an arsehole, shall we have another go?* You'd have laughed in my face. Or, knowing you, punched me in the bollocks. I thought I might have a chance when you asked me to sign up to RecycLove with you. Till you told me what you thought of me.'

She winced remembering that assessment.

'Then you started seeing that guy Thomas and it was going well . . . I couldn't lose my chance, because I am a different person now, Rachel. I've grown up. I used to think about a relationship and want my freedom. Now when I think about a relationship with you, it's all I want.'

He was staring into her eyes. 'Can you forgive me for what Sarah and I did?'

Forgive him?! She could hardly believe him. Screwy as his plan was, it had worked. She wouldn't have looked at him more closely if not for Sarah.

'Do you promise never to lie to me again?' She held up her hand when he started to object. 'To never lie to me again by commission *or* omission?'

He smiled. 'I do.'

'All right then, let's see about that. Whose drawings do you think were better?'

He opened his mouth but snapped it shut again. 'Mine. Yours are a close second, but I think mine are better.'

Ouch, but at least she knew he was telling the truth. As far as she knew he'd never lied to her. He'd been a constant and supportive friend, even when it meant him losing out.

And she was as nuts about him now as she was when they first got together.

'I forgive you.'

'Come here.'

Gently he pulled her face to his, and when their lips met she knew she was finally where she belonged.

Chapter Forty-Five

Sarah

Sarah was happy for Rachel and James but she couldn't help being a little disappointed that she wasn't getting her own happy ending. Not that she had any interest in James. He was great for Rachel, of course, but way too awake after nine p.m. for her.

Unfortunately, so was Jeremy.

So she pulled on jeans and a button-down shirt, tied her hair up, slipped on her purple trainers and went to meet him. It was only fair at this point, she figured, to show him who she really was.

His brow furrowed when he saw her. 'Did you come straight from Cambridge?' he asked.

Or from cleaning your house? his expression added.

'Nope. I was home working today.'

'Oh . . .' He found his smile again. 'Well, hi!' He kissed her. She'd miss those lips a bit.

The waitress in Ronnie Scott's showed them to their table for the late show. It was everything she imagined a jazz club would be – red walls covered with musicians' photos, a low ceiling that gave it an intimate feel and loads of tables lit with tiny lamps. 'This is nice,' she said.

As far as last dates went she couldn't ask for more, really. 'Have you never been before?'

She shook her head. Jazz people were nocturnal.

It was after midnight when the trio finished on stage and she'd been swallowing her yawns since the opening song. She'd liked the music, yawns aside, and the live gig hadn't given them much chance to chat except at the intervals, which was good.

But now, with the band packing up, she had to talk to Jeremy.

When the waitress came to settle up, Sarah made a grab for the bill. 'Please let me pay for tonight,' she said. 'You never let me do it and I'm putting my foot down.'

She couldn't add insult to injury by making him pay to be broken up with.

Her courage wobbled though when she glanced at him. He seemed to glow with the stage lights catching his blond hair. His pale freckled face was growing on her and she didn't even mind his height any more. They did have a nice time when they went out. There were more lulls in their conversations now that they'd been through most of the usual background questions, but there would probably be times when she'd prefer his company to *8 Out Of 10 Cats* reruns. Maybe that was enough reason to go on seeing him for a while longer.

But what was the point of that when she knew it wasn't going to go anywhere? He was okay, but she'd probably never like him any more than she did now.

Plus, she really wanted to start getting to sleep before midnight again.

'Jeremy—'

'J, you mean?' He smiled.

'Yes, J. I wanted to talk to you about something.'

'That sounds serious.'

She nodded. 'It's about us. Oh, that sounds melodramatic, doesn't it? I just wanted to say that we've been seeing each other for a bit now and . . . I wondered if you're seeing anyone else?' The question just popped into her head. 'I mean, we're both still on RecycLove, so I just wondered.'

He squirmed in his velvet seat. 'Nothing serious, just a few dates here and there. Why?'

'Then we're not too serious. Are we?'

Jeremy looked like a fox who's just heard the hounds behind him. 'Listen, Sarah, you're a great girl but I'm not really looking for anything serious at this point.'

'Neither am I!' Though her protest did sound hollow now that he'd just said the same thing. 'In fact, I've got to be honest. I've had fun with you but these late nights are killing me. And I think I've now got bunions.'

'You're blaming me for bunions?' There was the hint of a smile.

'Not you directly. But the shoes I've been wearing to get into the clubs to go dancing. I'm not really used to them. I'm not used to any of this. I have to drink a lot of coffee to stay awake after ten.'

He checked his phone. 'It's nearly one now.'

'I had a double espresso at Bar Italia on the way here. My point is that I don't think our lifestyles are very compatible. I like staying in and watching telly or just being with my friends. I'm really a very boring person at heart.'

'That's not true, Sarah,' he said. 'Maybe you're not a party girl but you're not boring either. I understand what you're saying though.' He seemed to think for a moment. 'Will you stay on the website?'

She nodded. 'Definitely. I do want to meet someone. He just has to be more my speed. Like, maybe, second gear.'

'Then here's to finding second gear,' Jeremy said, lifting

his nearly empty glass. 'I'm going to stay in overdrive for a while.'

It was after eleven the next morning by the time Sarah made her way down to the kitchen. It was quiet, blissfully quiet. After monthly promises to finish, Nate had finally kept his word. Yesterday they'd packed up their tools and even given the floors a cursory sweep. Finishing as they'd started, they'd scraped their tool bags along the wall in the corridor, waved a cheery goodbye and gone to wreak havoc on the next unsuspecting client.

The silence did feel weird to her ears. Would she miss them? She thought about the daily disinfecting and constant coffee duty, the wrongly torn down walls, the broken bathtub and missing banister, the neighbours' fire and electrical black-outs. There'd be no more poo bombs in their loo or anyone to stub out fags in their garden pots. She didn't have to be dressed before eight a.m. or take phone calls outside because of the noise. After a dozen or so cleanings the house would no longer look like Pompeii after the eruption.

But they'd survived. They'd lived with builders for over four months and had the grey hair and wrinkles to show for it. But they also had a beautiful house. The top two floors were transformed, ready to convert when the time came. She definitely wouldn't miss Nate and his team.

She did miss the hum of activity though, so, padding over to the ancient radio, she tuned in Radio Four and let the presenter's deep, calm voice wash over her. Then she got to work. Gathering the eggs, butter and carrots into her arms, she dumped them on the table. She got out the flour, sugar and spices and took down her mum's mixing bowl and sifter. As she worked through the morning muffin recipe, she thought about her mum and what she'd have said about the *Bake Off* audition. In the quiet of the kitchen, she could hear her. 'Dozy mare!' she'd say, going in for a hug. 'Better pull your socks up, girl, and next time do better.'

That's exactly what I'm going to do, Mum.

As the first batch baked she pulled her pencils and pad from her bag and started sketching. When she was finished she taped the page to the fridge. Next year she had a date with Paul Hollywood.

Mum's Morning Muffins

Cream cheese icing

Carrots AND candied fruit

**GBBO DEADLINE MARCH!

The second batch was just starting to smell delicious when Rachel shuffled downstairs in her dressing gown and slippers. 'Morning. Is it morning?'

'Coffee's in the thingy,' Sarah said, looking up from the table where she'd started typing on her laptop.

'What are you doing?'

'Baking muffins and looking at my new profile.'

'Ooh, let me see!'

As Rachel looked over her updated RecycLove page, Sarah braced herself to defend it. It was no longer slick or polished, but it was who she really was. So she liked *Grand Designs* more than grand restaurants and would rather be parallel on the sofa than paralytic in a club. If that wasn't good enough for a guy then he wouldn't be good enough for her.

'It's perfect,' Rachel finally said, sipping her coffee. 'It's perfectly you.'

Sarah relaxed. 'Thank you. I've got a couple of messages already that look interesting. I'll answer them later. I think my photo isn't bad either.'

It was one that Robin had taken the day they'd all gone to Brighton. Sarah's hair floated around her face where it had escaped from its elastic band in the wind on the pier. She wore her favourite stripy blue jumper and her usual goofy smile.

'What are we looking at?' Catherine asked as she came in, already washed and dressed.

'My new profile,' said Sarah. 'I figured I should update it to be more me, since I stopped seeing Jeremy last night.'

'Are you okay?' both women asked her.

'Oh yes, fine, really. He was nice but exhausting! I can't go to any more clubs. He wasn't upset when I told him.'

'As long as you're okay,' Catherine said. 'You're really sure?'

'Positive.' And she was.

'You will find someone who's perfect for you, you know,' Rachel said.

'I know I will. Look at you. It might take me four years and I might have to be tricked into it because I'm too thick to see what's been right in front of me all the time, but—'

'All right,' Rachel said. 'So don't be thick like me, then. Keep your eyes open and you'll find someone who's just as weird and lovely as you are.'

Her housemates drifted off to other parts of the house, leaving Sarah in the quiet kitchen to wait for her muffins. She'd called Sissy last night before she went out but she wanted to talk to her again.

'Sissy, it's me. What are you doing?'

'Drawing. What are you doing?'

'Making Mum's muffins. I'll bring some with me tomorrow. How is everything? You've had breakfast already?'

'It's almost lunchtime,' Sissy reminded her sister.

'Right. Will you have lunch with Ben? What's on the menu?'

'Turkey chilli. I broke up with Ben.'

'You did? Are you okay?' It was times like this that she wanted to be an easy journey away.

'I'm okay. Someone else will come along.'

Sarah smiled into the phone at her sister's pragmatism. She was definitely their mum's daughter. 'I have an idea,' Sarah said. 'Let's go away in a few weeks, just you and me. How 'bout that? A girls' holiday. We'll find somewhere with a beach and sun.'

There was silence on the line. 'Sissy?'

'You won't eat raw fish this time?'

'No, I promise.'

'Okay, then. I've gotta go, the bingo's going to start.'

'I love you, Sissy.'

'Love you too.'

The muffins were cool by the time Rachel came back into the kitchen. 'Those smell amazing!' Her hair was wet from the shower and she had on footless leggings and a pretty violet smock dress.

'Help yourself, I made a double batch. I'll take the rest to Sissy tomorrow.'

Rachel cut one in half, slathered it with butter and took a big bite. 'She's still settling in well?' she said with her mouth full. 'Sorry, gross.'

'She loves it.'

'Who loves what?' said Catherine, striding into the kitchen clutching her phone. When she went to the fridge for milk, she saw the *Bake Off* sketch. 'Good for you, Sarah Lee.'

As Sarah looked between her housemates, her two very best friends in the world, and thought about Sissy, and the *Bake Off* auditions next year, she realised she already had her happy ending. A like-minded boyfriend would just be the icing on the show-stopper cake. 'Thanks.'

'Can I have a muffin?' Catherine asked with her hand already hovering.

'Of course. We're talking about Sissy. She loves the new facility. Luckily. I was starting to think we'd have to get Nate to build a room for her.' Sarah laughed like she was joking, but the relief she felt was incredible. And not only because she'd nearly had an aneurism when they'd lost her in Brighton. Kelly was right. Sissy was sixteen and needed other teenagers around her, not just her twenty-nine-year-old sister and thirty-something housemates. Sissy was starting to feel her independence and one day she might want her own flat. So they could look into a supported living arrangement and get her close by in London when the time came. Till then she was happy and safe with Kelly and her friends at the home.

Catherine's phone rang. She glanced at the screen and ended the call.

Rachel and Sarah caught each other's eye. 'Who was that?'

'Nobody. Alis,' she said.

'Nobody Alis as in your client?' Sarah asked.

Catherine nodded. Then she told them about their night together. 'Obviously I can't see him,' she said when she'd finished.

'What's so obvious about that?' Rachel wanted to know.

'Well, duh,' Sarah said. 'Weren't you listening? He's her client.'

Rachel and Catherine both smirked. 'Yeah, I got that, Sarah, thanks,' Rachel said. 'I just think it's stupid to dismiss him out of hand if you really like him. You do really like him, don't you?'

The shutters rolled down over Catherine's face. 'It doesn't matter. I have enough other things to worry about. I've got to figure out how to get the money to buy out Richard.'

'Don't change the subject, and you're making excuses,' Rachel said. 'The valuers come this week, right? With the new layout you know it's worth a lot more than we paid. So back to Alis. Wait, where are you going?'

'Too much coffee,' Catherine said, standing up. 'I'll be right back.' She hurried upstairs before they could say anything else.

'She left her phone,' said Rachel, picking it up.

'She won't need it in the loo.'

Rachel began scrolling through the missed calls. Then she hit the text button and started typing.

'What are you doing?' Sarah said, eyes darting to the stairs.

'I'm helping.'

No one said anything about Alis when Catherine came back. Sarah knew it was pointless to try to get her to talk if she didn't want to. So they settled into their weekend routine, with the newspapers spread all over the kitchen table. They were halfway through the crossword when the doorbell rang.

Rachel glanced up. 'I don't have my shoes on. Will someone else get it?'

'I'm not dressed,' Sarah said. 'Catherine, please?'

As Catherine went to answer the door, Sarah said, 'Do you think she'll be mad?'

Rachel shrugged. 'She owns a matchmaking business. She can't be surprised when she gets a dose of her own medicine. Next clue. Sixteen down. Eight letters, starts with S, ends with E: something unexpected.'

Chapter Forty-Six

Catherine

Catherine did a double take when she opened the door. This was not what she was expecting to interrupt her calm Sunday.

'Alis, what are you doing here? And how are you *here*?'

She didn't need to point out that a client turning up on her doorstep wasn't the usual run of things.

He adjusted the bulging courier bag on his shoulder. 'Don't be angry. Your friend . . . Rachel? She texted me with your address.'

'How did she know your phone number?'

'She didn't. She texted from your phone.'

'My phone?' That sneaky cow.

'You haven't been taking my calls. Or texts, or emails,' he pointed out, like that was a perfectly reasonable explanation for stalking. 'Don't be angry with her.'

'I'm angry with you. You shouldn't be here.' But her tummy was betraying her words, the little traitor.

'Well that's where you're wrong, Catherine. That might not be something you hear very often, but it's true. You are wrong. I should be here because we've got unfinished business. I need to ask you a question and I'd like a simple yes or no answer, please.'

She crossed her arms.

'Would you like to go out with me?'

She sighed. 'It's not that simple, Alis.'

'I can't hear you. Was that a yes or a no?'

'I said it's not that simple.'

'Because I'm a client?'

She nodded.

'That's what I thought.' He grasped her hands. 'Catherine, you should know that I have the utmost respect for you as a businesswoman and your company is top-notch, but it'll come as no surprise to you that, between being stood up and set up with women who don't really want to go out with me, it's just not working. Plus, actually, I don't think I need the service any more. I've found an incredible woman on my own. So with all due respect, Catherine, you're fired. Now, let's go on a date. A real date.'

'You've got some nerve, asking me out when you've just fired me!' But she was smiling. 'You want to go now?'

'No time like the present.'

'Is your Mercury all right?'

'As it happens, it is, thanks. Come on, I have a plan.'

'What is it?'

'None of your business. Wait and see.'

She didn't notice Rachel and Sarah peeking down through the front room window. And she definitely didn't see them cheering when Alis slipped his hand into hers and led her away.

They hadn't gone far before he stopped at a row of city rental bikes. 'Just a sec.' Feeding his debit card into the machine, two little slips of paper were spat out that he used to unlock the bikes.

'You want to cycle on London streets?'

'Not on the streets. We're going along the canal, so you

don't have to worry about cars, and we can walk them on the pavement to the towpath.' He opened his bag. 'Here.' He handed her a round green helmet that was going to make her look like Cartman from *South Park*. 'I know you like to play things safe.'

It was a beautiful day to be outside, with the spring sun warming their backs as they pedalled along the canal towards the park. Lots of others had had the same idea, but the crowds didn't matter.

As they made their way along at a snail's pace, Catherine's smile grew. She'd forgotten how much she loved to cycle. She used to go everywhere on her bike at uni. They all did – big noisy groups of students on two wheels. She'd fallen out of the habit when she moved to Washington. It had started to seem frivolous and studenty and between the wedding and making a home for her and Richard, she had too many grown-up things to worry about.

But she'd quite liked that girl on the bike. As she pedalled along she realised she'd packed away a lot more than her bicycle in the name of adulthood. Now that seemed like a mistake and it was nice to know that the old Catherine was still inside. It felt like it might be time to let her out.

At a busy pinch point on the path they stopped to let a harried young woman pass them. She was trying to keep her three jolly dogs from diving after the ducks into the canal. As Catherine laughed watching them, she could imagine herself coming here again. Lately there'd been a lot of things she could imagine herself doing.

Inside the park, as they made their way toward an empty spot on the crowded grass, Catherine wondered aloud if he did this sort of thing often.

'No, I've never been on that stretch of the canal but I've been curious about the city bikes. They seem like a good idea for people without their own bikes, as long as you don't have to dodge the buses and taxis. They weigh about a thousand pounds though.'

'My housemate Sarah rides her bike everywhere. You too, I guess.'

He nodded. 'You don't though.' It was a statement, not a question.

'No . . . you and I aren't very compatible that way.' Hopefully that wouldn't be a problem. She wasn't about to turn up for dates with her trouser leg tucked into her sock.

He shrugged. 'It's just how I get around. It's not a way of life.'

'Unlike vegetarianism or astrology or feng shui.'

There were a lot of differences.

He pulled a bottle of white wine, two plastic glasses and a block of cheese from his bag.

'That's better than a magician's hat,' she said. 'What else have you got in there?'

'No rabbits, sorry, only these.' He unpacked some biscuits. 'I haven't got a rug to sit on though.'

'That's where the rabbits would come in handy.' She winced when she said it, remembering his veggie roots. 'Sorry, I don't mean to offend you.'

'Why would that offend me?'

'Well, animal rights and all, but it was just a joke. I promise I'd never use a live animal for a cushion.'

As he cut her a piece of cheddar with his penknife, the muscle in his forearm flexed beneath the tattoos.

'So, our first date,' he said. 'I think it's going well so far, don't you?' He popped another piece of cheese into his mouth. 'Don't be shy about digging in because I will eat the whole block. I have a weak spot for cheddar.'

Catherine smiled. 'I could live on cheese.'

'Maybe we'll do a cheese tasting on our next date. Assuming this one goes well.'

She had to admit it was going well, but . . . 'I feel like I should say something.'

'It might be a boring date otherwise.'

'I mean about us. We are very different. Does that bother you?'

'Just because we've got different interests doesn't mean we're different deep down,' he said. 'That's where the important stuff is. Not in how someone looks or what they eat for dinner.'

'I'm not talking about looks. But what if we have fundamentally different views on the world? You see lamb and think of one of God's creatures. I see it and think of mint sauce.'

'Must I eat a burger to prove my love?'

'You'd do that for me?'

'With bacon and cheese. So can you look past my compassion for sentient beings if I can forgive your murderous rampages on a plate?'

Why did she get the feeling that it was going to be very hard to argue with a man like Alis? She nodded, digging into the cheese.

He scooted across the grass until they were inches from each other. 'Then this seems like about the right time to kiss you. Any objections?'

'My mouth is full.'

'Is that an objection?'

She shook her head. 'It's a fact . . . okay, I've finished.'

When his lips met hers she was surprised at how soft his beard felt. It was nothing like kissing a groundhog.

As they snogged in the sunshine she knew she was nuts about that veggie-hugging, astrology-following, hairy, tattooed, kind, gentle, funny, smart, sexy, positive, engaging man. Finally, after sorting out everyone else's love life, it got to be her turn.

What was that expression? It's when you're not looking for something that you find it. Well, she wasn't about to put that on the Love Match letterhead, even if it was true. She had a business to run after all.

Later as they watched the sun setting over the trees, the wine long gone, she started to chuckle.

'What's funny?'

'I should probably make up something interesting and mysterious,' she said. 'But I'm thinking about house renovations.'

'That's very romantic.'

'It is, actually,' she said, thinking that they might need to ask Nate and the team back sooner rather than later to start on phase two of Rachel's plans. 'Or it could be. One day. When the time comes.'

Epilogue

The next year . . .

'Sarah Lee, it's starting soon!' Catherine shouted. 'Alis, is it recording?'

'It's recording. You realise you're conforming to stereotype, don't you? I know for a fact that you know how to record your own programmes.'

Catherine smiled. 'I just like to make you feel useful. Everybody comfy? Want the blanket?' It might be August but the house was chilly as usual.

Rachel and James sat to Catherine's right on the long sofa while Alis cuddled up on her left. 'Sarah!' she shouted again. 'It's like she doesn't even care.'

'Well, she was there after all,' said Rachel. 'She knows what happens. We're the ones in the dark about the details.'

They heard feet pounding down the stairs. 'I'm here, I'm here!'

Sarah threw herself over the back of the sofa, landing half in Catherine's lap and half in Rachel's.

'Too right,' said Rachel. 'James, Alis, move it. Drag those chairs around.'

Alis shrugged as he gave up his spot. 'It is their house.' He pulled two of the reading chairs within range of the telly.

'Where's Sissy? Sissy!'

There was more pounding, this time coming up the kitchen stairs. 'We're here,' she said. 'Ready? Close your eyes.'

Sarah grinned, screwing her eyes shut. She could hear rustling and Sissy saying, 'Higher. Higher. Higher. No, lower. Lower. Higher.' And then giggles.

'Okay, you can open your eyes.'

Sarah took in the large banner hanging between the windows. It was covered with improbably coloured cakes and the words 'Congrats Champ' mosaicked along its length.

'That's gorgeous, Sissy, really good. But you don't know whether I'm the champion or not.'

'You are,' she said.

'How do you know?'

'Because you're my sister.'

'Here, Sissy,' Catherine said, shuffling over. 'Sit next to Sarah.'

She launched herself at the cushions with the same gusto that Sarah had. It ran in the family. 'Where's Seamus sitting?' she asked.

Seamus stood a little awkwardly near the banner that he'd hung. 'I can sit on the floor in front of Sarah.' He plonked himself down, leaning against her legs.

'Young love,' said James. 'He'll be sitting in a chair like the rest of us this time next year. Your arse is going to fall asleep.'

'I'll risk the soggy bottom,' he said as Sarah chuckled. She reached over his shoulder so he could take her hand. 'I didn't think I'd be this nervous,' she said.

'It's not every day you see yourself on telly,' said Alis.

'It's starting!'

Mel and Sue addressed the camera, introducing this year's

Great British Bake Off as the twelve aproned contestants stood behind them.

'There you are!' screamed Rachel. 'This is so exciting! And there's Seamus on the end!'

Sarah watched the first part of the programme from behind her fingers, wincing every time the camera closed in on her. 'It's awful seeing yourself,' she murmured.

'They say the camera adds a stone,' James said helpfully. Rachel punched him in the arm.

Sarah shook her head. 'Baking non-stop for three months did that.'

'I love your cake handles,' said Seamus.

'Oh you big charmer,' Rachel teased. 'Hey, I just thought of something. Maybe we'll see the first *Great British Bake Off* wedding next year . . . What, too soon?'

Seamus smiled. 'Not too soon for me.'

'Me either.' Sarah could hardly believe it. She wouldn't have guessed in a million years that she'd meet someone like Seamus at the *Bake Off*. It had been enough of a long shot that she'd been chosen for the show in the first place. But to find someone so perfectly matched to her, who put crumpets before clubbing, and loved her as much as she did him?

She let herself imagine that she hadn't been selected. Then she'd be watching Seamus on telly for the first time this very minute. What would she think of him? Would his sandy blond hair and open smiling face still make her heart quicken with excitement? Would she hear his deep voice and Dublin lilt and know she could listen to him forever? Would his kindness and enthusiasm come across on camera? Or would she see him as Catherine and Rachel probably did – a cute guy with a deep love of cake?

Luckily she didn't have to guess at the answers because she *did* meet him, and they clicked from the first weekend of filming. It was intense, long and tiring, but they all went out for dinner after each day on set, and that's when they really got to know each other. Sarah managed to hold out until the third weekend, and then she kissed him.

She was under penalty of death (or at least in breach of an official confidentiality agreement) not to give away any details about the show, even to her best friends. But at least she hadn't had to keep Seamus a secret.

On the telly, Mary Berry judged Sarah's signature bake delicious and everyone in the sitting room erupted in cheers. Sissy threw her arms around her sister and they were soon whooping for Seamus too when Paul said his passion-fruit sponge packed a punch.

At the end, both Sarah and Seamus were still in the *Bake Off* tent.

But of course Catherine and Rachel already knew that, because the crew had come to the house to film the 'at home' segments for the final three contestants. They just didn't know if she'd won. That was a secret she'd promised to keep.

'Same time next week?' Alis asked as the programme ended. 'I'm inspired to bake now.'

'You just get better and better.' Catherine kissed him. 'Same time next week.'

'I'll bring wine next time,' James said. 'Or champagne. The bakers deserve champagne.'

'Sissy, should we keep the banner up till the end of the series?' Rachel asked.

Sissy nodded solemnly. 'Yes, because it's going to come true. Sorry Seamus.'

'That's okay, Sissy. I think she's a champion too.'

'Will you stay?' Sarah asked him. 'Or drive back to Cambridge?'

'I'd like to stay if that's okay. We can take Sissy back together in the morning. I don't have to be in work till ten.'

'I want to stay the night,' said Sissy.

'And I want you to stay,' Sarah replied. 'I want everyone to stay.'

'That's settled, then,' said Alis to Catherine. 'If Sissy says so then it's a sleepover night.'

'I wouldn't cross Sissy,' James said.

'You'd better not,' Sissy said, poking her finger into his chest. 'That's that then. We're all staying with Sarah tonight.'

Sarah beamed. It was the icing on her show-stopper cake.

THE END

Ready to do a little baking of your own?

Sissy's favourite chocolate chip cookies
Makes around 4 dozen cookies. Preheat oven to 180°C/350°F.

Ingredients
2 1/4 cups flour
1 teaspoon baking soda
1 teaspoon salt
1 cup butter, room temperature
3/4 cup granulated sugar
3/4 cup packed brown sugar
1 teaspoon vanilla extract
2 large eggs
2 cups semi-sweet chocolate chips (in baking section of
    supermarkets)*
1 cup chopped nuts (Sissy likes walnuts best)

In a small bowl, combine the flour, baking soda and salt. In
a large bowl, whip the butter with an electric mixer (electric

* You can also chop up chocolate bars but be sure they are dark –
they should have at least 50% cocoa or the cookies will be too
sweet.

whisk), then add the granulated sugar, brown sugar and vanilla extract. Add the eggs and mix well. With a spoon (not the electric whisk), stir in the chocolate pieces and nuts. Then gradually stir in flour mixture with a spoon.

Line baking sheets with greaseproof paper or foil. Use a teaspoon to make balls of dough and space evenly on the baking sheet so that 12 balls fit. They will spread into around 2-inch cookies while they bake.

Bake for around 10-12 minutes or until they are golden (time will vary depending on your oven). Take the baking sheet from the oven and let the cookies rest for a few minutes before moving them to a cooling rack.

Don't wait till they are completely cool to start eating them! One of life's joys is eating warm chocolate chip cookies.

Sarah and Sissy's Marbled Pound Cake
Preheat oven to 170°C/325°F. The recipe makes one 9-inch loaf. Be sure that the eggs are room temperature before you start, not cold from the fridge.

Ingredients
2 cups flour
3/4 teaspoon salt
1/2lb unsalted butter, at room temperature
1 1/2 teaspoons vanilla extract
1 1/2 cups sugar
5 large eggs (room temperature, not cold)
1 tablespoon unsweetened cocoa powder
9-inch loaf pan

If you want the cake to come out of the pan, then grease the bottom and sides and line bottom and long sides with baking paper, leaving about an inch of overhang on both sides. Then grease and flour the paper and pan, tapping out any excess.

Sift flour and salt together into a small bowl. Set aside. Put butter, vanilla and sugar in a large bowl and whisk with electric whisk on medium speed until light and pale. This could take several minutes. There's no raising agent in the recipe so getting air into the butter mix is what makes it rise. Then add eggs one at a time, beating well and scraping bowl between each. The air in the eggs also helps raise the cake.

Mix in flour gradually until it is fully incorporated; do not overmix or you'll beat all the air out of the cake. Divide the mixture into two bowls. Stir the cocoa powder into one of the bowls.

Using a spoon, add the vanilla and chocolate mixture to the pan in layers. Smooth top with a spatula (it will be thick), then drag a knife back and forth through the mix to make the marbled effect. Bake until a toothpick inserted in the centre of the cake comes out clean, about 1 hour and 15 minutes.

Cool cake on a wire rack for 15 minutes. Run a knife along unlined sides of pan and use baking paper to carefully lift cake onto wire rack to cool completely.

Sarah's Wedding Cupcakes

These cakes use oil instead of butter, which means they don't go stale after a couple of days. So they're perfect for baking ahead. This recipe makes about a dozen cakes.
Preheat oven to 180°C/350°F.

Ingredients for the cakes
1 1/4 cup flour
1 1/4 teaspoon baking powder
1/2 teaspoon baking soda
1/2 teaspoon salt
2 eggs (medium or large are fine)
3/4 cup sugar
1 1/2 teaspoon vanilla
1/2 cup oil (vegetable or canola/rapeseed)
1/2 cup buttermilk*
cupcake tin and paper cases
electric mixer (hand mixer)

* If you haven't got buttermilk, pour 1/2 cup regular milk into a cup and add 1/2 teaspoon of lemon juice or white vinegar to it 5 minutes before you add it to the mix.

Add flour, baking powder, baking soda and salt to a bowl.

In another bowl, use electric mixer to beat eggs for 15-20 seconds (they'll become a bit frothy), then add the sugar and beat on medium for around 30 seconds. The mix will become light, but don't over-beat or it'll start to look like meringue and the cupcakes will rise too much.

Add the oil and vanilla.

Add the flour mixture and buttermilk and mix till it's just blended together. The batter will be thin.

Fill the cupcake cases in the tin to 2/3 full and bake. Check them at 12-14 minutes (stick a cocktail stick in the middle of the cake – if it comes out dry, the cakes are ready). It could take up to 20 minutes for them to bake, depending on your oven.

Turn the cakes out on to a cooling rack, and don't ice them until they're completely cool.

Ingredients for the icing
16oz/450g icing sugar (confectioners' sugar)
1/4lb/110g butter (at room temperature)
3-4 tablespoons milk
food colouring if you want

Cream the butter with an electric mixer (electric whisk).

Add sugar slowly and keep the mixer on a low setting or the icing sugar cloud will overwhelm you :-)

Add a bit of the milk till you get the right icing consistency.

Loved *Match me if you Can*?

Then why not join *The Curvy Girls Club*?

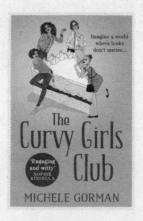

Can the curvy girls have their cake and eat it?

Meet best friends Pixie, Ellie, Katie and Jane.
Fed up with always struggling to lose weight, they start a
social club where size doesn't matter. Soon it's the most
popular place to be – having fun instead of counting
carbs. And the girls suddenly find their lives changing in
ways they never imagined.

But outside the club, things aren't as rosy,
as they struggle with the ups and downs of everyday life.

In this funny, heart-warming read about normal women
learning to love themselves, the curvy girls soon realise
that no matter what life throws at them, together,
anything is possible . . .